ISBN 0-7394-4000-4

Printed in the United States of America

Armando's Treasure

MELODY CARLSON

TYNDALE HOUSE PUBLISHERS, INC.
WHEATON, ILLINOIS

Chapter One

*A*rmando knew how to hot-wire an engine even before he knew how to drive. Not that he'd ever done it before. But Tio Pedro had taught him these sorts of things—"important stuff" that should help him through life's unexpected challenges. But his uncle was in jail right now, and as a result Armando was on the run. But he was tired of running and for that matter walking too. That's probably what made him notice the pickup from the road—a flash of blue within a sea of green. And he'd never seen so much green before. These thick layers of vegetation seemed to grow everywhere up here in Oregon—like a jungle of sorts. It would take some getting used to. At first he'd assumed the old truck had been abandoned in the middle of nowhere, but as he left the road and drew closer, he noticed signs of what appeared to be a farm, or rather used to be, a house and several outbuildings.

He pulled off his Dodgers cap and wiped the sweat from his forehead as he surveyed the overgrown acreage. Forgotten and neglected, it had the look of abandonment to it—like Tio Pedro's wife every time he'd taken off and left her with three hungry mouths to feed. Armando studied the ancient pickup parked out in the tall grass. Old and probably rusted out, it looked as dilapidated and forgotten as the rest of the place, but even so it drew him like a magnet. Not that he was actually planning on stealing it—no, he told himself, he just wanted a closer look. He shifted his backpack to his other shoulder and picked his way through the tall grass only to find it choked with blackberry vines. He growled as the greedy thorns clawed at his jeans, his best pair too. Seemed these stinking blackberries grew everywhere in these parts, but what good were they if they didn't even produce edible fruit? Or was it too early for berries up here?

His stomach rumbled as he glanced over his shoulder back toward the house. He hadn't eaten since yesterday, and that'd only been a couple of old cheeseburgers he'd dug out of a McDonald's Dumpster along the interstate, the best he could do before the "regulars" shooed him away with lots of cussing and threats of bodily harm. He swatted a buzzing fly from his face and put his cap back on, then squinted toward the house. It seemed used up and discarded and he doubted that anyone gave a hoot about this old heap of a pickup either. Likely no one would even care if it went missing, that is if it could even start, and he felt pretty uncertain about that.

"Go ahead," he could hear Tio Pedro's voice whisper into his ear, *"Piece of cake."* Armando had never actually stolen a vehicle before. Okay, borrowed maybe, then forgot to return for a day or two. But that was from someone he knew, and a long time ago. But today was a day of desperation, a day for giving up on trying to do things the right way. Where had that gotten him in the long run anyway? He looked over his shoulder, back toward the road. Why not?

He ran his tongue across his upper lip, savoring the taste of salt for a long moment as he studied the old aqua blue Chevy. Looked to be a '55, maybe '56. Pretty run-down, but nothing a little body-work and a fresh coat of paint couldn't fix up. Not one of those flashy colors like his friend Mickey Carrero went in for, hot pinks and lime greens. No way. If Armando got the chance he'd paint this baby a nice respectable blue, a little darker than the sky right before dusk on a summer's night. Now, if the engine would only cooperate.

He glanced once more at the old farmhouse, glaring back at him in the sunlight. Warped clapboard siding flaked off what once might've been yellow paint, shutters hung slightly cockeyed as if they'd given up, and greedy blackberry vines crawled up the foundation on one side like they'd devour the place before long. No doubt, they'd swallow up this poor old truck too.

"No way," he could hear his uncle telling him. *"This ain't stealing, boy. This is a rescue mission—an act of mercy even!"* Armando stepped over to the driver's side of the truck. What did he really have to lose anyway? It seemed the entire universe had turned against him lately. Who really gave a rip? He reached for the door handle.

"What're you doing there, boy?" yelled a shrill voice from the direction of the farmhouse.

He swallowed hard as he shoved his hands deep into his pockets and then slowly turned and stepped into full view. Not that he was afraid exactly; after all, he'd done nothing wrong—not yet anyway. He peered toward the house, squinting against the brightness of the afternoon sun, then finally spotted her, sitting right there on the porch, where she'd probably been sitting all along, slightly obscured by those blackberry bushes, just watching him and waiting for the right moment. From where he stood, she appeared to be a tiny scrap of a woman; her age he couldn't guess since a droopy straw hat cast a shadow that mostly obscured her face. But his stomach knotted as he was reminded of his own deceased grandmother, Abuela Maria.

He stepped forward now, chin up, ready to disarm the old woman with his famous Colgate smile. It usually worked on females no matter the age. He'd used it before to get out of a potential scrape, something else he'd learned from his uncle—turn on the charm and watch your problems melt away. But as he stepped forward and raised his hand to wave, he noticed the large black shotgun propped up against what appeared to be a plaster cast on her left arm. The cast went from forearm to wrist and looked like a large white *L* beaming angrily at him in the bright afternoon sun.

"Hey, there," he called out in his smoothest, calmest voice. "No need for that gun now, ma'am. I was just walking by and stopped for a minute to admire your fine-looking truck here."

"What d'you want?" she squawked, not flinching an inch as she peered down the barrel at him.

He kept walking toward her, slowly and carefully, still smiling big as he went. He'd survived fights in his neighborhood and cross fire in the city; no way he'd let some little old granny take him out with a stupid shotgun. Probably wasn't even loaded anyway. "Name's Armando," he called out. "I'm just passing through here. Looking for work. You know anybody who needs a good worker round here?" He paused for a moment, holding up his right arm as he flexed his muscles in a showy way, smiling even bigger now. "I'm strong and healthy and I know how to work hard." He took another cautious step.

"You stay right where you're at, boy." She lowered the shotgun down to her lap, but the barrel still pointed his way. He could see her face now and she looked to be fairly old. But her expression was tight and pinched, like she was in some pretty bad pain.

"You okay, lady?" He nodded to her cast. "How'd you break that arm anyway?"

"None of your business, boy."

"Looks like you're hurting." He took another careful step, but the gun popped right back up and he stopped and held his hands up in a show of surrender. Something about the steely look in those narrowed eyes told him she meant business. "I'm real sorry to bother you, ma'am," he said quickly, taking a step backward now. "But you look like you could use some help. You all alone here?"

"None of your business!" she snapped again. "Go away."

He nodded slowly, still studying her. Beads of sweat trickled down the sides of her wrinkled face and her lips puckered together in a tight pale circle. "Sure," he said, keeping his hands in the air, stepping back again. "I thought, you know, well, like maybe you could use a hand round here. Just for a few days, you know, 'til you get yourself back on your feet. Looks like that arm is really hurting you."

She shook her head, just barely, and in the same movement the heavy shotgun slipped from her hand and she collapsed, limp as a rag doll. Then, slumped over the arm of the old rocker, she moaned in pain. In one quick movement, Armando sprang to the porch and grabbed up the gun. He looked down at the tiny figure now hunched over like an old sack of beans.

"You okay, lady?" he asked, glancing quickly over her shoulder through the sagging screen door of the house. "Anybody else here with you?" But she said nothing, just kind of whimpered in a pitiful way that reminded him of when his old dog, Strand, had been hit by the UPS truck.

Armando swallowed hard. The cool metal of the gun had already grown warm in his hand. Obviously, this old lady no longer posed any threat to him. So what was he standing around waiting for? This was his chance to get out of here, and he might even be able to start up that pickup and get clean away before she ever came to her senses. If the truck had any gas, he could probably be out of the state before anybody even figured out he'd been here at all.

He peered down at her with curiosity. She was so old, she looked to be about a hundred and two, and for all he knew she could be half blind. She probably couldn't even describe him to the authorities, likely say some Mexican kid had taken her truck. That's how most gringos usually described his kind—to a gringo they all looked alike. The old lady moaned again. And for the second time today, he was reminded of Abuela Maria—it's as if he could see her brown wrinkled face looking down at him, and he could hear her soft voice telling him to be a good boy and help this poor woman. How could he disobey her?

With reluctance, he set down the gun and reached his arm around the old lady's back, then carefully drew her up to her feet. She was as light as a child and seemed barely conscious. "Let's get you inside, old woman. You need to get out of this hot sun." With one arm he supported her entire weight; with the other he opened the screen door, then half walked, half carried her into the darkened interior of the musty farmhouse. His eyes slowly adjusted to the dim light and he eased her down onto a sagging, old couch, taking care to slip a cushion beneath her head. He removed her straw hat and set it on the coffee table then looked around, unsure as to what to do next. He went into the nearby kitchen and quickly found a glass and filled it with tap water. It felt as if Abuela Maria were guiding his hand, and he even remembered her saying something about giving someone a drink of water was like giving it to the Lord Jesus. But what did that really mean? He shook his head as he returned to the living room. Lifting the old woman's head with one hand, he offered her a drink with the other.

To his surprise, she opened her eyes and took a long, slow swig. "Thanks," she whispered as he eased her head back down to the pillow.

He stood there with the half-filled glass still in his hands. What now? So he'd done his good deed for the day. Should he sneak away now? maybe take another look at that old Chevy? Or not. For some reason—maybe it was his grandmother—he felt fairly certain that pickup was going nowhere right now. For a long moment, he stood there, watching the old woman with an unexplainable curiosity. Who was she anyway? And what was she doing all by herself on this dilapidated old farm? Then again, what was it to him? Why should he care?

She had on faded blue jeans. Not the fashionable type he and his friends wore, but these looked like the kind that had once been dark and new and had slowly grown soft and worn by years of hard wearing and washing. It seemed unusual clothing for a woman her age. His grandmother had never been seen in pants of any sort. And this old woman also wore what appeared to be a man's work shirt, tucked neatly into her jeans and cinched in with a beaded leather belt, not so much unlike the one that his great-uncle used to wear. On her feet she wore dusty, old-looking tennis shoes, probably once white but now a nondescript gray, the back of the heels smashed flat like slip-ons. But the one stark contrast in this picture was the bright white cast on the old woman's arm. It looked perfectly clean, like it was brand-new. Was it possible she'd broken it today? And, if so, how had she gotten herself to the hospital for medical attention? That old truck sure didn't look as if it'd gone anywhere recently.

He walked back into the kitchen and set the glass into the deep enamel sink, then looked around. Neat and orderly. Cast-iron pots hung on the wall above the stove; colorful pottery dishes showed through the cloudy glass doors of the painted cupboards. Looked like some kind of cooking had gone on in here at one time. Maybe not lately, though. He ran his hand over the laminate top of the old-fashioned kitchen table. Clean, but slightly greasy. He helped himself to an apple sitting atop a bowl of fruit. Taking a bite, he walked back out into the front room and looked around. This home probably wasn't much by gringo standards, but compared to what he'd grown up in, it was pretty nice and fairly roomy to boot. It might be a nice place to crash for a while, to lay low until he figured out what to do next.

He paused in front of a small brick fireplace, flanked by floor-to-ceiling bookshelves that were crammed full of old books and magazines. A bunch of ordinary-looking photos were displayed on the mantel. The usual stuff, a black-and-white marriage picture of a couple from a time gone by—probably the lady and her old man. The guy had on an army uniform, and the woman, nearly a foot shorter, was petite and blonde and not half bad-looking, for back then anyway. He glanced at the other photos; nothing very spectacular, probably just the old woman's family. And yet it was interesting, gave a sense of history, belonging. He remembered his aunt's picture collection. All were recent color photos, and most of them of her girls—as if his family had no history—only the here and now. Although he knew that wasn't exactly true. In fact he still had a box of Abuela Maria's things, including some old photos, tucked under the cot he used to sleep on in Tia Marta's laundry room. He hoped she wouldn't mistakenly throw them out while he was gone.

Then his gaze quit moving and fixed itself on one particular picture. He picked up the silver-framed photo and stared into the face of one of the most beautiful girls he'd ever seen. She looked to be about eighteen or so, but who could tell with the way girls dressed nowadays. He knew some girls who looked like they were twenty-five but weren't even in high school yet. This girl had long, blonde curls falling loosely over her shoulders. But that face—it reminded him of something that he couldn't quite put into words. Maybe an angel. He stared for a few more seconds then quickly put the photo back, as if it might hurt him. A guy could go blind, he thought, staring at a face like that for too long.

Another groan from the couch made him turn around. Suddenly he remembered where he was and wondered why he had lingered so long when he could've easily been gone by now. The old woman held up her hand, the one that wasn't broken, then moaned and closed her eyes.

"Anything more I can do for you?" he asked blankly, quietly, not really expecting a response. He put the hand with the apple in it behind his back. "Otherwise I guess I'd better get on my way. Don't want to—"

She opened her eyes. "My pills," she said in hoarse whisper. "Get me my pills."

"Pills?" He looked around. "What—where are they?"

"By the sink."

He went back to the kitchen and looked around, and there next to the sink sat a small white bag and in it a brown prescription bottle. He read the label as he walked back to the living room. "Says these are for pain. Looks like you're supposed to take one every four hours."

She slowly pulled herself to a sitting position. "Give me one."

"When did you last have one?" His brow raised in suspicion.

"You a nurse?" She held out her small, wrinkled hand.

"Says you need to take these with food. When'd you last eat?"

She shrugged. "Just give me one."

"Hang on a minute." He returned to the kitchen and retrieved a spotty banana from the fruit bowl. "First you eat this; then I'll give you your pill." He opened the peeling on the banana and handed it to her.

She slowly took a bite, then chewed, eyeing him carefully the whole while, as if she didn't much trust him. "There." She set down the empty banana peeling and held out her hand. "Now give me my pill."

"Good girl." He handed her a pill followed by the glass of water.

After swallowing the pill, she leaned back into the sofa. A strand of pure white hair had escaped from where she'd pinned it back in some sort of bun and now rested across her wrinkled cheek. "Now, what's your name again, boy?"

"Armando."

"You a wetback?"

He patted himself on the back as if to check. "Well, I did get a little sweaty out there on the road today, but I think my back's pretty dry now."

"You know what I mean. You an *illegal?*"

He laughed. "I guess it depends on who you're talking to. But if you mean, am I a citizen of the good old U.S. of A.? Well, then the answer would have to be yes. Born almost twenty-one years ago in St. Joseph's Hospital in Los Angeles, California."

She nodded. "Well, that's something anyway."

"You feeling a little better now?"

"I think so."

He looked down at his feet. "Well, then I guess I better get out of your hair."

"Where you heading?"

"Treasure."

Her brows lifted. "Well, then you're here, boy. Only two miles to get into town."

"That's about what I figured."

"You on foot?"

He nodded. "Was hitching, but my last ride ran out about twenty miles back."

"That why you were looking so fondly at my truck?"

He felt his face grow warm. "Like I said, it's one fine-looking truck."

"It's a mess." She cleared her throat. "But it *was* a fine-looking truck, once upon a time. My husband, bless his soul, bought it brand spanking new back in 1956."

"So it's a '56 then."

"Yeah. And it still runs—well, mostly it runs. Needs some work though."

He shoved his hand into an empty pocket. "You interested in selling it?"

She firmly shook her head. "Nope. It's my only means of transportation. Not that I'll be driving it for a while. It's got a stick, you know."

"I noticed." He sighed. "Well, I better get going then."

MELODY CARLSON

"What brings you to Treasure anyway? Not much going on there that I can see."

"Just looking around."

She frowned. "That's not the truth."

He looked away.

"What are you looking for, boy? What's your true story?"

"You really want the truth?" He looked her in the eyes.

She studied him for a moment then nodded. "The truth's always simpler in the long run, boy."

He thought about that. "Well, the truth is I wanted to head someplace new—wanted a fresh start, you know. So I got me a map of the Northwest and I looked and looked and I saw this one town called Lucky up in Washington and I thought about going there, but then my luck's never been too good. Then I saw this other town by the name of Treasure up here in Oregon, and I thought it sounded more promising—plus it was closer. I thought maybe I'd find me a treasure in Treasure." He laughed.

She shook her head. "Boy, you don't sound too smart to me."

He shrugged. "Hey, I figure one place is pretty much the same as the next when it comes to getting away—"

"What're you running from? The law?"

He studied her. For an old lady, she seemed pretty sharp and pretty suspicious too. "It's a long story. I guess I'm mostly trying to start my life over—if I can, that is."

"Well, I suppose that'd depend on you now, wouldn't it?" She squinted slightly as she looked him up and down, as if she were adding him up and then subtracting it all over again. And with his luck it was amounting to less than nothing.

He wanted to think of some smart-aleck answer, something slightly sarcastic that'd put an end to this senseless conversation and let him get back on his way, away from this old woman and her pale prying eyes.

But then a knock on the door startled them both.

"Well, I'd better get going now." He glanced nervously toward the back door that he'd noticed in the kitchen.

"So you are running then?"

He pressed his lips together then returned her fixed gaze. "You know there's more than one kind of running, ma'am."

Chapter Two

Maybe it was the result of his uncle's early lessons on machismo or just his own foolish pride, but Armando rarely walked away from a dare. He still remembered the time Mickey Carrero had dared him to jump from the railroad bridge into the river below. Despite his fear of heights and having heard stories of various drowning incidents because of the sharp undertow next to the bridge pillars, Armando had jumped. But he never forgot that blast of the chilly water or how he plummeted like a stone into the dark depths below. Sometimes he still had nightmares where he frantically kicked and clawed against the pull of the undercurrent before he finally burst through the river's churning surface gasping for air.

And now, as he stood looking down on this frail old woman, he felt that she too had dared him; something in her eyes had the look of a dare to it. And suddenly he knew he wouldn't turn and dart out the back door like he wanted to, like he knew he probably should.

"It's only me, Mom," called a short man in a dark blue suit. He entered the room like he owned the place and set a plastic grocery bag on the end table next to the old woman. "Thought I'd better check on you. Olivia said that—" he stopped speaking when he noticed Armando. His face confused, he stepped back toward the door as if he were uncomfortable, maybe even frightened. "Who are you?" he stammered.

"That's Armando," said the old woman in a matter-of-fact voice, as if she were in the habit of entertaining young Latino men on a regular basis, and for all Armando knew, maybe she was. But at the same time he realized he didn't even know her name. She nodded to the man in the suit. "And this is my son, Charles."

Charles tentatively stepped forward and the two shook hands briefly. Armando sensed the reluctance in the man's grip, as if afraid to really grasp his hand, as if something unpleasant might rub off and soil him. But Armando just shrugged. It wasn't the first time a gringo had done that. He thought he recognized the man from some of the photos on the mantel, only it seemed the man was older now, balder, and more rigid-looking, almost as if his shorts were too tight, or perhaps he had indigestion from a bad lunch.

"I was just passing by, sir. I stopped to help your mother out a little." He glanced nervously at the old woman, worried that she'd blow his cover and say something about his eyeing her truck. But she didn't. "Anyway I should be going now."

"You *helped* my mother?" Charles looked even more suspicious now.

"Yeah, she was feeling a little worn-out I think, probably her arm bothering her some."

Charles turned back to his mother and scowled. "You mean to tell me you let a perfect stranger come in here to help you out?"

She made a shrugging motion then cringed at the obvious discomfort that brought to her arm. Armando felt bad for her. Here he'd been worried about how she could get him into trouble and now something he'd said appeared to have created more problems for her.

"You see, Mom!" The man's voice grew sharp. "This is exactly what I've been telling you. Just last week in fact. You can't keep living out here like this—" He paused, his gaze now resting upon the shotgun, right where Armando had laid it on the floor beneath the coffee table. "And keeping guns around where anyone can see them!" He glanced at Armando out of the corner of his eye. "Good grief, Mom, who knows what might happen to you!"

"Excuse me," said Armando, taking a step toward the door. "But I'd better be going now."

"No." She held up her good hand. "You sit down right there, young man." She nodded to an old recliner near the fireplace, and wordlessly Armando obeyed.

"If he needs to go," began Charles, waving toward the door, "why not let him get on his way?"

Her eyes flashed with cool blue flames. "Because he and I aren't done talking just yet."

Charles adjusted his striped tie and frowned deeply as he paced across the matted-down carpet. Armando suspected this suit-wearing man wasn't used to dealing with situations like this, and he wondered who was more frustrating to him—Armando or his willful mother? Suddenly Armando thought it might be amusing to watch this little scene unfold. He'd witnessed plenty of family fiascoes with his own hotheaded Latino relatives. It might be educational to see how gringos handled their little family disputes. And besides, the recliner felt soft and comfortable to his back, and it was cool in here, a nice break after walking for several long hours on the sunbaked road. He finished his apple and tossed the core into the fireplace then leaned his head back and listened with concealed interest.

"This is exactly what I mean, Mom! Here we are getting our-selves all worked up and worried about you. And you're so stub-born about staying out here all by yourself. Everyone knows you're not exhibiting a bit of good sense these days. And now you're all stove-up with a busted arm, and you go and let some stranger into your house. Well, what will happen to you next? Don't you get it? You can't keep living out here, Mom. You need help."

"Oh, phooey!" She waved her good arm at him. "I can take care of myself just fine. I was a little worn down from being at the hospital all day. You know how long it took them to figure out that this was a *broken* arm and then set the thing? Why, I had Olivia take me in first thing this morning, and it must've been past two o'clock before they ever put the cast on! I want to know what in heaven's name is wrong with our modern medical professionals when they gotta go through all sorts of ridiculous—and I'll bet expensive—procedures just to tell you what you already knew when you walked in there in the first place?"

"Quit changing the subject, Mom." He glanced at his watch. "Now, I've got Lester meeting me here in about five minutes. He's got some papers for you to sign and I don't want—"

"Not that real-estate weasel again! Charles, if I've told you once, I've told you a—" she was trying to stand now—"I do not want that slippery, slimy Lester Matson coming around my place again. Everyone knows his father was a no-account crook and I've no doubts that the apple doesn't fall far from the tree—especially in that family."

"That's not fair, Mom."

She was on her feet now, but swaying slightly. Armando moved to the edge of his seat, wondering if Charles had noticed or not. "Furthermore," she said, shaking her good fist high in the air, "when, and if, I ever want to sell this place, I will take care of the matter myself with my own attorney, thank you very much."

"You mean ol' Farley? Why he doesn't even practice anymore—"

"He does for me."

"But, Mom—"

"No *buts*, Charles."

Charles turned and looked nervously out the window. "Look, Mom, can't you listen to reason for a change? Lester's not at all like his dad; he's highly respected in his—that's him pulling up right now."

"Well, you can go out there and tell him to get off my place!" she shouted in a shrill voice, but she was starting to lean a little to her left, as if the weight of the plaster cast was pulling her off balance. In the same instance, Armando leaped from his chair and gently caught her before she toppled.

"What're you doing to my mother?" demanded Charles as he turned to see Armando easing her back down to the couch.

"None of your business," she huffed. Armando smiled to himself, remembering how she'd thrown those same words at him not more than an hour ago.

"I really should get going, ma'am." He spoke quietly to her, almost apologetically, and he did feel sorry for causing her any trouble. It seemed she had plenty already without his contribution. He adjusted her pillow and stood up straight, glad that he'd heeded his grandmother's voice and not made off with her truck after all.

"That's right," said Charles. "This is family business and doesn't concern you."

"Not so fast there, Charlie boy," his mother reprimanded. "Armando and I were discussing the possibility of him staying on here and working for me—just until I get better that is."

Armando kept a straight face, another trick he'd learned from Tio Pedro long ago—a result of losing his paper-route money playing blackjack with his uncle back when he was still a kid.

Charles scowled with skepticism. "You can't be serious, Mom."

"Why not? You're the one who's always telling me I need some-one to come live out here and help me—"

"But not a—" He stopped himself.

"Not a *what?*" She eyed her son sharply.

"Not a—well, not a complete stranger."

The old woman studied Armando as she spoke. "He's not a complete stranger. Armando was born in St. Joseph's Hospital in

Los Angeles, California. He's almost twenty-one. And he's trying to make a fresh start. He came to Treasure looking for a job. He's interested in old trucks and he's a hard worker."

Armando blinked. That was more than his own mother knew about him.

Charles studied Armando. "Is that true, boy? You're really looking for honest work?"

He nodded. "You bet. That's why I stopped." A lie perhaps, but then the old lady had lied too. And what was he supposed to say—that he had been about to hot-wire her old pickup, but got caught red-handed in the act?

Charles made a grunting noise as he headed to the door. "I better go talk to Lester."

"Tell Lester the Lecher to beat it!" She scowled down into her lap, rubbing her hand back and forth over her cast as if to ease the pain. But as soon as the door closed, she looked up eagerly. "Can you play along with me, Armando? Just 'til Charlie gives up and goes back home again."

Armando shrugged. "Sure, but doesn't sound like he gives up too easily."

"Yeah, he's a stubborn one."

"Wonder where he gets that from?" Armando peered out the window at the two men talking in the driveway. "Well, okay, then, if I'm supposed to be your new employee, you mind telling me your name?"

Her thin lips curled up slightly, the closest thing he'd seen to a smile yet. "I'm Dora Chase."

"Okay, then, Mrs. Chase, anything else I should know before your son comes back and starts grilling me again?"

"First of all, call me Dora. Always makes me feel old when people call me Mrs. Chase."

"Mind if I ask exactly how old you are?"

She held her chin up proudly. "Not at all. I turned eighty-one last February."

He whistled. "That's pretty old, ma'am."

"Maybe. But if Homer hadn't gotten under my feet today, I'd still be as fit as a fiddle right now." She glanced around the room. "Have you seen him anywhere?"

"Who?"

"Homer. My cat."

"Well, I did notice a big yellow cat out by the truck, right before you threatened to gun me down."

She nodded. "That'd be my Homer, the one that tripped me up. He didn't mean any harm though. I just need to watch my step better."

He studied her for a long moment, his arms folded across his chest. The idea of a place to sleep and food to eat was appealing. "Well, maybe you should think about having me stick round here for real—for a day or two, you know, 'til you get a little stronger."

She seemed to consider his suggestion then firmly shook her head. "No thanks. I don't need any help. I'm fine on my own."

"But what about Charles? Won't he find out that you lied to him about me? Then what?"

She frowned as she looked out the window. "I sure don't like my boy bossing me around like that. Acting like I don't have good sense or like I'm getting senile. Just because I'm old doesn't mean I'm crazy."

Armando glanced around the house with its old and worn furnishings. It wasn't a bad place really, but it was plain to see this woman wasn't living the "good life" that he often imagined most gringos enjoyed. And it sure didn't look like the set to any sitcom he'd seen on TV. "Hey," he began, "if it's about money, I'm okay working for food and a bed, just for a couple days—"

"It's *not* the money!" She looked down at her cast again, still rubbing it back and forth with her good hand, as if the motion some-how soothed her.

"Yeah, whatever." Not that he believed her. And what difference should it make to him anyway? Why should he suddenly feel so anxious to stick around this crummy old place? Had this strange old woman cast some sort of spell on him? His aunt used to talk about people who did things like that. But he'd never believed it was real. He stood by the window now, watching as Lester the Lecher climbed back into his car—a late-model Cadillac, black and sleek—pretty nice weasel wheels to Armando's way of thinking. Then Charles walked slowly back toward the house, his hands clenched by his sides in two tight little fists, and his face grim.

"Here comes Charlie boy now," Armando announced in a flat voice. "And he doesn't look too pleased."

"All right." Her face looked like someone who'd been dealt a bad hand of cards. "You can work here for room and board. Just a few days though. Just until Charlie settles down a bit and forgets all this nonsense about selling off my farm."

He leaned over and gently shook her good hand. "Okay, we got a deal then?"

She narrowed her eyes. "Deal," she said quickly as the door opened and her son walked in.

Chapter Three

$\mathscr{D}$ora felt herself grow drowsy as the two men in the front room continued to converse. It seemed they were having a disagreement of sorts, but their voices weren't raised exactly, and she couldn't quite make out their words. She squinted up at the taller one, but his image seemed slightly blurred as she tried to recall exactly who he was and why he'd come here. He had nice shoulders and, though lean, appeared strong. Was it her Henry? Talking to her daddy? Of course, she thought, closing her eyes in satisfaction, Henry was trying to convince Daddy that they were ready for marriage.

"But you don't have two nickels to rub together," her father had complained, stubbornly folding his arms across his chest. "I had expected more for my little girl."

"I know, Mr. Lawrence." Henry had taken a deep breath to bolster himself. "I realize that you're an important man in this town and—"

"My grandfather founded this town."

"I know that, sir."

"And do you know that Dora could have her pick of anyone—"

"I don't want anyone else." Dora slipped her hand into Henry's as she finally drew the nerve to speak. "Henry and I have been in love since we were kids."

"But you promised me—"

"I promised you I'd go to college, Daddy. And now I've obtained

my teaching credentials, but I've told you dozens of times that
I don't really want to teach school."

"But the Chase family has nothing. Henry has nothing." Charles
Lawrence ran his hand over his rapidly balding head.

"But we love each other, Daddy."

He grunted. "Well, love doesn't pay the milkman now, does it?"

Henry shifted uncomfortably. "I've managed to save up a little
money, sir."

Her father laughed. "And where do you keep all this money,
Henry? I haven't noticed any accounts in your name at the bank."

"Oh, Daddy!" Dora frowned. "Just because you're the bank's
president doesn't give you the right to go snooping—"

"Well, I'd like to know, Dora." He peered suspiciously at Henry.
"Where do you keep this big stash of cash, boy? In a sock or under
your mattress?"

Henry remained firm. "I have a safe place for it."

"And I suppose you've gotten rich from logging?" Mr. Lawrence
turned to his daughter. "So you really want to be a logger's wife,
do you? Clean his house, do his laundry, have a bunch of scraggly
kids and then get widowed before they're even out of grammar
school?"

"Oh, Daddy!"

"I don't plan on logging forever, sir."

"No, no, I didn't think so. I'm sure you have big dreams."

"Not big dreams maybe. But I have dreams."

"Henry wants to buy land, Daddy." Dora beamed up at Henry.
"He wants to be a farmer."

Mr. Lawrence hooted. "Now that's perfect! I thought logging
was bad, but you think you can get rich dirt farming?"

"I don't plan on getting rich, sir. I only want to make enough
to take care of my family and live comfortably."

"And you should see the wonderful garden he keeps at his

mother's house," said Dora. "He grows everything imaginable, and it's all weeded and nice."

Mr. Lawrence sadly shook his head. "A dirt farmer. My little girl wants to marry a dirt farmer."

Dora took in a deep breath and stood as tall as her five feet two inches could stretch. "For your information, I do not need your consent, Daddy. As you well know, I am twenty-one and I'm perfectly able to—"

Henry placed his hand on her arm to stop her. "Sir, we're not asking for your consent—we're asking for your blessing. We *do* plan to get married. But, for Dora's sake, it'd be nice if you could be happy for us. It'd mean a lot to your daughter."

Charles Lawrence grunted. "I guess I should be glad your mother isn't alive to see what a mess—"

"Daddy!" snapped Dora. "Mother always approved of Henry when we were kids. I think she would be proud now."

"Proud to see her daughter scrapping out a living with a poor dirt farmer?"

Henry cleared his throat. "Excuse me, sir, but I don't plan on growing dirt. I plan on growing good healthy food."

Dora nodded proudly. "And I plan on helping him."

"Well, I hope you two don't expect to get any help from me."

Henry firmly shook his head. "No, sir. This is something I intend to do on my own. I already have my eye on a couple pieces of property just outside of town, and I think if all goes well, I should be able to make a purchase before too long."

Charles narrowed his eyes. "Takes more than a parcel of land to make a farm. You need machinery and seeds and fertilizer—"

"Henry knows all that." Dora looked up at Henry with admiration. "He has lots of books on agriculture and he subscribes to all the farming journals. He knows what he's doing."

Charles Lawrence sighed deeply. "Well, I think it's a foolhardy thing to do, Henry Chase, and I'll never forgive you if you drag my daughter into rack and ruin. But I suppose there's no stopping you two." He rubbed his chin thoughtfully. "But how about if we make a deal?"

"What kind of a deal, sir?"

"How about if I give my blessing for your marriage after you bring in your first cash crop and deposit the money into my bank? And to show my approval I'll throw you kids a wedding that this town'll never forget. You'll be the talk of Treasure."

"Really, Daddy? You'd do that for us?"

"You bet. As soon as Henry gets his farm together and makes a real profit from it, I'll be proud to walk my little girl down the aisle and hand her over. But not until then." Charles stuck out his hand. "You agree, Henry?"

Henry seemed a little reluctant.

"Come on, Henry," urged Dora. "It's a fine idea."

So, on April 11, 1941, Henry and Charles shook on it. And shortly thereafter, Henry made a down payment on one parcel of property, the one with the tiny ranch house on it. The ever diligent Henry went right to work putting in a crop of late wheat, the quickest and cheapest thing he could grow on such short notice. But when harvesttime came, the wheat prices went down, and after he finally sold his crop he barely had enough money to make his payment and buy more seed for next year. It became clear that he would need to continue logging in order to support his small farm. Dora, sensing that their wedding date wasn't imminent, decided to take a teaching job in town. Her plan was to put every penny into savings—to be used for the farm.

* * * * * * * * * * * * *

When Dora woke up, the room was dim, and she could see by the rosy color of the sky that she'd been asleep for a while. It took her a moment to remember exactly what had transpired today—and to separate it from her vivid dream. But a sharp pain in her left arm brought her back to reality. Now where was that boy? Probably prowling around the place and stealing her blind. You could never trust those Mexicans. Oh sure, Henry had hired them upon occasion, and he seemed to trust them all right, and she didn't disagree that they were good laborers, but it had always worried her to have them in the house. And she had gone to great lengths to make sure they stayed outside. Until today.

"Armando?" she called out, trying to ease herself from the sofa. "Boy, where are you?"

Chapter Four

$\mathcal{A}$rmando could tell that Charles had been irritated by Armando's presence in his mother's home. And as Dora drifted off to sleep, he'd tried once again to talk Armando into leaving—even offering him a ride into town, a free meal, and a few bucks to send him on his way. As tempting as the offer was, Armando didn't want to give in to this pompous little man. And for whatever reason, this small victory gave Armando a sense of power as he grinned broadly from the front porch, calling out, "See ya round, Charlie."

Charles only grunted in return as he climbed into his shiny white Buick then drove, too quickly, creating a cloud of brown dust. Armando chuckled, thinking how Charles would need to wash his car now. He peeked back into the house to find the old woman sleeping soundly, probably a result of the pain pill he'd given her earlier. But it was probably good that she was resting. He glanced around the front room then quietly closed the screen door and returned to the porch.

Sometimes, especially lately, Armando imagined his uncle Pedro as that little horned devil he'd often seen as a kid in those old classic cartoons—the one who perches on a shoulder and whispers devious plans into its listener's ear. And right now Tio Pedro was on his shoulder again, suggesting that he grab a pillow-case and fill it with anything of value and then *"get outta there"*— maybe even in that old Chevy if he could get it to start.

But on the other shoulder, in the rounded form of a little old woman, sat his grandmother, Abuela Maria. She had always been a good woman, devout in her faith, and despite a life of hardship and disappointments, she'd been loved and respected by all who knew her. Her faith in the Lord Jesus Christ was as real as the tortillas she used to pound out with her flat wide hands, singing old hymns in Spanish to the rhythm of slap-slapping on the ancient tortilla stone that she'd carried with her from Mexico.

She'd raised Armando since infancy, scrimping and saving so he could attend a Catholic school where the nuns encouraged him to speak English "correctly" and to believe in himself and pursue his dreams. But when a heart attack removed his grandmother's good influence, Armando's life changed drastically. No more private school or hopes of college. Tia Marta, Abuela Maria's daughter, and her husband, Tio Pedro, took Armando into their small home. And although Tio Pedro was gone much of the time, when he was around his influence was anything but wholesome. And yet as a boy, Armando had always hungered for a father figure, and his uncle had been big and strong and macho. In the beginning, Armando looked up to him.

But it only took Armando a few years to discover and finally accept what his uncle was really made of, and in time he learned how to avoid Tio Pedro. A master of lying low, slipping out the back, and even protecting his young cousins from their father's unpredictable mood swings, Armando quickly learned how to not be fooled by this self-motivated man. He even tried to talk Tia Marta into leaving Pedro, promising that he'd work hard to support his aunt and cousins—hadn't he already? But she claimed she loved her devious husband, could never leave him. And so Armando had stayed on, helping when he could, and keeping a low profile when needed. He'd probably still be there right now if he hadn't finally allowed himself to be taken in by one of Tio Pedro's scams. And now he could never go back.

Still, it seemed that no matter how far he ran, hoping to flee his uncle's influence and now his wrath, there that stubborn man remained. So the battle between the good and the bad continued— with Abuela Maria and her lawless son-in-law, Pedro, bickering back and forth on Armando's two shoulders. It was a heavy load to carry.

Armando decided to walk around Dora's property, hoping it would distract him from these troubling thoughts and regrets. It was time to move on. To forget the past and somehow create a future. Since his earliest memories he had enjoyed being outside of the city. He'd felt especially comfortable in agricultural country and for some reason the idea of owning acreage had always fascinated him. Maybe it was in his blood. He knew that his great-great-grandfather had once owned a large ranch down in southern Mexico. It had supposedly been in their family for generations, but during some political uprising or property dispute or whatever, they had lost all their land. Back in the fifties, Abuela Maria and her husband had come to America in search of a better life. Unfortunately, her husband had found a better life in the form of a younger woman, and poor Maria had been left on her own to support her two little girls on a maid's wages and only a faint grasp of English. Yet she had always held her head high, as if she were still the daughter of aristocracy. And perhaps in her own mind she was. Armando still remembered her words shortly before she died. "I am going home to my Father soon." He had asked if she meant his great-grandpa, the one with the big mustache in the brown-toned photo that hung above her bed. She had smiled faintly. "No, *mijo*. I am speaking of God. He is my Father; I am His child." Then she had grasped Armando's hand and said, "He is your Father too." But Armando's concept of God steadily grew more and more cloudy as he grew older. And, of course, Marta and Pedro rarely attended church after Abuela Maria died.

Armando gave his head a hard shake, as if to dispel these old

memories. Hadn't he taken this walk to escape them? He took in
a deep breath and looked all around him, observing all the green
vegetation. During his early teens, before he'd gone to work at
Mickey's dad's garage, Armando had spent his summers earning
extra money doing farm labor. And he knew enough about agriculture to know that this property had once been a farm. But other
than a weedy vegetable garden and some scraggly flower beds, the
place seemed pretty neglected now, and it was hard to guess what
might've actually grown here at one time. It looked like it would
take some big machinery and real know-how to bring it back. But
he suspected it could be revived—if a person wanted to, that is.
But maybe Dora's son was right. Maybe this property would be
better off sold and placed in the hands of someone who could give
it the care it needed. Armando shook his head at the waste. Man,
if he had a place like this, he'd start whipping it into shape pronto.
He'd work night and day and give it all he had to make it into
something to be proud of—if it were his, that is. Some people
don't know what they've got.

After walking over the rise and down to the creek he turned
around and headed back toward the house. Despite the earlier
heat, the air was quickly growing chilly as the afternoon sun
dipped behind a stand of poplars near the creek. This cooler
climate might take some getting used to, but already he liked it.
The smell of damp soil and plants mingling with the fresh air gave
him a feeling of unexplainable hope. He paused by the vegetable
garden and almost without thinking stooped over and grabbed
a large milkweed. With the stubborn weed secure in his grip, he
gave it a strong twist and pull, extracting it from the dark brown
soil with its roots fully intact. He shook off the loose dirt and tossed
the weed aside. How could such a simple gesture bring such a
sense of power? He continued to pull weeds until his weed pile
grew tall and the shadows long. Then stretching his arms and back,

he stood and looked up in time to see the sky now glowing pink and rosy.

"What're you doing out there?" Dora called from the porch.

He'd almost forgotten the old woman, but now he waved to her as he approached the house. No sense in getting her riled. "Just checking the place out," he said as he stepped onto the porch, noticing that the board on the second step was dangerously loose.

She frowned. "Checking it out?" She seemed to consider this. "Or *casing it out* as I've heard them say on those TV crime shows."

He rolled his eyes. "Hey, I was looking around some. Seems like this might've been a pretty nice place at one time."

She peered beyond him, a faraway look on her face, as if she were seeing more than just the neglected acreage out there. "It *was* a beautiful place once. The best farm in these parts. My Henry worked hard to carve this place out of practically nothing. He put his heart and soul into it."

"What did he grow?"

She eased herself down into the rocker, cradling her cast in her good arm. "He started out with grain crops like wheat and barley and oats. But in time, he moved on to grow things like onions, broccoli, cabbages, beets, potatoes—you name it, and he probably tried it at least once. Henry loved farming."

Armando settled himself on the top step and listened to her rambling on and on; it almost seemed as if she'd forgotten he was there. But he didn't mind her chatter, and in some ways it reminded him of his grandmother, the way she would come home after a long day and tell him stories about the various guests who stayed in the hotel she worked for. He never really listened carefully, but the sound of her voice always reassured him somehow. Made him think that his world was a safe place. He watched the sky now as the sunset colors faded and slowly turned to a dark periwinkle blue.

"Why, there was a time when Henry grew a little bit of everything.

And his produce was so fine it was sold in the very best grocery stores across the Pacific Northwest. Chase Produce—people would actually ask for it by name." She finally paused as if waiting for something.

And he realized it was his turn to respond. "So what happened?"

"What happened?" She repeated his question with a look of confusion.

"I mean to the farm."

"Oh, you mean, how did it get so run-down?"

"Yeah."

"Well, Henry died."

Armando nodded in silence.

"Back in June of '83, he just died in his sleep one night. They said it was a brain aneurysm. But it was a complete shock to me. Why, Henry had never been sick a single day in his life. Still, if you have to go, I say, you might as well go in your sleep." She sadly shook her head. "I tried to keep the farm running back then, and I managed to produce for a few more years, but it was an uphill battle for a woman in her sixties. It wasn't long until I hired out my land, but by then market prices started dropping and we were getting too much competition from your people."

"*My* people?" He tried to conceal his aggravation now.

"Yes. Mexico, South America—you know what I mean. Anyhow I could see that it wasn't even worth it anymore. And finally, other than my little vegetable garden, I had to give up."

"Too bad."

"Maybe. But the fact is small farmers can't make a decent living in today's market. Sometimes I think it's a blessing that Henry died when he did because it would've killed him to see what's happened to family farms all over the country these days. I kept subscribing to his farm magazines for a time, but it got too downright depressing after a while, hearing how so many farms were going under left and right."

"Still, it seems like you could do something more here—grow something, I mean."

Dora stiffly rose from her chair. "It's getting a mite chilly out here. Best be getting inside and see what I can scratch up for our dinner."

He opened the door for her and followed her into the kitchen. "Maybe you should let me fix dinner," he suggested, noticing how her face was pinched in pain again.

"Humph. You really know how to cook?"

He shrugged. "You had a pill recently? I think the bottle says you can take them every four hours."

"Don't know that they do much good other than making me groggy. I think that little pill actually gave me a strange dream this afternoon."

"But the rest is probably good for your arm." *Besides,* he thought, *it will quiet you down some.* He opened the prescription bottle and fished out a pill then filled a glass with water. Then he remembered the thing about food. He glanced around the kitchen. "You got something light you could eat with this?"

"There's some crackers in that tin."

He fished a couple out and waited as she munched on them. Then, like an obedient child, she took the pill and handed the water glass back to him. "The doctor at the hospital says my bones are brittle so I'm supposed to start drinking milk."

"Do you want some?"

She made a face. "No. I told him I can't stand milk. So he gave me a prescription for calcium pills, but the man at the pharmacy said they're almost the same as Tums. And I already have Tums."

Armando nodded. "Maybe you should go sit down and rest a little while I see what I can fix for us."

"You sure you know how to cook, boy?" She peered at him

curiously. "Keep in mind that I can't be eating anything too spicy now. No tacos or chili for me; it upsets my digestion."

"Don't worry. I know how to cook gringo food too."

She narrowed her eyes. "What's that mean anyway? *Gringo?* Some kind of nasty Mexican slang for white folks?"

"Well, my grandmother told me it was from the old days when the white man first started taking our land—"

"*Your* land? What do you mean?"

"Oh, I'm sure you must know that Mexico used to be a lot bigger—it ran clear into Texas and California."

"Oh, right, but that was long ago." She waved her hand as if to dismiss this. "But what about that gringo business?"

"My grandmother said the white men used to go around singing, 'Green grow the rushes' all the time and the Mexicans started calling them 'green-grows', which later became *gringo.*"

She looked skeptical. "Sounds like nonsense if you ask me."

"Why don't you go rest some while I see what I can fix in here," he said again.

"There's some ham in the fridge," she called as she headed for the sofa. "And some asparagus that needs to be used up—you know how to cook asparagus? I don't like mine cooked until it's mushy."

"Yeah, yeah," he called from the kitchen, then more quietly, "I'm not an idiot, you know."

Abuela Maria had taught him to cook while he was a boy. "In Mexico, I was raised to believe that the kitchen was the woman's place," she had told him. "But now I think like an American—I think if you eat then you should cook." And so from an early age he had begun fixing their supper, having it all ready for her when she came home worn-out from a ten-hour day of cleaning hotel rooms. His favorite dishes were the authentic Mexican ones, but for the sake of time, he'd also learned how to fix some quick and easy American food—inexpensive things like macaroni and cheese and hot dogs and hamburgers.

He opened the refrigerator and removed the ham and asparagus. There was only one thick slice of ham, and he was hungry. But when he saw a carton of eggs, he decided to make *huevos rancheros*. He chopped up the ham and asparagus with a little onion and sautéed them in oil. Then he grated some cheese and whipped up some eggs, combining all the ingredients in a large frying pan. Now, tortillas would really taste perfect with this, but he would settle for bread. He dished up a plate of food and carried it out to the front room.

"What are you doing?" she demanded. "I never eat in the living room."

"I thought you might be more comfortable out here."

"Humph. I suppose it's okay just this once."

He spotted a nearby TV tray and moved it up next to her then set the dish and utensils down.

"What's this?" She frowned at the food. "I told you to use the ham and asparagus!"

"It's in there. What do you want to drink?"

"I like tea."

"I didn't see any in the refrigerator."

Her face grew puzzled. "Why would I keep tea in the fridge?"

Now he was confused. "To keep it cold."

Her eyes lit up. "Oh, you mean iced tea. No, I don't have any of that. I want hot tea. Do you know how to make hot tea?"

He shrugged.

"Just heat up the teakettle, fill a cup, and bring me a tea bag." She poked the eggs with her fork. "Is this some kind of omelet?"

"Something like that." He went back into the kitchen and turned on the teakettle then sat down at the kitchen table and hungrily devoured his supper, finishing even before the kettle whistled. Still slightly hungry, he went to the fruit bowl and helped himself to an orange.

"What're you doing in there?" she called as the kettle began to whistle.

Without answering, he poured her hot water, located the tin of tea bags, and returned to the front room. "Your tea." He set the cup on the TV tray then noticed that she'd eaten everything on her plate. "Did you like it?"

"Not half bad."

He took her empty plate back to the kitchen and, not wanting to sit out in the living room with her, he began to put things away.

"What're you doing in there?" she called again.

He stepped into the doorway, a dishrag hanging limply from his hand. "Cleaning up." He studied her face, not bothering to mask his own irritation, as he waited for her response. What did she think he was doing in there anyway? Pocketing the family silver? And maybe that wasn't such a bad idea. He'd already noticed a fairly substantial set in one of the drawers.

"Oh." She pursed her lips. "Well, there's some ice cream in the freezer that needs eating."

"You want some?"

"Yeah. It's got calcium, you know."

He found the ice cream and fixed them both a bowl then returned to the front room with hers.

"Aren't you having any?" she asked. "Don't you like ice cream?"

"I left it in there."

"Look, boy, it's not as if you're my slave. You can bring your ice cream out here to eat."

He studied her for a moment. "Then, if I'm not your slave, would you mind not calling me *boy* all the time?"

She chuckled then glanced over to the big TV console. "Suit

yourself, *Armando.* But while you're still out here, could you turn that thing on? It's time for my wheel."

"Your wheel?"

"Wheel of Fortune."

He turned on the TV, remembering how his grandmother used to watch it too.

"Well, get back in here with your ice cream if you want to play along too. But I'm sure you won't be able to keep up with me."

He would have preferred the silence of the kitchen but thought perhaps he should at least appear to be social. Not that she was particularly. He tried not to stare as she noisily scraped her spoon against her bowl, shouting out answers when they came to her. Some right, some wrong. She wasn't very skilled at eating with only one hand yet. And then before the show was half over, she began to doze off—probably the pill kicking in. He quietly removed the bowl from her lap, then leaned back in the recliner and watched the remainder of the silly game show, wondering what in the world he was doing here. And why didn't he just take off? Go while the going was good? But then where was he going to go? And maybe it was smart to lie low for a while—until he could figure things out. Besides, at least he had food here.

Chapter Five

*U*nlike Tio Pedro, who could watch mindlessly for hours, Armando didn't much care for television anymore. So when the game show ended and Dora still appeared to be asleep, he turned it off and returned to the kitchen. He stood for a long time, looking around. He went over to the hutch and opened the top drawer, the place where he'd looked earlier when searching for a clean dish towel. He picked up a sterling spoon and balanced it across his palm. It felt heavy. Probably valuable. He wondered what the whole set would bring? Several hundred perhaps? He sensed Tio Pedro's presence again. *"Go ahead, boy, get what ya can and get outta here."* He took in a deep breath as he blankly stared through the glass doors on the upper part of the hutch. Probably lots of valuable stuff around here if a person looked hard enough.

Then his eyes stopped on a set of porcelain salt and pepper shakers in the form of chickens. They reminded him of a pair his grandmother had used back when he was a boy. He opened the cupboard door and picked up the rooster, examining it closely. Identical. The voice of Abuela Maria came to him now, warm and comforting: *"You're a good boy, Armando. God has good plans for you."* He replaced the rooster and then the spoon, closing the drawer with a dull thud. He turned and surveyed the partially cleaned kitchen, and then almost mechanically, went back to cleaning up, as if his grandmother were right there looking over his shoulder.

After the last pan was scrubbed and hung back over the stove, he decided to explore the house—not snooping exactly, but seeing how it was situated. Dora was still fast asleep, her cat nestled at her side, as he tiptoed toward the hallway. He'd already used the bathroom, hadn't cared much for its matching tile and fixtures in an odd shade of pink, but was impressed with how neat and clean it was kept. Totally unlike his aunt's chaotic and messy little house, but then he knew it was tough with three little girls running all over the place. He had noticed the door to the right of the bathroom and suspected it was a bedroom, probably Dora's. Just slightly ajar, he gave it a nudge then glanced in. By the light from the hall he could see the walls were a pale shade of blue, a pleasant-looking room with its blond-colored furnishings that he guessed were from around the fifties because they reminded him of the old *I Love Lucy* reruns that his grandmother used to enjoy when he was a kid. The bed seemed carefully made up, probably done before Dora broke her arm, covered in a neat blue chenille bedspread and with pillows in an even row. Despite her age, Dora was definitely a careful housekeeper. He noticed an ornately carved box sitting atop a lace doily on the long dresser. It seemed like something from the Orient and he figured it was probably for jewelry, although he couldn't imagine that the no-nonsense little woman snoring on the couch went in much for diamonds or anything of great value. Still, you never knew.

Once again, he could hear Tio Pedro's persuasive voice, urging him to *"get the goods and get going."* Standing in the shadows, his hand still resting on the doorknob, Armando seriously considered this tempting option again. *"You gotta look out for the big numero uno,"* his uncle had been known to say, usually with a sly smile and always referring to himself. But maybe Tio Pedro was right. After all, who else was looking out for him? Besides that, this old woman surely didn't need most of this stuff, probably wouldn't even miss it—she might even consider it payment for all the help he'd given her today. Everyone knows that good help is hard to find. He thought about that silver set again, and whatever else might be hidden in that hutch. That set combined with a few pieces of gold jewelry could probably take him quite a ways—but where? Where would he go? What would he do? And why?

He shook his head as he silently pulled the door closed then let out a deep sigh as he stepped away from the bedroom. What was he thinking anyway? Tio Pedro was a complete fool—it was his fault that Armando was on the run even now. Why should he listen to the advice of someone like that? Hadn't he come up to Oregon for a clean start in the first place? To escape the grasp of Tio Pedro and others like him? He walked quietly back down the hall, this time pausing at the staircase. He wondered what was up there. Perhaps a place for him to sleep? He glanced over at Dora to assure himself that her eyes were still closed as he quietly stepped onto the first stair. But the second step squeaked in loud protest the moment he placed his weight upon it.

"What's going on?" she squawked from the sofa.

He turned in time to see her sitting up and blinking her eyes as if she were confused and didn't quite recognize him. The big yellow cat leaped from his comfortable spot and Armando smiled, hoping to disarm her. "Sorry to bother you, Dora. I . . . uh . . . I was wondering where I was supposed to sleep tonight."

"What?" She still looked startled and a little frightened with wisps of white hair sticking out on the sides of her head in a freakish manner.

"I didn't want to disturb you since you were sound asleep." He walked over to the sofa, wondering if she had any idea or what she would do if she knew what he'd been thinking. "How's your arm?"

She looked down at her cast then back at him as if she were

slowly recalling the events of the day. "Broken arm," she muttered. "Why'd I go do something so stupid as this?"

"I'm sure you didn't do it on purpose."

"Well, of course not!" She pushed herself up with her good arm, grunting in pain as she tried to rise from the sofa.

"Here, let me help—"

"I can do it my—"

But before she could finish, he'd already slipped his hand beneath her arm and eased her to her feet. "Steady now?"

"I'm perfectly fine. Just need to go to bed is all." She slowly shuffled toward the hallway, moaning as she went.

"But where do you want me to sleep?" he asked.

"Oh!" She stopped walking and turned around. With narrowed eyes she studied him. "Not in my house, that's for certain," she snapped. "Henry might've thought it was all right to have you wet-backs in the house, but not me."

Armando frowned. "Where then?"

"There's a room out there—out in the barn—you can use that if you like."

"Fine." He tried to conceal his irritation as he grabbed his back-pack and walked to the door.

"Just a minute, *boy.*"

He sucked in a tight breath at the sound of that word again. "What?" He turned with narrowed eyes to see her opening what appeared to be a linen closet.

"Come here and get yourself a pillow and some blankets to take with you." She stood and watched over him as he gathered up some things. "And don't forget to lock my door on your way out. And let the cat out. He doesn't like to be stuck in the house all night." Then she waited in the hallway, watching with satisfaction as he fiddled with the doorknob until it was twisted into a locked position. He pulled the door closed behind him, and even tested it to show her that it was really locked. Not that he couldn't get back in if he wanted to since the dead bolt wasn't locked.

He wished he'd thought to ask for a flashlight as he stumbled down the steps and into the darkness. But thanks to the light of a clear half-moon it was only a few moments before his eyes adjusted and he began to pick his way across the yard toward the barn, careful to avoid the blackberry vines.

"No wetbacks in the house," he growled to himself as he fumbled along the barn wall, hoping to find a light switch. "Who does she think she is anyway?" Finally he located a small box and flicked the switch that connected to an overhead light. He heard a scurrying sound across the floor as the interior of the old barn came to life in shadows of gold and brown. Startled by the noise, he peered around, but other than an ancient-looking tractor and a few dusty pieces of old farm equipment and tools, the barn appeared to be empty. He shook off his fear. Probably a rat—no big deal. He'd hoped to find some hay or straw to use as a bed, but realized since this farm had no livestock, there was little need for it. Then he noticed what appeared to be a boxed-off room or maybe a stall in a corner to his right.

"Must be the wetback sleeping quarters," he mumbled as he tried the doorknob. It was unlocked. In the dim light from the barn he noticed a string hanging down from the ceiling. He gave it a tentative pull, and the room was immediately illuminated by a flickering bare bulb suspended by a cord. He quickly surveyed the whitewashed room to see an iron bed frame complete with a dust-coated mattress, as well as a small chest of drawers topped with a cracked mirror and a straight-backed chair beneath the window. "Could be worse," he told himself as he returned to the barn to close the exterior door and turn off the main light.

He could tell by the various holes in the striped ticking that some form of rodents had been making good use of the mattress filling. Maybe tomorrow, if he decided to stay on that is, he could clean this place up a bit. For tonight it would have to do. Besides, he assured himself, it was better than sleeping on the damp ground like he'd done the past couple nights. He glanced at his watch to see that it wasn't even nine yet. Way too early for bed back in the city. But this wasn't the city and he was dog tired. He set his back-pack on the dusty chest of drawers, hopefully out of reach of rodents, and tossed the bedding on the mattress. Then he heard a meow outside his door and opened it up to see the big yellow cat.

"What do you want?" he asked. The cat walked in and rubbed against his legs. "You looking for a place to sleep?" He reached down and petted his back. "Well, I suppose you might be good at keeping the rats away. *Mi casa es su casa.*"

And, feeling slightly better about the rodent problem, he turned off the light and got into bed. Petting Homer's furry coat, he soon fell asleep.

* * * * * * * * * * * * *

The light woke Armando and he squinted to see the numbers on his digital watch. Only five-fifty! He hadn't been up that early since he was fifteen, back when Tia Marta had arranged for him to work on a melon farm for the best part of a long, hot summer. He glanced around the room to see that Homer had already left, hope-fully to catch a mouse. He noticed the sunlight pouring through a dirty window that apparently faced east and wished for a thick set of curtains to block it out. Maybe he'd nail something up there— that is if he decided to stay on, and only for another day or two. In the meantime he pulled the blanket over his head and tried to return to sleep.

The next time he awoke, it was to a loud knocking on the door. "You in there, boy?" called the old woman. "Or did you light out in the middle of the night?"

"What?" he answered sleepily, trying to remember where he was.

"You better get up if you want your breakfast."

He sat up and longed for a hot shower, a toilet, and a place to brush his teeth. Then he grabbed his backpack and sprang out the door, catching Dora outside the barn. "How's your arm doing?" he asked, hoping to sound more cheerful and awake than he actually felt. No need to alienate his only hope of getting breakfast this morning.

"Kept me up half the night."

"Did you take a pain pill?"

"Stupid old pills. They don't help much."

"But they help you to sleep."

She grunted. "I suppose."

"You didn't have to make my breakfast."

"I know, but since I was making oatmeal, I thought I might as well make enough for two. You do like oatmeal, don't you?"

He nodded even though he'd never actually tasted oatmeal before. It wasn't something his grandmother or aunt had ever fixed. "Was it hard to cook with only one hand?" he asked as they entered the house.

"Humph. I used to cook with one hand all the time back when I had babies to balance on my hip."

He nodded, setting his backpack in the corner. "Do you think I could take a shower . . . ?"

"Of course. You don't think I want you to go around smelling like a hog all day long, do you? Just as soon as you eat and clean up the breakfast dishes you can clean yourself up too. But use the bathroom upstairs. And don't be leaving a mess up there. I don't expect to be cleaning up after you." She pointed to the kitchen table. "Now, sit down."

He sat down at the plastic-topped table, smiling to himself as he noticed that she'd gone to a bit of trouble to put together what looked like more than just oatmeal. A small plate held several pieces of toast and there was also an unopened jar of peaches and another of jam on the table.

"You drink coffee?" she asked as she came to the table with a pot.

"Yes, thanks."

"Can you open those jars for me? That's one thing that's hard to do with just one good hand. I put those preserves up myself and I always make sure to get the lids on good and tight."

He twisted open the lid on the second jar as she sat down. But when he reached for his spoon, she stopped him. "Wait!" she commanded. "We must ask for the Lord's blessing first."

He blinked. "Sure."

She placed her good hand over the one protruding from the cast then bowed her head, and he followed suit, waiting as she quickly recited a short prayer. After she said amen, he crossed himself in the way his grandmother had taught him as a young boy. But when he looked up he noticed Dora was staring at him.

"Guess it just stands to reason that you'd be Catholic too." She shook her head as if it were a crime.

"Why's that?"

"Aren't all Mexicans Catholic?"

"Not all. But most, I guess. Is that a problem?"

She shrugged then reached for the milk carton. "My daddy used to say that you can't trust a Catholic any further'n you can throw him, and that they're all idol worshipers and just a step above a downright heathen."

Armando felt his brows rise. "And is that what *you* believe?"

She studied him carefully. "I'm not sure. Fact is, my daddy was wrong about a number of things."

They ate quietly, and to Armando's relief, the oatmeal wasn't bad once he'd followed her lead and added sugar and milk. He ate hungrily, barely bothering to speak or look up as he did. But as he finished his last bite of toast smothered in thick strawberry jam, he noticed that Dora had on the same shirt as yesterday—wrinkled, too, as if she'd slept in it. And it was no longer neatly tucked into her old faded blue jeans. Now it hung loosely over a pair of brown polyester pants. The pull-on type, if his guess was correct. Probably the only kind she could get into with one good hand. And her hair was no longer pinned up, but completely loose now, as if she'd been unable to get it back into place without two hands. It hung in witchlike strands around her face with two bobby pins haphazardly placed to keep it, he guessed, from falling into her eyes.

"Do you need help with your hair?" he asked as he began clearing the table.

She chuckled. "Don't tell me you can do hair too?"

He shrugged. "I'm willing to give it a try."

"Well, I might take you up on that."

He reached for the coffeepot. "More coffee?"

"Just half a cup."

He poured her coffee then continued cleaning, his back to her, but all the while he could feel her eyes watching him, as if she were studying every single move.

"That butter dish goes in the cupboard to the right of the sink," she called out. "It gets too hard in the fridge."

"Okay." He removed it from the refrigerator and placed it in the specified cupboard.

"And don't forget to wipe up the crumbs under the toaster."

"Okay." He rolled his eyes as he picked up the toaster and thoroughly wiped beneath it, noticing what appeared to be at least a week's worth of crumbs.

Finally, he was done washing the dishes and about to dry them when she jumped up from her chair. "Oh, no!" She snatched the tea towel from him. "I always let them drip dry—much more sanitary that way."

Armando looked her straight in the eyes. He was determined to control his temper, no matter how irritating she became. He figured she was his food ticket for the time being, and if he wanted to play things smart, he'd have to bite his tongue for now. "Okay," he said in a tight voice.

"You go take your shower now. I'll finish up in here."

He glanced around the already clean kitchen, then forced out another "Okay." Maybe that would be his word—*okay*— his way of saying, "Fine, you moronic old woman; have it your stupid way!"

The upstairs bathroom was a duplicate of the one down below except that its tile and fixtures were aqua and, in his opinion, prefer- able to pink. He showered and shaved and put on the cleanest change of clothes in his pack, then made sure to pick up after himself. He didn't want to hear Dora complaining about how she had to clean up after him in the bathroom—and with her one good arm. However, he doubted she ever came up here since this bath- room, though neat, was quite dusty and smelled of must and lack of use. He left the window open to air it out.

When he found her downstairs, she was kicking a full laundry basket with her foot, sliding it across the front-room floor.

"What're you doing?" he asked.

"Trying to get this thing to the laundry."

He picked up the basket. "Which way?"

"Back porch—off the kitchen."

"Mind if I wash some of my things too?"

"I suppose not."

He set the basket down and opened the washing machine.

"You know how to do laundry?" Once again, Dora looked skeptical.

"Don't you just throw your clothes in with some soap and turn it on?"

She shook her head. "Not so simple. First you separate lights from darks. Then you start running the water into the empty machine and put in some soap, so it can dissolve, you see? Then you put in a little bleach before you add your white items." She squinted up at him with what seemed satisfaction. "Didn't anyone ever teach you this?"

"Laundry was the one thing that both my grandmother and aunt insisted upon doing for themselves. I think they were afraid I'd ruin their machines or something. When I was older, I started taking my stuff over to the Laundromat once a week and threw it all in together. Seemed to come out okay."

She made a grunting sound as she placed the rest of the white items in the machine, and then waited as Armando dropped in a few of his own things.

She closed the lid. "You've mentioned a grandmother and now an aunt. Don't you have a mother, boy?"

He looked down at the basket now filled with only dark items. "Sure, I have a mother."

"Where is she then?"

He shrugged.

"How about a father? You got a father?"

He shrugged again. Why didn't this old woman mind her own business?

She pushed a loose strand of hair from her face. "Well, how about if we see what you can do with this mop of mine?"

Suppressing his anger, he followed her to the blue bedroom, and folding his arms across his chest, waited as she sat down on a padded bench in front of a wide dresser with a mirror. She handed him a brush. "There are the hairpins, in that little box. Do the best you can to get it pinned up and out of my eyes, will you?"

He tried not to think what Mickey Carrero would say if he could see him now, much less his uncle, as he pulled the bristle brush through the thin strands of white hair. Taking a deep breath, he began what quickly turned into an arduous chore. How could something as seemingly simple as pinning up hair prove such a challenge? He'd much rather be outside chopping firewood. And two hands were definitely not enough. Just when he thought he had one side ready to pin up, the other side would slip down again. Finally, after what seemed several hours, he managed to get it all pinned up at once. It actually looked okay from the front and on the sides, but he was glad she couldn't see the back and the mess of hairpins resembling a flattened porcupine.

Thankfully, she seemed fairly oblivious to the whole process. A good thing, for it would've only made matters worse if she'd started squawking and complaining in her usual aggravating manner. Instead she sat quietly, almost contentedly, as she stared blankly into the big oval mirror in front of her.

Chapter Six

*D*espite the frightening condition of the world at large, Dora had gone in for her late-afternoon hair appointment on December 9, 1941. To her relief, her friend Gladys had opened the shop as usual that day.

"Didn't know if you'd show," said Gladys as she draped the hair shawl around Dora's shoulders and turned the chair to face the gilt-framed mirror. "I didn't even open up yesterday, and today about half my customers cancelled on me. But the truth is I wanted to be open today—I thought it'd help to work, you know, to get my mind off of all this horrible news."

"It's so unbelievable," said Dora. "The children at school are so frightened and shaken by it. I try to act like it's okay and assure them that everything will be all right, but at the same time I feel every bit as scared as they are."

"John's signing up to fight." Gladys had already unpinned Dora's hair and now led her over to the wash station. "He said there's no talking him out of it, and that every self-respecting man under the age of forty ought to enlist and go kick the you-know-what out of those dirty blankety-blanks."

She shut her eyes as Gladys vigorously scrubbed her scalp with castile shampoo, chattering all the while. Dora listened in silence, pressing her eyelids tightly together. She felt the unshed tears burning back there and wondered how much longer she could hold them back.

"What about Henry?" asked Gladys finally, blotting Dora's hair with a faded pink towel.

Dora nodded sadly. "No different than your John, I'm afraid. He feels it's his patriotic duty to sign up too."

"Oh, did I get soap in your eyes, honey?" Gladys dabbed the towel on Dora's wet cheek. "I'm sorry. I guess I was distracted by—"

"No—" Dora choked back a sob—"it's not your fault. It's just that Henry and I put off getting married, you know, because of Daddy and all that business about the farm having to be a success, and now all this has happened and I . . . I . . ."

Gladys wrapped her arms around Dora. "Oh, you poor thing. I hadn't even considered that. Of course you don't want him leaving like this. You two have been waiting so long to get married. Well, as far as I'm concerned, there's only one thing left to do."

"What?" Dora peered up at her friend with watery eyes.

"Elope."

"Elope?"

"Of course. And it can be very romantic too." Gladys smiled dreamily. "Don't you remember how John and me drove all the way down to Reno right after high school graduation to get ourselves hitched?"

Despite herself, Dora smiled. "Yes, and you two were the talk of the town. What a scandal that was."

"But have you noticed how no one ever talks about it anymore? And what with the war going on and everything else, why, no one would think a thing of it if you and Henry hopped on down to Nevada to tie the knot."

"No one except my father you mean."

Gladys waved her hand. "Oh, your father will come round in time. After all, there's a war going on now. Things have changed. And Mr. Lawrence isn't a stupid man. I'm sure he'll be proud of his new son-in-law for doing the right thing."

Dora blinked. "You really think so?"

"You bet I do!"

Dora wasn't so sure, but later that evening, over a dinner of pork chops and peaches (her specialty at the time) she told Henry all about Gladys's far-fetched suggestion. And to her surprise, Henry loved the idea. So the following weekend, only one week after Pearl Harbor was bombed, they drove her little blue Buick down to Reno and repeated their vows in the Chapel of Love. After one unforgettable night in a fancy hotel, they even made it back to Treasure in time for her to be back in the classroom on Monday morning. And Dora had never been happier. For a while anyway.

Chapter Seven

So, what do you think?" Armando asked for the second time, hoping Dora wouldn't be too hard on his lack of hairstyling abilities. "I suppose I could probably do a little better with some practice."

She slowly blinked as if coming out of a dream or even hypnosis, then absently patted her hair. "Oh, it's fine." But she frowned as she leaned forward and peered into the mirror. "Land sakes, when did I get to be so old?"

Armando folded his arms across his chest and despite himself chuckled. She really was a crazy old bat.

With sad eyes, she shook her head. "Now, don't you be laughing at me, boy. It'll happen to you too. Just you wait and see. Old age catches up with all of us before too long. And it comes a whole lot faster than you'd expect, too." She reached her good hand up to touch her cheek. "I remember the day when my skin was as smooth as silk. That's what Henry used to say." She sighed. "Now it's as wrinkled and dry as old weathered cowhide."

Armando looked down on her and wondered how it would feel to be growing older and more helpless with each new day. It seemed impossible to imagine that it could ever happen to him. How could it? Despite the discouraging direction his life had taken lately, he was still strong and healthy. He felt invincible—almost immortal.

She sat motionless now, her good hand cradling her cast, staring hopelessly at the dismal reflection in the mirror. "Looks like I'll be wearing this shirt for a long time now."

"Why's that?"

"Can't get the stupid thing off. I even had to sleep in it."

He rolled his eyes. "I suppose you need some help with it."

Her lips formed a grim line and her eyes widened. "You proposing to undress me, young man?"

He glanced to the door, thinking he'd had about enough of this crazy lady. "No, no . . . I just thought maybe you could use a hand."

"Well, the problem is I don't know how to get this confounded shirt off without cutting off the sleeve. The nurse wanted to cut it off of me yesterday but I wouldn't let her." She sighed. "It's my favorite shirt."

"Good thing." He nodded. "Hope you still like it in a week or two."

She frowned and tugged on the sleeve, but it seemed obvious it wasn't going to slip down over the bulk of her cast. "Maybe you could try cutting it right along the seam. That way I could sew it back up to wear once my arm gets better. I've got a sewing basket over in the closet there. See if you can find it. There should be some shears right on top."

"Shears?" He looked at her curiously.

"*Shears,*" she repeated louder, as if he were deaf. She moved two fingers back and forth in a snipping motion. "You know, shears—*scissors*—to cut with."

"Oh, yeah, scissors." He quickly located the basket and returned with the scissors. "You want me to cut open your sleeve now?"

"Yes. Just be careful. I don't want to go back to that stupid hospital for stitches on my arm today. And try to cut right along the seam if you can, boy. I'd like to spare my shirt if possible."

He bent over her and carefully snipped, following the seam as best he could until he came to the armhole. Her arm was thin with pale skin hanging loosely. It reminded him of a raw chicken. The kind his grandmother used to boil for hours to get rid of the toughness before she made up a mess of chicken tamales.

Dora groaned. "You got it yet?"

"Almost. But I probably need to open it another inch or two more in order to get that cast through."

"Go ahead, boy. Do what you have to do. Just don't cut me."

At last he had the opening big enough. "There." He stepped back. "Do you want me to help you get it off?"

She harrumphed. "Go get me my housecoat first. It's hanging on a hook inside that closet door."

He returned with a pink-and-blue floral housecoat. Draping it over her in what he hoped was a discreet manner, he attempted to extract her from the shirt as painlessly and modestly as possible. But despite his best efforts she let out a little yelp of pain when he lifted her bad arm.

"What's going on here?" demanded a female voice from the hallway.

Armando jumped and turned, knocking the housecoat to the floor and exposing poor Dora with her blouse hanging half on and half off.

"Grandma!" exclaimed a young blonde woman. "What in the—" But before she finished her sentence, she had lifted up her purse and lunged at Armando with a primal fierceness. "Get away from her, you—you pervert!"

"Hey!" he cried out, holding up his hands to shield his head from the blows of her heavily beaded purse. "Wait!"

"*Olivia!*" screeched Dora. "Stop beating him for heaven's sake!"

The thrashing came to a halt, and Armando stepped back and stared at his attacker with a combination of fear and respect.

"What on earth is going on here?" demanded the young woman as she grabbed up the housecoat and quickly draped it back over Dora's thin frame. Then, like a mother lioness protecting her young, she planted herself between Dora and Armando and glared at him.

Dora slowly stood up. "Goodness sakes, Olivia, Armando was

only helping me to get my cast out of that shirt. Looked like I'd be wearing it forever otherwise."

"See, Grandma, you should've let that nurse cut off the sleeve yesterday." She turned to Armando with narrowed eyes. "Even so, this whole thing looks pretty suspicious to me."

"I apologize for my granddaughter's strange defense tactics, Armando," said Dora. "Now may I introduce you to Olivia."

"Uh . . . pleased to make your acquaintance." He kept a careful distance. "I . . . uh . . . I guess."

"Well, what did you expect me to do?" Olivia looked him defiantly in the eye. "I thought you were attacking my poor defenseless grandmother."

He raised his hands in mock submission. "Sure, yeah, whatever. I think I'll get outta here now."

"Where are you going?" asked Dora, her eyes hinting of concern, or did he only imagine it?

"Outside."

Armando grabbed up his backpack and hurried out of the house, a madhouse it seemed, eager to get away from those two crazy women. His head still throbbed from the pounding he'd taken. What'd she keep in that bag anyway? Rocks? He walked on out to the barn and into his room—"the wetback room." He threw his pack down on the bed and began to pace back and forth. He finally stopped in front of the dresser and leaned over as he pounded both fists on its surface of old powdery paint.

"Why not leave this nuthouse?" he asked himself, staring at his distorted image in the cracked mirror. The crack sliced diagonally across his face making it look like he had two noses. "Just pack it up and clear outta here, man. You don't belong here any more than a fish belongs in the desert." He sighed deeply. But then where *did* he belong? Back in L.A. where Tio Pedro, or his uncle's friends, could make his life miserable? And who knew what the law might do to—

"Hey, Armando!" yelled Olivia. "You out here?"

He opened his door and looked out into the shadows of the barn. "What do you want? You coming to beat on me again?"

She smiled, a little sheepishly maybe. "Oh, can't you forget about that?"

He rubbed his head. "Maybe in time. But not until the pain goes away."

"Hey, I'm sorry already. But it's only because I care about my grandma." She put her hands on her hips as if to look tougher. "And, just so you know, I don't let anyone take advantage of her—understand?"

He thought about that for a moment. "Is Charlie your dad?"

"*Charlie?*" She laughed. "*You* call him *Charlie?*" She slapped a slim jean-clad thigh. "That's hilarious. He must love you to pieces."

"Well, is he your dad?"

She nodded. "Yeah. Why?"

"Well, if what you're saying is true, if you don't let anyone take advantage of your grandmother, then how do you handle your dad?"

She waved her hand dismissively. "Oh, that's simple. I try to avoid speaking to him, whenever I can avoid it, that is."

"So, you know he wants Dora to give up her farm then?"

"Oh, sure. Everybody knows that. He's been at her for years to go to Shady Acres—" she put on an affected voice—" 'the premium retirement home for your elderly loved ones.' " She rolled her eyes. "But Grandma says that's where people go to die."

He frowned. "Sounds great."

"But don't worry about that. Grandma's been standing up to him for ages now." Olivia reached back and grabbed her mane of long blonde hair, quickly gathered it into a tail, and wrapped some sort of elastic band around it. "Anyway, she told me to come out here to check on you." She rolled her eyes. "She thinks you might leave now."

"Why's that?"

"She thinks I may have scared you off." Olivia took several steps toward him until they were only a couple feet apart then leaned forward. "I didn't, did I?"

"I dunno." He shrugged, his chin jutting out as if to signify he still had some pride left. "Maybe, maybe not. I never got beat up by a chick, you know."

"Hey, I said I'm sorry." She seemed to be studying him more carefully now. "But it looks to me like you could've held me off pretty easily if you'd wanted to."

"Maybe. But I was taught never to hit a girl."

She smiled. "Maybe I should thank your parents."

He shoved his hands into his pockets and stared at the ground, afraid to keep looking at her, worried that she might suspect something in his eyes. He already knew this was the same girl that was in the photo he'd admired on Dora's mantel. The one who had looked so like an angel to him yesterday but had a punch like the devil today.

"So are you going to stick around then?"

He looked back at her and knew that she alone was enough to make him want to stay. "Maybe. I promised Dora I'd stay a few days anyway. See how it goes."

"Good." She nodded. "I mean I'd stay out here myself and take care of her, but I have classes and she already told me she'd skin me alive if I miss any more school this term."

"What grade are you in?" He hoped this was a discreet way to determine her age since his best guess was anywhere from sixteen on up to twenty-six.

She laughed. "What grade? Hmm, let's see. It's my second year at junior college, but so far all I've taken is art and dance and theater. And I'm not in any program per se. I guess I don't really know what I want to be when I grow up."

"Who really does?"

"My brother. And my dad. They're both into banking, you know. They think money is where it's at."

"Maybe it is for some people."

"Not me." She rolled her eyes. "I think money's highly overrated."

"People who say that usually don't know what it's like not to have any."

"Well, according to my dad, I'm going to end up broke and homeless in the end." She laughed. "He already thinks I'm hopeless and utterly useless. Among other things, he calls me a grasshopper."

"A grasshopper?"

"Yeah, haven't you heard that story about the ants and the grasshopper? The ants work their little rear ends off all summer storing up food while the lazy grasshopper just plays around and has fun."

Armando nodded. "Then winter comes and the ants have lots to eat while the grasshopper is starving outside in the freezing cold."

"Yeah." Olivia pretended to shiver. "And then that poor, foolish grasshopper just bites the dust."

"Not in the version I remember," he corrected her. "In my story, the ants invite him in and the grasshopper entertains them all winter long with music and stories and dancing and stuff."

She looked puzzled. "You're kidding? Where'd you hear that story anyway?"

He scratched his head. "I don't remember for sure. Maybe I saw it on a cartoon or something when I was a kid. Isn't that the way it goes?"

She threw back her head and laughed. "I dunno, but I sure like your story a whole lot better than my dad's." She tugged him by the arm. "Come on, Armando, let's go assure poor Grandma that my little purse-whacking episode hasn't driven you away."

He smiled as he followed her back to the house. Second year of college? That would make her about the same age as he was. Not that it should matter. Because what would a gringo college girl like Olivia want with a loser like him? Still, you never knew. As Tio Pedro used to say, *"Where there is life there is hope."* And he certainly felt alive right now, especially as he watched her moving quickly up the porch steps in front of him. In fact, he felt more alive today than he had in ages!

When they got inside the house, they found Dora bent over on the sofa. Her face creased with pain as she clutched her cast with her good hand and moaned.

"What's wrong, Grandma?" Olivia knelt beside her.

"Just this arm."

"Have you had a pill today?" asked Armando. He waited a moment, but suspected by her lack of answer that she probably hadn't. Then he headed to the kitchen for the prescription bottle and a glass of water.

"Here." He dropped a pill into her open palm and waited for her to swallow it with the water.

"Where's your sling?" asked Olivia.

"It was hurting my neck."

"Oh, Grandma. The doctor said you need to wear the sling to help your arm heal faster."

"Where is it, Dora?" Armando used a firm voice.

"You two!" Dora shook her head then answered. "I guess I don't have a chance if you gang up on me. If you must know, it's in the linen closet."

Armando found a bundled-up piece of cloth tucked beneath a hand towel and, with the help of Olivia, managed to tie it in such a way that Dora thought it might be okay after all.

"I want to take a nap now," she snapped. "You two pests go away and leave me be."

Olivia laughed. "Fine. I have a ballet class at eleven anyway."

"And I'm sure I can find something to keep me busy."

He walked Olivia out to her car, a beat-up orange Volkswagen with a daisy painted on the left front fender. "Nice wheels," he said with an obvious tinge of sarcasm.

"What? You don't like Bugs?"

He grinned. "Hey, it's better than what I'm driving."

She glanced around. "What's that?"

He looked down at his worn Doc Martens. "My feet."

"Yeah, then don't go picking on me. I worked all summer for Grandma when I was sixteen, just so I could buy this thing." She climbed in and started the engine.

Armando was immediately enveloped in a cloud of thick blue smoke. He patted the roof, trying not to choke on the fumes. "Yep, and it runs like a top too."

She laughed. "Well, I suppose it needs some work."

"Bring it over here sometime and maybe I can take a look under your hood." He grinned, wondering if she suspected any double meaning here.

But she looked skeptical as she put the stick into reverse. "For your information, the engine is in the trunk."

"Yeah, whatever." He forced a smile and waved as she backed away. He hoped she didn't suspect that he felt like a complete fool right now. He hated feeling like this, especially in front of an extremely attractive girl. He shoved his hands into his pockets and tried to look macho as he walked back toward the barn—back to the wetback quarters.

Chapter Eight

$\mathscr{A}$rmando figured if he was going to stay here, even if it was only for a day or two, he might as well make himself comfortable. It's not like anyone else was about to. He dragged his threadbare mattress outside and hung it over an old hitching post, then beat it with a rusty rake until he was satisfied that most of the dust and straw and mouse droppings were gone. Then he left it in the sun to air out— a trick he'd learned as a boy from his grandmother. "The sun can clean most anything," she'd told him often enough. "And nothing smells better than sun-dried sheets." Remembering the clothes still in the washer and a clothesline he'd spotted over by the garden, Armando decided to give it a shot.

He slipped up the steps to the back porch and quietly loaded the wet laundry into a wicker basket then dumped the second load of dark pieces into the washer, careful to do it exactly the way Dora had shown him. No reason to get the old lady ruffled about laundry. Then he located a bag of clothespins and proceeded outside to hang the wet items on the line.

He suspected there was probably some sort of science to this whole process, but he wasn't exactly sure how it went. Still he did remember how his grandmother used to shake an item first, making an authoritative snapping sound like a soldier standing to attention, and then she'd pin the item securely to the line. With some frustration, he tried to imitate her. Only one towel landed in the dirt before he finally got the hang of it. He felt slightly uncomfortable when he came to Dora's underclothing, boxy panties and sturdy cotton brassieres—not the sort of things girls wore nowadays. Surely nothing Olivia, or even his aunt, would ever be caught in. But finally he clipped the last white pillowcase to the line and stepped back to survey his work. Not as neat as Abuela Maria's perhaps, but not bad either.

"What're you doing out there, boy?"

He turned to see Dora leaning over the back-porch railing, still wearing her housecoat over her brown polyester pants. "Just hanging the wash," he called as he picked up the empty basket and walked toward her. "I hope that's okay. I know you have a dryer and everything, but I thought . . ."

She nodded. "I like hanging my wash out in the sun. And it's not always clear like this in these parts. Best to make the most of the sunshine when you can."

He felt a strange wave of relief. It seemed there was so little he could do well enough to please this cranky old woman.

"Did you remember to wipe off the line first?"

He frowned as he walked toward her. "Wipe it off?"

She shook her head as if he were totally hopeless. "Should've known you wouldn't think of that. Clotheslines get awfully dirty during the course of a long rainy winter."

"Well, I never actually hung laundry before—"

"No matter." She turned slowly, heading back into the house. "Better than nothing, I suppose."

He set the empty basket on the washer and followed her into the kitchen. "I noticed some cleaning supplies out on the porch there," he began. "I thought maybe I could clean up that room in the barn. . . ." *The wetback room,* he was thinking.

"Sure, do whatever you like out there." She opened the refrigerator and looked inside. "I doubt there's much of anything you can hurt."

He clenched his fists and slowly exhaled, determined not to allow her tactless words to aggravate him. What did he care what she thought, anyway? She was just a foolish old woman. And he was getting free room and board in exchange for a little bit of help. Why should her opinion matter to him?

"We're going to have to go get some groceries tomorrow," she announced as she shut the refrigerator. "I'll make up a list while you start fixing us some lunch. There's a can of tuna fish in the cupboard. Do you know how to fix tuna-fish sandwiches?"

He shrugged. "Like grilled tuna?"

"Grilled tuna fish?" She looked up at him curiously. "Never heard of such a thing."

"Well, maybe you ought to give it a try."

"Don't know." Her brow creased stubbornly. "What if I don't like it?"

"Then I guess there'll be more for me."

She frowned. "Don't like the sound of that."

"Oh, come on, Dora, why don't you trust me with it? Try something new for a change."

She pressed her lips together. "I don't know . . . remember what they say about teaching an old dog new tricks."

Without responding, he started opening the can of tuna.

"Speaking of old dogs, would you feed Homer for me? His dish and food are out on the back porch."

Armando tended to the cat then returned to fixing lunch. He kept a careful watch as first the tuna, then the sandwich bread, browned in the cast-iron pan. As it turned out, he only got to eat one of the grilled-tuna sandwiches. Dora cleaned her plate right down to the last crumb.

"So, what'd you think?" he asked.

"Not half bad," she muttered as she stood to leave the table. "Just hope that grease doesn't upset my digestion."

He sighed as he filled the sink with hot water. Seemed to be no pleasing this woman. Why couldn't she admit that she liked the grilled tuna and get on with it? And why couldn't she simply say, "good job" or "nice try" or even "thank you"? Why was she so negative about every single thing? He considered the way she bowed her head to pray before each meal. Even that seemed an exercise in negativity, with her voice as flat as a griddle as she repeated the empty-sounding words. He wasn't even sure what her point was. Did she fret that God might never give her another meal if she forgot to pray? But why should any of this matter to him? He'd be gone by the end of the week anyway. It was only a matter of time until this grumpy old woman would be nothing more than a faint and curious memory. He heard her shuffling into the kitchen as he hung the frying pan above the stove.

"Here," she said, pushing a cardboard box across the linoleum with her foot. "Some things for your room."

"What's that?"

"Just some stuff you might need is all."

He stared at her, trying to figure out her motive in this gesture, but her eyes remained fixed on the box, refusing to meet his.

"Thanks," he said as he stooped to pick it up. Then, feeling her eyes on his back, he loaded himself up with the box and a mop and broom as well as some cleaning things to take out to his "quarters." Relieved to be in the privacy of his room, he opened the window and proceeded to sweep an amazing accumulation of dusty old cobwebs from the walls and ceiling, killing several startled spiders along the way. He thoroughly scrubbed down every surface including the insides of the drawers. The bottom drawer was jammed, but after several hard smacks, he got it open. And there, wedged in the back, he found a small bundle of letters and postcards and photos, all tied together with twine against what appeared to be an old Bible. He almost threw the whole dusty packet away, but then he noticed the writing was in Spanish. He hadn't read much Spanish since he was a boy, during an era when his grandmother had encouraged him to learn this skill from their lonely neighbor, Mr. Pescador, after his wife passed away. He examined the envelopes. All the letters were addressed to a certain Manuel Rodriguez.

He squinted at the top envelope's postmark to see it was dated in 1966—back when his mother would've been a little girl. He knew this packet must've belonged to a migrant worker, likely one of those wetbacks that Dora had complained about, but Armando felt slightly surprised that this person had been able to read and write, since many of the migrant farmworkers he'd known were primarily illiterate—especially the older generation. Armando removed the twine and set the letters and Bible on the chair. It might be entertaining to try to read them at a later time. For some reason, he felt mildly curious about the life of one who had occupied this dismal little room so long ago.

He continued to clean, taking time to scrub the cracked mirror and even the grime-encrusted window until they both almost shone. And finally he swept and mopped the wide-planked floors until the room smelled of wet wood and pine-scented disinfectant. He was hot and sticky by the time he finished, but felt pleased that the entire cleaning had taken him less than two hours. He emptied the buckets and returned the cleaning supplies, careful to put every-thing right back where he'd gotten it. No use giving Dora another excuse to complain.

Then he decided to check on the old woman and felt relieved to find her snoozing peacefully on the sofa, a thick book lying open in her lap and her reading glasses still perched on her pointed little nose. For some reason, despite her loaded bookshelves, he hadn't thought of her as a reading type of person. But then he'd only known her for about twenty-four hours. He stopped himself. Was that possible? Had he only been here for one day? For some reason it felt like a week or more. He turned away and tiptoed through the kitchen and out the back door. As he hung up the second load of wash, this time taking care to wipe off the line first, he could hear Tio Pedro mocking him. *"You are becoming a woman,"* his uncle tormented. *"You are a total wuss, a weakling, a loser. You shame me, nephew!"*

Armando tried to shake these words from his head as he snapped his blue jeans to make a loud popping sound. "*You* are the loser, Tio Pedro," he said aloud. "And if I lived my life for you, I would end up just like you, rotting away in prison." For the first time since leaving L.A., he was glad that Tio Pedro had been caught. Glad to be free of his uncle's influence—at least geographically. Still he had no assurance that his uncle's influence couldn't reach beyond the state line. What if the local police figured it out somehow? Treasure seemed to be an out-of-the-way place, but who knew how easy these things got with computer technology improving almost daily. Best not to think about it too much, he told himself as he clipped up the red T-shirt he'd been wearing that day. He considered taking the shirt down and tossing it into the trash, but maybe he was being paranoid. Besides, who would ever think to look for him up here, in the sticks of Oregon on some old lady's farm? This was a good plan. Just lie low for now. He pushed the hair from his forehead and looked out over the line and then at his watch. It was nearly two-thirty; hopefully his clothes would have enough time to dry before the sun went down.

"Woman!" His uncle's voice taunted so vividly that Armando actually glanced over his shoulder. Of course, Tio Pedro wasn't there. But the insults and threats continued. Armando tried to block out these disturbing thoughts as he walked toward the barn. He wondered what his grandmother would say now. Of course, she had always felt that laundry was a woman's work, but certainly she would see the bigger picture here. Surely she would be pleased that

he was helping someone else—a crippled old woman. He shook his head. But what was the real truth here? Wasn't he really helping himself? Taking advantage of her need, and waiting for his next opportunity to come along? Who was he kidding anyway? Perhaps when it was all said and done he'd find out he was just like his uncle after all. And just as guilty too.

The floor in his room was dry now and the strong smell of cleaning solutions had nearly evaporated, but he opened the window again to allow the fresh spring air inside. Then he retrieved his mattress from the hitching post. Throwing it over his shoulder, he hauled it back into the room and flopped it onto the metal frame. He made up the bed with care, actually using sheets this time, in the same way his grandmother had taught him to do. "Sleeping without sheets is for infidels," she'd told him one night after he'd sleepily climbed into bed atop a bare mattress. "Civilized people *always* use sheets."

For some reason it was important to Abuela Maria to be civilized, even though her daughter Marta would poke fun at her for her meticulous ways, saying, "Oh, Mama, why do you worry about what other people will think of you?" But Armando thought there was more to it than that. In fact, he liked to imagine it was Abuela Maria's family down in Mexico that had taught her these civilized ways, and that she was trying to pass down the traditions of her ancestors to future generations. Unfortunately it seemed to have missed Armando's mother altogether, and Tia Marta was like a bouncing rubber ball. Sometimes she was up and sometimes she was down. When she was up, she ran her home a lot like her mama. But when she was down, well, knowing she was probably very down right now . . . Armando didn't want to think about that today.

He emptied his backpack and placed the contents into the old dresser, along with his clean laundry. He considered leaving the pack full and ready to go, just in case, but at the same time thought he'd rather make himself comfortable, and maybe stay awhile. Then he set the cardboard box that Dora had given him on the bed. For some reason, he'd saved this for last, like a reward perhaps, corralling his curiosity until his work was complete. At the top of the box was a small windup alarm clock, the old-fashioned kind with two bells on top that clanged. The old woman probably wanted to ensure she didn't have to come out here and wake him every morning. He set and wound the brass clock and placed it on the dresser. Next was a large piece of rolled-up cloth. He opened it to discover what appeared to be an old pair of curtains in a printed fabric of faded green leaves and orange roses. He held them up to the window to find they were almost the right size. He wasn't sure about the next item. It looked like a small pitcher with a lid. But he removed the lid to find it was actually a drinking cup. It must be for water, he mused, perhaps for those times when you wake up thirsty in the middle of the night. Not such a bad idea, really. He also set this on the dresser. Packed between a couple hand towels was a dark green glass vase. He held it up to the light curiously. What was he supposed to do with this? He folded the towels and put them in an empty drawer, then set the vase on the dresser.

Near the bottom of the box were several books. The first one was *Treasure Island*. He'd always thought that was a kid's book, but felt surprised by the thickness of it. The second book was *Great Expectations*, a title he'd never heard of before. The third one was a paperback called *The Grapes of Wrath*. Now this one sounded familiar to him, but he wasn't sure why; maybe it was something he'd been assigned to read in high school but hadn't. He set these books next to the letters and Bible. He'd noticed that it was a Gideon's Bible, the kind you might find in a hotel room. He chuckled at this. Maybe Dora or her husband had thought this room was like some fancy hotel and needed a Gideon's Bible in the drawer. Hopefully, she wouldn't hand him a bill when it was time to leave.

There were two more items in the box. One appeared to be a framed picture of some sort, but was facedown. He pulled it out to see an old print of a pretty flower garden. Kind of girlish, he thought, but perhaps it was better than a blank wall. And on the bottom of the box was a colorful fabric item. He pulled it out to see that it was a small handmade rug. It appeared to be made of lots of strips of cloth in a variety of colors. This he set alongside his bed. And he had to admit that Dora's box of odds and ends did make the place seem more homey—almost as if she'd actually put some thought into it. As if she might care. Although that seemed unlikely.

He scrounged around the barn until he found an old hammer, a small tin of rusty nails, and what appeared to be an old broomstick, about the right length for a curtain rod. Then he proceeded to hang the curtains and the garden picture and stepped back to survey his work.

"Making yourself at home?"

He turned around to see Dora standing in the open doorway. "Guess so. What do you think?"

She looked around the room without speaking for a long moment then finally said, "This place looks better than I remembered."

"You should've seen it before—"

"Well, let's not stand here gawking all day, boy. There's something I want to talk to you about." She turned to leave. "Come on," she called over her shoulder. "We don't have forever, you know."

Feeling cheated again, he closed the door behind him and caught up with her. "How's your arm doing?" he asked in a forced effort to be cheerful. For some reason, perhaps it was the result of getting the room fixed up, but suddenly he found himself hoping that he might stay on for a while longer. Maybe even a week.

"How'd you think it's doing?" she snapped. "You ever have a broken bone before, boy?"

"Well, no."

"Then don't ask."

He glared at the ground and cursed her under his breath.

By now they were in the garden area and for a brief moment he thought maybe she was going to praise his weeding work from yesterday.

"First off, don't go leaving those weeds piled right next to the garden like that. They're full of bad seed, and the next thing you know a big wind comes along and *whoosh,* all those seeds get planted right back in your garden again. You understand me?"

"Okay." He scowled as he shoved his hands into his pockets and waited.

"Now see over there?" She pointed to the overgrown strip of land on the other side of the garden.

"What?" He peered over there, unsure of exactly what it was she was looking at. "All I see are more weeds and a bunch of blackberry vines."

She nodded. "That's right. At one time that was all vegetable garden too. But every year it just gets smaller and smaller."

"Uh-huh."

"And this year I want it to get bigger."

"Bigger?" His voice was skeptical.

"That's right. I want you to get out the old tiller, out of that shed over there." She pointed to a small, low building not far from the barn. "And see if you can make it work." She narrowed her eyes at him. "You know anything about engines, boy?"

"Yeah, I used to work at a garage."

"Good. Well, you get to work on that rototiller today. And then see if you can't get another patch of ground ready for planting by tomorrow. It's not too late to be putting in more seeds right now, but it's mid-May already and time's a-wasting."

"But why do you need a bigger garden?"

"Why not?"

He shrugged with indifference. "Okay. Guess it makes sense."

"You bet it makes sense. Now you get to work while it's still daylight out."

He glared at her back as she tramped back toward the house, restraining himself from saying, "Yes, sir!"

"And I'll fix supper tonight," she called from the porch.

"You sure you can do that?"

"I'm *not* an invalid!" She held up a fist with her good arm. "I've still got one hand, you know."

He shook his head as he turned toward the shed. Suddenly one whole week under her tyranny seemed like it would be an eternity. *Better take this thing one day at a time.*

Chapter Nine

$\mathcal{A}$rmando had just finished cleaning and oiling the tiller engine when he heard a car slow down on the road and turn into the gravel driveway. He peered up, hoping to spy Olivia's orange VW, but immediately recognized the car from yesterday as her father's white Buick. He sighed heavily. So what was old Charlie up to today? Not eager to interact with this pushy little man, Armando hunched back down over the tiller, hoping that Charlie wouldn't notice him in the shadows beside the barn. With a false intensity he rubbed the greasy rag over the metal casing that enclosed the tiller, cleaning and polishing the dark green paint until it finally began to gleam. A foolish gesture, since it would only become encrusted with dirt later. If the engine would even start up, that is, and he wasn't too sure about that, either.

He heard the car door close with a sharp bang, and then the sound of quick footsteps trotting up the steps of the front porch. Would Charlie notice that the loose board had been fixed? Dora hadn't.

"Mom?" Charlie called in an urgent-sounding voice, and in the same instant, the screen door slammed loudly behind him. Armando felt a tiny wave of pity for the old woman, probably about to have another go-around with her son. But on the other hand, the cantankerous pair seemed fairly equally matched, especially when it came to pure ornery stubbornness. Let the fight begin!

Armando wanted to test out the tiller, but at the same time didn't want to draw Charlie's attention to himself. So he decided to give himself a break and take a walk down by the creek. And today he would pay more attention to the lay of the land. He tried to imagine how it must've been back when Dora's husband kept things running smoothly. He wondered how much work it would really require to bring this farm back to what it had once been. Finally, he came to the secluded section that he'd noticed the previous day. It was a low, somewhat protected area on the southern side of a stand of birch trees, not far from the creek, and a variety of colorful blooms grew here and there where the blackberries hadn't yet reached. He'd assumed these to be wildflowers yesterday, but upon closer inspection suspected they might be something more.

He wasn't an expert on flowers by any means, but as he bent down to examine a dark green plant with a delicate pink flower, he thought it seemed familiar—perhaps like something his grand-mother had grown in a pot on her patio. But the poor plant was nearly choked by the undergrowth and weeds surrounding it. One by one he uprooted the weeds, careful not to harm the flower until it finally seemed the plant might be able to breathe again.

He stood and, folding his arms across his chest, surveyed this sheltered area, imagining what could be done here to enhance its already natural beauty. What would he do if this were his land? Finally, realizing the futility of such foolish thoughts, he satisfied himself by simply picking a nice bunch of flowers. He didn't know the names of the blooms or whether they were wild or domestic, but he thought the bouquet was quite colorful and would look nice in the dark green vase Dora had put in that box. And hopefully he'd been away long enough that old Charlie would be long gone by now.

But Charlie's car was still parked in the driveway as if it had every right to be there. Armando slipped around the side of the barn, retrieved the vase from his room, and filled it with cool water from the faucet beside the barn door. In the privacy of his room, he carefully placed his arrangement in the vase then stepped back to admire his creation. Then, still wanting to lie low, he pulled out his Walkman and headphones, slipped in a CD, and flopped down on his bed to await Charlie's departure.

He never heard anyone enter his room, but the unexpected sensation of someone thumping on his chest made him leap from his bed and actually yell out.

"Sorry," said Olivia, stepping back with her blue eyes laughing. "I didn't mean to give you a heart attack."

He jerked off the headphones. "What's up?" he asked, trying to regain some dignity and composure as he pushed his hair back and straightened his shirt.

"I thought I'd hang with you until Daddy dearest makes his exit."

"He's still here?"

She nodded, rolling her eyes. "Poor Grandma."

"Oh, I think she can hold her own with him."

Olivia glanced around the room. "Hey, I like what you've done with the place." Then she spotted the bouquet. "Wow, those are gorgeous. Who sent you flowers anyway? A girlfriend?"

He grinned. "No, I picked them myself."

"You're kidding? Where'd you find them?"

"Out past that bunch of trees over by the creek."

She nodded. "Yeah, I remember that spot. I haven't been back in there since I was little. But I remember it was pretty. I never met my grandpa, you know, but Grandma took me back there and told me about all the beautiful flowers he had planted there. I think he sold them to the florist in town or something like that. But I can't believe they'd still be growing after all this time."

"Well, they're barely growing. The place is mostly overgrown with weeds, but I think some of the plants must've survived." Armando nodded toward the vase. "You want these?"

"You're kidding? You'd let me take them?"

He shrugged. "Why not? I know where to get more."

"Yeah, I'd love to have them if you really don't—"

"What are you doing out here?" Charlie's voice boomed like a gun, as he shoved the partially open door fully open and stepped inside. His small narrowed eyes darted about the room in an obvious display of suspicion before they finally settled on his daughter. "Did you hear me, Olivia? What are you doing in here with—*him?*"

She rolled her eyes. "Oh, we're in here making wild passionate love, Dad; what do you think we're doing?"

Charlie glared at Armando then turned to Olivia. "I mean it, Olivia; I want to know what you're doing out here."

"Good grief, you are so paranoid. You think I'm out here putting the move on Armando? You know I already have a boyfriend. And what difference does it make to you anyway?" She planted her hands on her hips and took a step toward him. "Or maybe I should ask you, Dad; what're you doing out here? Did Armando personally invite you to come visit him?"

Charlie pressed his lips together, his eyes still darting back and forth between them.

"We were only talking, sir." Armando spoke calmly, ready to defuse this obnoxious man's suspicions. "Nothing else." Maybe it was the news of Olivia's boyfriend, or simply all those years of being taught to honor his elders, but for whatever reason he felt unexpectedly sobered. Besides, what good would it do for him to pick a fight with this hotheaded little man?

"Well, I don't like Olivia being here in your bedroom like this." Charlie straightened his tie. "It's not proper."

"Who says?" She flopped down onto Armando's bed and folded her arms across her front. "Can't you see we're just talking? Why do you get so freaked over nothing? Don't you remember what all this suspicious thinking does to your blood pressure? And besides, what are *you* doing here at Grandma's anyway? Heckling her to sell her place again? Why don't you lighten up?"

"I'm simply trying to talk some sense into the crazy old woman."

"Crazy, am I?" Now they all turned to see Dora standing in the doorway, a deep frown carved across her brow.

"Hey, let's have a party," said Olivia lightly. "Anyone else you want to invite into your room, Armando? Maybe the neighbors? Or I could call up some—"

"Olivia!" snapped her father. "Knock it off."

"Armando," commanded Dora, her eyes still fixed on her son. "I need your help inside the house."

"Excuse me," said Armando, relieved to step past Charlie and toward the door.

"You want to join us for supper, Olivia?" asked Dora, still glaring at her son.

"Sure, Grandma, I'd love to."

Armando fell into step beside Dora as they walked across the yard toward the house. He could still hear Charlie going on over by the barn, his voice elevated in its intensity, but the words were unintelligible from the distance. "Why's Charlie so mad, anyway?" asked Armando as they entered the house.

"Who knows?" Dora went into the kitchen where some things were sitting on the counter as if she'd already begun fixing supper. She sank into a vinyl-covered chair and leaned forward, her shoulders sagging downward like a limp rag doll.

"Are you okay?" He leaned over to look at her more closely. "Is it your arm? You need a pill or something?"

She peered up at him with her tired and faded eyes. And it might've been his imagination, but they seemed slightly moist too. "I don't know *what* I need anymore. Maybe I just need to be put down like Old Pete."

"Put down? Old Pete?"

"Yeah, *put down*—put out of your misery, you know? Old Pete was a good enough horse in his day, but when he got real old he was so bad off that Henry had to call the vet out here to put him down, so he wouldn't suffer anymore. Henry would've done it himself, but that old horse was like part of the family. Still, he was old and hurting, and it was the kindest thing to do."

"And you're suffering so bad that you think you need to be put down too?"

"Maybe so."

Armando scratched his head. "I always thought that it was a sin."

"What?"

"To take a life—a human life, I mean, not a horse's."

"It's legal, you know."

"Legal?"

"Yes. Have you been living under a rock, boy? It's called euthanasia, and in our state you can pay to have a doctor come right to your house and put you down if you want."

"You're serious?" He blinked. "A doctor will actually do *that?*"

She nodded.

"But you're not actually considering—"

"Why not?"

"It seems wrong."

"Guess that depends on where you're standing."

Despite himself, Armando felt sorry for her. Sitting there on the verge of tears and acting as if her life were no more valuable than an old horse's. He shook his head. How did people get themselves into such pathetic places? Then he narrowed his eyes. "Is this something Charlie's trying to force you into?"

She sighed. "Not in so many ways."

"Well, what then?"

"Oh, it's the same old thing—he wants me to go into a *home*. He's even got a room reserved for me right now. He wants to pack me up and move me over there tonight of all things."

"But that's crazy."

She laughed, but not with humor. "Crazy? Why you heard him. According to my son, *I'm* the one who's crazy. And he's certain he can prove it."

"Prove it?"

"Prove what?" asked Olivia. She walked into the kitchen and picked up an apple then rubbed it across the front of her T-shirt. "Are you guys talking about Dad again?" She took a bite, munching loudly.

"Is he still here?" asked Dora in a bitter voice.

"Yeah, he's poking around outside. He said that he's moving you to Shady Acres tonight, that you agreed to—"

"I *what?*" Dora stood now, fire replacing the unshed tears. "Why, I did no such thing!"

"Well, he seems to think you did." Olivia took another bite then glanced over her shoulder. "He told me to come in here and help you pack."

Dora looked Armando right in the eyes. "It's all on you now, boy."

"Huh?"

"You've got to convince Charlie that you're staying on here— indefinitely."

"Indefinitely?"

"Yeah, more than just a few days, like Charlie thinks—" She stopped talking, and they all listened as the screen door squeaked open and then slammed. They waited as his footsteps thudded across the living room and down the hallway toward the back bedroom.

"Olivia?" Charlie called loudly. "You getting your grandmother's things all packed up now like I told you?"

"Nope," she yelled from the kitchen. "Grandma's not going any-where."

Dora sat back down, her good hand balled into a tight fist. "Come on, Armando," she hissed quietly as she thumped her fist on the table.

"What's going on in here?" asked Charlie. "I thought I told you two to get ready. I promised the manager at Shady Acres that I'd have you over there before eight o'clock tonight."

Armando tried to remember his grandmother's favorite movie hero as he took a step toward Charlie. How would one of John Wayne's characters handle a situation like this? "Looks like that's a promise you won't be able to keep, sir."

Charlie glared at him. "This is none of your business, boy."

Armando folded his arms across his chest. "Well, according to Dora, it is. I guess you didn't know that she's hired me on here to be the caretaker . . . and that we have a . . . uh . . . a gentleman's agreement. Like a contract, you know. And I'm not going anywhere and neither is she." He glanced over his shoulder in time to see a tiny smile play across Dora's pale lips. "And, if you don't mind, it's time for us to be fixing supper. You know how important it is that your mother eats her meals on a regular schedule." He turned around now, his back to Charlie, and actually winked at Dora.

"So, unless you're planning on joining us for supper, Dad—" Olivia stepped up and put her arm around her father's arm, as if to escort him out—"we'll just let you be on your merry little way. I'm sure Mom's wondering what's keeping you by now."

"But I—"

"Now, don't you worry about a thing," she interrupted as they walked through the living room. "Grandma's in fine hands with Armando here. And they've got big plans for this place. You go about your own business and let them go about theirs and every-thing will be just fine and dandy."

Armando could hear Charlie's protests as Olivia ushered—or perhaps even pushed—him out the front door. But when the solid wood door closed with a loud thud, Olivia burst out laughing.

"That takes care of that," she said as she stepped back into the kitchen, pretending to slap the dirt off her hands.

"For today anyway," muttered Dora. "But he's a stubborn one, you know."

Armando suppressed an observation about family traits.

"Why don't you go rest on the sofa now, Grandma," suggested Olivia. "You look a little worn-out."

"But I was going to cook—"

"Don't worry. I can fix supper tonight," offered Olivia.

As it turned out, it was Armando who got supper ready since Olivia didn't appear to even know how to boil water and was easily distracted. Still, he had to admit, she was rather good company in the kitchen and she did manage to set the table, although he had to instruct her as to which sides the knives and forks really went on.

"Didn't your mother teach you anything?" he asked.

"Apparently not." She shrugged. "Or else I just forgot."

Chapter Ten

$\mathcal{D}$ora felt her weary body sink into the sofa like a leaden weight. She couldn't remember when she'd felt so tired and drained. But stressful situations had always done that to her. In fact, she'd spent much of her life trying to avoid the exchange of hotheaded emotions where hurtful words were tossed about like leaves in the wind. Like that December night back in 1941 when her father had learned of her elopement. Now that was a confrontation of epic proportions. Of course, she'd had her good-natured Henry to help buffer the storm, but even he hadn't known what he'd gotten himself into.

"You are no longer my daughter!" Charles Lawrence had cursed at her as he stood on the rickety front steps that blustery winter night, his fist waving in the wind. "You are a disgrace to your family."

"Daddy, come inside," she pleaded, tugging on the sleeve of his overcoat. "Let's talk—"

"I don't want to talk! I have nothing more to say."

"Please, Daddy," she cried. "Don't do this to—"

"I'm glad your mother's not alive to see what you've done with your life—how you've thrown yourself away like this."

"Please," she begged. "Let's just talk."

"Come inside, Mr. Lawrence," urged Henry calmly. "Acting like this won't resolve anything."

Charles glared at his new son-in-law. "I don't want to resolve anything. And I don't want to hear another word from you. You are nothing but a liar and a cheat, Henry Chase, and I don't care who hears me say it."

"Daddy!" Dora grabbed Henry's arm, clinging to him protectively. "How can you talk like that? Henry's been nothing but honorable throughout this entire—"

"Honorable? You call running off in the middle of the night and secretly marrying my only child behind my back honorable?"

Dora wanted to stand up to him, to boldly defend her husband, but she felt herself collapsing inside, caving like the house of cards when the queen of hearts gave way. She knew she was succumbing to the spineless weakness that she'd been indoctrinated into over the course of her lifetime. No one ever opposed Charles Lawrence. How could she possibly expect to stand against him now? Everyone knew he was a rock, an immovable fixture in the town of Treasure. And unfortunately most of the citizens admired him for these very qualities. As if her legs were listening, her knees became weak and she noticed the porch light growing dimmer as if it, like her, was being sapped of all strength. The next thing she knew, both Henry and her father were inside the small house, standing over her as she lay limply on the sofa.

"Are you okay?" asked Henry, gently wiping a damp cloth across her forehead.

Her father looked concerned too. As if a tiny chink of his armor had been popped loose. And she wondered if perhaps he cared about more than just his own reputation.

"What happened?" she asked.

"I think you fainted," said Henry, glancing over his shoulder toward her father.

"Harrumph," Charles snorted. He looked around the tiny house— their first home—and made a sour face. "It's no wonder she's fainting like that, having to live in a horrible hole-in-the-wall like this."

She sat up. "Oh, it's not so bad, Daddy. It came with the land. And besides it's only temporary—"

"No child of mine should live in such pathetic squalor." He turned to Henry. "It's plain to see you were never prepared to support my daughter in the manner she's been accustomed to. You should be ashamed of yourself, Henry Chase. You had no right to inflict your poverty onto my daughter."

"I know it's small," Henry began patiently, "but it's clean and it's sound. And like Dora said it's only temp—"

"Look, Henry." Charles almost seemed to soften. "I know your people lost most everything they had in the Depression, and this place might even be a small step up for you. But can't you see this shack is uninhabitable? It's not fit to keep animals in!" He held his hand against the wood planks on the wall. "I can actually feel the wind coming between these boards right now. Are you crazy, man?"

Henry looked down at the floor and Dora felt her heart breaking for him. She knew she had to say something. "You can't blame Henry for this, Daddy." She stood up, clutching Henry for support. "It was all my idea to elope in the first place. Honestly, Henry didn't like the thought of me living here much more than you do, but I talked him into it. And I promised that I'd help to fix it up. I can put up some wallpaper and sew some curtains—"

"Wallpaper and curtains?" Her father hooted. "You think you can fix this hole up with wallpaper and curtains? Theodora Olivia Lawrence, I thought I raised you better than this. You're an educated woman, but you're acting like a complete fool."

She took a step toward him, her chin up, eyes defiant. "I am *not* a fool, Daddy. I love Henry, and I begged him to go away with me to get married. And I'm not sorry. Can't you see how we've waited and waited, and now the war is on and Henry's got to go off and fight and—" She pressed her fist against her lips, fighting to hold back the tears.

Henry's arm slipped around her waist, like a steadying force, an anchor, and then he spoke. "I am truly sorry that you can't give us your blessing, sir. Not so much for my sake as for Dora's, since she still cares about what you think. But I am *not* sorry that we got married." He turned and looked into Dora's eyes. "And I promise that I will do everything humanly possible to take the best care of her. I'll work hard and I'll do anything to protect her—"

"A pretty little speech!" snapped Charles. "But how're you going to take care of her when you're thousands of miles away, far across the ocean and hunkered down in the trenches? Who's going to come out here when the pipes freeze up or there's no wood for the fire or the electricity goes out?"

Henry looked perplexed. "I . . . I haven't figured that all out yet, sir."

"Of course not!" boomed her father. "You haven't thought of anything but yourself!"

"I can take care of those things," said Dora, knowing full well that she couldn't. "Henry will show me how everything works around here and I'll get along perfectly fine when he's gone. You'll see, Daddy."

"We will see, won't we?" Then he laughed in that harsh cynical way and, turning on his heel, stormed out of the house, leaving the rough plank door open behind him with the wind rushing in. Henry quietly closed the door, sliding the wood bolt tightly shut. But when he turned toward her, she could see the pain and humiliation in his eyes.

"I'm so sorry," she said softly, slipping her arms around him and burying her head into his chest. "My father is a proud man. And I don't think he understands the first thing about true love."

* * * * * * * * * * * * *

Unwillingly, Dora opened her eyes and looked around the room. She was in another house now and someone was calling her to come eat—it sounded like the voice of a young woman. Oh, yes, that was Olivia standing in the doorway to her kitchen. Dora closed her eyes again. She didn't want to eat supper; she wanted to finish this dream—if it was a dream. It had seemed so real. And she wanted to remember what it was that Henry had said to her after that.

"Supper's ready, Grandma, and it looks yummy." Olivia was helping her to stand now. But in that same instant, Dora remembered what had happened next. Oh, not Henry's words so much, but the way the two of them had warmed up that little house on that blustery December evening. Theirs was a fire that needed no firewood but burned brightly all on its own and kept them toasty warm throughout the night and during the years that followed. She smiled to herself as she allowed Olivia to lead her into the kitchen.

"You look happy, Grandma," said Olivia. "Feeling better now?"

She nodded. "Much better."

Chapter Eleven

$\mathcal{T}$he following morning, Armando got up when the alarm clock sounded and quietly slipped into the house to take a shower. He had just finished in time to see Dora shuffling down the hallway still in her housecoat.

She stopped and stared with what appeared to be suspicion or maybe even fear, as if she'd forgotten who he was, but slowly a look of realization crossed her face. "You up already?"

"Got lots to do today."

"Like what?"

"Don't you remember that you wanted me to till that piece of ground to make more garden?"

"I did? Why do I need more garden?"

He studied her closely. Perhaps her son wasn't too far off the mark when it came to her mental faculties. "I thought you said you wanted to grow more food."

She scratched her head, causing her already mussed hair to look even wilder. "Oh, yeah," she said slowly. "I remember now. Sometimes I forget little things like that. Comes with being old, you know."

He nodded. "So I've heard."

Fortunately she hadn't forgotten how to make oatmeal. But this time he watched her so he could make it too. He was surprised at how simple it was. "So you boil the water and pour in the oats?" he repeated.

"Don't forget to toss in a little salt," she reminded him as they sat down. "Can't abide the taste of oatmeal with no salt." Then she bowed her head and recited her funny little prayer.

After breakfast, Dora asked Armando to help her with her hair again. "But I've got an idea that will be easier for you to do and I think it'll stay put better too."

He followed her into the bedroom then waited for her to situate herself at the dresser and explain her plan. "Back when I was a young thing, and I was busy being a mom and helping Henry on the farm, I started wearing my hair in a ponytail." She chuckled. "Of course, I never went out in public looking like that. People would've thought I'd lost my mind, and despite some things, I did like keeping up appearances at least a little—mostly for Henry's sake."

Armando nodded. "So, is that what you want then? A ponytail?"

She put her hand over her mouth and made a noise that sounded almost like a suppressed giggle. This was a side of her that he'd never seen, never imagined even existed. "Do you think it would look silly on an old woman like me?"

He shrugged. "It sounds okay to me. Just tell me what to do."

So she proceeded to explain how he needed to comb all the hair back into one section and to hold it with one hand and then wrap the rubber band around it several times. It took him several tries to get all those flyaway wisps of white hair pulled neatly back, but finally he managed. "Okay, now, where's the rubber band?"

"Oops."

"No rubber band?"

"I might have one in the bathroom," she said, slowly standing. "Now, can you hold on to that and follow me at the same time?"

So, feeling slightly ridiculous and hoping that Olivia didn't suddenly pop in and assume he was doing something horrible, Armando held on to Dora's skinny white ponytail and slowly trailed her into the bathroom, where she fumbled through a drawer until she finally located a rubber band.

"Here you go!" she exclaimed victoriously.

At last he had the band wrapped securely around the tail, and he stepped back to see how it looked.

"Well?" she demanded.

"It looks okay." He suppressed the urge to laugh at the ridiculous hairdo.

She seemed doubtful. "Maybe you should tie something around it, like a scarf or a ribbon. I used to do that sometimes, and Henry always thought it looked nice."

She located an old pink chiffon scarf in a drawer, and Armando did his best to tie it around the scrawny ponytail. "Very chic," he proclaimed, thankful that Dora lived a secluded life out here on the farm.

She reached up and patted it with her good hand. "Good."

"Now, if you don't mind, I'd like to go out and try that tiller."

"Don't you forget to mow down the grass and weeds before you start to tilling."

He frowned. "Why's that?"

"Don't you know anything, boy?"

He sighed deeply then looked right into her eyes. "Do you mind not calling me *boy* all the time, Dora?"

"Did I call you *boy?*"

He nodded.

"Well, don't see that it should matter much. I mean, look at you—you're not much more than a boy. I don't mean anything personal, you know."

"Maybe not, but it really bugs me."

"Well, don't be so thin-skinned, Armando. If you're not a boy, if you're really a man, you should be tough enough not to be bothered by such minor things."

"Listen, Dora, it's not minor to me!" He knew his voice was too loud now, but maybe he didn't care anymore. It's not as if he hadn't tried to get along with the old bat. And he'd even had brief moments when he thought this could work, when he'd hoped that she might really be starting to appreciate him and want him here. But who was he fooling? This whole thing was hopeless. The sooner he got on with his life the better it would be for everyone. He'd probably overblown that whole business down in L.A. It was Tio Pedro's problem, not his. And the police? Well, what did they really have on him anyway?

"Look, Dora, maybe it's time for me to get on my way. Maybe this isn't such a good arrangement after all."

"What do you mean?" She scowled at him. "You running out on me already?"

He shrugged. "Guess so."

"Well, have it your way then. If you're going to just whine and complain every time I accidentally call you *boy.*"

He started for the door. Part of him—something ingrained in him since childhood—felt the need to apologize to her. But at the same time he felt that she was the one to blame here. She had goaded him, dissed him, made him feel like a nothing, a nobody. She might not be a criminal, but in many ways she was as bad as his uncle.

He heard her footsteps shuffling down the hallway behind him. But he was not going to look back. He reached the front door. He was finished here.

"It's your choice," she called out after him. "If you leave right now you'll never know about it."

He sensed the bait in her voice and he knew that for some reason she was trying to stall him now. What was it with her anyway? Some sort of cat-and-mouse game? He turned and looked back at her, taking in her cockeyed ponytail tied in the garish pink scarf. "Be seeing you," he said as he opened the door.

"Fine." She held up her chin. "Go ahead and leave. But you'll never find out about *the secret.*"

He studied her closely. Was she serious or just plain loony, as Charlie seemed to think? That spark in her eye was intriguing. But his grandmother had often reminded him that curiosity killed the cat. Still, he was game. "Okay, and what is that?" he asked in a flat voice.

"Oh, I'm not sure that I can trust you with it, especially if you're thinking of running off on me already."

"Like I said, I don't like being called *boy.*"

"Well, I'll try to remember that." She eased herself down into the recliner.

He glanced out the door. The idea of freedom held a certain appeal. And yet there was something about this place, maybe not Dora and her confusing ways, but there was something about the farm—something he wanted to belong to. He turned back and looked at her. "Okay, so what's the big secret?"

She smiled mysteriously. "Well, you know the name of our town is Treasure, right? But I'll bet you don't know why they called it that. Very few people know the *real* reason for the name, but my family settled here way back in the beginning. So *I know.*"

He could sense he was being reeled in but decided to play along anyway. Maybe he should stick around long enough to have some lunch. "So, tell me, Dora, why do they call it Treasure?"

"Because long, long ago, a gold miner was passing through these parts. He was on his way home from the Alaskan gold rush. And he liked this area so much that he buried his gold round these parts before he lit off to California to fetch his family back here to settle down."

Armando shrugged. "So?"

"So . . ." She leaned forward as if someone else were trying to listen. "The gold miner never made it back here. He was killed by Indians or smallpox or something." She lifted her brows as if to make her point. "And some folks believe that his fortune in gold is still round here somewhere."

He shook his head. "Why are you telling me all this, Dora? You want to go out treasure hunting now?"

"Well, my late husband, Henry, happened to think that it was buried right here on our property, on this very farm."

Armando studied her. This was obviously a stupid come-on, her feeble excuse of an enticement to keep him here, working for her like a slave. "You really expect me to believe that, Dora?"

She nodded with a pleased and somewhat daffy expression. "That's right. The treasure is right here on my land."

"Well, that's real interesting and all . . ."

"Stick around, Armando. You might get lucky."

He laughed sarcastically. "Yeah, you bet."

She frowned. "You don't believe me?"

"I'm not sure what I think of you, Dora."

She narrowed her eyes. "You think I'm crazy?"

He shrugged.

She sighed and shook her head. "Oh, why not. Everyone else seems to think so. I might as well call Charlie right now. Tell him to send somebody over here to give me those injections, or whatever it is they do to sorry old worn-out and useless folks like me."

He noticed her chin trembling slightly and her eyes filling with tears. Was this the real thing or just more theatrics to keep him here? "Look, Dora, I don't mind sticking around awhile, until you get stronger, you know. But—"

Her head snapped back up and she looked him in the eye. "Okay then. What was it we were talking about in the first place, back before you got all put-out at me for calling you *boy?*"

He thought for a moment. "I think I was asking you why I need to mow first? Why can't I till the grass and weeds all under at once?"

"Take it from me, it'll go a whole lot easier if you mow first. The mower's out in the shed by the—"

"I *know* where the mower is." He quickly exited, allowing the door to slam firmly behind him. Okay, maybe he had been manipulated by her. Or perhaps he was the one doing the manipulating. After all, how far would he get with less than a dollar to his name? At least he had food to eat here and a roof over his head. Who was working whom here?

Fortunately the mower started up after only a few tries. He cut and even raked away the grass and weeds, careful to put these, as well as the piles he'd made from before, in a heap behind the barn; he hoped to burn the pile later. Then he divided the rest of the morning between tilling the ground and tweaking the tiller engine to keep it running smoothly. He considered Dora's crazy treasure story as the tiller was clawing its way into the soil, and for a brief moment he thought maybe he'd hit some old treasure chest buried down there. And yet he knew it was all a silly hoax to keep him here. She was a crafty old crow. And even if there had been a treasure here at one time, surely old Henry would've found it long ago with all the plowing and farming he'd done over the years.

By one o'clock, he'd turned over a good section of turf, and he shut off the tiller and stooped down to feel the texture of the soil. He scooped up a handful of moist dirt then rubbed it between his fingers and even lifted it up to his nose to smell before he tossed it back down. He wasn't even sure why he'd done it, but somehow it seemed right. And strangely enough the soil smelled clean and fresh to him. But when he stood up, he noticed that Dora was standing on the porch and staring at him like maybe she thought he'd taken leave of his senses. And maybe he had. He walked over, preparing himself for more criticism.

"What were you doing there?" she asked in sharp voice.

"You mean tilling?"

"No, just now, when you were bent down like that?"

"Feeling the dirt."

She frowned. "How did it feel?"

"Like dirt." He shrugged. Then he noticed that she was wearing some strange kind of dress. The fabric looked slightly tropical with bright red flowers and turquoise birds printed all over it, and it had deep wrinkles, as if it had been packed into a box for about a century. "What's that you're wearing, Dora?"

She held up her chin and almost seemed to smile. "It's called a muumuu."

He nodded. "Like they wear in Hawaii?"

"Yes. And I was able to get it over my head and around my cast all by myself." She pulled on the fabric to show how the sleeve was open and loose. "See?"

"Yeah. That was a good idea."

"I thought so. It took me a long time to find it and I'm afraid I made a mess of my closet doing so, but at least I could dress myself without any help today." She moved from side to side to watch the flowing skirt move. "My Henry was stationed in the Pacific, you know. He sent this to me along with lots of other fine things during the war. I almost forgot I even had it."

"Guess I better go inside and clean up now," said Armando.

"Yes, and then you can fix us some lunch." She pressed her lips together to make a smacking sound. "I'm hankering after one of those grilled-tuna sandwiches."

"Right."

"Leave your muddy shoes on the porch," she chided sharply, sounding more like her old self again. "And after lunch we'll go into town to get some groceries."

"In the old pickup?"

"Well, we're not going to walk, boy—" she put her hand to her mouth—"I mean, *Armando.*"

After lunch was finished and cleaned up, Dora handed him a key. "Drive the pickup around front, will you?"

"You sure it'll run?"

"Why shouldn't it run?"

"When was the last time you started it up?"

"Oh, heavens, I don't know. But whenever that was, it ran just fine."

Armando wasn't so sure as he picked through the overgrown blackberry vines to make his way toward the neglected truck. He wondered what he could've possibly been thinking that day when he thought he could actually hot-wire this old thing. But after several tries, and fiddling with the carburetor and a loose battery cable, the old engine amazingly turned over. But even then it looked like the gas tank was on empty. He revved the engine then drove over to the front of the house, keeping the motor running while he dashed inside to get Dora. He fought to keep a straight face when he saw her coming down the hallway. If the muumuu and scarf-tied ponytail hadn't been enough, the old woman now had on several strands of beaded necklaces and carried a large basket-type purse adorned with pink and orange flowers.

"You look like you're going to Tahiti," he said as he held the door for her.

"I thought your people always dressed in bright colors like this."

"My people?" He scowled as he opened the truck door then helped her climb inside.

"Oh, you know what I mean. Don't Mexicans like vivid colors?"

He rolled his eyes as he climbed into the cab. "Yeah, I'm sure some do." He shoved the gearshift into first. "But not everyone."

She sat her purse on the seat beside her. "I got this purse down in Mexico, you know, in Tijuana. Henry and I went down there one year after Charles went off to college. You ever been to Tijuana before?"

"Sure. My uncle used to take me there for a good time." He eased the gear into second and started down the driveway.

"A good time?"

Armando shook his head. "Well, my uncle thought it was a good time. I'm not so sure what I think anymore."

"Was this uncle related to your mother or your father?"

"He was my mother's sister's husband." Armando looked straight ahead.

"No relation to you then?"

"Right." He answered her question in a brisk way as he shifted into third, a hint that he didn't want to continue this line of questioning.

"So whatever happened to your—"

"You know, we'll need to get some gas first thing, Dora." He shifted into fourth now, wanting to see how well this old truck could perform on the open highway. "The needle's way below the *E* right now."

"There's a Shell station as soon as you get into town. We can get two dollars' worth there and then fill it up at the discount station on the other end of town."

"Okay."

"Say, I forgot to ask if you have a driver's license."

"Would it make any difference if I didn't?"

She seemed to consider this.

"Rest at ease, Dora. I have a valid California driver's license that doesn't expire until next year."

Satisfied, she nodded and turned to look out the window. Armando relaxed a little as he gripped the steering wheel. Man, it felt good to be riding above a set of wheels again! Way better than walking. And, as Dora would say, this truck wasn't half bad either.

It was only a few minutes before they reached the outskirts of town. Armando felt a small surge of pleasure to spy hints of civilization as he spotted first a big neon sign for a Jack in the Box and then another for the Shell station. The last few days had made him feel as if he'd been trapped in a time warp. Maybe it was better than jail, but it was a prison of another kind just the same. He stopped the pickup at an intersection to allow a young redheaded woman in a very short skirt to cross the street. She glanced his way then moved as if she wanted his eyes to remain on her. And he obliged. As he turned into the Shell station, he thought perhaps the world hadn't really stopped turning after all.

Dora had a number of places she wanted to go, and Armando maneuvered the pickup in and out of tight parking spaces, feeding a variety of coins into the old-fashioned meters. He helped her in and out of the pickup, trying not to notice the curious stares they received from passersby. Whether they were staring at the brightly clad granny sporting the stringy ponytail or the dark-skinned young man accompanying her, he couldn't be sure. And although he told himself he didn't care, he didn't believe himself very much. His biggest concern was the law. And yet he thought it unlikely that a small town like this would be much interested in something that had happened down in L.A.

He thought Dora might've been pushing things a little too far when she went into the bank where he knew her son reigned supreme but, hey, it was her business not his. And if old Charlie wanted to come out and make a big scene, well, that might be something worth seeing. Armando leaned against a big column and waited while she tended to her business with the patient-faced teller who'd obviously dealt with her before. But even as he waited, he sensed the eyes of the security guard fixed tightly on him, as if the old coot thought Armando might be concealing a handgun, or maybe even a knife in his boot, and was about to attempt an armed robbery. Not that he couldn't use the cash.

Still it was this kind of suspicion that had always aggravated him—as if the mere fact of being Latino was a guarantee to do something stupid. This especially troubled him right now since he really wanted to maintain a low profile. Suddenly he could imagine himself completely snapping, heeding Tio Pedro's warped advice and attempting something totally crazy—just to show them.

Finally, Dora finished her bank business and they went to the grocery store, a run-down Safeway that smelled like overly ripe produce. And what should've been an easy task turned out to be an ordeal, when hidden in Dora's cavernous straw bag was a myriad of dog-eared coupons, and the crazy old broad seemed determined to use every one. But since she'd neglected to bring along her reading glasses, Armando was forced to stay at her side and read the fine print aloud, making sure to take special note of the expiration date since many of the coupons were too old to be redeemed in the first place.

"Says this Best Foods mayonnaise coupon expires the end of this month," he told her, loud enough to be heard over the tinny music system. At the same moment he noticed the attractive woman he'd observed earlier, the one who'd crossed the street with such flare. But now she simply tossed a concerned glance his way—like maybe she felt sorry for him, as she picked up a bottle of Italian salad dressing and quickly made her way toward the next aisle.

Dora paid for her groceries in cash, but it took her a while to figure out how much to give the clerk as she fumbled with her one good hand to remove the money from her wallet. She counted out the correct amount, and Armando tried not to stare as she clumsily dumped the remaining bills loosely into her enormous purse. How he wished he had a couple of those for himself. And once again he heard Tio Pedro urge him: *"Go ahead and grab a couple twenties while the old crow's not looking. She'll never even miss them."*

Armando picked up the bags of groceries and headed toward the door, trying to push his uncle's bad advice far away from him. Besides, he asked himself in defense, what do I need money for right now anyway? *"Cigarettes,"* his uncle whispered into his ear. *"And booze."*

Armando smiled to himself as he followed Dora outside. Tio Pedro was wrong. He'd quit smoking a couple years back. Now booze, that might've been more tempting if he didn't think too hard about it. But if memory served him right he'd decided, after one too many hangovers, that his money was better spent elsewhere. Tio Pedro would have to come up with something better than that to lure him across the line. And why go looking for trouble in this quiet little town? Problems with the law up here would surely lead to connections down there. And he'd much rather be poor and free in Treasure than locked up in L.A.

Chapter Twelve

$\mathcal{A}$rmando loaded the grocery bags into the back of the truck, taking time to pull off some blackberry vines that were still entwined around the tailgate. He tried not to think about what he and Dora must look like driving through town in this dilapidated old truck partially covered with vines. What if his friend Mickey could see him now? At least there were some benefits to being a stranger in town. He climbed into the driver's seat and turned on the ignition. "I'll bet this truck could use an oil change and some minor maintenance," he said as he put it into reverse and backed out. "Do you want me to stop by the automotive store over there and get some things?"

"I'm worn-out," she said, leaning against the seat. "You can get that stuff some other day. I want to get myself home now."

"Okay." Disappointed to delay the much-needed maintenance, he quietly headed down Main Street toward the highway.

"Stop," she said suddenly, pointing across the street. "Pull into the Kentucky Fried Chicken. I want to get some chicken to take home for supper tonight."

"Okay." He pulled into the parking lot and waited for her to tell him what she wanted before he went inside to order. While he sipped his Pepsi and waited for their food, he overheard a couple of guys in a booth near the window.

"Get a load of that chick in that old Chevy out there," said the one in a ball cap.

The other guy turned his head to see then laughed. "Hey,

I thought you were serious, man. That *chick* looks like she's about a million years old."

"Yeah, but check out that hairstyle."

"But how about that truck? It's not so bad."

"Yeah, it'd be all right if it was fixed up some. I wouldn't mind getting my hands on an old pickup like that."

"First off, I'd paint it fire-engine red, throw some flames on the hood."

"Yeah, and maybe jack it up, or chop the top, get some duelies and—"

The kid behind the counter called out Armando's number and he stepped up to take the bags. Then, avoiding the glances of the two guys at the table, he quickly ducked out the door. He could only imagine what they'd have to say when they saw him joining Dora. But he didn't really care. Or at least that's what he told himself. And why should he? But they were dead-on about this old pickup. It did have potential. And suddenly he had an idea.

Later, after they'd finished their chicken dinner, he decided to mention it. "I've got an idea, Dora," he began as he cleared the table.

"An idea? About what?"

"Yeah. You know how I told Charlie that we have a contract for me to stay on and work for you on the farm?"

She waved her good hand in the air. "Oh, that's just talk. Something to shut him up and make him go away and leave me be."

"Yeah, I know. But the truth is you do need some help round here. And there's lots I could do to fix this place up. But I don't think it's fair to make me work for just my room and board—"

"Oh, here it comes." She scooted her chair back and slowly stood. "I knew it would come down to this sooner or later. Now I 'spect you're going to try to get some money out of me."

He followed her into the living room, waiting as she sat down on the sofa. "No, Dora, I'm not talking about money."

She narrowed her eyes. "What do you mean then?"

"I'm thinking about your old truck. How about if I work here for a few weeks for the pickup? It's not like you can be driving it anyway. And if someone doesn't do some work on it, it won't be long until it's good for nothing."

"But what about when I get well and need to get to town?"

He shook his head. "No way you could drive that thing, Dora. It doesn't even have power steering or power brakes. I don't see how you could possibly manage it. When was the last time you drove anyway?"

She frowned. "Don't rightly recall."

"So how about it? Can I take the truck off your hands in exchange for some good hard labor?"

"That was Henry's favorite truck."

He forced a hopeful smile. "Then I think Henry would be happy to see it getting saved."

She considered this and finally nodded. "Okay, it's a deal."

"Should we agree on how much time I need to work?"

"Well, you've already put in a couple of good days. . . . How 'bout working till the end of this month?"

"Sounds fair to me." And so they shook on it.

"You probably need to rest some now, Dora. I think I'll go outside and work on some things. Maybe clean up that truck a little and check on the engine."

"Make sure you get that tiller and mower put away first," she called. "The weatherman says we're going to get some rain tonight and I don't want my tools getting all soaked and rusted."

"Don't worry. I'll take care of it." He wanted to add, "I'm not a complete moron, you know," but thought better of it. Still, he wished she'd lighten up a little. Didn't she think he could do anything without being told explicitly how and when and where?

Thick gray clouds were already starting to gather overhead. And he quickly cleaned up the mower and tiller and returned them to the shed. Then he spent some time whacking away on blackberry vines around the house before he went off to work on the pickup. He imagined what he might do with a truck like this if he had a little cash in his pocket, and he became so absorbed in cleaning the spark plugs that he almost didn't notice when a car drove into the driveway, but he could tell by the sound of the engine that it was probably Charlie's car. Would that man never give up?

He slammed down the hood and looked toward the house in time to notice a flash of color moving around the area where he had tilled earlier today. Dora must've gone out to check his work. He decided to join her, to perhaps warn her, before Charlie started up another one of his tirades. But as Armando hurried over there, he noticed that Dora appeared to be dancing in the freshly tilled soil. Her feet were bare and she was smiling. He suppressed a chuckle.

"What're you doing there, Dora?" He glanced over his shoulder to see Charlie quickly approaching.

"Feeling the soil," she said with a contented expression. "My feet used to be able to tell me whether or not—"

"*Mother!*" exploded Charlie. "What in heaven's name are you doing out here—walking around with no shoes on?" Just then it started to rain, great big raindrops splattering onto the soft dirt like pellets.

Armando ignored Charlie. "Here comes your rain, Dora."

"Have you lost your mind, Mother? You're going to catch your death out here." He tugged on her good arm. "Get inside right now."

"Don't you go telling me what to do, Charlie." She pointed her finger at him. "Don't forget, I'm *your* mother."

"Then quit acting like a demented child." He continued pulling on her.

"Why don't you let Dora go back into the house when she's ready," suggested Armando. He stepped up to Charlie and looked down at him in an effort to intimidate.

Charlie released Dora's arm and scowled. "We're getting all wet, Mom. Can we please go inside?"

She looked up at the sky. "A little spring rain never hurt anyone." Then she sniffed the air. "And just smell that. Is there anything as delicious as rain falling in May? Your father used to love evenings like this, Charlie. Don't you remember—"

"I remember my father working from dawn till dusk and always having black lines of dirt beneath his fingernails."

"Well, it was *clean* dirt." She looked at Armando and nodded. "All right, I'm ready to go inside now." She stopped on the porch. "But what're you doing here again, Charlie? I thought I made it perfectly clear to you yesterday that I'm not going anywhere."

"I only want to talk to you for a few minutes," he said quietly.

"Just talk?" She looked skeptical.

"Alone." He glanced at Armando. "Just a nice little chat between you and me, Mom. Is that all right?"

She seemed to think about this then finally agreed. "Yes, I think that would be okay."

Armando had a bad feeling about this visit as he walked back to the barn, but what could he do? It seemed wrong to interfere in family business without Dora's invitation. The rain was falling harder now and by the time he reached his room his shirt was completely soaked. He stripped it off and hung it over the chair then sat down on his bed and looked around the room.

The vase of flowers was still on the dresser. With all the excitement yesterday, Olivia had forgotten to take the bouquet home with her. He'd even considered going out and picking her a fresher bunch in case she stopped by today, but then he'd remembered that bit about a boyfriend and thought, *Why bother?* Why should he care if she did have a boyfriend anyway? Why shouldn't a good-looking girl like Olivia have a boyfriend or even two or three? Besides, he told himself, she wasn't even his type. Not that he really knew what his type was exactly. And she seemed a little flaky, or maybe it was flighty. But sometimes he got the feeling that she didn't even know her own mind.

Not that he'd ever felt concerned with the minds of girls he'd known in the past. Give him a pretty face and a body to go with it and he was usually happy, for a while anyway. But that was before he'd left that and so many other things behind. In his new life he had this longing to find a girl who had more going for her—some-one he could really talk with and share his dreams with—someone who wouldn't laugh at him for wanting something more. His girl-friends down in L.A. didn't understand the "something more" bit. They thought he meant something more as in fancy clothes and a hot car, or maybe even a house or a boat or a motorcycle. But those material things weren't it either. Not really. He wanted something more than that.

He laughed at himself. "You are totally full of it, man." As he dug in a drawer for a clean dry shirt, he noticed the bundle of letters still sitting on his dresser where he'd moved them last night. He looked out the window to see the rain now pouring down in sheets and decided this was as good a time as any to brush up on his Spanish.

He flopped down on his bed, took the first letter out of the enve-lope, and attempted to read it.

> *Dearest Manuel:*
>
> *My heart misses you so much. I want you to be with me now. But I know it is not possible. Thank you for the money. It is inconceiv-able that you are paid so well in America, as much as a physician*

here. I want that the children and I come join you but know it is not to happen for Mama needs me now. Mama is very sick. The money you send buys medicine but she does not get better.

The children send their love to you. Manuel Jr. is doing well in arithmetic. Little Rita lost a front tooth and baby Carlos is taking first steps. Tio Luis took photos for me to send for you to remember your family. It is very good that Mr. Henry is kind to you. I pray rosary for him and his wife every night before I sleep. They are good and generous people. God is watching us.

All my love,
Your Elisa

Armando carefully, almost reverently, refolded the letter then removed the two black-and-white snapshots. One was of three big-eyed children, their ages ranging from toddler to school-age. They were dressed in similar outfits of striped fabric. The second photo was of a smiling woman, and very beautiful. He flipped it over to read "Elisa, 1966" on the back. Manuel was a lucky man. Or maybe not so lucky. It must've been frustrating for him to be so far from his family—in a foreign country even. He imagined this man, stuck in this small room, probably isolated from social relationships because of his ethnic difference, and doing menial farm labor in order to survive and feed his family. No, Armando decided, Manuel was definitely not so lucky. And the image of the lonely Mexican man, all by himself in this little room disturbed him. More than he cared to admit.

Just then his door cracked open and the cat strutted in. "Hey, amigo, you're starting to act like you own the place." Homer jumped onto his lap and purred contentedly as Armando petted his slightly damp coat. "Still raining out there?"

He looked out the window again and then at the little alarm clock. He'd spent half an hour translating that short letter into

English. He wondered if old Charlie was still around, and what it was that he'd wanted to say to his mother in private anyway. Hopefully he wasn't convincing her to leave her farm and go live in the old folks home. Because, as bad as this little room was, it was better than getting soaked in the rain. And as prickly as old Dora could be, staying here with her was a whole lot better than being homeless and on the run. Besides, he really wanted the chance to work for that old pickup truck, and the end of May wasn't all that far off. He set Homer aside and went out through the barn and peeked through the door to see Charlie's white Buick parked stubbornly in front of the house. Apparently they were still talking. How could there be so much to say? Was Dora giving in?

* * * * * * * * * * * * *

Dora rubbed her hand back and forth over the smooth surface of her cast. She was trying to decide whether her son was on the up-and-up right now or simply trying to manipulate her into having his own way again. Charlie was so much like his grandfather that she found it hard to believe he'd only been a boy when her father had died of a heart attack back in the early sixties. But this she knew had to do with genetics. Even Henry had pointed that out to her more than once. Still, it was confusing. And, sometimes when Charlie was talking to her, like right now, she got mixed-up and actually thought it was her father speaking, and as usual he was telling her what to do and how to think.

"Mom," Charlie spoke in an aggravated tone that suggested she hadn't been listening again. "Can you hear me?"

"I hear you just fine. I'm thinking about what you're saying, trying to make sense out of it."

"It makes perfect sense to me," he continued. "The farm is going downhill fast. But if you let me bring some guys in here, they can start fixing things up. Remember how much Dad loved this place? Don't you think he'd like to see it fixed up?"

"But I don't know why *you're* so interested in fixing up the farm all of a sudden." She peered over at him curiously, wishing she could see into his mind. What ever happened to her sweet little boy? Was he still in there somewhere, or had this conniving, uncaring man replaced him forever? "You never cared a whit about the farm before. Not when your dad was alive and not after he died. What's going on now?"

Charlie smiled. "I simply think it's a good piece of land that needs to be taken care of."

Now she was getting it. He was thinking of the *value* of the land, how much money he might be able to get for it if it wasn't in such a bad state. "But I thought you said farmland was worthless."

He waved his hand dismissively. "Oh, that's not what I meant. No land is really worthless, Mom." He stood now. "Well, I really need to get going. I promised to meet Audrey at the country club."

"You still go to that snooty place?"

"It's a good place to do business." He smiled. "And you know I never drink—the church would frown on that. So you don't mind if I send some guys out here to start working on the place?"

"I never said that, Charlie."

He scowled now. "Come on, Mom."

"I already told you I have a deal with Armando, and I—"

"You're not going to go on about that lazy Mexican again. He's a freeloader, Mom. You don't need him hanging on and—"

"He's a hard worker, Charlie. And I happen to like him."

Charlie laughed, but not with humor. "Yes, and my secretary told me how you two were seen all over town acting like a couple of lunatics today." He frowned at her colorful dress then spoke in a snide tone. "Maybe you think Armando's your new boyfriend."

"Don't be ridiculous, Charlie."

"Well, I can't believe you traipsed all over town dressed in that silly getup. Good night, Mother, what could you have been thinking?"

She looked down at her dress, smoothing the fabric with her good hand. "Your father gave me this dress."

He exhaled loudly. "I know, I know."

"And I could get it on over my cast without help."

"Look, I'm sorry, Mom. I shouldn't have said that. But I'm frustrated about the farm. Won't you agree to let my guys come out and start doing some work?"

"Okay, under one condition."

Charlie's eyes lit up. "Sure, anything. You name it."

"Armando is the foreman."

Charlie swore.

"Charles Lawrence Chase!"

"Armando as foreman? You *must* be crazy."

She shook her head. "Then just forget the whole thing."

He held up his hands. "Okay, okay. Have it your way. Hire an ignorant wetback to be the foreman if you like." He rolled his eyes. "Whatever it takes."

"Armando is the foreman then?"

"Yeah, yeah. Your boyfriend can play Mr. Foreman." Charlie was already to the door now. "But I want to talk to him first and make sure he understands what's going on and what's expected of him."

She smiled now. "That's fine."

* * * * * * * * * * * * *

Armando jumped when he heard the sharp knock on his door. "Who is it?" he asked as he got up from his bed.

"Mr. Chase."

Armando thought about that for a moment, trying to decide if he was willing to play the subservient Mexican or not. Not. "Oh, *Charlie.*" He opened the door to see Charlie standing stiffly, as if he were uncomfortable in a barn, or maybe he didn't like having to knock on Armando's door. "What do you want?" he asked.

"I've just had a talk with my mother."

Armando sighed. So this was going to be it then. Charlie was here to give him his walking papers. "And?" Armando leaned against the door casing, pretending to be bored, as if anything Charlie had to say was completely inconsequential to him.

"I want to do some improvements to the property," Charlie began. "And I plan to send some men over here to work."

"And?"

"And my mother insists that you're to be the foreman."

Armando brightened a little. "Does she?"

Charlie cleared his throat. "Now, don't you start thinking that means anything, because it doesn't. I'm only trying to please her. These guys know what they're doing, and they don't need any *foreman* to give them orders. So try to stay out of their way and concentrate on things like keeping the grass mowed and the laundry done, and everyone will be perfectly happy."

"Including your mother?"

Charlie rolled his eyes. "Look, it's no secret that my mother is getting a little senile these days. Call it Alzheimer's or old age or whatever, but the old lady's clearly losing her marbles."

"I don't know about that. She seems pretty normal to me."

"Didn't you see her out there dancing barefoot in the mud tonight? Surely you don't think *that's* normal." Then Charlie laughed. "Well, maybe it is where *you* come from."

Armando could only recall a few times in his life when he really wanted to pound someone. And this was such a time. His fists curled, causing his short nails to bite into his palms, but even so, he kept his arms down at his sides as he spoke in a tight but controlled manner. "Where *I come from,* family members are loyal to one another, and children respect their parents."

But Charlie shook his head as if the words had washed right over him. "Just remember what I said, boy. The men I'm sending over don't need to be ordered around—especially by the likes of you. You stay out of their way and everything will be peachy." Then he left.

Armando closed the door with a bang and took in a sharp breath. He turned to his bed and pounded his fists into his mattress, again and again, pummeling so hard that the poor bed frame finally gave in and he had to pull the mattress off and reattach the metal springs back into the iron bed.

By the time he'd restored his bed and cooled off a bit, he decided to distract himself with another one of Manuel's letters. In this letter, Manuel's beautiful wife pleaded with him to give up his labors in Oregon and return to Mexico. Money meant nothing, she said. And she promised him that if he came home they would both work together for a better life, as well as other things, romantic things. Armando refolded the letter and returned it to the envelope. Stupid Manuel! He should've left this place and gone back to his family. Some people just didn't know when they had it good.

Chapter Thirteen

$\mathcal{A}$rmando was already frying bacon when Dora shuffled in for breakfast. "Morning," he said in a forced yet cheerful voice. He had gotten up early, taken a walk, and was determined to remain positive today. No more taking offense from Dora's callous comments. No more feeling sorry for himself. Besides, things were looking up for him. He flipped the bacon then noticed Dora still wore the old muumuu. Only today it was even more wrinkled and rumpled, as if she'd slept in it. And with her white hair sticking out like a fright wig, she was really a sad little sight.

"You got the coffee going yet?" she muttered.

He smiled as he pulled out a chair for her. "I'll get you a cup."

"What're you so happy about?"

He set the steaming cup in front of her. "I don't know. Maybe I'm starting to see that life's got possibilities."

She sniffed. "Must be nice to be young."

"Yeah, I guess so. And it won't be long until I have a truck to drive, and—" he glanced at her—"I hear I've been made foreman."

She took a sip of coffee and groaned. "That may be so, but I sure don't like the smell of it."

He frowned. "What do you mean? You don't think I'll make a good foreman?"

She waved her hand. "No, no, that's not it. Fact is, I don't know whether you'd make a good foreman or not. I just don't know why Charlie's gotten so interested in working the farm all a sudden. Why, he's never wanted anything to do with it before. I know it sounds terrible for a mother to say, but truth is I don't completely trust my own son."

He nodded. "How d'you like your eggs?"

"Over hard."

Armando considered her little confession as he cooked breakfast. As a child, he'd always been taught to be loyal to family—simply because they were family—and yet he, as much as anyone, knew there came times when a member of your own family could mess you over but good.

He set the plates on the table and sat down, waiting for Dora to pray. But to his surprise, she didn't. She picked up her fork and started eating.

"How come you didn't bless the food?" he asked.

She shrugged. "I don't know. Sometimes I wonder why I even bother at all. Oh, I know it's because that's the way Henry did things, but I'm thinking if I'm not doing it for myself, well, why do it at all?"

Armando bit off a piece of bacon. "Guess that makes sense."

"I'm not saying I'm never going to bless my food again. I'm just not sure, is all."

"Was Henry a very religious man?"

"A *religious* man?" Dora pondered over this. "No. I doubt anyone ever would've said Henry was a religious man. Now my son, Charlie, he might be what you call a religious man."

"How's that?"

"Well, he goes to church at least once a week and sometimes more. And he's a deacon too—anyway, I think that's what he calls it. But my Henry, well, up until the end of his life, he hardly ever went to church. But he was a *good* man. Good through and through. And he treated people—*all* people—with dignity and respect."

"Sounds like he was a nice guy." He peered over his coffee mug at her. "Not everyone believes all men are created equal."

She frowned. "You making an insinuation?"

He shrugged, wondering why he'd bothered to go there, especially after his resolve to have a good day.

"I treat all people with dignity and respect."

"*All* people?" he asked. "Even the wetback Mexican migrant workers that you never allowed to enter your house?"

"You remember me saying that, do you?" She got a sly look. "Well, I just made that up."

"Made it up? Why?" He wiped the edge of his toast through the egg yolk puddled across his plate.

She studied him for a long moment. "Well, I suppose I was a little uneasy with you staying here at first. How was I to know whether you planned to kill me in my sleep or rob me or who knows what? So I made up that little fib about wetbacks not coming in the house. But the truth is, Henry always regarded his workers as friends. He even invited them in for a meal on occasion. Why, they sat right here at this very table and ate food that I cooked."

"How did you feel about that?"

She set down her fork. "Well, to be perfectly honest, I wasn't completely comfortable with it at first. I hadn't been raised that way. And out of respect for my feelings, Henry didn't push me too hard on this. But I came round over time."

"Sounds like Henry *was* a nice guy."

"Yes, he was."

Armando had barely finished the breakfast dishes when Dora came back into the kitchen. "Do you think those worker men will be coming out here today?" she asked nervously.

"I don't know. It's Saturday, you know. Maybe they won't come out here until next week."

"Maybe not." She pressed her lips together. "Can you get Olivia on the phone for me? It's near impossible for me to hold on to the phone and push those buttons with only one hand."

He punched in the numbers then handed her the phone.

"Olivia?" she began. "Yes, I'm feeling better, dear. But can you do me a favor? I haven't had a real bath since the day before I broke my arm and I can't hardly remember how long that's been now. Do you think you could be an angel and—" she paused—"oh, thank you, dear. Yes, ten is just dandy."

Armando started to leave.

"Not so fast."

He looked at her. "You're not going to have me do your hair again, are you? I mean since Olivia's coming—"

She shook her head. "No, that's not it. I wanted you to get some seeds out of the freezer."

"The freezer?"

"Yes, it keeps them from going bad. They're in a blue plastic tub, way in the back. I want you to set them out, to warm them up, you know. And then I want you to plant them in that new patch before it starts to rain again. Do you know how to plant seeds?"

He thought about that. "Well, not exactly. Don't you just make holes and put them in?"

"Something like that. But all seeds are different. They need to be planted at different depths, and some you plant in groupings and some in rows. But you do know how to read, so I 'spect you can read the fine print on the back of the seed packets and then follow the directions. You do know how to follow directions, don't you?"

He nodded, noticing the grin at the corner of Dora's mouth. "Yes. I'm pretty good at following directions." He looked her in the eye. "You should know since you're so good at giving them."

She blinked. "Are you suggesting I'm bossy?"

"Well, you *are* the boss, aren't you?"

"That's right. I'm glad we understand each other." Armando saw a twinkle in Dora's faded eyes.

He opened up the freezer and poked around until he spotted the plastic tub clearly marked *Seeds*.

"And," she called over her shoulder, "you keep a watch out for those worker men. I want to know when they get here and what they're up to."

"Gotcha."

Armando carefully read the directions and planted the seeds as instructed. And he couldn't help but feel a sense of anticipation, wondering how long it would take them to grow, and what the plants would look like. His work in agriculture before had always been on the harvesting end of things. He'd never actually grown something from a seed before. Well, other than marigolds in a paper cup back in first grade with Sister Luciana.

Just as he finished the last row of carrots he heard Olivia's Bug pull into the driveway. He waved and waited for her to walk over to him. Today she had her hair pulled back into a ponytail—like she was following Dora's latest fashion trend.

"Hey, Armando," she called. "You're still here."

"You thought I'd left?"

"Well, Dad keeps saying you'll be gone soon."

"Hopeful thinking, I guess." He studied the color of her eyes and decided it was the same shade as the Oregon sky on a clear day.

"You still wanna do a tune-up on my car sometime?"

"Sure. I could take a look at it today and see what it needs."

Olivia looked up at the sky. "Looks like it's about to rain again."

He glanced over to the barn. "Well, I was planning to do some work on the pickup today if the weather turned bad. I figured to park it in the barn. I can do the same with your Bug."

"Cool. The barn'll make a great garage."

"I'll go open it up and you can pull right in."

* * * * * * * * * * * * *

Dora stood on the shelter of the porch watching the two young people converse in the driveway. Then Olivia got back into her little orange car and drove it into the barn. Raindrops were starting to fall as Olivia dashed across the yard and up to the porch.

"Armando's going to give my car a tune-up," explained Olivia, giving her grandmother a hug.

Dora nodded wistfully. "That's nice. Henry used to work on the cars and tractors in the barn when it rained sometimes too."

"You ready for your bath now?"

"Am I ever."

Olivia touched the fabric of Dora's muumuu. "Cool threads, Grandma. Where'd you get this?"

Dora smiled. "Your grandfather got it for me during the war. I put it on yesterday because I could get it over my cast."

"Well, I think it's very chic."

"Your father doesn't agree. He was embarrassed that I'd worn it into town yesterday."

Olivia rolled her eyes as she led Dora inside. "Oh, you know how he is. You need to let it go and ignore him."

"Is that what you do, Livvie?" Dora sat down on the toilet seat and watched as her spry granddaughter bent over the tub to rinse it out.

"Sure. I couldn't survive him otherwise." She turned and studied her grandmother. "Isn't that what you had to do with your father, Grandma? You're always telling me that those two men are like two peas in a pod."

Dora pressed her lips together. "Unfortunately, I was never very good at standing up to *my* father. I suppose it's just how we women were trained to be back in my day. And to my way of thinking my father was a powerful man. As a result, I'm afraid I was pretty spineless."

"But then you had Grandpa."

Dora smiled. "Yes. I had Grandpa. But strangely enough he rarely stood up to my father either. But then I suppose he didn't need to." She looked at Olivia. "He was more like you, dear. He could let my father's orneriness run off him like water off a duck's back. Of course, there were a few occasions when Henry did stand up to him. But only when he felt something had hurt me. That's when Henry would put his oar in."

"Smart man." Olivia turned off the water. "Okay, I'm going to go get a plastic bag and some tape to keep your cast dry."

"Good thinking."

Soon Dora's cast was encased in a garbage sack, and Olivia was helping her ease into the tub. "How's the temperature?"

"It's fine."

Olivia dug around in a drawer until she emerged with a new bar of lavender soap. She sniffed it. "What are you saving this for, Grandma?"

"Oh, for company, I suppose."

"When did you last have company?" Olivia slipped the bar out of the box and dipped it into the water then lathered it up. "Here, lean forward and I'll scrub your back a little. And then I'll go and leave you in peace." She gently rubbed the aromatic lather into Dora's back and then handed her the soap. "Doesn't that smell absolutely delicious?"

Dora inhaled deeply. "I always did love lavender. Such a peaceful smell. It reminds me of summer."

"Why don't you grow some lavender plants?" Olivia added a little more hot water to the tub.

"Your grandpa used to have some. He had them shipped here

from France. There might still be a few out there, out beyond the aspen grove."

"I'll have to watch for them. Armando found some beautiful flowers back in there. You should see the bouquet he made."

"What do you think of our Armando, Olivia?"

"I think he's pretty cool, Grandma. I think you should keep him around for a long, long time."

Dora smiled. "Okay, now off with you before my bathwater gets cold." Then she propped her plastic-wrapped cast on the side of the tub and relaxed into the hot sudsy water. She sighed as she breathed in the sweet earthy fragrance of the soap. When was the last time she'd so enjoyed a soak in the tub?

Of course, there was that memorable bath back in February of 1942. Henry had been at war, serving in the Pacific for two long months, and she had missed him dearly. But, like so many of the servicemen, he'd left a little something behind. She hadn't actually told anyone about her pregnancy yet, not even Henry. It just seemed too soon; plus she didn't want anyone thinking that she and Henry had *had* to get married. Tongues had flapped well enough without adding additional fuel to their fire. But her tiredness and nausea matched the descriptions she'd read in the prenatal section of a health journal in the public library, and somehow she knew it was true. And after missing two monthly cycles she was certain. She felt excited and happy, but also a little scared. It was one of those difficult passages in life when she severely longed for her mother.

Henry had done all he could to insulate their little house before he'd left. He'd chopped what looked like a mountain of firewood as well as a large mound of kindling. And he had taken the time to install a new propane-powered water heater. But their tiny added-on bathroom consisted of a toilet, a small sink, and a coffin-sized shower that dribbled more than it actually sprayed. After three months of living in such spartan conditions, Dora had craved a real bath even more than she craved dill pickles and peanut butter.

It had been a long, wet winter with no end to the chilling rains in sight. The students in Dora's class were antsy and distracted; like her, they wished for spring and sunshine. And by the end of February, she felt drained and exhausted. She stopped by the bank on her way home to deposit her check as usual—half in savings and half in checking—and she noticed her father's office was dark and empty. Worried that something was wrong, she approached his secretary, Mrs. Standish.

"Oh, no need to worry, dear. He's up in Seattle at some bigwig bankers' conference," the older woman told her. "He'll be back on Monday." Then peering at her more closely, she asked, "How're you doing, Dora? You look a little peaked."

"I suppose I'm just tired."

"Well, it's that time of year, isn't it? You know, I don't think I've hardly talked to you since you got married. Congratulations, by the way."

Dora smiled. "Thanks. But I'm feeling fairly single again these days. I sure do miss Henry."

"You're not alone there. I miss my William too."

"Your son's in the service? But he's only a boy."

"Eighteen last summer."

Dora shook her head. "Well, they do grow up, don't they?"

She nodded. "Do you want me to tell your father you asked about him?"

Dora considered this. They hadn't actually spoken since December during the night of the storm. "No, no . . . I wanted to make sure he was okay. You know he has that high blood pressure and all."

"Don't I know it. I'm always reminding him to take it easy. But does he listen to me?"

Dora laughed. "Does he listen to anyone?"

"Well, you take care now. And get some rest this weekend."

As Dora left the bank it occurred to her that she still had a key to her father's house—and her father's house had not just one, but *four* full-sized bathtubs. The mere thought of being in her old room again, with its spacious adjoining bath, sounded like pure luxury. A forbidden pleasure even. All the way home she imagined how good it would feel to spend a couple of days in her old home. And Mrs. Standish was right; she did need to take care of herself. She was bone tired and weary.

So that night, after dark, Dora packed a small bag and drove to her father's house. Discreetly parking her car in the back, she let herself in, and feeling like a thief in the night, she crept up the stairs. Thanking God for blackout curtains, she turned on the lights in her bedroom then began to draw a hot bath. She knew she should eat something, but her stomach had been upset for most of the day. Perhaps after a relaxing bath, she would raid her father's kitchen, careful not to leave any traces of her presence behind.

Finally, she slipped into the foaming bath, sighing with pleasure as the hot water wrapped itself around her thin body. She knew she'd lost a little weight due to her lack of appetite. But that should be reversing itself soon enough. Already she could feel a small rounding to her belly. She leaned her head back and closed her eyes, dreaming of days in late summer or early fall when perhaps Henry would be allowed a leave of absence to come see his wife and newborn son—she was certain it was a boy.

Dora was never completely sure how long she soaked in the bath, and for that she would chide herself later. She did recall adding fresh hot water several times to warm it. After a while, she came to with a start as a sharp pain stabbed and twisted in her abdomen. She clutched her belly in fear. What was happening? The pain subsided for a few minutes, and she thought perhaps she'd only imagined it. But then it returned with even more force. It felt like menstrual cramps. She had no idea what it meant or what she should do.

She considered calling Aunt Bertha, her father's sister, but knew that would expose her as a trespasser and her father would surely hear of the whole thing later. And then she thought perhaps it was simply a normal condition of her stage of pregnancy. But somehow she wasn't convinced.

She stood and reached for a towel, but in the same moment was clenched with another intense cramp, and this time she doubled over in pain and actually cried out, "God, help me!" She stayed in that position until the pain finally subsided. Then she stood and took in a deep breath. It was too late.

The image of stained bathwater burned itself into her memory that night. She knew she had lost the baby in that pool of blood. With as much certainty as she had known she was pregnant, she now knew she was not.

She couldn't remember much of the other details of that night. Somehow she managed to clean everything up so that no one would ever know she was there. And the next day she got into her car and drove back to the farm. That was the last night she ever spent in her father's house.

At first she blamed herself for the miscarriage. She thought perhaps her lengthy bath had brought it on. But later she learned, through reading, that it hadn't.

Then she blamed her father. She felt it was his bitterness that had poisoned her that night. His hard and unforgiving nature had stolen the unborn child from her body. Oh, she knew this was crazy thinking, but she believed it anyway. And although she never shared her conviction with anyone and never told anyone about the miscarriage, she held it against her father until the day he died—and even afterward.

There were times when she had almost told Henry about the lost child. But she knew it would only make him feel bad, as if it were somehow his fault for not having put in a bathtub or the other little luxuries he always felt guilty for depriving her of. Besides, it wasn't long before he made up for these small deprivations, after the war, when he built their real home, the one she had lived in for more than half a century. And of course, he always made up for it by loving her dearly, tenderly, completely. Oh my, how Henry had loved her!

Chapter Fourteen

Armando made a few minor adjustments on Olivia's car engine then composed a list of items she would need for a real tune-up. He didn't know if she could tell the difference between a spark plug and an oil filter, but at least she could hand over his list to the clerk at the automotive store. He wondered what her boyfriend was like and whether or not he knew anything about engines. Probably not. Or else he wasn't a very thoughtful boyfriend. Armando was cleaning his hands when Olivia came back out.

"So what's the prognosis?" she asked as she took a pack of cigarettes out of her purse.

"Prognosis?"

"You know, my car. Is she going to live?"

He laughed. "Yes, I think so. But unless you like walking, you might want to take better care of the old girl."

"I figured as much." She offered him a cigarette.

He took it and gently rolled it between his fingers. He lifted it to his nose and smelled the pungency of the tobacco then handed it back to her. "Thanks, but I quit."

"You sure about that?"

"I am for today. It's one of those things you can only guarantee yourself by the moment. I smoked for more than seven years, and believe me, it wasn't easy to stop."

She made a smirky face. "Well, *good for you.*"

"I'm sorry. I didn't mean to sound superior or anything. And I don't mind if other people smoke."

"That's a relief." She blew out a long puff. "I thought you might be one of those obnoxious guys who get on their soapbox and make everyone else feel like slimeballs because *they're* still smoking."

"Nope. That'd be inviting trouble."

"How's that?"

"Well, it's something my grandmother used to say. But she said it in Spanish. You speak Spanish?"

She shook her head as she blew smoke over her shoulder.

"Let me see, it was something like 'don't think too highly of yourself or you'll be sure to fall flat on your face.' It sounds more poetic in Spanish, but it means something like that."

"I like that." She knocked the ash off her cigarette. "So have you ever fallen flat on your face?"

He grinned. "Sure, lots of times."

"And you're willing to admit it?"

"Why not? There's no shame in falling down, as long as you get back up. And hopefully learn something from it."

She peered at him curiously. "Are you some sort of religious fanatic or something?"

"Me?" He laughed. "Are you kidding?"

"Well, you seem so good sometimes. Like too good to be true, you know. And you know what they say about that."

"No. What do they say?"

"That if it *seems* too good to be true, then it probably is."

Armando shrugged. "Don't worry. I've got plenty of problems. I try not to drag them around with me all the time, if I can help it, that is. But for some reason it feels important to do the right thing these days."

"The *right* thing?" Olivia studied him.

"Yeah, that probably sounds pretty lame, but I've seen what happens when you don't."

"So have you been in some kind of trouble?"

He frowned. "Maybe."

She nodded with satisfaction. "Just as I suspected."

"Yeah, well, there's all kinds of trouble, you know. Things aren't always what they seem." He pushed the memory of that last day in L.A. away from him. Nothing about it seemed to make much sense anyway.

"So are you running from something then?"

He shrugged. "I don't know exactly. Sometimes it seems like it. Then sometimes I wonder why I even care. Like it's *nada*—nothing. The thing is, I came up here looking for a fresh start."

"A fresh start?" She snuffed out her cigarette beneath her sneaker. "Is that really possible? I mean no matter where you go or what you do, you still bring yourself along with you, don't you? How can that be a fresh start?"

He decided to redirect this line of questioning. "You saying you want to get away from yourself? You don't like yourself?"

"Oh, I don't know. Sometimes I despise myself. Or maybe it's just the things I do that I'm not so crazy about." Olivia threw back her head and laughed suddenly. "And that's as much as I'm going to say about that. Good grief, I'm starting to feel like this is a confessional or something. Hey, I'm not even Catholic."

"Something wrong with being Catholic?"

"No, I wasn't suggesting that. I only meant that—"

He waved his hand. "Aw, forget it."

She glanced back to the house. "I told Grandma I'd fix lunch today."

"But you don't know how to cook."

"Hey, I happen to make a mean grilled-cheese sandwich, and I can heat soup pretty well."

He grinned. "Hidden talents."

"Yes. I like to keep it that way. Helps me stay out of the kitchen."

He handed her his list. "This is what you need for your car— to get her running better."

She frowned at the list. "I don't even know what these—"

"Give it to the guy at the automotive store. He'll know what it means."

"Will they cost a lot?"

He shrugged. "Guess it depends on who you are." He smiled. "To me it would be a lot since I'm basically broke. But for you, well . . ."

Olivia peered at him. "You're broke? Like totally broke? How can you be on your own like this and not have any money?"

"Guess I'm kind of a bum."

"I didn't mean—"

"No, it's okay. Right now I'm working to earn the old pickup—"

"Grandpa's truck?"

He nodded.

"She's giving you Grandpa's truck?"

"Not *giving*—I'm working for it."

"I always wanted to have his truck. She never even offered it to me."

"But you have your car—"

"But it's not the same—it's not *Grandpa's.*"

Armando studied her for a minute. Was she going to throw a temper tantrum? He looked down at the floor and considered his situation. Should he back out of his deal with Dora and suggest that Olivia take the truck? But that didn't seem fair. Olivia already had everything. Rich parents, college tuition, a family—even a boyfriend

"Dora and I have an agreement," he finally said. "And the truck's in pretty bad shape right now. It'll take a fair amount of work to get it running and looking good. You really want to do all that?"

"Maybe not." She sighed. "I guess I'm jealous."

He laughed. "Now, that's funny."

"Well, don't worry. I'll get over it. But you better promise to let me drive it once you get it all fixed up. And please tell me you won't do anything ridiculous to it, like paint it some sherbet color or put those stupid-looking tailpipes out the back end."

He smiled. "No, I'm not into that. It's not like I want to embarrass the poor truck; I only want to fix it up. And then drive it."

"I guess it's okay then."

"I was wondering . . . " Armando didn't want to sound too nosey, too interested. "Isn't your boyfriend into cars?"

She laughed. "Ben? Are you kidding? He thinks anything that burns petroleum products should be outlawed. *He* rides a bike."

He nodded. "Well, that's cool."

"Yeah. And Ben doesn't wear leather either. He's a vegetarian and totally into environmentalism and world peace and, well, you name it. My dad basically can't stand him."

Armando laughed. "Yeah, that sounds about right."

Olivia grinned mischievously. "That's probably why I'm still with him."

"You mean Ben?"

"Yeah. If my dad liked him I'd probably drop him like a tough chemistry class." She started walking away. "Lunch'll be ready in about half an hour."

Armando moved her car out of the barn and the pickup in. It was starting to rain again when he closed the big sliding door. He planned to finish cleaning the engine and start doing some body-work. He figured it would be something to keep himself busy during the evenings or when the weather was bad. He'd noticed some old cans of oil-based paint in the back of the shed and planned to ask Dora about using them. He wanted to get the rusty spots sanded and primed as soon as possible. And hopefully, he'd find a way to earn some money to buy the items he'd need to get the truck into really good shape.

After thirty minutes of puttering around on the pickup, Armando dashed across the rain-soaked yard to the house. When he got inside, it looked as if a hurricane had hit Dora's living room. "What happened?" he asked as he surveyed the piles of clothes and miscellaneous household items strewn all over the room.

Dora dropped a pair of old high heels into a box. "Audrey's help-ing with a rummage sale at her church next week and she asked me to gather up some things to donate."

"Audrey?"

"Charlie's wife." Dora held up an ancient-looking man's sport coat. "Don't suppose this would fit you, would it? You seem to be about the same height and build as my Henry."

"That's a fantastic idea, Grandma," said Olivia as she appeared in the kitchen doorway. "Some of those old fifties threads would look really great on Armando. I can't believe some of the incredible things I've already found for myself."

"Really?" Armando frowned at the strange garments splayed across the old sofa then back at Olivia. Was she just stringing him along?

"Definitely." Olivia picked up what looked like an old bowling shirt in a pale shade of blue. "Like this." She held it up to Armando. "Totally cool."

He looked down at the shirt. "Yeah, I kinda like it too."

Dora smiled. "Henry loved bowling. He was pretty good too. I think I still have his old bowling ball around here somewhere." She started heading toward the hall closet.

"Not now, Grandma," ordered Olivia. "First we eat. I didn't slave away in this kitchen to let it all get cold."

Midway through their meal, Olivia stopped eating and looked

over at her grandmother. "Hey, I just realized that you never prayed before we ate. What's up with that?"

Dora shrugged. "Oh, I don't know. I guess I've been thinking that if I'm going to pray I should really mean it. I'm not sure I have lately."

Olivia chuckled. "Better not let Dad hear you talking like that. He'll think you've become a heathen or lost your marbles for sure."

Dora stuck her chin out. "I don't care what Charlie thinks. Whether I pray or don't pray has nothing to do with him—or anyone else for that matter—except for me, that is."

"And God?" Armando ventured.

Dora considered this. "Well, yes, I suppose that makes sense."

"Do you *really* believe in God, Armando?" asked Olivia.

"Sure. No reason not to."

"No reason not to . . . " Olivia repeated those words slowly, as if mulling each one over in her mind. Then suddenly she looked at her watch. "Oops, I gotta run. Do you mind cleaning up for me, Armando?" She wiped her mouth on the napkin and pushed back her chair. "Ben expects me to meet him at his exhibit by two."

"Exhibit?" Armando asked.

"Yeah. Ben's a sculptor—pretty good too. And he's got an exhibit that opens tonight at Marlowe's."

"Is that the new art gallery I read about in the paper a while back?" asked Dora.

"Yeah. I promised Ben I'd help him set up today."

"Are you putting your things in there too?" asked Dora.

Olivia laughed. "Nah, I'm not good enough to show yet."

Dora scowled. "Says who?"

Olivia leaned over and kissed her grandmother. "Certainly not you, Grandma."

"That's right. And thanks for the bath, dear. I feel almost as good as new now."

"Maybe Armando can help you with the rest of that rummage-sale stuff. Mom'll probably be by later this afternoon. At least I think that's what she said."

For such a simple meal, Olivia had really managed to make quite a mess in the kitchen. The girl obviously didn't cook much. Armando remembered what she'd told him when they'd first met—how her dad called her a grasshopper. And maybe old Charlie wasn't too far off there, for Olivia did seem fairly fickle and irresponsible. But perhaps that was the result of having life too easy. Maybe she was just spoiled.

"Armando," called Dora, as he finished scrubbing the last pot, "come see this."

He dried his hands and went into the living room. "What's up?"

She held a small pink dress in her hand. "This was Susan's."

"Susan?"

"Our little girl." Dora sat down on the sofa, right in the midst of the clothing piles. "Our dear little girl."

"I thought Charlie was your only child."

"Charlie came along after we lost Susan." She pressed the small garment to her cheek. "He never even knew his sister."

"How did she die?"

"Polio."

"People died of polio? I thought they just got crippled."

"Susan got it clear into her lungs. She slipped away quickly."

"I'm sorry."

Dora studied the dress. "I thought I'd given everything away. My friend Gladys had a baby girl the following year and I boxed up all of Susan's clothes and gave them to her. It was easier than seeing them hanging on their little hangers."

"Yeah, that makes sense."

"Armando, could you help me get up those stairs? I think I'd like to look at Susan's room. Maybe you'd like to see it too."

He wasn't so sure that he wanted to see the room of some long-lost child, but supporting her good arm, Armando slowly helped Dora climb to the top of the steps. She was out of breath by the time they reached the landing. "I haven't been up here in years." She steadied herself. "It's that door on the right."

Feeling like a character in some old horror flick, Armando walked over and slowly opened the door, preparing himself for the appearance of a ghost child or even a haunted nursery. But all he saw was a little yellow bedroom. The only pieces of furniture were a twin bed and a small white dresser.

"Nice room," he said.

Dora walked over and sat down on the bed. She still had the pink dress in her hand, and she glanced around the room with an expression of wonder on her face. "It looks exactly the same."

He nodded, unsure of what to do next. "You want me to go down and start packing up all those things for when . . . uh . . . Charlie's wife gets here?"

"Yes." She didn't look at him. "Yes, that would be helpful. And if you see anything you can use, just set it aside. No sense sending away perfectly good clothes when someone in the family can use them."

"All right." As he walked downstairs, he thought about what she'd said: "when someone in the family can use them." Had she really meant those words? It was the closest thing to warmth he'd heard escape her old lips, coming in his direction, that is. Perhaps the memory of her long-lost baby girl had touched a soft spot in her. He would be careful not to take her words too personally.

Just the same, as he worked his way through Henry's old clothes, he set aside more items than he would've if she hadn't said that. And to his surprise, he found some pieces he actually liked, including an old pair of red-and-blue bowling shoes that were a little on the large side. He put some of the clothes in the washing machine to freshen them up and remove the stale odor. Then he continued to box and bag the rest of the stuff, wondering who on earth would be interested in buying some of these weird items that hadn't seen daylight in decades.

Chapter Fifteen

*D*ora lifted the small pink dress to her nose and inhaled deeply. Could she detect the slightest lingering trace of baby powder and sunshine still tucked between its threads? She remembered sewing this dress for Susan during several hot summer afternoons while the baby was napping. She'd hand-smocked the bodice and trimmed the collar and sleeves with dainty white lace that she'd salvaged from an old blouse. The dress was for Susan's first birthday— July 30, 1947.

Henry had been back from serving overseas for some time by then—long enough that his absence during the war seemed like a distant memory. He'd started clearing land for their home as soon as he'd returned. Constructing the one-and-a-half-story house in stages, he'd finished the downstairs section the spring before Susan was born, and the upstairs would be nearly finished by the time she turned one. Not that Dora was in any great rush to move the child upstairs. That could come later when Susan was old enough to safely make her way up and down the stairs. For now Dora kept the stairs securely gated from the toddler. But she'd already picked out the color for Susan's room—a warm buttery yellow—and Henry planned to have it painted in time for the child's first birthday.

Dora had never been happier. Henry was devoted to his "two girls" and had worked hard to keep up with all the latest agricultural technology. As a result, the farm now produced enough income to modestly support their small family. Oh, sure, they didn't have the luxuries Dora had grown up with, but that was a small sacrifice to pay for such happiness. Not only that, but she'd even been going out of her way to restore her relationship with her father. Not so much for herself, because there were still things she could never forget or perhaps even forgive, but she didn't want Susan to grow up without family. And Charles doted on his beautiful fair-haired granddaughter—he called her Suzy Sunshine and was even threatening to buy her a pony.

"Not yet, Daddy," Dora had pleaded over the phone a week before Susan's birthday. "She's much too young."

"But I found the most beautiful palomino, and this way she can grow up with a pony and never know any fear of horses."

"No, it's too soon," she insisted firmly. "Maybe in a couple of years."

He made his usual *harrumph* noise, but then said, "Well, if I can't give my granddaughter a pony, I insist that you let me throw her a birthday party."

"But I wanted to do something simple out here on the farm."

"Oh, you can do that any day, Dora. But how many times do I have an excuse to throw a party and show off my pretty granddaughter? And you know I never did get to enjoy a wedding. . . ."

Dora exhaled slowly. Again with the guilt. Well, she was not going to let her father spoil her happiness now. What would it hurt if he did throw a little party? Think of the money it would save them. And besides, it would be fun for Susan. "Okay, Daddy," she finally agreed. "But don't get carried away."

Of course, he did get carried away. He had a clown (no pony) and balloons and cake and ice cream and all the trappings and trimmings for an unforgettable first birthday party. The hit of the party was a small wading pool he'd had specially constructed in his backyard, complete with a spraying fountain. And since the temperature was in the nineties, even the adults were caught dipping their toes into it.

When the party was over, Dora thanked her father as well as her lucky stars that she didn't have to clean up that awful mess. His hired help would tend to that. She and Henry loaded a sleepy Susan and all her birthday loot into the car and headed happily for home.

The heat wave continued during the next few days. When Susan seemed more tired and fussy than usual, Dora just attributed it to overdoing it at the party combined with the heat and humidity and teething. But one morning, Dora got up to find Susan strangely quiet, burning up with fever, her limbs rigid.

"Henry!" screamed Dora. But he'd already gone outside to work. Dora grabbed up the phone and dialed the pediatrician—a number she knew by heart.

"We need to see her immediately," the doctor said after his receptionist finally got him on the phone. "There are several cases of polio in—"

"Polio?" Dora felt her world caving in. "No, it can't be—"

"I'll send an ambulance and meet you at the hospital."

Dr. Peters's diagnosis was correct. Susan had contracted polio and the small child's body was unable to fight the brutal virus. By that evening her tiny lungs had succumbed to the disease and she died the following morning.

"She was probably exposed at the birthday party," suggested Dr. Peters as he tried to console the stricken parents. "Everyone knows that swimming pools are highly contagious—"

"Everyone knows?" sputtered Dora. *"I* didn't know."

"Well, there's nothing you can do now." He squeezed her hand. "Be thankful she didn't suffer much, Dora."

Thankful? How did he expect Dora to be *thankful?*

Somehow Henry carried her through the next few days—Henry and a prescription of Valium. Even to this day, Dora had difficulty remembering the funeral or what was said. Except for one particular incident.

After the miniature casket was covered with dirt and only immediate family remained at the grave, Dora had lunged at her father. "It's all your fault!" she had screamed. "You ruin everything for me! It was your party that killed my baby!"

Henry had pulled her off and ushered—perhaps even carried— her back to the car, where she crumpled into the seat and sobbed all the way home. She felt as if a part of her had been buried with her baby that day.

And it would be years before she spoke to her father again.

* * * * * * * * * * * * *

"Dora?" called Armando quietly, unsure as to whether she might be napping.

She slowly opened her eyes, pausing to dry her wet cheeks with the back of her good hand before she finally sat up on the bed and blinked at him.

"Are you okay?" He came over and studied her closely. She'd obviously been crying. "Maybe it's not such a good idea to be up here like this."

She sighed and shook her head. "No, it's all right. I have places I need to go right now—places I haven't been to in years."

"Huh?" Did she want him to drive her somewhere?

"Things come back to you when you get old."

"Things?"

"Old memories and such." She waved her hand. "I don't know why. Maybe I'm just getting ready to die."

"To die?" He sat down next to her. "I hope not."

"We all gotta die sometime, Armando. And my time's probably right around the corner now."

He looked down at his hands. His nails were still dirty from planting the seeds and working on the engines. He wondered what he'd do if Dora suddenly died. Sure she was a cantankerous old woman, but he'd come to depend on her—and perhaps if he were honest with himself, he even cared about her. Was it possible she was really going to die soon? "Are you feeling bad, Dora? You need to see a doctor?"

She turned and looked at him. "No, silly. Other than this arm, I'm perfectly fine. But I'm old, Armando. Doesn't take a genius to see that. And I 'spect it's about time I face up to the likelihood of my own mortality."

He considered this. Of course, everyone would die eventually. Yet that brought no comfort. "Are you ready to die, Dora?"

She made a cackling noise that sounded a bit like laughter. "Ready? Is anyone ever ready?"

He thought back to when Abuela Maria passed away. "I think my grandmother was."

She peered up at him. "Really? How can you know that for sure?"

"Well, I know she didn't like leaving me—she was like a mother to me, you know—but she told me she was ready to go to heaven and see God and reunite with her loved ones who were already there."

"And you think she really meant it? You think she actually wanted to die?"

"I don't know that she *wanted* to die. But I believe she was ready."

"Are you ready, Armando?"

He firmly shook his head. "No way. I'm not good enough to get into heaven yet. I think I'll have to figure a few things out before I kick the bucket."

"Oh, phooey, you're a good boy, Armando. And you said today that you believe in God. Why on earth wouldn't you be good enough for heaven?"

"I don't know for sure. But I feel pretty certain I'm not."

Her face grew sad. "Well, if you're not, then I'm probably not either."

Armando didn't know what to say. Already, he felt way over his head when it came to *real* matters of faith. What did he really know about things like God and the hereafter anyway? Sure, his grandmother had told him things—things she believed with her whole heart. And the nuns had taught him his catechism and things about the church. But other than a strong feeling here and there, he'd never really experienced real honest-to-goodness faith firsthand. Never really wanted to.

"Can you help me downstairs now?"

He took her arm and slowly guided her down the stairs. She still had the little pink dress in her hand. "I don't think I'll ever go up there again," she said when they reached the last step. "It's too hard."

She went back to her bedroom, and Armando moved his load of wet clothes from the washer into the dryer. It was too rainy to use the clothesline today.

As he stopped to get a drink of water at the kitchen sink, he saw a car pull up in front of the house. It was a cherry red, late-model Thunderbird, the style that resembled an old classic. He drank his water and watched as a youthful-looking blonde woman climbed out. She had on a lime green pantsuit that looked like something straight out of the seventies but at the same time seemed stylish on her trim figure. She held what looked like a magazine over her head as she dashed through the rain toward the front porch and pounded on the door. But before he could get there, she'd let herself in.

"Dora?" she called. "I came to pick up the—"

"She's in her room," he told the woman, who upon closer inspection appeared to be in her late forties but still familiarly attractive. "You must be Olivia's mother."

She stopped in her tracks and stared at him. "Why, you must be the . . . uh . . . the one Charlie told me about."

He forced a smile and stuck out his hand. "I'm Armando."

She returned the smile, her perfectly painted lips separating just enough to reveal a set of unnaturally white teeth. "I'm Charlie's wife—Audrey." She shook the rain off her magazine and took his hand. "Nice to meet you, Armando."

"Thank you, ma'am. Do you want me to get Dora for you?"

"Is she resting? I don't want to disturb her."

"I'm not sure. She seemed a little worn-out."

"Don't bother her. I only wanted to pick up the rummage-sale things and drop off the latest issue of *Good Housekeeping*—it's Dora's favorite magazine."

"I'll make sure she gets it."

Audrey looked down at the boxes and bags littered across the floor. "Land sakes! Am I supposed to get all that in my car?"

"I'm happy to load them up for you, ma'am."

"Oh, I'd so appreciate that. The rain is absolutely destroying my hair today. And I just got it done for the art exhibit tonight."

"It looks nice."

"Why, thank you." She patted the back of her head. "You know, I don't know why Charlie made such a big fuss. Why, you seem like a very nice young man to—"

"Is that you chattering away in there, Audrey?" Dora called out from her room.

"Yes. Are you fit for company, honey? I brought you a magazine."

"Come on back then," called Dora.

"Excuse me, Armando." She tossed him another brilliant smile.

"No problem. I'll start loading these up now."

It took several trips and some real engineering strategy to get everything into her small car, but somehow he managed. By the time he finished, Audrey was getting ready to leave.

"Thank you so much for your help. I can't believe you got all that into my car."

"Well, I had to put some of the stuff on the seats. I hope that's okay. I spread a blanket over your upholstery to protect the leather."

"Why, you're a very thoughtful young man."

He smiled self-consciously.

"Now, if only I could take you with me to unload all this junk at the church."

He shrugged. "Hey, I don't mind going along, but then you'd have to drive me back."

She actually giggled. "Oh, I can hear Charlie now. He'd throw a perfect hissy fit. First his mother is seen all over town with you—and then his wife! And you're such a good-looking young man." She winked at him. "And can you just imagine how those church ladies' tongues would wag? Oh, the things they'd say!"

"Like that you have good taste in younger men?" He grinned.

"Oh, you!" She patted him on the arm. "I don't know why my daughter doesn't toss that Ben Sheraton aside and take up with you."

"That'd be okay with you?" Armando studied her expression closely.

Audrey shrugged and she reached for the door. "Truth is, I don't agree with my husband on a lot of things. I happen to believe the good Lord loves each and every one of us the same no matter what we look like or where we come from."

He nodded slowly. "And is that what your church believes too?"

"As a matter of fact, most of them do. I believe you'd be welcome there on any day of the week."

"Would Charlie welcome me too?"

"Oh, you can't worry too much about how he acts. Despite him thinking he's such a leader in the church and all, well, let's just say he's got his own baggage to carry."

The rain had stopped now, and Armando walked her out to the

car then opened the car door for her. "It's been a real pleasure to meet you, ma'am."

"Why, thank you." She smiled. "Say, are you coming to the exhibit tonight? It's open to the public, you know."

"Well, I didn't really think—"

"Oh, *do* come. I'd love to see you there. I'm sure Olivia would too. And then you could meet Ben. He's really not so bad. A little too serious for me is all." She winked. "I like a little spice and color."

He closed her door and waved, then stood watching the flash of red disappear as she sped down the highway. *Nice wheels!*

Chapter Sixteen

While clearing the table after supper, Armando casually asked Dora if she wanted to go to the art exhibit. Although he was curious about this Ben character, he didn't want to appear overly eager to go.

"I'm awful tired and this arm is paining me something fierce tonight." She drained the last bit in her coffee cup and sighed.

"I understand. But I thought you might like to see the exhibit." He set the supper dishes next to the sink and began running the water.

"Nah, I don't go out much in the evenings. It wears me out. I'd rather stay home and watch my *Wheel*—or fall asleep reading a good book." She looked up at him as he refilled her coffee cup. "But you go on ahead. Take the truck and go, if you want to. Goodness knows, it must be frightfully boring staying out here on the farm with the likes of me all the time."

"No, that's not—"

"I *want* you to go, Armando." Her voice grew persuasive. "That way you can tell me all about it tomorrow morning. You probably have already guessed that I'm not terribly fond of Olivia's friend Ben. Nice-looking enough, but he's too quiet and somber for my taste. Don't fully trust him. And sometimes I get the feeling he's looking down on all of us, like he thinks he's too good to even sit at the supper table with you. Can't abide that in a person. Never could."

He knew this all too well. "Yeah, I know what you mean."

"Just the same I wouldn't mind hearing how his big fancy art show goes."

"So you really don't mind if I go?" He rinsed out a glass.

"Aren't you listening to me, boy? I *want* you to go."

He tried not to bristle at *boy* as he rinsed another glass. "You sure you're all right on your own, Dora? You seemed a little down this afternoon."

She waved her good arm at him. "That was then. Naturally, I was feeling sad about my little Susan—feeling things I haven't felt for ages. But I'm fine now."

"Well, okay, maybe I'll drop in there and see what Ben's sculptures look like. Might be interesting." He scrubbed a plate with the dishrag. "You know, I did some sculpting myself back in high school."

"Is that so? So you're an artist too?"

He laughed. "No, not at all. But it was kind of fun and my art teacher thought my stuff was okay. I haven't done much of anything you could call artistic since then."

"Well, it's not too late to try your hand at it again. You know, Olivia's a fine artist, but she just doesn't take herself seriously enough."

"Sometimes it seems like Olivia doesn't really know what she wants to be when she grows up." He regretted his words when he saw the shadow cross Dora's face. Who was he to slam her only granddaughter? Especially considering the fact that his own life was pretty much going nowhere.

But Dora smiled. "Well, it's fine and dandy with me if that child never grows up completely. I love my little Livvie just the way she is."

Armando thought about her words as he washed the rest of the dishes. Sure, it was nice that Dora felt that way, but wasn't everyone supposed to grow up eventually? Didn't they all need to take responsibility for their lives? Or was he just starting to think too much like stuffy old Charlie now? He took his time wiping off the stove top and kitchen counters and table, waiting until Dora was comfortably situated on the sofa with her favorite game show playing before he went out to his room to get ready to go—if he was going that is. He still wasn't sure.

He tried to imagine what he'd be setting himself up for. He'd be the obvious outsider there tonight, the stranger in town, perhaps even unwelcome at what might be a snooty affair where someone like him could never possibly fit in. He wished he'd been able to bring more of his things from his aunt's house—like his black leather jacket; for some reason that always made him feel more confident. He glanced at the diverse pile of old clothes splayed across his bed and scratched his head. Maybe it was time to play dress-up. He picked up Henry's old sport coat, a charcoal herringbone, and slipped it on and looked in the mirror. Not bad, although it looked out of place with his faded sweatshirt. He pulled out a pair of dark gray pleated trousers with cuffs and then a shiny blue shirt that looked to be from the forties or fifties—like something Ricky Ricardo might've worn on a *Lucy* episode.

Finally, he stood before the cracked mirror and studied himself and thought he actually looked pretty good. His Doc Martens looked a little out of place and he considered wearing the old bowling shoes but thought that might be a little over the top. He wasn't really trying to make a spectacle of himself tonight. "Lighten up, man," he told his reflection as he combed his hair. "You're going to a dumb old art show."

It felt good to be behind the steering wheel again, by himself this time. And he immediately dismissed the voice of his uncle that kept pestering him to *"just keep going, man. Hit the road and don't look back."* No, he knew that would be stupid and wrong. He was on the right track now and he planned to stick to it. And besides, how could he do that to Dora, or Olivia?

He felt his palms grow clammy as he slowly drove into the town.

He wasn't completely sure where the gallery was, except that it was on Main Street, but he quickly spotted a shop that was well lit and had a large sandwich sign that read "Marlowe's—Special Exhibit Tonight" placed predominately on the sidewalk. He parked the truck a couple blocks away and strolled toward the building. He squared his shoulders and held his head high and, taking on a nonchalant air that felt as foreign and phony as his strange attire, he walked through the opened doorway.

"Armando!" said Olivia almost as soon as he stepped inside. She had on a long flowing dress with lots of vibrant colors and glass beads and fringe—very exotic looking. "I'm so glad you came." She glanced over his shoulder and whispered, "I'm the official greeter tonight and I'm getting a little sick of it."

"I see." He smiled and hoped he appeared at ease. "Your grand-mother thought I should come see Ben's work."

"And so you shall." Her eyes quickly skimmed over him. "By the way, you look mahvahlous, dawling." Then she nodded over to a food table in a corner. "Better go get yourself some eats while there's still some of the good stuff left. I'll introduce you to the *arteest* later."

He winked at her. "By the way, you look pretty good yourself."

Armando moved through the crowd more easily than he'd expected. Olivia's welcome made him feel almost as if he belonged here. Almost. Still, he couldn't help but notice how wealthy most of the patrons of the arts appeared, at least to him. And he wondered if they suspected him to be a fraud—just sneaking in off the street for free food and fun. Although, in his opinion, neither of those cate-gories had all that much to offer. The art, well, it was okay, but noth-ing to make such a fuss over. And although he couldn't think of the right words to describe it, it seemed almost as if the artist was trying too hard—as if there were too much something about absolutely nothing. But then that was his uneducated opinion and what did he know? Just the same, he couldn't help but wonder how Ben had been able to form some of his metal sculptures without the aid of some sort of petroleum power, like a propane torch for instance? But then maybe he stoked up a big wood fire, or perhaps coal, and did these things the old-fashioned way. But Armando thought not.

"There you are!"

Armando turned to see Audrey working her way toward him as she balanced a glass of punch in one hand and a small plate of appetizers in the other. Tonight she had on a satin suit of peacock blue, quite stunning really, especially against the contrast of her platinum blonde hair. "Hello, Mrs. Chase," he said in a formal voice. He wasn't sure why he didn't call her Audrey, but somehow that kind of familiarity didn't seem quite right, especially amidst all these strangers.

"Please, call me Audrey," she reminded him. "I'm like Dora when it comes to that Mrs. business—it makes me feel old. And who wants to be old? So, tell me, Armando, what do you think of our Ben?"

"Well, I haven't met him yet. But it looks like he's a pretty good artist."

She nodded over to the far corner. "You see Charlie over there in the dark suit? That tall skinny man next to him is Ben."

Armando studied him for a moment. "He looks older than I'd imagined."

"Oh, yes. He's nearly thirty, I believe. I felt he was too old for Olivia at first. But we got used to the age difference after a while." She looked back at Armando and smiled. "Now, you certainly look handsome tonight. Has my daughter laid eyes on *you* yet?"

"She met me at the door. Official greeter, you know."

"Oh, that's right. Maybe I should go offer to relieve her so she can mingle with the crowd." But in the same instance, something else had caught her eye. "First let me introduce you to Ruth." She took a few steps then waved her punch glass and called out. "Ruth, dear, come on over here. There's someone I want you to meet."

A pretty dark-eyed brunette turned around and walked toward them. "Hi, Audrey. What's up?"

"This is Armando—" She stopped and looked at him with a perplexed expression. "Why, for heaven's sake, Armando, I don't even know your last name."

"Garcia," he answered solemnly.

Audrey laughed. "Yes, of course, Armando Garcia. And this is a good friend of ours, Ruth Michaels. She went to school with Olivia and was like a part of the family." She gently nudged Ruth with her elbow. "Armando is living out on the farm with Olivia's grandmother right now, helping out while she recovers from her broken arm."

Ruth looked directly into his eyes and smiled brightly. "Olivia told me about Dora's fall. Is she okay?"

"She seems to be better. But I think it makes her tired."

"I should come out and visit her. Dora's been like a grandmother to me. Please tell her I said hi, okay?"

"Ruth works at the bank with my husband," said Audrey. "Well, not with him exactly. But she works there as a loan officer—the youngest one they've ever had."

"It didn't hurt having an inside track." Ruth grinned. "And Charlie's a pretty good boss. I work in smaller loans like auto and second mortgages. So, if you ever need some money, just look me up."

Armando laughed, remembering the security guard's suspicious glances at the bank last week. "Sure, I'll keep that in mind." Then he sensed someone's eyes on him and knew he was being watched. He glanced back to the far corner to spy Charlie now glaring in his direction.

"Oh, here comes Olivia now," said Audrey happily. "She must've been relieved by someone else."

"All the crab quiches are gone," Olivia complained as she joined them. "That was the only thing I really wanted—"

"Hush, child," said her mother. "Now, if you'll keep quiet, I'll tell you where I hid some away for you—in the back room under a yellow tea towel on the counter."

Olivia's eyes lit up. "You did? Oh, Mommy, you're the best." She looked at Armando. "Did you try any yet?"

He shook his head. "I haven't even—"

"Come with me." She grabbed his arm.

"Nice to meet you," he said to Ruth as Olivia pulled him away.

"Later," she called.

The back room felt quiet and safe after the noisy confines of the crowded main gallery. Armando was glad to escape the curious eyes of onlookers—mostly Charlie's. He leaned against a post as Olivia scavenged around the dimly lit storage room and framing workshop.

"Here they are!" she exclaimed, handing him a small pastry.

"These have crab in them?"

She'd already taken a bite. "Yes, aren't they lovely."

He followed her lead then nodded. "Yeah, they're really good."

They were starting into their third ones when her father appeared. "What're you two doing back here?" he demanded.

"What's it look like we're doing, Dad?"

"Well, you shouldn't be back here."

"Why not? It's not like you own the place."

He puffed out his chest slightly. "Actually, I do happen to own some shares in the gallery. And, as your father and a shareholder, I'm saying you two shouldn't be back here."

She rolled her eyes at him then turned to Armando. "Poor man. He's so consumed with appearances that he doesn't even realize how he looks like a complete fool sometimes."

"Olivia?" Ben pushed through the swinging door. "Is this a private party?"

She chuckled. "No, but if you were hoping for a crab quiche you're completely out of luck. Armando and I just polished off the last ones."

Ben looked at her sternly. "You *know* I don't eat animal flesh."

She laughed. "You really think crabs are animals? Aren't they more like insects what with their shells and creepy claws and stuff?"

"Of course they're animals. Besides that, has it ever occurred to you that crabs are the garbage collectors of the ocean? They scavenge across the sea floor devouring every dead and rotting thing they can put their claws onto."

Olivia grabbed her stomach in a pretense of horror. "Oh no, stop. I think I'm going to barf."

Ben looked away from her in obvious exasperation and turned to Armando. "Aren't you going to introduce me to your friend, Olivia?"

"I'm sorry." She faced Armando now and pointing to her boyfriend said, "This is the famous *arteest* Benjamin James Sheraton the Third." She made a mocking bow. "We gather tonight to honor him and his amazing work." Then she turned to Ben. "And this is our new friend Armando Garcia—my grandmother's knight in shining armor, well, of late anyway."

Charlie cleared his throat. "Olivia, have you been spiking the punch?"

"*Moi?*"

He blew air through his teeth then turned on his heel. "Excuse me. I think I'll go find my wife."

"What's bugging your dad tonight?" Ben asked after Charlie was out of earshot.

She waved her hand dramatically. "Oh, you know, whatever it takes."

"Probably me," said Armando. "Maybe I should go now."

"No!" Olivia clutched his arm tightly. "You should definitely stay. Right, Ben?"

Ben nodded. "Of course. Stay as long as you like, Armando." He cleared his throat. "Do you *like* art?"

Something about the tone of Ben's voice felt slightly patronizing. It reminded Armando of a creative writing teacher he'd had as a junior in high school. She'd said that Armando had real talent, but it felt like what she really meant was "for someone of your ethnic background." And unfortunately it had soured him on writing altogether. "Sure, I *like* art." He smiled stiffly at Ben.

"What *kind* of art do you prefer?" Ben held his chin high as he sipped his punch.

"The *good* kind." Armando looked him in the eye.

Now Ben laughed. "Well, that's pretty subjective, isn't it? I mean some people think Elvis painted on black velvet is good—" Then suddenly Ben looked very uncomfortable. "I mean . . . I wasn't . . . I wasn't suggesting . . ."

"Oh, Ben!" hooted Olivia. "That was rich, especially coming from you, Mr. Politically Correct about absolutely everything and everyone." She bent over and held her sides as she laughed loudly.

"I didn't mean how that sounded." Ben's previously pale face was steadily reddening, starting from the neck up, until even Armando felt a little sorry for him.

"Hey, it's okay, Ben." Armando waved a dismissive hand. "I have an aunt down in Los Angeles who actually has a velvet painting hanging right above her king-size water bed. Not Elvis though. She's not into the King like some of our folk are. No, I think it's of a horse or a unicorn or something mythical. But it's still pretty hideous. Of course, that's only my opinion. She happens to like it a lot."

Ben put his hand on Armando's arm. "Hey, man, I'm really sorry. I don't usually say stupid stuff like that. It's just this show; I think it's got me wound a little too tightly."

"I'll say," chimed in Olivia.

"Really, it's no big deal," said Armando. "I thought it was pretty funny. But like I said before, I should probably get going."

"Thanks for coming." Ben still looked a little unnerved.

"Yeah. Cool show. I hope you sell lots of stuff."

"See you around," said Olivia. "I'm glad you came tonight."

Armando went back out through the gallery, trying to avoid Charlie's gaze, which seemed fixed like an infrared scope directed into the center of his forehead.

"Leaving already?"

He turned to see Ruth. "Yeah, I think I've pretty much seen it all."

Her eyes lit up. "Me too."

He wondered if this was a hint, like was he supposed to invite her out for something—but what? A drink, a cup of coffee, a soda perhaps?

"So what do people do in this town for fun?" he asked.

"Are you kidding?" She shrugged. "If they're looking for fun, they usually have to look elsewhere."

He smiled. "How about you?"

"Me?" She stepped closer and looked up into his eyes with slightly raised brows. "Well, I live a pretty quiet life. I go to work and afterward I sometimes hang with my friends—the ones who still live here that is, and there aren't many. Or I sit at home and watch TV. Pretty pitiful, isn't it?"

"Sounds better than my social life recently."

"Olivia says you're from L.A. You probably used to have lots of fun down there."

"I guess. But after a while it didn't feel that much like fun anymore."

She nodded, yet didn't seem entirely convinced. "Do you expect to be in Treasure for long, Armando?"

"I'm not sure. I mostly came up here for a change of pace."

She laughed. "Well, you certainly came to the right place. I'm sure Treasure is about as far removed from L.A. as anything—well, other than outer Siberia maybe."

"After being on Dora's farm for a week, Treasure is starting to feel like a bustling metropolis to me."

"Oh, yeah. The big city in all its glory."

"Well, I noticed you do have a bowling alley and a movie theater and a few eating places. What more do you really need?"

Ruth nodded. "You know, you may fit in just fine around here after all." She looked over her shoulder to see who was calling out to her now. It was an older woman in a black pantsuit. Ruth waved at her then turned her attention back to Armando. "Well, if you do stick around, you might give me a call sometime— if you ever get bored, I mean. Maybe we could go . . . uh, bowling." Then she laughed and he wasn't totally sure if she was serious or not.

"See ya around."

"Hope so." She smiled brightly.

Armando felt a mixture of emotions as he walked back to his truck. Ruth had obviously been flirting with him, and although it wasn't the first time a woman had come on to him, being the new guy in town, it should've been something of a lift to his spirits. But it wasn't. That little episode with Ben and Olivia had left him feeling frustrated and slightly deflated. He wasn't sure if it was due to Ben's stupid remark about the velvet painting or simply because it disturbed him to see those two together—to know without a doubt that they really were an item, a couple. Was he actually jealous? And if so, why? Or maybe it just tweaked him that Ben seemed so totally wrong for someone like Olivia. But then again, who was he to judge such things? What did he know?

It was past nine when he got back to the farm, and he was surprised to see the house lights still on. Dora usually went to bed by eight-thirty, and he felt worried that something could be wrong.

All her talk of death today had left him feeling uneasy. He decided to check on her before he called it a night.

He knocked quietly on the door, but when no one answered he let himself in. Dora was asleep on the sofa with the TV playing one of those nighttime magazine shows where a heavyset man insisted that he was innocent in the sort of way that made you think he was anything but. Armando switched off the TV and turned back to Dora. Her face seemed so quiet and pale that for a moment he feared she had actually passed away while he'd been gone. His heart pounded in his throat as he knelt beside her and looked closely. Then he sighed in relief as he noticed the faint up-and-down movement of her chest. She was only asleep.

"Dora?" he said softly. "Time to go to bed now."

She slowly opened her eyes then smiled. But it was unlike any smile he'd seen from her before, like maybe she thought he was actually someone else—someone she was very glad to see. He suspected she wasn't fully awake yet, or perhaps just dreaming—but at least it seemed to be a pleasant dream.

"Okay, let's stand you up and get you to bed." Not wanting to completely disturb her pleasant dream, he gently helped her up and, placing one arm securely around her waist, slowly guided her down the hall to her room. He eased her onto the bed then removed her slippers and helped her lie down, with clothes still on. It wouldn't be the first time she'd slept fully dressed since breaking her arm. He pulled her blankets and chenille coverlet to her chin and noticed that her eyes were closed but she was still smiling.

"Good night, Dora." He turned out her light and tiptoed away.

Chapter Seventeen

Dora sighed. Henry had always looked so handsome in that herringbone sport jacket. Almost like a movie star. She remembered the first time he'd worn it—and how he'd swept her heart away that evening.

After losing Susan, she'd felt certain she would never bear another child—she didn't want to. It was too painful to lose them. Still, and although he never pressed the issue, she knew Henry hoped she would change her mind in time. She still remembered the night it must've happened. It was in 1949—almost two years after losing Susan—that she became pregnant with their third child (third because she always counted her miscarriage as the first).

It was a Friday afternoon in early June, warmer than usual but not unpleasant, and Henry had come in from the fields early.

"What's wrong?" she asked, looking up at his face with concern.

He smiled. "Nothing. I thought we might need to take some time to smell the roses today." Then he pulled a small bouquet of wild-flowers from behind his back and handed them to her. "Picked these down by the creek."

She sniffed the flowers then peered up at her handsome husband. "You sure you're feeling okay?" It's not that picking her some flowers was so unlike him, but quitting work this early, and especially in June, well, that was a little unusual.

"I'm fine, Dora. Just want to go take a shower and I was thinking maybe we could have an early supper then go catch a show."

"Okay," she said uncertainly. "As long as you're feeling all right."

He grinned at her. "You shouldn't worry so much, my sweet Dora. It'll wrinkle up your pretty face." Then he kissed her and headed down the hall to the bathroom.

When he came to supper, he had on the herringbone sport jacket she'd found on sale for him at Brewster's last month. "Well, now don't you look like a dandy?" She set his plate before him and sniffed the top of his head. "And cologne too?"

"Yep. I felt like dressing up to take my best girl out."

She let the dishes sit in the sink that night and hurried back to her room to change her clothes. She wasn't about to go into town wearing a plain housedress with Henry all gussied up and looking like Cary Grant. She pulled out a red dress that she hadn't worn in years. Its skirt had been too long during the war (when hemlines had shrunk) but it was about right for now. She knew the shoulders were a little out of fashion, but by adding a scarf and a belt, she hoped no one would notice.

Henry let out a long low whistle when she came into the living room. "Woo-eee!" And he swept her into his arms and kissed her with passion. "Maybe we should just stay home tonight," he teased.

She frowned. "But you said—"

"I know, doll. I'm pulling your leg."

It was a balmy evening and they drove into town with the windows of the little blue Buick wide open. As they walked down Main Street, the air felt like warm velvet and smelled like the locust blossoms blooming on the trees that grew in the park. They chatted with some friends as they stood in line to buy tickets to the new comedy *Adam's Rib,* featuring the amazing Katharine Hepburn and Spencer Tracy. And for the first time in ages, Dora felt almost like herself again, and for a few hours her sadness seemed to slip away like a heavy winter garment that's been cast off in the first days of summer.

A month later, she realized it was that same romantic evening that induced her current morning sickness. With tears streaming down her face, she clutched the edge of the shell pink toilet and longed to reverse the clock and take back that deceptive evening. Hadn't they been doing all right—just the two of them? Sure, she wasn't exactly happy, but she was content, wasn't she? She didn't *want* any more children. She couldn't survive another loss—and she felt absolutely certain it would happen again. She was cursed as a mother—a curse that flowed from her own father when he'd refused to bless their marriage. And both her losses—first the unnamed baby and then her sweet little Susan—she believed came directly from her father. And, in her heart, she blamed him for all her misery and knew she would never forgive him.

She kept her pregnancy secret for nearly two more months, fearful she might lose this child before her waist even had time to thicken. But by the end of August, she told Henry her disturbing news. "I'm expecting a baby," she said quietly as she set his breakfast before him.

He leaped out of his chair and wrapped his arms around her. "What? What did you say?"

She felt her cheeks growing warm. "I said I'm pregnant, with child, expecting."

"Oh, Dora! That makes me so happy! Oh, my sweet, you sit down right now. Let me get your breakfast for you." He pulled out her chair and eased her into it as if she were suddenly made of delicate bone china.

Despite herself, she laughed. "Don't be silly. I feel perfectly fine."

He dished up a generous portion of bacon and eggs and set it before her. "Coffee?" he asked.

"No. I'm mostly over the morning sickness now, but I still don't care much for coffee."

He sat down and smiled in a silly way, as if he were still taking it all in. "A baby!" He sighed. "So when's the big date? Do you know yet? Have you made a doctor's appointment?"

She sighed and looked down at her plate. "Well, I've done the math. The baby should be due in mid-February, I think." She didn't mention how much this due date disturbed her. She'd lost her first baby in the same month.

"A Valentine's baby?" Henry laughed. "Maybe we can call her Val or Sweetheart or Cupid."

"Her?" She raised her brows.

He nodded. "Of course, it will be a girl."

She frowned. "I don't know." She wanted to say she didn't know if she would even be able to carry the baby full term, what with the curse that was on her and all. Still she kept these worrisome thoughts to herself.

But to her amazement, her pregnancy continued without complications of any kind. "Looks like a good-sized baby you're growing in there," Dr. Weibert announced in January. "I'm still predicting late February. But it could be sooner."

Dora was relieved to go into labor on the twenty-first of February. She'd been dreading the twenty-fourth like the dickens (the day she'd lost her first child eight years earlier). She'd been awakened by the first contractions in the wee hours of the morning, well before sunrise, just a gentle tightening around her swollen abdomen, but familiar. And after a couple of hours the pains grew stronger. But at least she had a chance to warn Henry before he went outside and got beyond earshot.

"I think this is the day," she told him as she set their oatmeal on the table.

"The day?" He absently picked up his coffee mug. Then he turned and looked at her with raised brows. "You mean *the* day? For the baby?"

She nodded. "But don't get yourself all worked up. We can head into the hospital after we finish breakfast."

"You mean you're going to just sit here and eat your breakfast like everything's normal?" His eyes were wide now.

"Maybe a little oatmeal. It takes strength, you know, to birth a baby."

She was able to drink some orange juice and get down a few bites of oatmeal, but poor Henry could only sit there and stare. "You ready to go now?" he asked when she finally stood up.

She had to remind him twice to slow down on the way to the hospital. "No sense in getting into a wreck or getting a ticket," she said. "Besides, I heard there's been black ice this week." Still, she could feel the pains growing closer and more intense and she suddenly wished that she'd skipped her foolish pretense of breakfast altogether.

The bit about black ice slowed him down. But he urgently honked his horn as he pulled up to the hospital entrance, then leaped out of the car and ran to help her out. By the time they were halfway into the emergency room an orderly was coming toward them with a wheelchair.

Her labor was longer and more intense than it had been with Susan. "It's because this baby's bigger," said Dr. Weibert as he gave her another shot to dull the pain. During her delivery with Susan, she'd disliked the numbing effects of the drugs administered to her because she'd wanted to be fully awake and aware when she gave birth. She'd wanted to be the first one to look into her baby's eyes and to hold her. But this time she didn't even care. This time she knew that it was only a matter of time before her father's curse would interfere once again, and she would lose the baby anyway. It seemed foolish to become attached or hope for anything more.

Dora remembered waking up and asking the nurse, "When will this baby be born?"

But the nurse simply laughed and said, "He's already born. He's soundly sleeping in the nursery right now."

Then Dora reached down to her midsection to discover that it was indeed a little flatter although still pouchy. "He?" she said.

"Yes. You gave birth to a whopping nine-pound, twelve-ounce boy." The nurse looked at her chart. "At exactly 1:57 this afternoon."

"A *boy?*"

"Yes, and he's the cutest thing we've seen in a long time. Chubby cheeks and big blue eyes. He's even got curly hair. He's the darling of the nursery."

Dora tried to imagine all that, but the effects of the drugs were still at work in her system and she wasn't even sure if it was real or if she was simply dreaming the whole thing up.

"Your husband would like to see you now," said the nurse.

"Yes, please." Dora nodded eagerly.

"Congratulations, darling," said Henry as he sat an enormous bouquet of yellow roses on the table beside her. Then he leaned over to gently kiss her forehead. "The doctor said it wasn't easy bringing a boy that size into the world, but that you were a regular little trooper."

She nodded sleepily. "I don't remember much."

"He's a beauty. Everyone's saying how good-looking he is." He nodded to the roses. "I wish I could say those were from me, but they're from your father."

"Dad's here?"

"Yep. He's outside the nursery window right now, handing out cigars and bragging to anyone who'll listen about his beautiful new grandson."

Dora frowned.

Henry squeezed her hand. "It's time to move on, Dora. You can't hold what happened to Susan against him forever. You know it wasn't his fault."

She felt tears filling her eyes but said nothing.

Henry kissed her again, this time on the cheek. "You did good, honey. I'm real proud of you."

She nodded, swallowing to keep the lump from growing in her throat.

"I'm sure you need to rest. The doctor said not to wear you out today, that you've been through a lot."

She nodded again. "What about names, Henry? We'd only discussed girl names since you were so certain it would be a girl. How about if we call him Henry?"

He made a face. "I never cared much for the name myself; don't know why I'd stick it on my son."

"I think it's a lovely name."

He smiled. "You would." Then he scratched his head. "Don't care for my dad's name either."

She shook her head. "No, I definitely don't want a boy named Herman." She closed her eyes and sighed. "Henry, I'll trust you with this. You pick his name and I promise I'll be happy with it."

He leaned over and gently hugged her. "You rest up and get strong."

Henry came back later that evening. "Well, it's done," he said as he pulled a chair next to her bed.

"Done?"

"Our baby has an official name."

She nodded. "And that would be?"

"Charlie."

She stared at him. "Are you serious?"

"Oh, Dora, you should've seen your father's face when I told him. Charles Lawrence Chase. Isn't that a fine-sounding name?"

Dora was speechless.

"And it has a history with it. No reason to deprive our son of his family roots. The Lawrence family has been a cornerstone in this town forever. And little Charlie should be part of it."

She shook her head. "I can't believe it. After everything my father's done to us—to you—that you could actually want to name our son—"

"We've got to forgive and move on, Dora. I know he's made some mistakes, but your father loves you and he loves his grandson. Already he's talking about setting up a college fund—"

"That's enough!" Dora held up her hands. "I can't hear any more."

"I'm sorry you're upset, honey. But you told me I could name him."

"I know. I know." She shut her eyes and covered her ears with her hands. "I don't want to hear any more. I need to rest."

After only four days in the hospital Dora wanted to go home.

"Are you sure you're ready?" asked Dr. Weibert. "I usually keep my new mothers in for at least a week."

"I feel perfectly fine," she assured him. "And I think I'll rest better at home."

"But you'll have the baby to look after."

"I know."

He looked at her chart. "I see you've chosen not to nurse. That should make it a little easier on you." He chuckled. "You might even get Henry to take a feeding or two if you're lucky. Some daddies like to do that."

"I'm sure he'd be happy to help out."

"Well, okay, then." He looked at her. "I guess I'll release you. But to be honest, I'm concerned."

"Concerned?"

He nodded. "Yes. You don't seem very happy about your new baby. The nurses say you haven't spent much time with him."

She turned and looked at the bright yellow roses. They seemed to be mocking her with their sunny faces. "I've been resting like you told me to do, Doctor, getting well enough to go home."

"I know it was hard on you losing Susan," he said kindly. "But I hope you won't let that affect how you feel toward this child."

She said nothing.

He squeezed her hand. "Well, I'm sure you're going to do fine. You just need to go home and start getting yourself back to normal." He looked out the window. "And it looks like spring's right around the corner too. I'm sure that will lift your spirits."

The nurse helped Dora into the wheelchair and then set the baby in her lap. "Henry has your bag and he's just pulling the car around to pick you up," she said, reaching for the bouquet of roses. "I'm sure you'll want to take these home. They still look gorgeous."

"No, I don't want them," said Dora. "Why don't you keep them?"

"Really? Are you sure?"

"Yes. They'd only get in my way."

"Well, thank you very much."

Dora looked down at the fair-haired child resting contentedly in her lap as the nurse rolled her down the hall. Certainly, he was good-looking. And he seemed to be a good baby. Strong and healthy too. But you could never tell about these things. Some unusual sickness or freak accident could strike at any moment. She knew as well as anyone how life could change in an instant.

She shook her head. No, she must stop thinking that way! Dr. Weibert was right. She couldn't allow what had happened in the past to hold her hostage like this. But how? she wondered. How could she not?

Fortunately, as time passed, Dora became so caught up in caring for her baby that she thought less and less about her father's curse. But she fretted about little Charlie just the same. A cough in the middle of the night could send her heart racing. Even the slightest fever, and she was on the phone to the doctor.

During the first year, she never took Charlie off the farm for any-thing other than his regular pediatrician visits. And she never invited anyone out to visit them. Even Charlie's first birthday was celebrated quietly and uneventfully at home with just the three of them. And although her father sent an extravagant gift—a hand-carved rocking horse that was too big for Charlie to use yet—at least he didn't show up uninvited. That was something.

Chapter Eighteen

By now Armando knew that Dora considered Sunday to be the Lord's Day and a day of rest. His grandmother had also held to that tradition, spending much of her time within the confines of the church—usually attending both morning and evening services. It wasn't a traditional Catholic church; at least that's what people said. Armando couldn't be sure since it was the only one he'd known, but he'd always felt fairly comfortable and welcome there. And although he didn't attend the number of services that his grandmother did, he was faithful to go regularly. But on Sundays he never quite knew what to do with his free time. Abuela Maria would always remind him to keep the day holy. But what did that really mean?

Now it felt as if the clock had been turned back on him—like he was a little boy again. "So did you and Henry go to church on Sundays?" he asked as he finished rinsing the last plate.

"Truth is, we hardly ever went to church back when we were younger. Oh, we'd go on holidays sometimes, for Susan and then later Charlie. It seemed important, somehow. We went to my family's church back then, the same church that Charlie and Audrey still attend now. But then, just a few years before Henry passed, we started going to church more regular-like. But not to the old family church."

"Where'd you go?" He rinsed out the sink.

"Well, Henry had been spending a fair amount of time with his old buddy Howard Farley. And one day Henry decided that he wanted us to try out Howie's church." Dora slowly stood up and pushed the chair back into place. "And so we both went there for a few years. But once Henry passed, well, I quit going."

"Why's that?" He hung up the towel and turned to look at her.

"Well, me and God . . . you know, we haven't always been on such good terms." She laughed. "Oh, Howie likes to come over here and preach at me on Sunday afternoons, after he's gotten himself all fired up at his church service. He usually has some good things to say. But I don't know; that church is a lot more lively than what I was brought up in, and it just wasn't for me. I guess I don't have much use for religion."

Armando nodded. "I sort of know how you feel."

She started shuffling toward the living room.

He waited for her to get settled on the sofa before he spoke again. "Uh, Dora?"

She looked up.

"I noticed there's a nice patch of land over by the creek, past those aspen trees. . . . "

"Yeah, what of it?"

"Well, would it be okay if I worked on it some?"

"Worked on it?" She peered up over her reading glasses at him. "What'd you have in mind exactly?"

"Oh, maybe do some weeding and landscaping and see if I can rescue some of the flowers and—"

"Sure. Why not?" She waved her hand. "That was one of my Henry's favorite spots. He never actually planted any crops over there, other than the flowers, that is. But it was beautiful back in its day."

"That's what I thought. And I think some of those flowers might still be alive and growing."

"That's what Olivia said." She opened her book. "Help yourself to whatever you can find around this place to work on it with. Goodness knows I can't do a thing with it myself." She groaned as she shifted into a more comfortable position. "Can't hardly do a thing for myself anyway these days."

"Oh, you're getting better every day, Dora. You'll be back to your old self in no time."

She grunted. "Don't know how you'd know anything about that."

So, telling himself this wasn't real work—or disrespectful of the Sabbath—Armando headed outside and rounded up a wheelbarrow and a selection of garden tools and went down to the area by the creek. But before he actually started in, he sat for a long time and looked at the place, imagining what it might've once been and what it might someday become. And then he walked around and studied the lay of the land, the way the trees grew, the flow of the creek, and the lower place that seemed to hold water, where nothing much grew. And before long, he thought he had some ideas.

Dora hadn't seemed terribly concerned about what he might do here, and he figured anything would be an improvement anyway. So finally after about an hour of contemplation he started to work. First he dug up some beds and heaped up some mounds, and then he carefully removed and transplanted any plant that looked of interest to him. For all he knew he could be wasting his time moving some interesting-looking weeds, yet somehow he didn't think so. And slowly, the image in his mind started taking shape in the ground. Or so it seemed to him. By midafternoon, he had hot blisters on his hands, but it felt like he had actually accomplished something. He also realized it must be well past noon and time to check on Dora. He quickly heaped the tools into the wheelbarrow and walked back toward the house.

But as he came around from behind the barn he noticed a car in the driveway. And not one he recognized. It was a light blue Cadillac, an older model, probably from the seventies—the era where cars had been long and low, and this one probably rode like a boat. Armando parked the wheelbarrow by the barn then went over to admire the car. The paint job and everything else on it looked to be original and quite well maintained, like someone appreciated this old-timer and probably kept it parked in a garage most of the time.

"You like my car?"

Armando squinted to see an elderly man in a pale gray suit and a white straw hat. He was standing in the shade on the porch, with Dora sitting in her old rocker next to him.

"Yeah," called Armando. "Pretty cool wheels you got here."

"Go ahead and open it up and take a peek inside if you like. She's a real cream puff."

Armando opened the driver's side door to see pristine, cream-colored-leather interior. He whistled long and low. "Man, she's a beaut," he said as he shut the door and walked over to the porch.

"This is Armando," said Dora. "I told you about him."

The old man stretched out a wrinkled and spotty hand. "I'm Howard Farley. I just stopped by to say hello to my old friend here."

"I would've offered Howie some iced tea or lemonade." She made a sad face. "But I'm a little stove-up just now."

"I'll get you something." Armando smiled. "What would you like?"

"I'd like a little lemonade," said Dora in a voice that sounded almost childlike.

"Sounds good to me." Howard smiled, revealing a gold tooth that glinted in the sunlight.

"And could you bring out some of those gingersnaps that we got at the store last week?"

Armando nodded. "Have you eaten any lunch yet, Dora?"

She pressed her lips together then shook her head.

"I'm sorry, Dora. I should've come back sooner. I got so caught up with working—"

"He's fixing up Henry's old flower patch," Dora said quickly. "Not actual farmwork, you know, since this is Sunday and all."

"Well, that's nice." Howard sat down next to her. "I always liked it over there by the aspen grove. You remember how the four of us used to picnic there in the summertime?"

She laughed. "Yes, and I recall that time when Daisy and I took a little dip in the creek."

"Yes. You two said you were going wading and came back drenched from head to toe."

"It was a hot day."

Armando cleared his throat. "How about if I make you and Mr. Farley some sandwiches to go along with that lemonade?"

Dora nodded. "Now that sounds right nice."

So he went in and washed his hands then set to work in the kitchen. He'd been steadily rearranging a few things in the cupboards to suit himself and it was starting to feel more like his kitchen. At first Dora had put things back her way, but after a while she appeared to give in. It seemed only fair since he did most of the cooking and cleaning anyway.

As he opened the refrigerator and took out sandwich fixings, he fought back the sharp onslaught of familiar words (in his uncle's voice) that echoed through his mind. Words like *houseboy* or *kitchen slave* or *wuss*. And once again he reminded himself there was more honor in doing kitchen work than in being locked up in jail. At least he was free to come and go at will. Well, sort of.

He arranged the food and drinks on a large tray that he had discovered in a high cupboard and took it out to the porch.

"Don't know how you could say that, Howie." Dora pointed to a small table off to her side for Armando to place the tray on. "Why, I'm perfectly comfortable with the idea of dying."

Armando glanced at her as he served their lemonade. *Since when?* he wanted to ask as he unloaded the tray, but instead he turned to leave.

"Aren't you going to join us, Armando?" she asked. "You haven't had any lunch yet, have you?"

"Well . . . uh . . . I just thought—"

"Come on," urged Howard. "Pull up a chair and grab one of these delicious-looking sandwiches. I'd like to get better acquainted with you."

"Okay." He scooted a wooden chair closer to them and sat down. But with his sandwich halfway to his mouth he realized that Howie was praying—asking God to bless their food and their friendship and the beautiful day and then finally he said, "Amen."

"So," continued Howie, hardly missing a beat, "Dora's been telling me that she's ready to go meet her Maker—anytime now. What do you think about that, Armando?"

He swallowed his bite and peered at Dora. "You mean, do *I* think she's ready to go?"

Howard shrugged. "She or you or even me? Are any of us really ready to go?"

"Well, I'm sure not." Armando took another bite.

Howard nodded. "I can understand that. Most of the time I think I'm all ready to go. I gave my heart to Jesus back when I was just a kid, and the idea of leaving my earthly life to begin my heavenly life has never bothered me. Why, I can imagine flying through the sky to meet my sweet Daisy and my parents and Henry and all the others who have gone on ahead of me. But then God goes and sends down a beautiful spring day like this, and I think, well, maybe—just maybe—I'd like to stick around here for a little while longer." He laughed. "But I suppose when you get right down to it, I won't have much choice in the matter when the time comes along. God's the one who calls the shots, you know. And I expect I'll be raring to go by then."

Dora quietly ate, nibbling the edges of her sandwich like a little mouse.

"I'd *like* to be ready," said Armando. "I'm not sure how to do it. Ever since my grandmother died, I've hardly gone to Mass, and even less to Confession."

"So you're Catholic, then?"

He nodded. "I guess I still am."

Howard chuckled. "Well, eventually I don't think any of that's going to matter too awfully much."

Armando looked up. "Huh?"

Howard waved his hand. "Oh, you know, all the different denominations and religious beliefs. I think the day will come when it won't matter worth a hill of beans exactly what *religion* we believe in."

"What on earth do you mean, Howie?" asked Dora.

"I mean the only thing that'll matter is *who* we believe in. That's the ticket. The Bible says, 'In this new life, it doesn't matter if you are a Jew or a Gentile, circumcised or uncircumcised, barbaric, uncivilized, slave, or free. Christ is all that matters, and He lives in all of us.' If we believe in Jesus and invite Him into our hearts and have a personal relationship with Him, and then live our lives for Him . . . well, I think that's all that really matters."

Armando considered this. It seemed a lot to take in.

Howard nodded and picked up another sandwich half. "Yep, the Bible says whoever believes in Jesus will live forever. It doesn't say anything about being Catholic or Baptist or Methodist or even Buddhist."

Dora scowled. "You really believe that, Howie? You honestly think God'll let Buddhists into heaven?"

"If they believe in Jesus."

She shook her head. "Maybe that's what trips me up."

"Believing in Jesus?" Howard took a long sip of lemonade.

"Yeah. It's not that I *don't* believe in Jesus. Of course, I believe that He was a real man and lived on earth. But the way you say it, Howie—you say we've got to *believe in* Jesus, like we've got to believe He's standing here right in front of us right now or some- thing. That's the part I don't understand."

"I know." Howie patted her hand. "It's because you've got things you haven't let go of yet, Dora. When you're ready to let go of them, you'll open your eyes and you'll see Jesus standing right in front of you. Oh, not with your earthly eyes. But you'll know He's there all right—that He's been there all along. He's just waiting for you to give in to Him."

"I've tried to live a good life," Dora said. "I haven't done too much that's terribly wrong. Not that I know of, anyway."

"I know, Dora," Howard agreed. "But like I've told you before, it's not being good that gets us into heaven. It's believing in God's Son, Jesus Christ."

They ate quietly for a while with nothing but a couple of bicker- ing blue jays to break up the silence. Armando felt curious about what it was that Dora couldn't let go of, but he knew it wasn't his place to ask. He hoped she'd say something or give him a hint. But she just continued to eat in silence.

"That was a fine lunch you fixed for us, Armando," said Howard with a wide smile. "And I'm sure glad I got to meet you. I can see my dear friend here is in good hands."

"Thank you, Mr. Farley." Armando stood and brushed off his hands.

"Oh, you don't need to be so formal." Howard grinned. "Why don't you just call me Howie, like everyone else does."

Armando nodded.

"Now you said something a little while back, Armando." Howie peered up at him with a penetrating gaze.

Armando shrugged and leaned against the porch railing.

"You said you'd *like* to be ready." Howie leaned forward in the rocker, tipping his head back so that his face was even closer to Armando's. "You know that it doesn't matter how old you are, son. God could come calling your name at any given moment. Why just last week a young man over in Clover got run over by a semi— the driver had fallen asleep at the wheel. Now, I'm sure this fellow didn't expect that it was going to be *his* last day on the planet when he got up that morning. But just the same it was. The thing is, Armando, we've all got to be ready."

Armando began stacking the empty plates, eager to get away from this conversation that was becoming increasingly more uncomfortable.

"I'm sure Dora already warned you about my little sermons." Howie laughed. "I can't help myself sometimes. Anyway, I'd like to invite you to come on over to my church. You'd be most welcome there. And if you could talk Dora into coming along with you, I'd be much obliged."

"Oh, Howie," said Dora. "You never give up on me, do you?"

"Not while I'm still down here on earth, living and breathing God's fresh clean air." He reached over and squeezed her hand. "It's a promise I made to Henry, you know."

Dora looked down at her lap and frowned.

Armando moved toward the door. "Can I get you anything else?"

"Not for me, young man." Howie stood. "I best be getting on my way."

"And you'll come back out here like I asked and go over my legal business with me this week?" said Dora.

"You can count on it." He tipped his hat and walked down the steps. "You two take care now."

She sighed and reached out her good arm. "I'm weary, Armando. Can you help me into the house?"

* * * * * * * * * * * * *

After getting Dora settled and cleaning up the lunch things, Armando slipped back outside to continue working on his project— his secret garden. Well, it wasn't actually a secret, but he liked the idea of working unobserved and unnoticed.

As he worked he thought about what Howie had said about religion not mattering. It was a new idea to Armando, but somehow it made sense. Not to his mind perhaps, because the rules and routines of Catholicism were ingrained into him like washing your hands before you eat. But it made sense in another part of him— maybe it was his heart. And somehow he hoped Howie was right.

He remembered the Bible he'd found in his room. He'd begun reading *Treasure Island* a couple days ago and was about halfway through the story now, but he hadn't even considered cracking open the Bible. Maybe he'd give it a try.

He remembered how his grandmother used to read her Bible in the evening sometimes. "We didn't have a Bible in the house when I was a child," she had told him once. "We always went to Mass, but Mama felt it was wrong to have a Bible in our home, and the priest was against it too." She had laughed. "I'm sure glad that Father Miguel sees things differently now." Armando thought about what Howie had said about believing in Jesus. It's not that Armando didn't believe in Jesus. But like Dora, he didn't believe in Jesus in the same way as Howie. He didn't feel like he was living his life for Jesus. He'd been trying to do things right, trying to please Abuela— in case she was watching—but the idea of living his life for Jesus, well, that was something entirely new.

By late afternoon, clouds were beginning to gather, and Armando suspected they would be having another spring shower before long. He patted the soil down around a group of hyacinths that he'd just transplanted. The flowers would probably appreciate a little rain right now. Then finally, as the first drop smacked him on the forehead, he started packing it up.

He noticed Olivia's little orange car parked in front of the house. Dora was having a busy day. Instead of going straight in, Armando took a few moments to clean up. First he washed his hands and face in the freezing water from the faucet by the barn; then he went to his room to change his shirt and shoes and comb his hair. He hurried over to the house and went inside to find Olivia and her grandma chatting in the kitchen.

"We're having a tea party," said Olivia. "Want to join us?"

Armando smiled. "Sure."

"Hey, Armando."

Armando turned to see Ben coming down the hallway. "Hey, Ben."

The two shook hands; then Ben smiled. "Thanks again for coming to my show last night."

"Did you sell some things?"

Ben shrugged. "Maybe. We'll see."

"I brought pastries," announced Olivia.

"Did you make them yourself?" teased Armando.

Olivia laughed. "Not hardly."

"Oh my!" exclaimed Dora as Olivia set a loaded plate in the center of the table. "Those look yummy."

"They're from the Blue Hat."

"The Blue Hat," Dora said the name fondly. "I haven't been there in ages. I almost forgot about that little place. Does the Harvey family still run it?"

"No way," said Olivia as she filled the teapot. "They've been gone for ages. A young couple named Rosetti runs it now. They've made it really cute in there too with antiques and plants and things."

Armando got some small plates and cups from the cupboard and began setting four places at the table.

"Oh, you don't need that many," said Olivia when she saw what he had done.

He frowned. "Aren't there four—"

"Oh, Ben's not joining us."

He glanced over his shoulder into the living room to see Ben seated in the easy chair with the newspaper spread across his lap. "Why not?"

"He doesn't eat white flour or sugar." Olivia giggled. "And that's pretty much all that's in these pastries."

"That stuff'll kill you," called Ben in a dry voice. "Not that Olivia cares."

"What about tea?" asked Armando.

"It has caffeine in it," said Olivia lightly. "Ben doesn't do caffeine."

Armando wondered what exactly Ben *did* do, but thought it better not to ask.

So the three of them sat down to a pleasant little tea party. And Ben read his paper in the other room.

"Grandma says you're working on the piece over by the aspen grove," said Olivia as she filled his cup. "What are you up to?"

Armando smiled mysteriously. "Oh, just a little cleaning up is all."

"Hmm? I'd like to see it."

"Why don't you wait until it's finished," he said quickly.

"And when will that be?" asked Dora.

"Oh, I don't know." Armando looked at the window that was now being pelted by nickel-sized raindrops. "It's something I plan to do in my spare time, when I'm not on the time clock for you."

"So, you're actually working for Grandma then?" Olivia took a bite of a cream puff covered in powdered sugar.

"Yep." Armando grinned then used his napkin to wipe off the white powder that dotted her nose.

"Thanks." She smiled. "But what exactly are you doing?"

"He's my foreman," said Dora. "He's going to supervise the men that your dad is sending out."

"Dad's sending out men?" Olivia frowned. "What's up with that?"

Dora shrugged. "Don't rightly know. He says it's because the place is going downhill and he wants to help fix it up."

Olivia shook her head. "That sure doesn't sound like Dad to me."

"What men?" asked Ben. He leaned in the doorway to listen in, the folded newspaper now under his arm.

"Like I said, I don't *know,*" said Dora in an aggravated tone. "Ask Charlie for yourself if you're so concerned. All I know is that he said he was bringing in some men, and I insisted that Armando be their foreman. I sure don't want a bunch of strangers working around here and messing things up."

Ben looked at Armando. "And you're okay with this?"

"I don't know why not."

"Do you know what they're going to be doing?" asked Ben.

"Charlie didn't get too specific." Armando chuckled. "But he did tell me to stay out of their way."

"*Harrumph!*" Dora set down her cup with a clunk. "Well, don't you forget you're answering to *me,* not Charlie."

"So are you paying Armando now?" asked Olivia. "Are you giving him a fair wage?"

Dora didn't answer.

"I'm working for the old pickup."

"Well, I know that." Olivia rolled her eyes. "But are you getting paid too? I mean as much as I love that old truck, well, it's not exactly worth much."

"You should be getting paid," added Ben.

Armando looked up at Ben and thought maybe he'd been judging this guy too harshly.

"He *will* get paid," snapped Dora. "And for your information, it's between him and me."

Olivia laughed. "Settle down now, Grandma. I'm just trying to be fair here."

"Are you suggesting I'm not fair?"

Olivia patted her grandma's shoulder. "No, Grandma. You are always more than fair. You're a very generous woman."

Dora nodded. "And Armando will get his fair recompense. In due time."

"In due time?" Ben leaned forward. "And what exactly does that mean?"

"It means whatever I mean it to mean."

Armando cleared his throat. "Hey, I'm not a bit worried about Dora not treating me fairly." He smiled at her. "I feel thankful just to be living here right now."

Olivia finished her tea. "Well, don't underestimate the value of your work here, Armando. It's not fair for Grandma to make you into her slave."

Dora's eyes flashed. "He is *not* my slave."

"Oh, I know, Grandma. But you need to make sure you don't take advantage of Armando's good nature." She winked at Armando. "Grandma's used to having sharp businesspeople all around her—the people in her family usually try to take advantage of her as well as everyone else."

"Your grandfather was never like that," said Dora. "My Henry was a good man, and always fair. He never took advantage of anyone, no matter who they were."

Olivia nodded. "That's true. Everyone who knew him, other than Dad that is, says my grandpa was a truly good man. The salt of the earth, they say." She glanced at Armando. "And even though I never knew him myself, you make me think of what he must've been like."

Armando didn't know how to respond to that.

"Oh," said Dora as she pushed herself to her feet, "Armando's just a boy. Henry was a mature man."

Olivia laughed. "I'm sure he didn't start out that way, Grandma."

Chapter Nineteen

The following morning, Armando heard the vehicles pull up as he finished in the kitchen. "Sounds like Charlie's boys might be here," he called to Dora as he dried his hands. He headed outside, but paused on the porch as he watched the fancy rigs park next to the barn. Those wheels obviously didn't belong to farmworkers. Armando knew what farmhand rigs looked like—old beater cars and pickups usually coated with dust and piled high with junk. But here were a pair of new-looking SUVs—one navy and one gray— both shiny and clean with lots of gleaming chrome that shouted *money!* And the men climbing out didn't resemble farm laborers either. One man even wore a suit and carried a briefcase. The others wore nice jackets and neatly pressed pants.

"Hello," called Armando as he caught up with them. "What can I do for you?"

The man in the dark suit frowned, but a guy in a khaki jacket stepped over and shook his hand. "You must be Armando. Mr. Chase said you'd be around to help us if we need it." He glanced over to the barn and the field beyond it. "But I think we'll be okay on our own. Mr. Chase drew us a rough map of the place. And we'll be making some of our own measurements and whatnot. You just feel free to go about your business as usual. Don't mind us."

Feeling dismissed by these important-looking men, Armando started to walk away. It was plain these guys wanted him to make himself scarce. But suddenly he stopped and turned around. "Well, *my* boss, Mrs. Dora Chase, the woman who owns this property, has asked me to stick around and help you guys out." He shoved his hands in his pockets and waited.

The man in the khaki jacket turned to the others. "Guess Armando here wants to hang around."

None of them seemed too pleased about Armando's presence, but this in itself only increased his suspicion and made him more determined to keep close tabs on them. If they weren't up to anything why should they care whether he stayed or not? Besides it wasn't their land. So, feeling like a stray dog, he followed the men around Dora's property. By now he knew every fence line himself. And he couldn't figure out why certain areas seemed to interest them more than others. Without making himself too much of a nuisance, he tried to stay close by. Still, they were constantly on the move, and it seemed they were intentionally trying to make it difficult for him to hear any actual conversation as they looked and took photos, and measured and wrote down notes and even took what appeared to be soil and water samples.

Finally, after several tedious hours, they climbed back into their expensive rigs and left. It didn't slip past Armando's attention that none of them had bothered to introduce themselves or to even say good-bye. None had said more than a few words to him all morning. He knew they thought he was a pain, and some of them, like the man in the suit, probably considered him nothing more than an ignorant Mexican with no right to even walk on the same ground as them. He could sense it in their eyes—those fleeting glances where they would stare at him one moment, then quickly look away the next. Like he disgusted them. And while these observations disturbed him—even hurt him—he was more troubled by their overall consuming interest in Dora's little farm. But it didn't seem to be an agricultural interest. And when they had carelessly tromped through the area he'd been working on, actually walking right across a freshly planted flower bed, he had to fight to hold back his rage. But somehow he did.

"Something's not right," he told Dora as he heated up some tomato soup for their lunch.

"What'd'you mean?" She leaned into the counter and peered up at him.

"Those men were definitely not farmhands."

She nodded. "I didn't figure they would be."

"So what do you think Charlie is up to?"

She shook her head. "I'm not sure, but I don't think it's good."

"They said some other guys would be back later on, maybe this week."

"To do what?"

"They didn't say."

"Guess I better give Howie a call."

That evening Olivia and Ben showed up as Dora and Armando were finishing their supper. "You kids want something to eat?" asked Dora without getting up. "Armando made some kind of Mexican food tonight. What'd you say it was called again?"

Armando laughed. "It's just bean enchiladas and one of the easiest things to make—I learned it from my grandmother."

"*Bean* enchiladas?" asked Ben. "No meat?"

"Not tonight." Armando held out the pan for him to inspect. "I sometimes make them with chicken or beef."

"Sure, I'll try one," said Ben as he sat down.

"Me too," said Olivia. "Care if I make a fresh pot of coffee?"

"Go ahead," said Armando. "What's there is pretty bad."

"Well, I've got some news for you, Dora," said Ben. "Are you ready?"

Armando glanced curiously at Olivia as she filled the coffeepot with water. Was this going to be some kind of engagement announcement? But her expression revealed nothing.

"What is it?" asked Dora with interest.

"Have you ever heard of CompKing?" he asked as he forked into an enchilada.

"CompKing?" She shook her head. "No, can't say that I have. What's it got to do with me?"

"It's a computer company based in the Northwest. They produce parts and software and stuff. I heard they've been looking around Treasure for a new site for their manufacturing plant."

"*And . . . ?*"

"I heard from a reliable source that they might be looking out here." Ben turned to Armando. "Hey, this is good."

"That's probably those men who were out here today, Dora." Armando sat down at the table.

"They were *already* here?" asked Olivia. "You mean the worker guys that Dad was sending?"

"Yeah, but these worker guys were well dressed and carried briefcases and testing equipment, not to mention they drove some pretty expensive rigs."

"Is that coffee ready yet?" asked Dora as she rubbed her cast with her hand.

Olivia came over and filled her cup. "And this doesn't bother you, Grandma?"

Dora shrugged. "Sure, it bothers me. But there's nothing to get all excited about."

"Well, you're sure a lot calmer than I was when Ben told me. I wanted to go kick some—"

"Everyone knows that Charlie's been pestering me for the last few years to sell this place. Don't know why we should be surprised that he's taking the bull by the horns now."

"But it's *wrong*, Grandma!" Olivia hit the table with her fist. "Dad has no right to try to sell your land right out from under you."

"He's just like his grandfather," said Dora in a low voice. "He only sees what he wants to see, and then he wants what he sees."

"But you won't let him get away with this, will you?" asked Olivia, her eyes bright with anger.

"Yeah," chimed in Ben, "that CompKing plant would be a serious disaster for the natural environment and the delicate ecological balance around here. They'd probably ruin your creek and upset the—"

"They aren't going to touch my land!" said Dora in a firm voice. "Henry carved this place out with his own two hands. He put everything he had into making this farm work. And it wouldn't take all that much effort to really bring it back. Already, Armando's making good progress."

"Well, I don't know about—"

"Oh, hush! Besides, you've only just started. If you keep at it, who knows what this place might look like in a year or so."

"So what are you going to do, Grandma?"

"Howie's coming by tomorrow morning. I'll work it all out with him."

"Good. I was thinking you need some trustworthy legal advice right now." Olivia held her fork in midair and grinned at Armando. "These *are* good."

That night, Armando read a chapter from *Treasure Island* then looked over at the Bible sitting at the bottom of the stack of books on the chair by the window. He had never actually read from a Bible before, although he remembered his abuela reading hers sometimes. She seemed to enjoy reading it and even thought it made sense. He took the Bible out from the bottom of the stack and placed it at the top. Maybe tomorrow he would open it.

* * * * * * * * * * * * *

The next morning, as Armando was getting ready to go outside to work, Dora called for him. He went back to her bedroom to see what she needed.

"I want you to reach up there and get down that hatbox for me," she told him. "The round pink one up on top."

He stretched as tall as he could to reach it, but not realizing it was heavy, he barely had it in his hands before it toppled and spilled onto the floor. And there, splayed like a green carpet across the hardwood floor of Dora's bedroom were what appeared to be hundreds of bills. Tens, twenties . . . he even spotted several fifties! Armando turned to Dora with wide eyes.

"Oh, don't just stand there gaping. Pick 'em up."

So, with slightly shaking hands, he got down on his knees and started to pick up the money. He stacked the bills into neat piles and placed the stacks one by one back into the hatbox and finally replaced the lid. He stood with the full hatbox in his hands and just looked at her. But she said nothing.

"Where do you want this?" he asked.

"Just set it on the bed."

He put the box on the bed then turned to her. "Do you mind if I ask why—"

"Oh, fiddlesticks!"

He held up his hands. "Okay, okay . . . I won't ask."

"It's for Howie—to pay my legal fees."

"Oh." He nodded and started to leave.

"Oh, I know what you're thinking. You're thinking this crazy old bat is off her rocker to keep this much cash in her house. Well, go ahead and say it. That's what you're thinking, isn't it?"

"I . . . uh . . . I don't know."

"Well, I do keep some of my money in the bank. You saw me in there the other day. But I don't completely trust banks, you see. I grew up in the Great Depression and I saw plenty of people, including my husband's family, go broke."

He nodded. "Yeah, I guess that makes sense. But have you ever considered a safe?"

She waved her good hand. "Oh, no one would ever think to go looking in my hatbox for money."

Armando sighed.

"Well, get on with you then. Weren't you going to work on the tractor and get that parcel next to the barn ready to plant this week? But keep an eye out for Howie. I want you to stop what you're doing once he gets here, clean yourself up, and get in the house. Understand?"

He made a mock salute. "Yes, ma'am."

"And another thing."

"Yes?"

"Don't you go telling anyone, not even Olivia, about this, you hear?"

He nodded. "My lips are sealed."

But as he went outside, he felt uneasy. Slightly sick even. In his mind's eye, all he could see was all that cash splayed across Dora's bedroom floor, and all he could hear was his uncle's voice, berating him for his stupidity.

"You are a complete failure, Armando! You shame me! You work like that old woman's slave boy—and for what? A beat-up old truck? You are worthless, boy! And you work for nothing, even though the old woman has money to burn!" Armando shook his head sharply as he marched into the barn, trying to repress that nagging voice. But still it haunted him as he pulled out Henry's old toolbox. *"Take these tools! Take the money and the pickup, then run, bambino! No one will ever believe that old bat when she tells about her money. Who would believe she had it in the first place? Keeping it in an old box like that. She's loco. And everyone thinks she's loco. This is your chance, boy. Take the money and vamoos!"*

Somehow he managed to block out the words as he focused all his attention and energy on the old tractor. He cleaned and adjusted the carburetor and plugs and tuned and retuned, and finally got it running fairly smoothly, revving its engine again and again, loudly, hoping to completely drown out his uncle's voice. But when he finally turned it off, the voice came back at him again—with even more persistence. *"Take the money and run, boy!"*

"Shut up, man!" Armando stood and yelled, shaking his wrench in the air. "I am *not* your boy!" Then he threw the wrench down and watched it go spinning into the far corner of the barn. *"Just leave me alone!"* Taking a deep breath, he stepped outside and glanced nervously around to see if Farley had arrived or was near enough to hear him yelling at himself like a madman. He wondered who exactly the crazy person was here. Him or Dora? But the driveway remained empty.

Then cursing to himself, he decided to walk down to the creek to cool off. "Just chill, man," he said to himself over and over as he slowly walked through the sunlit field. "Just chill." This field was still overgrown with weeds and blackberries and in need of some real work. He tried to think about the steps it would take to get it into any kind of shape for planting. He wondered what Dora planned to put in there and if it would really grow. By the time he reached his garden much of his anger had melted away and he felt a little more like himself—except for the frustration. That remained. And it churned inside his chest like a pent-up tornado, going round and round and pummeling him with its intensity.

"I don't *want* Tio Pedro's life," he finally said as he walked around and examined his newly made beds. The transplanted flowers looked better than before; they seemed to be thriving from their thinning and Sunday's rain. And even though they weren't really *his* flowers and this wasn't really *his* garden, there was some- thing curiously satisfying about the whole thing—nurturing the tender plants and watching them grow. He sat down on an old stump and looked toward the creek.

More than anything else right now, he wanted to be completely free of Tio Pedro's influence—his thinking and his crooked ways. Armando had spent his teen years observing Tio Pedro. At first, Armando had admired his uncle with his slick talk, cool clothes, and hot cars. But it didn't take long before Armando realized that Tio Pedro seldom came by his money honestly. Armando noticed how his uncle spent most of his time and energy trying to avoid actual work. Whether it was mowing the tiny backyard lawn or fixing a leaking faucet, his uncle managed to slip out of almost anything that involved labor. But he was Johnny-on-the-spot when it came to a scam or a deal or any other promising moneymaking scheme. Yet he always made his profit at the expense of someone else.

Not only that, but Tio Pedro's entire focus in life was always centered on money. And as quickly as he got it, he spent it. Mostly on himself. But maybe that's the way it is when you're born into poverty and grow up poor the way they all had. Maybe it was the curse of the poor to be obsessed with money. That was all Tio Pedro ever seemed to think about. Money, money, money! And once again, in his mind's eye, Armando saw those bills spread like a green blanket all over the floor. And he could still feel the soft texture of the bills, their furry edges, as he stacked them neatly, trying not to mentally calculate how much they were worth.

He leaned forward, his head in his lap, and sobbed. "I don't want to become Tio Pedro! I want to be free." He sat there crying for a long while, but when he finally stopped, he felt stupid—like a big baby. He glanced around, worried that someone might've sneaked up and seen him like this, but he saw no one and all he could hear were the birds and the sound of the creek's rushing water. He sighed deeply and wondered what his grandmother would tell him right now. What would her advice be?

Of course he remembered her usual advice. It was the same thing she'd told him every morning before he went to school, the same thing she told him in the hospital the last time he had seen her alive: "Now be a good boy, Armando. And do your best. Be honest. Trust in the Lord Jesus and remember to say your prayers." This was usually followed by a hug and a kiss.

Armando smiled. But how did a person manage to live that way and do those things consistently? Especially when temptation seemed to lurk around every corner—and when voices like Tio Pedro's haunted him like they had today. He thought about his grandmother's advice again—taking it apart piece by piece. Okay, he'd been trying to be a good boy lately. Really trying. And he had been doing his best; he'd been working hard and accomplishing things he hadn't even known he could do. Like getting that tractor running. Sure, he'd had automotive experience, but never with an old tractor. And now it looked like it was working fine.

Next he considered his grandmother's view on honesty. Thanks to her husband, who had so severely betrayed her, she could never abide dishonesty of any kind. And she had been quick to say that lies were lies—black or white, they all were lies. And maybe, if Armando was completely honest with himself, he would realize that he wasn't always truthful. Not even with himself. But how was it possible to change that?

And then there was that praying thing . . . and the stuff that Howie had said about Jesus. He shook his head. He couldn't even remember the last time he'd truly said his prayers. Probably right before his grandmother left him for good. He remembered being in the hospital chapel, lighting a candle, and praying the Rosary. But what good had that done? He frowned up at the sky. "Why pray to You?" he asked, seeing only the clouds above him. "Do You even listen?"

Chapter Twenty

$\mathcal{D}$ora sat down on the bed next to her faded pink hatbox, slowly removed the lid, and stared down at the stacks of bills. She smiled. Until today, no one had known about her secret stash. She hadn't meant to reveal her little nest egg to Armando, but somehow— although it could be foolish—she thought she could trust him. She reached in and fingered a pile of bills, feeling the softness of the old money.

She tried to remember when she had first started this strange method of saving. Probably shortly after her marriage, when Henry was away at war and times were lean and hard. She would put some of her teacher's salary in the bank to use for paying bills, but the rest she would request in cash, to be placed in her box. Her plan was to always have something set aside for a rainy day, because she never wanted to have to go crawling to her father for help. She never wanted to hear him say, "I told you so. See, Henry is no good. He can't make the farm pay off." And she supposed it gave her a sense of satisfaction to know that her father's bank, the only one in Treasure, wasn't holding on to her money, and that her father's eyes (known for peeking into private accounts) wouldn't be privy to this secret savings fund.

"I don't know how you do it, Dora," Henry had said one spring day when she produced a crisp fifty-dollar bill for him to use for new tractor tires when she'd noticed the old ones were so worn that they could hardly grip the soil anymore. "You are the best money

manager that a husband could hope for." He grinned. "I guess banking is in your blood."

She frowned at that. "I'm sure it would make my father proud,
but that's one compliment I could just as easily live without."

Then Henry hugged her. "We're not doing so bad, are we, darling?"

"We're doing fine, Henry."

"And if things keep going this way, we'll not only be keeping
this little boat afloat, but we'll be making some pretty dandy profits
to boot."

"You're a good farmer, Henry."

He leaned over and kissed her. "And you're a good wife and
a good mother."

She laughed. "Not according to your son. This morning, before
the bus picked him up, he made it clear that he thought I was a very
bad mother."

Henry frowned. "Charlie said that?"

She smiled. "No, not those exact words. He wasn't too happy
about his lunch today."

"What's wrong with his lunch?"

"Well, as usual, I made his sandwich. Today it was leftover roast
beef on bread."

"And what on earth is wrong with that?"

"He said that all the other kids have *white* bread on their sandwiches, store-bought white bread. And he's embarrassed to hold his
old-fashioned homemade brown bread up in front of them. He says
they tease him about it."

"Goodness gracious!" Henry shook his head. "What's this world
coming to?"

She laughed. "Oh, you know how it was when you were a kid.
No one wants to be different. I promised Charlie that I'd start baking
white bread, and we'd try to slice it nice and thin so it looks just like
store-bought."

"Store-bought!" Henry rolled his eyes. "I'll take your good home-made bread any day of the week over store-bought."

As Charlie grew older his need to fit in with the other children became more and more important. Dora struggled with herself many a time. Was it right to waste money on silly lunch boxes with pictures of cartoon characters on them? Did it really matter what kind of tennis shoes or jeans they wore? But it mattered to Charlie, and despite herself, Dora found herself giving in more than she liked. She had to admit, it was sometimes easier that way. It seemed to keep the peace better. And it made life easier on Henry too. So during those growing-up years she found herself going more and more into her pink hatbox—for Charlie.

Then her father died unexpectedly. And to her surprise, since they had continued to be estranged, he left everything to her. Of course, she was his only child, but she had honestly expected he might leave everything to his brother and nieces and nephews. She'd been dumbfounded when the lawyer had called her, even before the funeral, and informed her of this windfall.

"I don't want it," she'd told him.

"Now, Dora, we all know that you and your father had your differences. But you need to know that he loved you. He regretted some of the things that he'd said and done to you, but you know he was a proud man."

"That's the truth."

"And I think by leaving you this, well, it's his way of saying he was sorry—and that he loved you."

"To bad he waited until he was dead to say all that."

"I know this is hard, Dora. But in time I think you'll understand."

But time passed and she didn't.

And when she told Henry of her new inheritance his face fell. "I don't want your father's money," he said sadly. "I've made it fine on my own so far, and to use his money now—well, it would feel

like I'd failed somehow, or like the success of my farm was somehow because of his money and not my work. I couldn't live like
that, Dora."

She nodded. "I know, and I totally understand. The truth is,
I don't want it either. I told the lawyer so today. But he wouldn't
listen. So what do we do with it? Give it away? Make a big bonfire
and burn it?"

Henry scratched his head. "Well, there's Charlie to think of,
and it's his grandpa's money. Fact is, college is only about six years
away, and more than anything I'd like to see him go. And, you
know, some of that money rightly belongs to him."

She nodded. "You're right."

So she transferred all of her father's accounts into Charlie's
name. And she planned to do the same with the proceeds from the
sale of his house. She'd already removed everything she wanted—
mostly just sentimental items that had belonged to her mother—
since they had no room in their little farmhouse for the rather large
and imposing pieces of furniture. She had decided to sell the house
furnished, for a price that had been suggested by her Realtor friend,
Jackie Jordan, and deposit the money into the accounts she was
setting up for Charlie.

But just as she was setting the For Sale sign in the immaculate
front yard of her family home, Dora remembered something. She
recalled a conversation she'd had with her mother long ago, as a
little girl, only a couple years before her mother passed away. She'd
almost forgotten all about it. It had been a sunny spring day and
they'd been planting petunias in the big cement flower boxes that
lined the walkway to the house.

"Daddy says you should let the garden man do this," Dora had
said as she dug another hole with her child-sized spade.

Her mother had thrown back her head and laughed. "Oh, that
daddy of yours. He just doesn't like me to get my hands dirty." She

wiggled her ungloved fingers. "But I can't help it. I like the feel of the fresh spring soil."

"Me too!"

"And besides, I used to plant petunias with my own mommy back when I was a little girl like you."

"Really? What colors did you plant?"

"Just like these, red and white and purple. That way they look all nice and patriotic in time for the Fourth of July."

"Where did you live when you were a little girl?" Dora asked her mother.

Her mother smiled. "Why, right here."

"Right here?"

"Sure. This was my mommy and daddy's house. They left it to me."

"Left it? You mean when they went up to heaven."

Her mother smiled. "Yes. That's sort of how it happened."

"So this is the only house you've ever lived in?"

"Well, Daddy and I had another house for a while, back when we were first married and your grandma and grandpa were still alive. But then we came here, and you were born. So most of my life I've lived right here in this very house."

"And this is where I want to live for my whole life too."

Her mother laughed again. "You might change your mind if you get married someday. You might want to live somewhere else with your husband."

Dora firmly shook her head. "No. I will never get married. I will stay here in this house with you and Daddy forever."

"Well, that'll be just fine. And one day this house will belong to you."

"To me? Why?"

"Because it's my house and one day I will want to give it to you." Mother patted the soil around a petunia seedling.

"When?"

She used the clean back of her hand to push a stray strand of hair from Dora's face. "Oh, not for a long, long time, Dora."

Dora walked back to the sidewalk now to make sure the sign was clearly visible from the street. Her mother's house! Why, she'd almost forgotten. After her mother's death, the Fourth of July petunias were replaced with more stately geraniums and English ivy. And over the years, Dora had come to think of the place as her father's house. Now it was hers, just as her mother had promised. And here she was selling it.

But then she didn't want to keep it. She had no use for a huge house like this, and in town. Yes, selling it was the right thing to do. But Dora no longer objected to keeping the money herself. She realized now that it was what her mother would have wanted for her.

"Why can't *we* live here?" Charlie had complained on the day she took him over to pick through his grandfather's things before the sale was finalized. "It would be so close to my friends' houses, and I could even ride my bike to school from here."

"It would be too hard to keep up this house and the farm too."

"That dumb old farm!" Charlie put his grandpa's prized baseball, signed by some ballplayer that Dora had never heard of, into a cardboard box. "Why do we have to be stupid old farmers anyway?"

"Farming is *not* stupid, Charlie." She used her stern voice this time. "Your father works very hard and—"

"But Gramps was rich and Tommy Spangler told me that he left you enough money to—"

"*Charlie!*" She raised her voice. "Just because your grandfather was wealthy does not mean that anything about our lifestyle is going to change."

"Aw, Mom. You and Dad are old stick-in-the-muds."

She shook her head. "I know you're about to become a teenager, Charlie, but you still need to respect your parents. I don't like hearing this kind of talk from you."

"Isn't that how *you* talked to *your* dad?" He looked at her accusingly.

"I always tried to respect my father." She pressed her lips together.

"Aw, Mom, everyone knows you and Gramps didn't get along at all. He told me that it all started when you and Dad got married."

"He told you that?"

"Yeah. He said that he didn't think it was a very good idea to start out with, but that he thought it was okay now."

"He did, did he?"

"Yeah. And maybe you need to let bygones be bygones, Mom. Gramps has been dead for almost a month and you still act like you hate him."

"I do not hate him." She picked up a framed photo from his desk. It was one she'd overlooked, from her parents' wedding day. "We just didn't see everything eye-to-eye."

"Well, I don't get that," said Charlie as he placed a hunting trophy in his box. "I think Gramps was fun and—" he choked up a little—"I *miss* him."

She put her hand on Charlie's shoulder. "I know you do."

But he pulled away and looked at her with fierce blue eyes, eyes that looked frighteningly similar to her father's. "No, you don't, Mom! You and Dad aren't like me at all. I'm like Gramps. He's the only one who ever understood me."

She didn't know what to say to that. And so, taking the wedding photo with her, she went outside to wait, leaving Charlie to his gathering and his memories. But in all honesty she wondered if Charlie would miss his grandfather or just his money. Her father had been very generous to his only grandson. And Dora couldn't help but think it was his feeble attempt to buy the young boy's affections. Unfortunately it seemed to have worked—only too well.

She didn't tell Charlie that he would be the recipient of his grandfather's money until his last year in high school. And even then he got mad.

"I can't believe you kept this from me!" he'd exclaimed. "All this time I've had money and I've been living like the kid of a poor dirt farmer."

Fortunately, Henry had not been there to hear his words. Nor was he there to see his wife slap his son's face. She still regretted losing her temper like that.

"Your father is *not* a poor dirt farmer!" she shouted back at him. "He is a highly respected man. And he's turned a bunch of previously worthless land into what is now a thriving farm."

Charlie just stared at her with those fiery eyes, a sharp red mark emblazoned across his cheek.

"And the reason we kept quiet about your inheritance was because we hoped that living out here and working the land would build character in you and make you a better person. Unfortunately, it seems we were wrong!"

"This farm stinks! And so do you! As soon as I graduate I'm gonna get as far away from here as possible!" He had stormed out, slamming the door behind him.

It was on days like that Dora had been thankful that she'd kept all the money from the sale of her mother's house and put it away. She knew Charlie would have more than enough money to make himself totally miserable with—and what he did with it would be up to him. She still remembered the look on the banker's face when she'd presented the check for the sale of the house.

"You want this to go into savings or checking?" he'd asked.

"Neither," she told him, holding her head up with an air of false confidence. She felt nervous about what she was about to do, almost as if she expected her father to burst out of his office and demand that she put it entirely into savings or bonds or some other wise form of reinvestment. "I want it in cash, please."

"Cash?" his eyes grew wide. "How about a cashier's check?"

"I want cash."

"That's a whole lot of cash, Mrs. Chase."

She nodded. "I realize that. But I have my reasons. Is it a problem? Does the bank have insufficient funds?"

The banker glanced over his shoulder. "Well, no, I don't think it's a problem. Usually a transaction this large would require a signature, but since we all know you, and you are, after all, Mr. Lawrence's daughter . . ." He smiled. "No, I suppose there's no problem."

He was gone for a while then finally returned. "I'm sorry I can't give this to you in all large bills. But I did the best I could with such short notice."

"That's just fine." She watched closely as he slowly counted the money out. And then she placed the bills into her oversized handbag that she'd brought along expressly for that purpose. "Thank you very much."

He nodded, his eyes still wide. And she could tell he was dying to ask her what she planned to do with all that money. He probably thought that she was going to leave the country or pay off her gambling debts or something else equally ridiculous. But she took it all home and when Henry was out tilling the north field, she put most of it in her big pink hatbox, and she hid some of it in a few other places as well. No sense in keeping all your eggs in one basket!

But lately, since she was getting on in years now and one never knows, it was starting to worry her. And with Charlie nosing around more, and always greedy for money, she felt she had reason for concern.

Oh, it wasn't that she didn't love her son. Goodness knows she did. But she just didn't understand him very well, and it seemed they grew further and further apart with each passing year. And she did *not* want Charlie getting his hands on her money. He'd already had his inheritance, which had been considerably more than this. Maybe he hadn't used it all that wisely. She still didn't know for sure. According to Olivia, he often got himself into one kind of financial squeeze or another. But then he usually managed to come out of it eventually. Or so it seemed. But even if he didn't, Dora was determined that he would not get her money—or Henry's farm. And it wasn't to punish him or to teach him a lesson. She didn't think it would do him a lick of good.

Chapter Twenty-One

$\mathcal{A}$rmando noticed Howard Farley's car pulling up just as he finished washing his hands under the faucet. It was barely past noon and he wondered if the old guy was expecting lunch again.

"Hey, there," Armando called as he caught up with him.

"How're you doing, Armando?"

"Okay, I guess."

"Okay, you guess?" Howie paused at the top of the porch steps, perhaps to catch his breath. "Why, if I was a handsome young feller like you, I'd be doing a lot better than 'okay, I guess.' "

Armando smiled. "Is that how you felt when you were my age?"

Howie chuckled. "You make a good point there, son. The truth is I was struggling to work my way through college back then. And at that time, I didn't think life was much fun either. What are your plans for the future, son?"

He shrugged. "I don't really know."

"You seem like a bright young man. Do you ever think about going to college?"

He shrugged again. "Maybe. But, like you, I'd have to work to put myself through. And since I don't even know what I'd be going to school for, well, it's a little hard to get motivated."

Howie studied him for a moment. "Well, what do you enjoy doing?"

"I like working with my hands. I was a pretty good auto mechanic down in L.A. But after a while, the smell of grease and exhaust got to me." He looked over to the vegetable garden and smiled. "I like the smell of farming a whole lot better."

"Dora says you're a natural-born farmer."

Armando brightened. "She really said that?"

Howie nodded. "Well, you don't have to let on that I told you."

"I don't know much about farming yet, but I like learning."

"Henry used to have lots of agricultural books. I'll bet they're still around here somewhere. You should crack some open while you're here."

Just then Dora opened the door. "Well, it's about time. What are you two standing out on the porch and yacking about?"

Howie laughed. "I was telling Armando here that Henry used to have all kinds of agricultural books and journals, and that maybe he should read some of them."

Dora peered at Armando. "You'd really want to read those old things?"

"Sure. I'd like to learn as much as I can about farming."

Then she looked at the clock. "I don't know about you two, but I'm getting fairly hungry." She glanced over to Howie. "You eaten yet?"

He waved his hand. "Oh, don't worry about me. I had a late breakfast."

"Armando, you think you could whip up something tasty for the three of us?"

He tried not to eavesdrop as he worked in the kitchen, but portions of their conversation drifted his way, especially when Dora got worked up about Charlie.

"He thinks this land belongs to him!" she shouted. "But he's *dead wrong.* He never wanted anything to do with the farm when his father was alive, or even afterwards, for that matter. It's only now that he sees the possibility of turning over a profit that he's taken on this sudden keen interest."

"Well, Charlie's like his granddad. He knows the value of a dollar, and he likes to make his money work for him."

"That's what irks me. They both think that the world owes them a living, yet neither one of them could bear to get their hands dirty with an honest day's work."

"Now, that's not entirely fair, Dora. You know that your father worked hard making the bank what it is today. And Charlie works hard too. It's just a different kind of work than your Henry enjoyed."

"You can say that again. There wouldn't have been enough money in this entire town to pay Henry to go to work at that confounded bank. You know my dad tried to talk him into it once." She laughed. "It was when Charlie was still a boy. In fact, I'm sure it was Charlie who put him up to it. My dad came out here one wintry evening, and sitting right where you're sitting now, he told Henry he'd give him a good position in the bank with enough salary for us to move into town and live like normal folk. I'm pretty sure those were his exact words—*normal folk*. As if we were some sort of sideshow freaks living out here in the country like this. Like he thought we spent our spare time out here just a-wallowin' with those hogs Henry happened to be raising about that time."

Howie was still laughing over that when Armando poked his head out and announced, "Lunch is ready."

Howie had barely finished saying a blessing when Dora returned to their previous conversation. "It gets my goat, Howie, that my own flesh and blood could treat me this way."

Howie chuckled. "I don't see why, Dora. Honestly, some of the worst battles I've ever seen fought were within families. Blood may be thicker than water, but it spills out as easily."

Dora shook her head. "Well, I don't want to see any blood spilling. I just want Charlie to understand that what's mine isn't necessarily his. Anything wrong with that?"

"Not at all. That's why we have lawyers and wills and such." He set down his soupspoon. "Can I be really frank with you, Dora?"

"Well, of course! Why'd you think I asked you to come in the first place?"

"Well, I've heard some talk in town. And it may be only that— nothing but talk." He glanced over to Armando. "I 'spect you're still not used to this small-town living yet, son, but gossip runs rampant like wildfire in a town the size of Treasure."

"Go on, Howie," she demanded. "What are the good townsfolk of Treasure saying now?"

"Well, there's rumors going round that a certain elderly woman might be—oh, how can I put this gently—might be losing some of her marbles."

Dora laughed. "Now, why doesn't that surprise me?"

"It wouldn't be such a big deal," continued Howie, "except that something like that could play right into Charlie's hand—if he wanted to push it, you know."

"Are you suggesting that Charlie could accuse me of being batty?"

"Normally I don't like to imply something like that, but as your attorney, I feel it's my responsibility to let you know it's a distinct possibility."

"And just what have I done, pray tell, to give anyone the notion to think I'm losing my marbles?"

"You want me to repeat what I've heard?"

"Yes, Howie, I do. Goodness knows no one else is going to tell me."

"Well, first of all, it's rumored that you took a strange young man right off the street to live with you." He glanced at Armando. "No offense, son. But this is a small town with some small minds. And the fact that you're of a different ethnicity doesn't sit well with some folk."

Armando grinned. "Like I've never experienced *that* before."

"Yeah, I'm sure you've seen it all—"

"So what?" interrupted Dora. "We've had Mexicans working on the farm before."

"But this isn't exactly a working farm anymore."

"Well, it's going to be. What else are they saying?"

"There's also been some talk that you came to town not long ago wearing some strange sort of getup. And that you go around walking barefoot in the dirt—"

"Aha!" Dora nearly toppled her soup bowl. "That one had to come directly from Charlie's own lips." She pointed to Armando. "You remember that day he came out here, right after you'd worked up that new section of garden, and he caught me walking barefoot through the soil."

"Yeah." Armando shrugged. "Didn't seem like such a big deal to me. In fact, none of this seems like any big deal. I'm thinking if you were sixty years younger and doing these exact same things, no one would even pause to notice."

Howie nodded. "An excellent point, son. And it's true that people don't treat the elderly the way they do young people. I mean, think about it. Young people go around doing all sorts of wild and crazy things, but if you're over seventy and you pull some of the same stunts you get locked up as senile."

"That's exactly right," agreed Dora. "If I get a little forgetful, Charlie is suddenly accusing me of having Alzheimer's and trying to get me locked up at Shady Acres."

"In my culture, we're taught to respect our elders," said Armando as he refilled their coffee cups. "At least that's what my grandmother taught me."

Dora held her cup up high. "Well, here's to your grandmother."

Howie followed her lead. "A good woman, indeed."

Armando laughed. "Not that all her children followed her teaching. My family's had more than enough of its own problems."

"You haven't said much about your family," said Dora, setting her cup down. "Other than your grandmother, that is. What happened to your parents?"

Armando thought for a moment. This wasn't something he normally wanted to speak of. In fact, other than with his grandmother, he'd kept this pretty much to himself. "It's kind of a long story . . . " He glanced over at Howie. "And I know you have business to discuss."

Howie waved his hand. "I think we've almost wrapped it up, haven't we, Dora?"

"Pretty much." She turned back to Armando. "I'd like to hear your story, if you're willing to tell us. It seems like you've seen most of my family's dirty laundry lately." She laughed. "Actually, you've been doing *all* of my laundry lately."

Armando wondered where to begin. "Well, I never knew my mother. She didn't get along very well with my grandmother. My grandmother said that my mother thought she was too religious and old-fashioned. I think my mother left home right after high school and she worked to put herself through secretarial school and got a pretty good job. My grandmother always told me that my mother was very smart. But maybe she just wasn't very wise. Anyway, my grandmother got a call from a hospital one night and my mother had been taken to the emergency room. She'd been badly beaten and, as it turned out, raped—" As soon as he'd said that word—out loud—he choked. How could he tell such an awful story?

Dora reached over and placed her good hand on his arm. "It's okay, son."

"And, well, you know what can happen. . . . " Armando sadly shook his head.

"Did she get pregnant?" asked Howie.

He nodded. "No one knew at the time. I guess there was a pill she could've taken, but she was unconscious and my grandmother wouldn't allow it. Plus, I guess everyone said that it was very rare for . . . for that . . ." He clinched his fists and looked down at the table. Why was this so difficult?

"Sometimes bad things happen," said Howie, "and the good Lord sees fit to turn them into something good."

Armando looked up at him. "My grandmother used to say something like that. Anyway, my mother was real angry when she found out she was pregnant, like it was somehow my grandmother's fault. She'd been unable to work while she was recovering from the beating, and my grandmother took care of her. But when my mother wanted to get an abortion, my grandmother wouldn't hear of it. I guess they fought and fought for days." He looked at both of them. "And then my grandmother did something that might sound a little strange."

"What's that?" asked Dora, her eyes still fixed on him.

"Well, my grandmother was Catholic, you know, and she thought it was a horrible sin to have an abortion . . . so she offered my mother all the money in her savings if my mother would have her baby. I guess it wasn't a whole lot of money to some people, but it was everything to my grandmother, and my mother had lost her apartment and all." He pressed his lips together. "My mother agreed, and my grandmother took care of her until I was born. And you'd think—" he looked from Dora to Howie—"you'd think that my mother would've appreciated her mother's help so much that she wouldn't have taken the money."

"But she did," said Howie with a knowing expression.

Armando nodded. "Yeah, and she left me for my grandmother to raise."

Dora raised her coffee cup again, but this time her hand was trembling slightly and there were tears in her eyes. "Here's to your grandmother. What a remarkable woman she must've been."

Howie shook his head in what appeared to be amazement. "A truly remarkable woman."

"She didn't tell me all this until shortly before she died. And only because I begged her to tell me the truth about my real mother. My aunt had said some things to make me suspicious, but I had no idea that it was such a miserable story."

"It's not so miserable," said Dora, blotting her eyes with a napkin. "We've all made mistakes along the way, Armando. Just look how fine you've turned out. I think your grandmother would be proud."

He looked down at the table. "I don't know about that."

"You know what amazes me most?" asked Howie.

Armando looked at him. "What?"

"You don't seem to have even a trace of bitterness in you. Why is that?"

Armando shrugged. "My grandmother told me over and over, and even on her deathbed, that I had to forgive my mother—" he swallowed—"*and* my father."

"And did you really do that?" asked Dora.

"I tried to, at the time. And I guess I keep trying even now. To be honest, it's not always easy. But it was important to my grandmother, and I promised."

"God's the only one who can *really* help us to forgive," said Howie. "We take the first step, by being willing. And then if we ask Him, He will intervene and help us."

Dora pushed herself up from the table. "*Humph.* I'm not so sure about that. Some things are pretty hard to forgive."

"You're right," said Howie. "Lots of things are hard to forgive. Anything worth forgiving is usually pretty hard to forgive. Right, Armando?"

"Yeah, I guess so."

Dora shuffled over to the sink and set her bowl in it with a clank. "Well, maybe some things are just plain *unforgivable.*"

"Only when we refuse to forgive," said Howie in a gentle voice.

Armando started clearing the table, still slightly incredulous that he'd just sat there and told these two people about his strange parents. And yet it didn't feel so bad. In fact, he almost felt better for having spoken.

They went out into the living room, and Howie asked Armando to witness Dora's signature by signing his name below hers.

"Do I need to read these papers first?" asked Armando. He knew enough to know that you should never sign anything without reading it first.

"No. See where it says 'witness to signer'?" Howie pointed it out. "All you're doing is saying that you saw Dora actually sign her name, and no one was forcing her to do it."

"Okay." Armando signed the documents. "Do you need anything else?"

"Not that I know of," said Dora. "Did you get that old tractor running yet?"

"Yeah, didn't you hear it?"

She shook her head. "My ears aren't as good as they used to be."

Armando headed for the door.

"Say, Armando," she called after him, "I'll show you where those farming books are after supper this evening."

"All right."

"Now, you take care, son," called Howie. "And thanks for the delicious lunch. If Dora ever gets tired of your company you can come to my place anytime and work for—"

"Enough with you, Howard Farley," said Dora sharply. "Armando is perfectly happy working for me." She lifted her brows. "Aren't you?"

He smiled. "I couldn't ask for a better job."

But as he walked toward the barn he wondered. Sure, it was great being here on the farm, and he loved working on the place and watching things grow. But what was he really doing here? Buying time? Waiting for old Charlie to launch some horrible lawsuit or put Dora away in an old folks home? And what then? Howie's talk of college made Armando realize that he needed to look toward his own future. He needed to start establishing some sort of a plan. And maybe that meant finding out how things had turned out for his aunt and his cousins back home. But was it really safe to make contact yet? Or perhaps the reason Tio Pedro kept haunting him was meant to be a warning of sorts? Maybe it was better to just keep lying low for the time being.

Chapter Twenty-Two

The rest of the week passed uneventfully. No more of Charlie's boys dropped by to measure or speculate or photograph. Olivia didn't pop in unexpectedly with her tempting pastries. And even old Howie kept his distance, although Dora mentioned that he'd called once just to check in.

Armando hadn't really minded the quiet week, because it allowed him to get some real work done. He'd removed most of the blackberry bushes, cut back piles of weeds and grass, and even done an initial plowing of the field next to the barn, but he suspected he'd need to go over it another time or two before it would be ready to plant. He still wasn't sure what Dora intended for him to put in there, but being that it was late May—and he'd been reading up in Henry's old farming books—there would only be so many options to choose from.

"Sure quiet around here," he commented as they were finishing up their lunch on Friday.

"Too quiet, if you ask me." Dora pushed her empty plate away. "Makes me wonder what's cooking in town these days. You think my boy's up to something?"

He smiled and leaned back in his chair. "Now, you don't want to start getting all paranoid. Maybe old Charlie decided it wasn't worth the fuss to sell your place against your will. Or maybe that computer factory found something they liked better."

"Better than my farm?" She looked indignant.

He shrugged. "There might be some practical reason that your land isn't suitable for a factory."

"That's true enough. And that reason being that *I'm not selling.*" She picked up her fork and started to scratch inside her cast again.

"Dora," he reminded her, "I don't think it's good for you to do that."

"But it itches something fierce in there. And my arm is feeling just fine now. Don't see why the doc can't take this fool thing off sooner."

"I thought you said it would be only another week or so."

She nodded. "But I want it off *now.*"

He smiled. "Guess I'll have to go hide all the hacksaws."

She stood up and straightened her dress, the same colorful muumuu that she'd worn so much lately. "Well, I think we should go to town today."

"Really?" He frowned. "I thought I might have time to go over that field one more time."

She got a sly look. "Well, it won't do you much good to keep tilling that field if you don't have anything to plant in it."

He brightened. "You mean we're going to get some seed?"

"That's right. That and a few other things too. Can you be ready soon?"

"You bet." He hopped up and gathered their empty plates. He considered suggesting that Dora wear something a little less flamboyant but then wondered why. Why shouldn't she feel free to dress in any manner she chose? It's not as if the dress were indecent—it trailed nearly to her ankles. And like he'd told her and Howie, people wouldn't think anything of it if someone his age wore something like that. Olivia was known for her outlandish getups and nobody ever thought she was crazy. Or if they did, they didn't seem to care. It didn't seem fair to treat old folks any differently.

"I want you to drive by my old house," Dora told him shortly after they'd driven into town. "Turn down that street." Then she directed him toward what seemed a pretty nice section of town.

"You lived over here?" he asked as he took in the large and expensive-looking older homes.

"The house was in my mother's family," she told him as she pointed for him to turn left at the next corner. "Just another block. There it is. That big white one with the columns on the front porch."

Armando let out a long low whistle. "Wow, your family must've been really rich."

She sniffed. "Well, money isn't everything, you know."

"Believe me I know." He parked the truck across the street and looked at the imposing house, clearly the largest one in the neighborhood. "Did you like living there?"

She seemed to consider this. "Well, when I was a little girl, when my mother was still alive, I liked it. But she died when I was nine— and, well, my dad was awfully busy with his banking business and city affairs. Of course, we had a maid who looked after me—her name was Hilda, and she was quite nice. She even taught me to speak a bit of German, although I can't recall a single word right now. Well, other than *danke,* and that means 'thank you.' "

Armando studied the little white-haired woman sitting next to him and wondered what had suddenly brought about this change in her. It's as if she were suddenly sitting straighter; even her voice seemed different, more proper somehow. Maybe it had to do with the house and the way she'd been raised.

"Where did Henry grow up?" He wasn't quite sure why he asked it, but he was curious.

"Oh, he lived on the other side of town. What some people might call the wrong side of the tracks—although the railroad doesn't run right through our town. But his place was torn down some time ago. It was just a little two-bedroom house. Henry's people didn't have much in the way of monetary things—but they were good people, all the same. Very good people." She sighed. "Well, I guess that's enough of that. I was curious about the house. I hadn't seen it in years. And it looks pretty much the same. Except for the door. My mother always liked it painted a deep brick red. She thought it made it look more friendly."

"I think I would agree with your mother," said Armando as he started the engine. "That black seems a little unfriendly to me."

Dora chuckled. "You and me, Armando, we think a lot alike."

They went downtown and did their errands, much like the last time they'd been in town, except they didn't go to the bank today. Armando had hoped they might have a reason to stop there because he thought he might see Ruth Michaels, the girl he'd met at Ben's art show. He supposed he could still go over there and say hello to her by himself, but then he wondered if that would seem odd and decided to let it go. Maybe some other day.

As he loaded the groceries into the back of the truck, he saw Olivia walking toward them, waving.

"Hey," she called, "I thought I saw your truck over here." Then she went over and hugged her grandmother.

Olivia had on a lime green dress with big orange flowers all over it and next to her grandmother she looked almost startling. He almost wished he had some sunglasses—or maybe a camera.

"I would've been out to see you this week, Grandma, but it's dead week, the week before finals, you know, and I thought I better get some things done," she lowered her voice, "or risk getting put on academic probation. You'd think there wouldn't be any such thing when you're only taking art and ballet and drama—easy breezy classes like that. But even those teachers have their standards." She turned to Armando. "How's it going?"

"Okay."

"You get any more work done on your special garden?"

"I'm not saying." He smiled smugly.

"We came to town to get seed for the south field." Dora nodded toward Armando. "He's almost got it ready to plant now."

"You're kidding! You're actually going to plant something?"

Dora nodded. "That's right. And I don't mind if you let your father know."

Olivia laughed. "Like I even talk to him. But how's that going, Grandma? I mean has he sent any more of his boys out there sniffing round the place?"

"No, but I had Howie write him an official letter, warning him that the land still belongs to me, and that it's *not* for sale."

"Good for you." Olivia patted her on the back. But Armando noticed that Olivia's hands seemed to be shaking, and he wondered if something was wrong. Maybe she was nervous about her finals.

"Maybe. Still I'm not sure if it'll do much good. Charlie can be pretty stubborn."

Olivia nodded. "That's for sure."

"What about that computer company?" asked Armando.

"CompKing?"

"Yeah, have you or Ben heard anything more about it?"

She drummed her fingers on the tailgate of his truck. "Actually I haven't seen much of Ben this week. But, hey, you could give him a call and see if he knows what's up."

"Nah, that's okay. I was just wondering." But what he really wondered now was *why* hadn't Olivia seen much of Ben this week? Were they breaking up? Of course, he wasn't about to ask something like that.

"Well, I better let you guys go," she said quickly. "I'll try to stop by this weekend, Grandma. Maybe you'd like another bath."

Dora smiled. "Oh, that would be nice. I'm getting sick to death of these stupid sponge baths." She held up her cast. "And I'd give anything to have this thing off right now."

"Isn't it about time?"

"Next week." Dora nodded. "I think I'll throw a party."

Olivia laughed. "Good idea, and I'll bring along my dancing shoes." Then she turned to Armando. "Speaking of parties, some friends are getting together at my place tonight. I need to celebrate the end of dead week. Remember Ruth? I think you met her at Ben's opening last week. She'll be there, as well as a few others. Anyway, if you'd like to come by—around sevenish."

He glanced at Dora. "Oh, I don't know—"

"Well, of course you should go." Dora sighed. "Good grief, Armando, a young fellow who works as hard as you needs to have a little fun sometimes. You know what they say about all work and no play?"

"Okay then." He nodded. "Sevenish?"

"That's right."

They stopped by Foster's Feed & Seed on their way out of town.

"I think I'll wait here in the truck," said Dora. "I'm feeling a little tuckered out just now."

"But what sort of seed am I supposed to get?" he asked. "And how much?"

"Land sakes, I don't know. You'll have to ask the boys in there. They know everything there is to know about anything when it comes to farming. Just explain what you're working with."

"You'll be okay then?"

"Sure. It's a nice shady spot you picked to park, and I've got the window wide open. I might lean back and take a little snooze."

Armando walked around inside the Feed & Seed for several minutes, studying things and taking it all in, before an older man wearing denim overalls approached him.

"You looking for something in particular?" the man asked, looking at Armando with what almost felt like suspicion. Did the guy think he was going to try to make off with a rake or perhaps a bag of grass seed?

Armando put those thoughts aside, deciding it would be better to use his charm to lighten the situation. He smiled at the man and extended his hand. "Hi, I'm Armando Garcia, and I'm helping out around Mrs. Chase's farm—"

The man nodded. "Oh, you're that boy old Dora's got working for her." He shook his hand. "My name's George Foster and this is my business. I've known the Chases for years. Henry and my dad were good friends. Fact is, I helped out with the farm for a few years right after Henry died. But then I got too busy and had to quit. Even now, I have to hire out my own farmwork. So what can I do you for?"

"I'm not really sure." Armando frowned and looked around. "Dora had me plow up this field, not a real big one, I guess. She said it's a little less than two acres. But it's almost ready to plant now."

"Little late in the year to plant most things."

Armando nodded. "I realize that, sir. But Dora really wants to see something go in there. It's important to her."

George scratched his head. "Well, if you were raising any stock I'd suggest you go with hay or alfalfa. That'd be simple enough. You got any livestock?"

Armando shook his head.

George grinned. "Hey, I got plenty of baby chicks that I could let you have real cheap."

"I guess I could ask Dora about it."

"But that's not going to solve this problem." George pressed his lips together and looked around the tall shelves surrounding him, as if searching for clues then finally said, "How about sunflowers?"

"Sunflowers?"

"They grow pretty fast."

"What do you do with them?"

"Well, you can harvest the seeds, of course. But if you get a real nice variety with lots of colors, you could sell them to the florist market. I hear they're pretty popular these days. Do you want to check with Dora first?"

Armando considered this. "No, she said that you guys would know what's best. Just give me enough for about two acres."

"You want me to put it on her account?"

"Sure, I guess so."

"And you'll be wanting some fertilizer." George started writing these things down. "And what are you using to get rid of the weeds and the blackberries out there? Last I saw the place was pretty infested."

Armando held up his hands, now calloused and stained. "These. As well as the tractor some."

"There's easier ways to eradicate. I know that place has gotten pretty far out of hand." He smiled. "But it's sure nice to know that Dora wants to save it. Too much farmland is being lost these days." He lowered his voice. "And from what I hear around town, even her land might not be safe from the hands of certain developers."

"Not if Dora has anything to say about it."

"Good for her. Now, I'll write all this up for you. In the meantime, why don't you go over there and take a look at those work gloves in that barrel. I've got 'em marked down 30 percent and I'll bet you could use a couple pairs."

By the time Armando finished up in there he had enough stuff to fill the rest of the pickup. "I hope it was okay to have them put everything on your account," he said as he backed the truck around to be loaded.

"That's fine. Was George there to help out?"

"Yeah. He seems like a real nice guy."

"Fosters are good people."

As they were driving home, she asked him what kind of seed he'd chosen. "Sunflower seed," he said, glancing to see her reaction.

"Sunflower seed?" She seemed to consider this then nodded. "That should be real pretty come August."

Armando was careful not to overdress for Olivia's gathering that night. He didn't expect it to be as formal as Ben's opening. So after a quick shower, he decided to put on Henry's old bowling shirt. He remembered how Olivia had particularly liked it. It was already past seven, but he didn't want to be there too early or to seem overly eager. He knew there was something to be said about being laid-back. So he sat down in the living room and watched the last half of a game show with Dora.

"You want to shut that thing off now?" she said as the show ended.

"Sure."

"Well, now, look at you. Don't you look nice," she said as he got up to turn off the TV. "Henry always loved that shirt. It was his lucky bowling shirt. You ever bowl, Armando?"

"Yeah, a little, back when I was a kid. I haven't been for a long time."

"You should take it up again. I'll bet you'd be good."

He smiled. "Maybe."

"I was never much good at it myself. But I didn't mind going and watching Henry bowl with his buddies. Some of us wives would sit and drink coffee and just shoot the breeze." She smiled. "It was fun."

He nodded. "What else did you do for fun?"

"Oh, you have to learn to make your own fun in a small town like this. But we had a few good friends. We liked playing cards and bowling. Then once Charlie was grown up and gone, we took a few trips with Howie and Daisy—that was fun too."

"You and Henry had a good life, didn't you?"

She frowned now. "Well, some of it was good. But some of it

wasn't so good. The early years were a lot of hard work. Wasn't much fun going on back then."

"But you still had each other."

She got a wistful look on her face. "Yeah. That we did."

"I think if you had someone you really loved beside you, well, you could probably go through a lot of hard times, and maybe it wouldn't be so hard."

"You're sure right about that." She looked at the clock on the mantel. "Hadn't you better be going now?"

"Guess so." He stood and stretched. "Anything I can get for you before I leave?"

She smiled up at him. "Nah, I've got my mystery book here. I'm fine."

"Hey, I've been reading those farm books you gave me."

"Learning anything?"

"Yeah. Lots of things."

"Good for you."

"See ya, then."

"Have a nice evening, Armando." She waved with her good hand.

* * * * * * * * * * * * *

Dora leaned back into the couch and lifted her book, but instead of seeing the words, it was Henry she saw, smiling down at her. "Got on my lucky shirt," he said.

"Going bowling, are you?"

"Not without my lucky girl."

She laughed. "You got your lucky shirt, your lucky shoes, and your lucky ball. Isn't that enough?"

"Not hardly!" He wrapped his arms around her waist. "I can't even break a hundred without my lucky girl by my side."

She untied her apron and smoothed her skirt. "Do I have time to tidy up?"

"You bet. And why don't you put on that red sweater I got you for Christmas. I like the way it shows off your shape."

She shook her finger at him. "Why, you old—"

"Don't you go calling me old," he warned her with a wink. "Just because our one baby chick has gone and left the nest, doesn't mean we're over the hill. Why, look at you, Theodora Olivia; you're nothing but a spring chicken yourself."

It some ways it was the happiest season of their lives. The farm was running smoothly and not even taking too much of Henry's time since he always managed to get good help these days. And Charlie seemed happily settled in college—an expensive one back east. Dora didn't even mind the distance between them. She'd sent him regular care packages until the day she got a short letter from him asking her not to send any more. "It's a waste of postage," he'd explained in the typewritten note. "And the baked goods only go to waste here since we have a perfectly good bakery a block away." In other words, he still preferred store-bought food to her home-made items. Well, that was his choice. And if he didn't appreciate her old-fashioned ways, she had no intention of wasting her time and energy for nothing. Still, it hurt her feelings. She often wondered how she'd failed to raise a more thoughtful and sensitive son. Why hadn't he turned out more like her Henry?

And even though they knew he could afford it, Charlie never came home for holidays. He spent summers vacationing with friends, sending an occasional postcard, not so much to communicate, it seemed, as to boast of his recent whereabouts and escapades. Places like the Mediterranean or Acapulco or even closer to home the summer he sailed the San Juan Islands on a forty-foot yacht, but even then he hadn't bothered to stop by home and say hello. It's as if he were punishing them. And it was during that time that Dora had taken to planning little getaways of their own. She could well afford it on the money she'd stashed away from the sale of her mother's house. She and Henry went with Howie and Daisy to places like Victoria, BC, Puerto Vallarta, and even Hawaii to see the Pearl Harbor Memorial. And all this while, they tried to push from their minds how their only son had seemingly abandoned them.

"What's Charlie up to these days?" asked Daisy as the two women sipped drinks beneath a coconut-thatched roof on a sunny beach outside of Honolulu.

"Well, you know he graduated with his master's degree in business last spring," said Dora, adjusting her wide-brimmed hat to fend off the reflection from the water. "And now he's taken a job in a big bank in Seattle."

"Banking?" Daisy laughed. "Well, if that boy isn't bound and determined to follow right in his grandfather's footsteps."

"You sure got that right."

"Sometimes I think the good Lord has the best sense of humor."

"How's that?"

"Oh, I don't know. Maybe it's the way He tosses the genetic dice."

Dora frowned. "Genetic dice?"

"You know, the way He creates us in our mothers' wombs. He grabs a little of this and a pinch of that and voilà—a brand-new person emerges. Only sometimes that brand-new person has some of the very same traits as one of his ancestors. And that can be a little irritating." Daisy chuckled. "Especially to someone like you, Dora. Someone stuck in the middle."

Dora smiled. "So are you suggesting that God's playing some kind of little joke on me. First He gives me Daddy and then He gives me Charlie."

Daisy nodded. "Funny, isn't it?"

"Maybe to you. I don't know if I can see the humor in it just now."

"Well, I figure there's a lesson in there somewhere."

"A lesson?" Dora took a sip of her fruity drink.

"Oh, sure. You know God doesn't waste anything. If Charlie's a repeat of your dad, it's probably just God's way of giving you a second chance."

"A second chance for what?" Dora made a face. "To endure more heartache?"

"It's my experience," said Daisy, "that folks can't hurt you unless you let them."

"Are you saying it's my fault that Daddy treated me the way he did? Or that Charlie never comes home to visit or doesn't stay in touch?"

"Not exactly. I guess what I'm saying is that sometimes we set ourselves up to be hurt. Sometimes we hang on to old things that would be better laid aside."

Dora had considered her friend's words as the sun slipped into the sea. She knew perfectly well what Daisy was getting at. It was something that Henry had to remind her of often enough. But it was all too easy for them to say. They weren't walking in her shoes. They didn't know what it felt like to have both a father and a son who looked down on you and treated you like you were somehow less than worthy simply because you were married to a farmer. Oh, she'd tried to hide these sorry facts from Henry. She didn't want him to feel the hurt and rejection that she'd lived with on an almost daily basis for most of her adult life. Certainly, Henry was a good man, living a good life. It wasn't his fault that not everyone could appreciate it. But she did. And, of course, he did too. And maybe that was all that really mattered—in the long run anyway.

Chapter Twenty-Three

Sometimes, like tonight as he was leaving to go to Olivia's party, Armando wished he had said something more meaningful to Dora. Like something as simple as "thank you" or "you really mean a lot to me" or "I appreciate your kindness." But he was never quite sure how to get the right words out without sounding phony or pretentious or like he was schmoozing. And he knew Dora well enough to know she was sharp as a tack when it came to that, plus she wouldn't take kindly to what she might suspect to be false compliments any more than she gave out real ones. Still, he wanted her to know how much her friendship meant to him. And he worried that one day it would be too late for him to express his gratitude. For some reason he felt like maybe he was living here under borrowed time. Like one morning he was going to come into the house and find her—well, unable to wake up. And this disturbed him more than he cared to even think about.

"Well, just forget about that for tonight," he told himself as he started the truck. "Tonight is for having fun. No thinking and acting like an old man tonight, Mr. Garcia. You are going to a party!"

He'd never seen Olivia's place before. In fact, before today, he'd simply assumed that she still lived with her parents. But she'd given him the address of an apartment. And now he wondered if perhaps she didn't share this with Ben. And why not, especially if they'd been going together for a couple years now? It's not as if that would be so unusual. And besides, he knew she didn't work to support herself since she was going to school, so how could she afford to pay for an apartment? Of course, he told himself, her wealthy parents might be footing the bill. As he parked the truck and looked at the apartment complex, he knew the bill couldn't be too cheap either. He shook his head and thought that some people have all the luck.

He followed the sound of music to the second floor and quickly found her apartment. Several burning candles were artistically arranged with some branches and flowers on a small table outside the door. He rang the bell and waited.

"Hey, you came!" said Olivia as she flung the door wide open. *"Entrez, s'il vous plait."*

"Nice apartment," he said in a voice loud enough to be heard over the blaring music. He glanced around the living room to see what looked like maybe a dozen or more people gathered here and there. Several were smoking, as was Olivia, and the alcohol appeared to be flowing freely. In some ways, it didn't appear much different than many of the parties that he and Mickey used to attend back home. Only smaller and classier perhaps, and, of course, he was the only Latino in this pale-faced crowd.

Olivia took him by the arm and proceeded to introduce him to several people both inside her apartment and out on the patio. But the names came and went and he chastised himself for not trying harder to remember them. Ben was there as well as Ruth. So he wasn't completely on his own.

He passed on a beer and took a can of soda, moving outside to join Ben on the patio that overlooked the pool. "Nice view out here."

"And the air's a lot better too."

Armando chuckled. "Yeah, that's what I was thinking."

Ben shook his head. "I wish she'd just give it up."

"Huh?"

"Oh, you name it. But take smoking for instance. It's so disgusting. I don't understand why she insists on such destructive habits."

"Speaking from experience, smoking is a hard thing to quit."

"You used to smoke?"

He nodded. "Yeah. I was up to two packs a day before I finally got smart."

Ben glanced at Armando's soda can. "You don't drink either?"

He shrugged. "I'm driving tonight. Dora's truck, you know."

"You seem like a good kid, Armando."

Armando knew that was meant to be a compliment, but for some reason it felt more like a dig. Still, he decided to ignore it. "So how's your art show coming these days?"

Ben sighed deeply. "Don't ask."

"That bad, huh?"

Ben leaned over the railing and looked down to the pool area below. "Sometimes I wonder why I go to so much trouble."

"Isn't that how an artist is supposed to feel?"

He glanced at Armando out of the corner of his eye, but didn't answer.

"Hey, have you heard anything more about that CompKing outfit? Are they still thinking about locating here in Treasure?" Armando asked.

"According to my sources they've still got their eye on Treasure." Ben made a groaning sound. "And apparently they did their research well. Our county happens to be one of the few in the Northwest with some outdated and really lenient development laws. A real boon for an outfit like CompKing. I mean they could care less what they do to the environment."

"Oh, Ben!" Olivia exclaimed as she joined them. "Don't tell me you're out here whining at Armando about stupid environmental issues again. Can't you lighten up and just party?"

He turned around and glared at her. "Can't you take life

seriously for one single moment? Olivia, you live your life like you think you're the female version of Peter Pan, dancing your way through never-never land like tomorrow will never come. *Don't you get it?*"

"I get that you enjoy being a great big wet blanket."

"Well, maybe I'll just take my blanket and leave now!"

The noise level from the party, other than the music, suddenly grew quieter and Armando felt slightly embarrassed for both Ben and Olivia. But they didn't even seem to notice.

"Fine!" she said loudly. "No one will miss your gloom-and-doom attitudes anyway. Will we, Armando?"

"Hey, Ben and I were only talking—"

"Forget about it, Armando," snapped Ben. "With Olivia everything is 'my way or the highway.' And I for one have had about enough!"

"Join the crowd!" she shouted. "I've had it up to here with your strict dietary rules and your no-nonsense ways. I'm tired of continually trying to cheer you up. If you insist on living like life is so totally miserable, then go do it by yourself."

"Fine, I will!" Ben slammed down his glass so hard on the tile-topped table that it shattered into pieces; then he turned and stormed inside.

Armando stood watching Olivia. Would this ruin her party? Would she regret her hasty words? But as soon as the front door slammed, she threw back her head and laughed loudly.

"Welcome to my world, Armando." She held up her wineglass in a toast. "Here's good riddance to bad rubbish!" Then she emptied her glass in one big gulp.

He didn't know what to say. But already several of her friends were clustering around her, telling her not to worry, that Ben would be back, or to forget about him, or that she was better off without him—whatever advice seemed to best suit the particular giver's state of mind. And Olivia seemed to devour their words like a hungry child left alone in a candy shop.

"Did you enjoy the fireworks?" came a quiet voice from the other side of the patio.

Armando turned to see Ruth at his elbow. "Uh . . . I'm not sure—"

"Oh, don't worry." She waved her hand in dismissal. "They do this all the time. Olivia says it's what keeps them going. Kind of like cleaning the air or taking out the trash. And they really seem to get off on doing it in public too. Kinda kinky if you ask me. But, hey, whatever trips your trigger."

He nodded. "Yeah, I have an aunt and uncle who are a little like that."

"Isn't that fairly common among—" she stopped herself briefly then continued, perhaps more carefully—"well, you know . . . I mean with Hispanic people. Don't you guys tend to be fairly open with your emotions, just cutting loose with all that fire and passion?"

Now he realized this was one of those less-than-sensitive comments that a person could easily take offense at, but once again he wondered what good that would do. And it's not like Ruth was being intentionally rude. Besides, what she'd said was partially true, like most stereotypes. "Yeah, I suppose a lot of Latinos are like that. But not everyone. And not me."

"Yeah, you seem pretty cool and laid-back to me." She spoke in a flirtatious voice now, looking up at him with overly wide eyes. "But there must be some hot Latino passion hidden in there somewhere, Armando." She tapped his chest. "I'll bet you could get fired up under the right conditions."

Olivia turned around and jabbed Armando with her elbow, then with a sly smile, like she'd been listening, said, "You must be kidding, Ruth. Armando's one of the coolest cucumbers I know. I've never seen him lose it. Not once."

"Oh, I'm sure I could lose it all right—if someone pushed me far enough. But I guess I try to avoid that kind of conflict."

"You mean you don't enjoy a good fight?" Olivia's eyes seemed overly bright and she held a fist up like a boxer. "You don't wanna go a few rounds with the champ?"

He shook his head. "Nah. I got to see too much of that garbage growing up."

"Not with your sweet little grandmother?"

He laughed. "No. My grandmother never lost her temper, at least not when I was around. Maybe that's where I get it from. But I was telling Ruth just now that you and Ben reminded me of my aunt and uncle back home. I used to live with them and they fought all the time. But whenever they started to blow, I'd usually try to get outta there in order to avoid the fallout. But I always felt sorry for their little girls. It was kinda hard on them."

"Maybe that's *my* problem." Olivia took a sip of another drink, no longer in a wineglass. It looked like she'd moved on to the hard stuff now.

"What's that?"

"Maybe my parents should've fought more. Instead of just sweeping all their garbage under the rug. Then maybe I wouldn't be such a feisty lass." She laughed. "Or not. Who knows?"

"Your parents fought sometimes," Ruth reminded her. "I remember that time I went to Yellowstone with you guys and they had that big old fight over that one motel that your mother insisted was a fleabag."

Olivia laughed. "Yeah. You're right. They did fight every once in a while. But usually about something totally irrelevant and moronic. The rest of the time they just avoided things. You know what my shrink told me?" She waved her now empty-glass in front of Ruth's face. "She said that every single family has a pile of stinking garbage sitting in the middle of their living room. But the difference between a functional family and a dysfunctional one is that the functional family will get out their buckets and shovels and try to clean it up, but a dysfunctional family will throw a rug on top, and then add a table and a pretty vase, and just pretend it's not even there."

Ruth laughed. "Yeah, I guess that makes sense."

"Hey, bartender!" yelled Olivia to no one in general. "Get me another drink."

"I'll get it for you, Livvie," offered a guy named Tim or Tom or Todd; Armando couldn't remember for sure.

Armando noticed Ben's broken glass still littered across the small table and bent over to gather it up into his napkin.

"Not so fast there, *amigo!*" said Olivia, slapping his hand. "No one invited you here to play houseboy tonight."

He looked up at her. "I just didn't want anyone to—"

"This is *my* party!" she shouted. "You let me worry about the messes." Pushing him aside, she started grabbing up the broken pieces.

"Careful," he warned.

With a loud curse, Olivia suddenly drew back her hand to reveal what looked like a deep cut in the center of her right palm. It was already starting to bleed.

"Let's get you to the kitchen," said Armando quietly. He led her inside and pressed a path through her oblivious guests and guided her over to the sink, then gently rinsed her cut with soap and water, ignoring her cries of protest and pain.

"That looks pretty bad, Olivia. I think you might need stitches." He grabbed what looked like a clean towel and packed it into her palm. "Hold this tight." Then he grabbed another towel and wrapped it tightly around her whole hand.

"Here's your drink," said a guy as he handed her a full glass of amber liquid.

"Haven't you had enough?" asked Armando.

"Oh, don't you start acting like Ben!" Olivia took a big swig. "I need this now more than ever—painkiller, you know."

"Is she okay?" asked Ruth, joining them.

"I think she needs stitches," said Armando, taking the half-empty glass from Olivia's other hand.

"Hey!" Olivia glared at him.

"You want me to take her in?" offered Ruth.

Armando glanced at the empty drink glass in Ruth's hand and wondered just how much alcohol she'd consumed. "No, it's okay. I can do it."

"Do you even know where the hospital is?"

"I've seen the signs in town." He was walking Olivia to the front door now, and fortunately she no longer resisted his help. "Why don't you take care of things here, Ruth," he called over his shoulder. "Play hostess until we get back."

"Oh, sure. I can handle that."

Armando put his arm around Olivia's waist to support her as he walked her to the pickup. Her steps felt loose and weak to him, as if she might topple at any moment. And he supposed it was possible she could go into shock. Or else it was simply the alcohol. In some ways it reminded him of helping Dora in those first few days, back when her arm had been troubling her so much. He helped Olivia into the pickup and leaned over to buckle her in.

"Hey," she said with a crooked little smile. "Better watch yourself, sailor."

"Just being safe." He slammed the door then ran over to the driver's side.

"Yeah, sure," she slurred, "tha's what they all shay."

"You okay?" he asked as he started the engine and pulled into the street.

"Oh, yeah, I'm juz peashy keenie, hunky-dory." And then she started singing some goofy kid's song about a little white duck. Not one that he'd ever heard before, but he felt pretty sure she was getting the words all mixed up because they made absolutely no sense to him. At least she wasn't going into shock or passing out.

Keeping his speed in control, he followed the signs and drove quickly to the small community hospital. He parked in the well-lit area right in front of the emergency entrance and helped her inside. She seemed even more wobbly now. "You sit down and wait here," he told her as he went to the desk. "I'll take care of this."

"I brought my friend in," he explained to the receptionist. "I think she needs stitches."

The woman looked at him then shoved a clipboard across her desk. "Have her fill out this paperwork."

"But she's bleeding." He glanced over to see Olivia slumped forward, her hair hanging over her face like a curtain.

"Did she sever a main artery?" The woman's tone sounded bored and slightly sarcastic.

"I don't know." He glanced around the nearly empty waiting room. "But can't someone take a look at her while I start filling this—"

"She'll have to wait her turn just like everyone else."

"How long will that be?"

She shrugged. "Depends." Then she studied him closely. "Do you people even have insurance? Or is this supposed to be a freebie?"

"What?"

"Do you have insurance?" She spoke the last word slowly and loudly as if he were a small child. *"Yo Comprendo?"*

"Look—" he tried to contain himself—"I'm sure my friend has insurance—"

"Then have her fill out the paperwork. Can she read?"

"Of course!"

"Does she speak English?"

"Yes!" Now, despite all that earlier talk about remaining cool-headed, Armando suddenly felt very close to losing it. In fact, he could even imagine himself reaching across this woman's tidy desk, wrapping his hands around her flabby neck, and squeezing hard until her small beady eyes bulged right out of her head.

But instead he took a deep breath. "Look," he paused to read her name tag then spoke slowly, as if she were the one who had a problem understanding English, "Ms. Thurman, my friend's name is Olivia Chase. Her father is Charles Chase, the president of the First Bank of Treasure, and if she passes out or bleeds to death in the lobby, it's going to be on your head—"

"Well, why didn't you just say so?" She nodded toward a closed door to her right. "Take her right through there. We have all Miss Chase's medical information on computer." She rolled her eyes. "In fact, she was here less than a month ago."

Armando hurried over to Olivia. "Here." He offered her his arm. Her eyes were big now and her face looked as white as the wall behind her. "Let me help you." He gently eased her up. "Now let's get you in—"

But before they even reached the door, she bent over, clutching her stomach, and vomited all over the light beige carpet. He steadied her as she stood there retching and sobbing, waiting until she was finally finished.

"Oh, good grief!" exclaimed the disgusted receptionist.

But Armando smiled and said, "Guess you'll take care of that." And then he walked Olivia into the ER, where a male nurse met them and quickly ushered them into a small room and helped Olivia get settled onto the examining table. She flopped backward and sighed deeply.

The nurse pushed up her sleeve and wrapped a blood-pressure cuff around her arm. "Having a bad night, are you, Ms. Chase?" He peered down at her pale face.

"Do you want me to stay with her?" asked Armando.

"Not unless you want to."

Armando looked at Olivia. But her eyes were still closed. He turned to the nurse. "I . . . uh . . . maybe I should let you know that she's been drinking . . . uh . . . in case you want to prescribe something for the pain, just so you'll know."

The nurse nodded. "Thanks, man. We sure don't want her ODing on us again."

"Again?"

The nurse got a strange look. "Hey, I'm sorry." He glanced over at Olivia. "I shouldn't have said that."

Armando waved his hand. "It's okay. I'm a friend of the family. It's safe with me."

"Okay, then, while we're on the subject, was she doing anything else tonight?"

"Anything else? Like what—"

"You know, like any other substances we should be aware of." He was removing the blood-soaked towel now.

"I don't really know."

The nurse glanced at the still-bleeding cut, shoved a large piece of gauze into it, and quickly wrapped it with more gauze.

"Aren't you going to have someone stitch it?"

He nodded. "Yeah. But this could be the least of her problems."

"What do you—"

"Her blood pressure is low." He turned to Olivia and spoke loudly. "Ms. Chase? Can you hear me? I need to ask you some questions."

But she didn't respond.

"I'm getting the doctor." And in the same instant he turned and left.

Armando stepped closer to Olivia. "Olivia?" he spoke loudly too, imitating the nurse. "Can you hear me?" He leaned closer, concerned that she might not even be breathing.

"Move out of the way," demanded a doctor with the nurse right behind him and another medical person following with a gurney.

"We've got to move her," the nurse told Armando. "You'll have to clear out of here now."

Armando managed to slip past the three of them and returned to the waiting area where a janitor was cleaning up Olivia's mess. He paced for a few minutes, then wondered if he shouldn't inform them about the fact that she had already thrown up. He glanced at the receptionist and then went back into the ER. He found another nurse at another desk and quickly explained the situation to her.

"Thanks," she told him. "The doctor will want to know that."

Then, remembering his truck still parked in the driveway, Armando decided to go outside and move it. He slowly drove to the nearby parking lot and parked along the perimeter. He turned off the engine and sighed. It was dark now. And for a few minutes, he sat in the cab, looking up at the sky and watching the stars. He sat there, wondering why on earth someone with so much going for her, like Olivia seemed to have, would want to mess it all up with alcohol and, well, whatever. But it's not like this was anything new. It was common enough where he'd come from and he knew that kids all over the country, from all economic and ethnic backgrounds, struggled with the same kind of garbage. He'd been there himself not so very long ago. Maybe not with drugs; he'd seen enough of his uncle's messes to steer clear of that trap. But he and Mickey had done their fair share of alcohol consumption and bingeing during their teen years. Maybe he was a faster learner. Or maybe he just didn't enjoy pain and discomfort that much. Because it hadn't taken too many hangovers (hanging over the toilet is the way he remembered it) to make him realize that it wasn't worth it in the end. Even tonight, he'd been tempted to guzzle a beer—thinking, *how much could one single beer hurt?* But he knew from his own personal experience that one beer led to another and then another and pretty soon he'd lose count altogether. And so, more than ever, he was thankful that he'd abstained tonight. Maybe he was finally growing up after all.

But what about Olivia? What would it take to make her grow up? He remembered how Ben had called her the female version of Peter Pan earlier tonight. And wasn't Peter Pan's theme song "I Won't Grow Up"? Or maybe he was getting it confused with being a Toys "R" Us kid. He couldn't quite remember. Still, he knew something was wrong.

Chapter Twenty-Four

As Armando drove Olivia home from the hospital, he wondered if the party would still be going on. Somehow he didn't think so, but then it was barely past two in the morning, and he could remember parties that had lasted clear until dawn in L.A. Of course, people were usually pretty wasted by then, and it hadn't taken him too many times before he discovered there were better ways to experience the sunrise.

He glanced over at Olivia again. Her face was drained of all energy and emotion, but her eyes were still wide-open—probably a result of medicine she'd been given. He'd waited for hours while she'd undergone treatment and then observation before the staff doctor finally released her. And even that came with a stern warning that Armando had been forced to hear.

"You're playing with fire, Olivia," the doctor had told her. "You were lucky again tonight. But the time may come when your luck runs out. You could be all by yourself next time, and there won't be anyone around to cart you into the hospital." He pointed to her bandaged hand. "And if you hadn't cut your hand and been forced to come in, it might've even been tonight."

Her eyes were wide and her face unusually sober as she listened to him.

"You need to get into some kind of a treatment program. I'll give you the brochures and information again. I know your parents can afford it. So the problem has to lie with you." He leaned over and peered into her pale face. "Do you really want to keep living like this?"

She shook her head and looked down at her lap.

"Then do something. Before it's too late." He turned and looked at Armando. "You must be a pretty good friend, right?"

He nodded. "Yeah, I'd like to think so."

"And are you into this crud too?"

Armando firmly shook his head. "No way."

"Then maybe you can help her."

"I'll try."

"Good." He turned back to Olivia. "But the bottom line is, it's up to you, Olivia. No one can do this for you. It's your life and you've got to want it. Your friend here can help you out if you let him. But you've got to be willing."

"I know." Her voice sounded small and faraway, as if someone else were speaking, not the usual self-assured and devil-may-care Olivia.

He shrugged and closed his clipboard. "Well, I guess that's all I can say. I just don't want to see you in here again—not for this anyway."

Without saying a word, Armando parked the truck and silently accompanied Olivia back to her apartment. He wanted to make sure she was safely inside before he went home.

"Thanks, Armando," she said as they reached her darkened door. The candles were out now and all was quiet. "I owe you one."

He nodded. "But what about what the doctor said?" he asked as she fumbled with trembling hands to get her key into the lock and open the door.

"Yeah, I know." She went inside, flipped on the light, then tossed her keys onto a table. "Come on in."

He went inside, leaving the door partially open, as if to signal he wasn't staying long. "Are you going to do it?"

"A treatment facility?" She sank onto the couch, leaned her head back, and sighed loudly.

"Yeah. The doctor said you need help." He glanced around the apartment in disgust. No doubt there'd been a party here tonight. And it didn't appear that anyone had lifted a finger to clean up either. Not even Ruth, apparently.

"I need help." She repeated the words slowly, almost mechanically. "I *do* need help."

"So, you'll get it then?"

She pressed her hand into her forehead and closed her eyes. "Oh, I don't know, Armando. I'm too tired to think about this right now. My head is killing me."

"Yeah, I can understand that. You've been through a lot." He went over and helped her to stand. "You need to get to bed."

She smiled sleepily. "You coming with me, sailor?"

He shook his head. "No."

He set her down on the bed and bent over to slip off her strappy high-heeled sandals. He was amazed that she'd been able to walk in them considering her condition. Then he gently leaned her back onto the bed. She reminded him of a worn-out rag doll, and her eyes were closed even before her head touched the pillow. He laid the patchwork quilt over her and hoped she didn't mind going to sleep with her jeans and T-shirt still on, but he felt it would be improper to attempt to help her remove them. It was bad enough helping Dora with various stages of her dressing, but with Olivia it would be entirely different. He stood there for a moment, just watching her. He couldn't help but think how this was exactly the same sort of thing he had done for Dora so many times in the last couple weeks. Was this to be his lot in life, helping injured women into bed? He leaned over and pushed a blonde strand of hair from her face then whispered, "Good night, Olivia." But she was clearly asleep already.

He went back to the living-room area and began straightening a bit. He picked the colorful silk pillows from the floor and lined them back on the long white sofa. Then he began gathering the empty drink glasses that were littered everywhere and put them in the dishwasher. At first, he'd only meant to clear things up a bit— just to make it safer for her, in case she got up in the middle of the night. Of course, he knew it wasn't his responsibility to clean up Olivia's messes. Hadn't she made that perfectly clear earlier, before she'd sliced her palm on the broken shard of glass?

But then he decided he wasn't sleepy anyway, and he might as well do a thorough job of cleaning. Maybe it would encourage her to trust him better as a real friend, and perhaps to even take his advice (along with the doctor's) and get some real treatment. Finally, he had the all counters and surfaces clean and the dish-washer quietly running, and he decided to take a few minutes to straighten up her bathroom before he left. And this is when he may have taken it a step too far. He knew it could be a mistake, and perhaps he was even risking her friendship, but suddenly he no longer cared. Because when he discovered what was obviously a cache of illegal drugs—an assortment of uppers and downers— something in him just snapped, and almost without thinking, he flushed them all down the toilet.

By now he felt fairly certain that Olivia lived alone in the apart-ment. Oh, there were a few signs of Ben's presence there, like an extra toothbrush, shaving cream, and cologne, but not enough to suggest that he was more than an occasional guest there. And with her irritating smoking habit, it made perfect sense that Ben would have his own place. So Armando had felt fairly certain the pills were Olivia's, but even if they were Ben's, he knew he still would've thrown them away without feeling guilty. Was he inter-fering? Probably. But somehow he just didn't care.

It was getting close to 5 A.M. when he left the apartment and he knew it wouldn't look good, if anyone were around to spy him, to be seen leaving her place at this hour. But fortunately the parking lot seemed quiet and deserted of any forms of life, other than a stray cat that streaked past him in a blur of black and white. Yet, even as he hurried to the pickup with his head down, unwilling to be seen, he wondered why he should even care. It was obvious that Olivia didn't give a hoot. If anything, she seemed to thrive on her bad-girl image. And yet she had that face of an angel!

He hit his fist against the steering wheel as he drove back toward the farm in the predawn gray. Why did life have to be so messy? Why did people with everything going for them throw it all away for nothing? And why did people with nothing throw away what little they had to get what really amounted to nothing? Why couldn't everyone just be happy? Why couldn't *he* be happy?

He'd been reading that old Bible lately. Not a lot, but enough to make him wonder. He suspected it was the very same Bible that old Manuel Rodriguez had read when he stayed in that room and helped run the Chase farm. Apparently Manuel had written to his wife about a Bible that Mr. Chase had given him to read because she had responded back to him about it. She told him she was glad he was working for good Christian people.

The eastern sky was just beginning to glow pink as he pulled into the driveway. He hoped the sound of the engine wouldn't awaken Dora. He didn't really care to explain pulling an all-nighter. Especially with her granddaughter.

He considered going to bed for a couple of hours, but knew he'd have a hard time getting back up. So he loaded some gardening tools into the wheelbarrow and walked over to the area by the creek and continued working on the project that had occupied his evenings during the past several days. He decided to throw all his frustrations into digging this morning. And by the time he finished, he felt a little bit better. He stepped back to survey his work and smiled. It wouldn't be long now.

It wasn't until later that day that the little orange Volkswagen pulled into the driveway. Armando was still on the tractor, tilling the soil one more time before it would be ready to plant. He waved toward Olivia, but she didn't even glance his way, just went directly to the house. And he could tell by her posture that she was purposely ignoring him. In fact, she seemed angry. He turned the tractor around, away from the house, and tugging his cap down low against the glare of the afternoon sun, he continued to till. That was her problem if she wanted to be mad. Stupid gringa! If she was so messed up that she couldn't even tell when someone was trying to help her—well, why should he let it bother him? But, of course, it did.

Her car was still there when he finally turned off the tractor. He glanced at is watch. It was half past six already, time to be getting dinner started. He pulled off his hat and wiped the sweat from his brow as he walked to the outside faucet to wash off some of the dirt. Then cupping his hands, he took a long thirsty drink of cool water. He stood and looked back toward the house, and for the first time since coming to Dora's farm he decided he'd had it. Maybe he was just tired, but he'd had it with playing houseboy to a couple of somewhat unappreciative and totally unpredictable women.

"I'm *not* going to do it!" he said out loud, snapping his encrusted ball cap across his knee to dislodge some of the dirt. "Let them cook their own stinking supper tonight." He turned around and marched to his room. Without even taking off his boots, he collapsed across his bed and fell soundly asleep.

When he awoke it was dark in his room and his stomach rumbled with hunger, but he noticed a pale sliver beneath his door, like someone had left the light on inside the barn. When he went to turn it off, he nearly tripped over the tray sitting outside his door. He could tell by the dim light that it was a meal and probably meant for him. He glanced around the barn, wondering if someone now lurked in the shadows, but all was quiet and still with only the sounds of crickets and frogs to disturb the evening's peace. He walked to where the light switch was located, over by the door, and peered out to the driveway, but Olivia's car was gone now. And the house looked dark and quiet as if Dora had gone to bed.

Then he went back, picked up his tray, took it to his room, and began to eat. He knew it must be Olivia's doing, since it wasn't all that good. The tuna sandwich was soggy and the bananas in the fruit salad had already turned brown. But he was hungry and he couldn't complain about the giant-sized, maple-bar pastry. He suspected that Olivia had stopped by the Blue Hat Bakery again. Satisfied, he washed the whole thing down with a tall glass of milk. He remembered the time when Olivia had teased him for drinking milk. She'd acted like she was so much more mature, saying how she'd given it up as a child. Too bad she hadn't given up being a child then as well.

He set the tray on his dresser and sighed. He sure wished he could sneak into the house and take a nice long shower. But he didn't want to disturb Dora. He looked at his watch. It was barely past nine and he no longer felt sleepy. He left his room and started poking around in the barn. While working out in the garden today he had come up with an idea. It seemed a little crazy perhaps, and he wasn't even sure if he could pull it off, but he thought it might be worth a try. So he scrounged around the barn and the various sheds until he gathered up an interesting assortment of odd items—things like metal pipes and bailing wire and chicken fencing and a couple old bags of concrete and some odd-sized pieces of old rusted sheet metal. And then he began to work. He worked until well past midnight, and even then he had to force himself to stop and go to bed. "Tomorrow's another day," he said as he turned out the barn light.

* * * * * * * * * * * * *

Armando got up early the next morning and slipped quietly into the house and took a long hot shower, scrubbing off what felt like a week's accumulation of sweat and dirt and dust. Then he tiptoed down the stairs and began fixing breakfast.

"That you, Armando?" Dora poked her head into the kitchen. Her hair was sticking out in all directions, but at least she was smiling.

He grinned. "Yep. Sorry I missed supper yesterday."

"Oh, that's all right." She came in and sat down at the table. "Olivia explained the whole thing to me."

He turned and looked at her then went to get the coffeepot. "The *whole* thing?" he asked as he filled her cup.

"Sure. She told me how she'd cut her hand at her party and how you took her to the hospital and stayed with her until they fixed it up." She took a sip of coffee. "Stupid hospital! Don't know why on earth it should take them hours and hours to put in nine little stitches."

He nodded. "Yeah, things seem to move pretty slowly over there."

"And Olivia told me how you took her home and even straightened up her place while she was sleeping." Dora nodded with satisfaction. "You're a good boy, Armando."

He studied her, wondering how he should react to this unexpected compliment. "Thank you, Dora. That means a lot to me coming from you."

She waved her good hand. "Aw, you must know you're a good boy."

He set a plate of eggs and toast in front of her then turned back to get his own. "I'm not so sure about that."

"Well, isn't that what your grandmother used to tell you?"

He smiled. "Yeah, something like that."

She took a bite. "I figured she would."

He sat down with his breakfast. "You know, Dora, I've been wanting to tell *you* something."

She looked up from her eggs. "What? Is something wrong?"

"No, nothing like that. I've just been wanting to let you know how much I appreciate you taking me in like this. I never thought I'd end up staying on this long. And, well, I realize you'll be getting your cast off pretty soon and you might not want—" he sighed— "well, I know our little agreement was really only until you got back on your feet, so to speak."

"Oh, that." She took a bite of toast.

"And I know the main reason you needed me out here was to keep Charlie off your back. And, well, that all seems to be pretty much under control. . . ."

"So, are you thinking that I'm all done with you now, and that I'm ready to set you off on your merry little way?"

He shrugged. "I don't know. I guess I want to be careful and not overstay my welcome, you know? Leave the party before they throw you out."

She laughed. "No need to worry about that. Like I said, I *need* someone to keep running this farm for me. Now, do you suppose that once you get that field planted that's all there is to it? Or did you fancy I was going to get out there and drive around on that old tractor and just tend to things all by myself?"

"I wasn't exactly sure what you had in mind."

"Goodness knows I'm not going to be around forever, Armando." She reached for the jam jar. "But for some reason it's become important to me to do everything I can to get this farm back into the same kind of shape it used to be in."

"The *whole* farm?"

"I know, I know, that probably sounds crazy. But it hurts me to see how I've let it get away from me like I have. I know how disappointed Henry would be—he worked so hard on this place. I don't even remember how the years passed so quickly after Henry died. It's like I'd fallen asleep or something." She chuckled. "Just like Sleeping Beauty, fast asleep while all the briars and weeds and thorns grew up all around me like a great big wall."

"And I'm supposed to be the prince," he asked with a grin, "hacking away the blackberry vines to find my way to the castle?"

"Well, I guess we'd make a fairly odd couple, now, wouldn't we? And don't you go getting any silly notions about kissing me to wake me up." She laughed loudly now. "Wouldn't *that* give the townsfolk something to cackle about!"

"So do you really want me to keep working the place?"

"Of course I do. And I even plan to pay you too. I guess the old pickup rightfully belongs to you this week. I'll sign over the paperwork tomorrow."

He smiled. "Cool."

"And I'll pay you a fair wage too—less room and board, of course."

"Of course."

"And as soon as I get this cast off, you won't even be expected to help out with the housework and cooking anymore." She stuck her knife down inside the cast and scratched an itch.

"Oh, I don't mind helping."

"Well, we can discuss all that later."

"I've really enjoyed working on that area over by the creek in my spare time."

"How's it coming?"

"I think it looks pretty nice. Naturally, there's still lots to do, but those flowers I moved are really starting to look good."

"You really like flowers, don't you?" She looked over her coffee cup at him, her pale blue eyes glinting with interest.

"I think I really do." He leaned forward. "You know I've been going through Henry's books, the ones you gave me, and he has this one that's about having a landscaping nursery as a business. And, I don't know, but I think it sounds really good. I wonder how hard it would be to get something like that going."

"You know, Henry considered doing that very thing. Not long before he died too." She smiled. "He'd go on and on talking about greenhouses and steam-heating systems and solar power and, well, all sorts of newfangled things. I 'spect if he'd lived it would've all happened too."

"Wouldn't it be great if we could make it happen now?"

Dora's eyes lit up. "Oh, it would, Armando! It surely would."

"I'm anxious to plant those sunflower seeds. George said the crop could be harvested for the seeds, either to use for sunflower oil or to eat. But if the flowers turn out nice and pretty, we might even sell them to florist suppliers."

"To florists?" She shook her head in wonder. "Now, isn't that interesting? I always did think sunflowers were about the happiest things. I guess I could see someone putting them in a cheerful sort of bouquet."

"You know it'd probably take a whole lot of time and planning to really do it right, Dora—I mean to have a nursery as a business. And I'm guessing it'd take a fair amount of money too—to build greenhouses and get all the equipment it takes to grow flowers and shrubs and trees and stuff. It might be a pretty big undertaking."

She scowled. "You worried you're not up for it?"

"No, no, that's not it. I just hate to get you going into something that could—"

"Well, you figure things out, and you get them written down on paper, and then we'll talk about the next step. That's what Henry always did. He'd write down all his ideas and what he needed and how much things would cost and then he'd go to work."

"Sounds like a good plan."

She sighed. "I always did like flowers."

He started clearing the table, anxious to get back outside in the fresh morning air.

"So what are you planning for today?" She slowly stood and walked over to the sink.

"Well, I know you don't like me working on the Lord's Day and all." He studied her expression closely. Would she waver this time? So often her views on religious issues seemed to fluctuate like the weather. "So I guess I won't be planting those sunflower seeds like I'd like to do. . . ."

"They'll be perfectly fine until tomorrow."

"Then maybe I'll do some things down by the creek. That's not exactly work, you know." He smiled. "It's more like fun."

"Well, have yourself a good old time." She held up her cast. "I'd like to bust this thing off and work in my flower beds today."

"I weeded them already." He started running water in the sink.

"Yeah, I know. But I'm just a-hankering to get my hands dirty."

"You can get your hands dirty pretty soon, Dora."

She sniffed. "It reminds me of when I was a kid."

He rinsed a glass. "How's that?"

"Next week. It always seemed a long ways off when I was little. And now that I'm so old and decrepit I sometimes wonder if I'll even be around next week."

He turned and looked at her. "You don't seem all that old to me, Dora. In fact, I'd say that you seem younger now than when I first met you. Remember that day, right after you broke your arm?"

"You're right. I was feeling a mite poorly that day."

He turned back to the dishes.

"Maybe old Howie's right," she said as she shuffled toward the living room. "I suppose only the good Lord knows the real number of our days."

Armando scrubbed stubborn egg yolk from a plate and hoped that Dora's number would be a generous one. And if he'd been a regular praying person—like his grandmother had wanted him to be—he would've asked the good Lord to lengthen Dora's days right then and there. But as it was, he still wasn't sure whether or not God listened.

Chapter Twenty-Five

*T*ime seemed to evaporate like the morning dew when Armando worked on the garden by the creek. It was past noon when he finally paused to glance at his watch. His digging project was nearly complete now and he planned to test it out later in the week.

But before that, he wanted to finish his sculpture in the barn. Then he planned to load it onto the wheelbarrow and cart it over here and put it in a special place. He felt fairly self-conscious about his creative efforts and hoped that he wouldn't fall under Ben's or even Olivia's critical artistic eye. After all, he knew he wasn't an artist, and he hadn't even meant for his "creation" to be an actual work of art as much as just a simple garden accent. The garden seemed like it needed something a little different, something to set it off somehow. He recalled doing yard work back when he was fourteen, for the Tanningers, a wealthy family with a full acre of well-maintained garden, and tucked here and there in this beautiful garden were numerous sculptures. To Armando's way of thinking, it just seemed to make the place more interesting. So if people wanted to take a poke at his little art project, well, that'd be their problem. He'd have to slough it off.

Before he headed back to the house for lunch, he paused to pick a nice bunch of flowers. He wanted to give them to Dora. Maybe it would help encourage her until next week when she'd get her cast off and actually be able to get her hands dirty too.

He halfway expected to see Howie's old Cadillac parked in front of the house. Or maybe even the orange Bug. But the driveway was conspicuously empty today. And Armando felt disappointed. For Dora's sake, he wished someone would drop by to visit and break up the monotony of her day. It seemed that ever since she'd started feeling better and staying awake more, she also seemed a little lonelier too. Or maybe that was his imagination. Maybe he was the one who felt lonely.

He arranged the flowers in a light blue vase he'd found beneath the sink and then set it on the coffee table before he went upstairs to wash up before he fixed lunch. He wasn't sure where Dora was, but suspected she was in her room. Maybe resting or reading or poking around through old closets like she sometimes liked to do. He'd just taken out a brick of cheese, deciding upon grilled-cheese sandwiches, when she called out. "Put that thing away."

"Huh?"

"We're going into town to eat lunch today."

He turned to see her then suppressed a smile. "What's that you're wearing, Dora?"

She grinned and looked down. "Why, I felt like dressing up today."

He studied her slightly wrinkled red-and-white, polka-dot dress, and the clever way she'd tied a bright blue-and-white scarf over her cast. He smiled. "Well, you look . . . uh . . . very patriotic. Kinda like a flag."

"That's right." She nodded. "I 'spect you know that tomorrow is a holiday."

He frowned. "A holiday?"

"Well, it's not Memorial Day proper. That'll be on Wednesday the thirty-first, but you know how the government always changes these things to Mondays so regular working folks can have a three-day weekend. Anyway, I thought we could get a jump start on the holiday and go visit the cemetery today." She glanced toward the living room. "Oh, my, will you just look at those flowers!"

"They're from the garden spot by the aspens."

"Well, good for you. We'll take them out to my Henry, if you don't mind. I know he'll appreciate them."

He didn't mention that he'd meant the flowers to be for her. But maybe it was right for Henry to have them. After all, he was the one who had originally planted them out there. Armando glanced down at his dirty jeans. "Maybe I should clean up a little too."

"Suit yourself. I'll be waiting on the porch."

So Armando put away the cheese and hurried out to his room to change. Somehow he couldn't bring himself to wear any of Henry's cast-off clothing today. For some reason it seemed disrespectful in light of their going to visit his grave. But he did put on his best jeans and a clean white shirt before he went out and started up the truck. He drove slowly, so as not to stir up the dust, as he circled around to the porch. The pickup was running better than ever these days, and Armando had dreams of investing every cent that Dora might eventually pay him to fix it up to look as good as new. At least he'd do that for a while. Then maybe after he got the truck painted, he'd try to put some money away. Maybe he'd even follow Dora's example and keep it hidden away in a box somewhere.

He chuckled to himself when he saw Dora sitting on the porch. She now had on a wide-brimmed straw hat with a faded red bow. This combined with her vivid red, white, and blue outfit and the bouquet of bright-colored blooms, and she was really a sight to be seen. He wondered what the townsfolk would have to say about this.

"Let me help you with that," he said as he took the vase and opened the door for her then helped her inside.

"I think we should eat first," she said once they got onto the highway. "And I'd like to go to Perkins. I haven't been there in ages."

"Is that the family restaurant on the other end of Main Street?"

"That's the one. It's been there for as long as I can remember. They barely survived the Great Depression, but once that was over, they were the most popular restaurant in town. Until all those other places came along that is. But as far as I know they're still in business. I think the granddaughter runs it these days, but goodness sakes, she must be close to sixty by now."

He parked on the street and helped Dora down from the truck. The restaurant had a few customers but wasn't what you'd call busy, and they were quickly seated by a young redhead with a tattoo on her wrist. "Where's Bernice?" asked Dora as the girl filled their water glasses.

"Bernice?" The girl frowned. "Oh, you mean the lady who used to own this place. I think she and her husband retired and moved to Arizona a few years back. The restaurant is owned by Jim Kelly now."

"But they still call it Perkins?" asked Dora with a confused expression.

"Yeah, Jim's afraid people might quit coming if he changed the name."

Dora looked slightly saddened by this news. "I see."

They both ordered the daily special—pork chops and applesauce. But Armando thought the meat was dry and the meal, well, just so-so. Still, he kept these thoughts to himself.

"This place has gone downhill," said Dora in a voice loud enough for anyone within twenty feet to hear. "Henry and I used to love eating here. Good simple home-style cooking." She made a face. "But this—this tastes like something you'd feed your dog— if you didn't like your dog, that is."

He laughed uncomfortably. "Must be the new ownership," he said in a quiet voice.

"Well, I'm not about to leave a tip," said Dora as they stood to go.

Armando felt a little bad for the waitress because she'd actually been pretty nice, especially to him, and the quality of the food didn't really seem to be her fault. But he was flat broke and it was Dora's money paying the bill, so he knew she could do whatever she liked.

"Thank you for the meal," he said once they were back in the truck.

"Good night!" Dora exclaimed. "I should be apologizing to you for making you eat such bad food."

"Oh, it was okay." He pulled out into the street. "Sometimes even a poor meal beats cooking it yourself."

She laughed. "Now, that's the truth, isn't it?"

Then she directed him toward the cemetery. It was just out of town a ways, a peaceful-looking area with green rolling hills. "You can take that road right there—" she pointed—"and it will get us through the center of it and nearly to the right spot without having to walk too far."

Finally he parked and helped her climb out. "Watch your step," he warned. "This road is kind of rocky and uneven."

"You fetch the flowers and follow me," she commanded. "And I'd appreciate it if you kept quiet too. I don't like much chattering when I'm visiting the cemetery."

He smiled to himself as he picked up the vase. That suited him just fine. He wasn't much into chattering himself. Out of respect, he followed several feet behind her. He sensed this was a special time for her and didn't want to spoil it. Finally she stopped at a very large headstone and what seemed to be one of the more impressive gravesites in the cemetery. The family name "Lawrence" was engraved in ornate, bold letters across the top of the granite. And he could tell by the numerous blank spaces on the large stone that there must still be several vacant graves here.

"This is the family plot," she said in quiet voice. "My grand-parents are buried here on the other side, and Mother and Father are right here." She pointed to the two marked graves then sadly shook her head. "But will you look at how the caretaker lets this place go to ruin? And to think of the good money my family paid for these plots and the monthly maintenance. It's a perfect scandal."

"I could pull out some of those weeds. . . ."

"Nah, don't bother." She paused. "Well, okay, maybe just the ones on Mother's grave. She always hated having weeds in her flower beds."

Armando stooped down and quickly pulled a dozen or more of the oversized dandelions growing near the gravestone marked "Theodora Olivia Lawrence, beloved wife of Charles Harrison Lawrence." He discreetly piled the weeds off to one side and turned to Dora. "Are you named after her?"

She nodded. "Yes. And Olivia is too. I don't think Charlie meant it as a compliment to me so much as it was his attempt to connect with the Lawrence side of his family—that was always important to him."

"I see."

"Here, let me pick some of the flowers from that bouquet."

He held the vase down low for her to select from and she chose several of the big, fluffy, pink blooms, the ones that reminded Armando of roses, although the smooth green stems had no thorns.

"Mother always liked peonies," she said.

"Those are peonies?"

She nodded. "We're going to have to teach you all the flower names." She walked over and laid the pretty blooms at the head of her mother's grave. She stood there quietly for a couple minutes before she returned, wiping a tear from her eye. Then she turned and walked a little farther. Armando followed, still carrying the vase. She stopped at a smaller gravesite. Although it too had one large stone with the family name "Chase" engraved across the top, it was not as impressive as the previous one, but substantial just the same.

It appeared to be designed for four graves—two empty, two filled. Armando read the smaller plates to discover that one grave was for the daughter, Susan Olivia Chase, and one was for Henry Herman Chase. He held out the vase and waited as Dora removed a handful of delicate blooms and tenderly laid them on Susan's grave. Then awkwardly, but using both hands despite her cast, she took the whole vase and turned toward Henry's grave.

Armando walked about thirty feet away, hoping to give Dora the space she needed to feel like she was truly alone with her dearly departed, since he suspected that was what she had meant when she'd dictated "no chattering." He watched discreetly as she slowly bent over Henry's grave. She struggled to set the vase down, looking for a level surface for it. Finally, when she seemed satisfied that the vase wasn't about to tip over, she slowly stood up, pausing to rub her back with her good hand. Then she turned and went over to the nearby cement bench directly across from the gravesite and sat down, laid her hands in her lap, and looked silently toward the two graves.

* * * * * * * * * * * * *

Dora remembered the day she'd found him as if it were today. At first, she'd thought he was simply sleeping in that morning, a rare occurrence but probably much needed, so she'd quietly slipped out of bed and started cooking his favorite breakfast of eggs and ham and blueberry hotcakes, expecting he would pop in and join her any moment. Then finally, as the eggs were starting to get cold, she went back to their bedroom and stood next to the bed and gently nudged his shoulder. "Henry?"

Somehow she knew instantly—as if a hidden place inside her was suddenly empty and aching and alone. In fact, she wondered later on if she hadn't known all along, even before she'd gotten out of bed in the first place. Maybe she'd just been trying to fool herself into thinking he was still breathing, or maybe she thought if she pretended it wasn't so, it simply wouldn't be. But the sorry truth was that Henry was dead. And although it was a warm June day, she could feel the cold emptiness in the room pressing in all around her—and throughout her. Her Henry was gone. And she was all alone.

She'd never told anyone how she'd climbed back into bed with him. Who would understand? Or how she'd wrapped her arms around him and lay there silently, trying to convince herself it wasn't so. She'd cried herself back to sleep, and when she awoke she thought perhaps it had all been a bad dream—a nightmare.

Howie and Daisy had been her source of strength during those days. Howie had arranged the funeral details with the pastor of their church and taken care of the newspaper obituary and flowers and headstone. All Dora had done was to pick out Henry's best suit and show up at the funeral. But she'd been stunned to see her son, Charlie, there that day, already seated conspicuously in the front row, wearing a navy three-piece suit and a striped tie, as if he thought he belonged.

"Who told Charlie?" she whispered to Howie as they stood in the back, waiting to be ushered to the front row where the family and close friends were meant to be seated.

"I thought you'd want him here," said Howie. "He's Henry's son."

She shook her head. "He's never acted like it."

"Henry loved him, Dora."

She frowned. "Yes, that's just it. Henry loved Charlie with his whole heart, but I never saw Charlie love him back—not once, not even as a little boy."

"Of course Charlie loved his daddy. And even if he did get a little big for his britches when he left home, Henry never held any of that against him, Dora. He never had a single bad word to say about his son."

She sniffed. "That's because Henry was a good man."

"Well, for Henry's sake, let's make Charlie welcome today."

She tried to be civil, and she wanted to act like a loving mother, but despite her best efforts she still resented her son's unexpected appearance at his father's funeral. Why, he hadn't been home in nearly a dozen years. All they'd ever heard from him was the occasional postcard or sometimes a Christmas card. And even when he married, they'd received only an announcement—not an invitation. Of course, he later explained that it was a very small wedding, just close friends and immediate family. As if she and Henry weren't *immediate* family. No, of course, they were *removed* family.

When Charlie and his wife had children—first a son, and then later a daughter—all they got from them was an announcement. And it didn't appear that he'd brought any of them with him today. She suspected it was because Charlie was still embarrassed by his parents and their countrified ways. He'd certainly made the implications more times than she cared to recall. Sometimes she thought he was even worse than his grandfather had been.

Oh, she was well aware of how she'd taken to talking and acting more and more like a farmer's wife over the passing years. Sometimes she thought she'd done it on purpose just to show snooty people like Charlie and her father that their opinions meant nothing to her. And then sometimes she thought that maybe she'd always talked that way. But that's not what Henry said. She still remembered the evening when he asked her about it. Not all that long before he had passed away.

"You've changed over the years, Dora," he'd said as they sat out on the porch together, watching the sunset.

"Of course." She smiled. "We've both changed. But I like the changes."

"But sometimes I feel sorry to think that maybe you changed yourself to fit in with me, Dora. That makes me feel bad."

"What in the world are you talking about?"

"Oh, it's nothing horrible. It's really just little things." He shrugged. "And, don't worry; it doesn't bother me none. But I guess it makes me a mite curious. I remember back when you were a girl in school and you were always so prim and proper and you spoke like you'd been educated in the finest academies." He smiled. "And I guess I kind of admired that in you."

"Oh, you did, did you?"

"Yes. I sort of looked up to you. And I even thought I wanted to become more like you. You know how I've tried to improve myself and my grammar over the years." He chuckled. "But I reckon old habits are hard to break and easy enough to slip back into if you're not paying close attention."

"So are you saying it's a bad thing if I've come to be more like you, Henry Herman Chase?"

He shook his head. "Nooo, no . . . it's not a bad thing."

"I happen to think you're the finest man I've ever known. I only wish I was a whole lot *more* like you."

He laughed. "I happen to like you just the way you are, darling."

"Well, then—" she winked at him—"what're you complaining about, old man?"

Even though they were past sixty by then, they still appreciated a night of passion and romance from time to time. And on that particular warm spring night, they turned off the porch light and slipped into the house and went to bed early. Dora smiled to herself. Henry Chase had been a very good man!

If things had gone differently they could've enjoyed many more of their golden years together. But for some reason Henry's life had been cut short. He was only sixty-three when he died.

Even now, Dora felt it had been unfair. Oh, she knew what people like Howie said: "Just be thankful you had someone you loved so much that it hurts to lose them." But she'd already lost her mother and Susan, and even her first unnamed baby. And she supposed if she were completely honest with herself, she might even include her father and Charlie on the list—although that seemed more their fault than hers. But all that losing of the ones she loved still seemed as unfair as ever before.

Howie could talk and talk till he was blue in the face about God's wanting to heal us from our hurts and disappointments, and about how Dora needed to forgive Charlie and her father and every-one else who had hurt her, and probably even God, for that matter. But the way Dora saw it, God owed her something in exchange for everything He had taken away from her. How could He expect her to give up even more—to give up the anger and bitterness that was all she had to hold on to these days?

She looked up and sighed. "Armando!" she called suddenly.

He came rushing over. "What's wrong?" he asked.

She was standing now. "Oh, nothing's wrong. I'm just ready to go home is all. I guess my work here is done now."

Chapter Twenty-Six

By the end of the following day, Armando had the sunflowers all planted in fairly straight rows about a foot apart. He hoped with practice his rows would become straighter and more even. Nevertheless, he was pleased. He stood next to the dark furrowed field and looked on with satisfaction. How long would it be before the seeds would wake up and send tiny green shoots through the soil?

"You all finished?" called Dora.

He turned to see her slowly walking his way. "Yeah, it's all planted."

"You made fairly good time—for a beginner, that is."

He nodded. "I wanted to get done today. I can't wait to see them growing." Then he frowned at her. "That was a pretty long walk for you to make."

She grinned. "I'm getting myself back into shape."

He tapped her cast, now worn and gray from wear. "Eager to get that thing off?"

"Don't you know it! My appointment's for ten o'clock tomorrow; now don't you forget."

He laughed. "So you've told me about a hundred times already." He glanced at his watch. "Guess I better clean up and get supper started."

"No need."

"Why's that?"

"Olivia called. She's coming over to talk to me about something or other and I asked her to pick up some Kentucky Fried Chicken for us."

Armando smiled. "Sounds good to me."

"And you might have enough time to take yourself a shower before she gets here too." She made a face as if she smelled something bad. "Not that you need one." Then she laughed and turned back to the house.

He barely had enough time to put the tractor away and run inside to take a shower before he heard voices talking downstairs. He knew Olivia was here but he felt nervous about seeing her. They hadn't actually spoken since that night he'd taken her to the hospital and he still couldn't be too sure about how she'd handled his intervention with her pills. He knew that someone like Tio Pedro would be absolutely furious about that kind of interference. But he hoped Olivia would be different. Still, you never knew how people might act when it came to things like drugs and addictions.

"Supper's on the table," called Dora as he came down the stairs. "Come and get it while it's hot."

He set his backpack by the door then joined them. "Smells good."

The table was unexpectedly quiet as they ate. Olivia's usual cheerful chatter seemed noticeably absent. And Armando, for the life of him, couldn't think of a single thing to say.

"Armando's got the sunflower field planted," said Dora as she buttered a biscuit.

"That's nice." Olivia took a serving of coleslaw. "I bet it'll be pretty when it starts to bloom. I might even try to paint it sometime when the light is right."

"Wouldn't that be lovely." Dora nodded. "I'd like to see you get more serious about your painting, Olivia. It's a shame to waste such good talent."

Olivia shrugged. "I'm not that good, Grandma. Ben says I just play at being an artist."

"How is Ben?" asked Armando, suddenly wishing he hadn't since it seemed that Olivia's face darkened at the mere mention of his name.

"I wouldn't know," she snapped.

"Aren't you two getting along?" asked Dora. Armando wondered if he didn't detect a note of hopefulness in her tone. But then she'd always made it clear, at least to him, that she wasn't overly fond of the man.

Olivia shook her head. "Oh, you know, just one of our many lovers' quarrels. It's what keeps things interesting."

Dora frowned. "I don't understand that. Sometimes I'll read one of those silly books that your mother's always giving me; you know the ones—where the hero and heroine are always fussing and feuding and acting like a couple of complete nincompoops, and I think to myself, why waste all that precious time fighting? Why, your grandpa and I—we hardly ever quarreled, and to this day I am eternally grateful. I would hate to think that I wasted one precious moment by being angry at that dear man."

Armando smiled. "I like your thinking, Dora."

Olivia scowled at him and then picked up her still half-filled plate. "I'm full," she said abruptly. She went over and dumped her uneaten food in the trash.

"Well, that's the way it is," continued Dora absently, "when you love someone, I mean. You don't want to waste valuable time fighting. In fact, Henry and I made a promise to each other, real early on." She chuckled. "We'd had the most ridiculous fight over something or other—I can't even recall what it was anymore; that's just how silly it was. Anyway, we'd gone to bed madder than wet hens and then got up the next morning all grumpy and tired and just plain upset. And that's when we decided it wasn't worth it, and we promised each other to never go to bed angry again. And I don't think we ever did. Or if we did it wasn't more than a time or two."

"That's nice, Grandma," said Olivia in a sharp-edged tone. "But what worked for you and Grandpa might not work for everyone else."

"I don't know about that," protested Dora. "I think if you really love each other, it should work—"

"Excuse me!" Olivia turned and left, slamming the front door behind her.

Dora glanced at Armando with worried eyes. "I think my girl is feeling a little troubled. Do you suppose it was something I said?"

"I . . . uh . . . I don't know."

"Well, go catch her, Armando." Dora nodded toward the door. "Please, tell her I'm sorry and to come back."

So he wiped his hands on the paper napkin and got up to see whether or not she'd left already. And the truth was, he almost hoped that she had. Olivia seemed to be in a pretty foul mood right now, and he couldn't help but think it might be partially his fault.

But she was still there. Standing out in the driveway with both her hands, one still bandaged, placed on the top of her car, almost as if she'd just been arrested and was about to be frisked for weapons.

"Hey," he called out in what he hoped sounded like a casual greeting.

She didn't answer.

He kept walking toward her, then stopped when he was about ten feet away, like he was afraid to get too close. "Your grandma told me to tell you she's sorry—"

"She's sorry?" Olivia turned to face him now and he could see two streaks of tears streaming down her flushed cheeks. *"You're* the one who should be sorry!"

"Why?"

She narrowed her eyes at him. "Because you . . . you stole my stuff."

"I didn't *steal* anything—"

She pointed her finger at him. "When you cleaned my apartment—you went into my bathroom and took my . . . my . . . well, you know what you did."

"*Your drugs?* You think I *stole* your drugs?"

She nodded. "Yeah. I didn't think you were like that—"

"Hey, I didn't *steal* your pills, Olivia." He tried not to laugh. "I just flushed them down the stupid toilet."

Her eyes grew wide. "*You flushed them down the toilet?* Don't you know how much that stuff costs?"

"I know what it costs you." He folded his arms across his chest and looked evenly at her.

Her eyes flashed with blue heat. "But you had no right—"

"I know." He nodded. "I realize I stepped over a line there. And I guess I'm a little bit sorry. But not too sorry. The truth is I didn't want to see you messing up your life anymore."

"Look, Armando, if I want to mess up my life, it's my business! Not yours!"

He took a step toward her. "But can't you see how you made it my business that night when I took you to the hospital? Can't you see how you made it my business when you made me care about you—" He stopped himself.

"You *care* about me?"

He shrugged, glancing uncomfortably back at the house. "Sure, of course I care. You're Dora's granddaughter. Why shouldn't I care?"

She rolled her eyes. "So you're saying you care about me just because I'm Dora's granddaughter?"

"No, that's not it." He looked up at the sky for a moment, searching for the proper answer. "I care about you because you're you,

Olivia. You're a person. And nobody should live like that. Didn't you hear what the doctor said?"

She slammed her fist on the top of her car. "He doesn't *know* about my life! He doesn't *know* how I feel or what I need! He doesn't—" Then she leaned into her car and started sobbing.

Armando stepped closer. "Olivia." He spoke quietly now. "I *really* want to help you if you'll let me."

She didn't look up. "Just go away, Armando. Just leave me alone. Maybe you can help my grandma, but you can't help me."

"Why not?"

"Can't you see I'm a lost cause? That's what my dad's always telling me—a lost cause . . . hopeless . . . a disappointment." She sobbed even louder.

"You're *not* a lost cause, Olivia. That's ridiculous."

"Yes, I am. Everyone says so."

Armando wanted to reach out and touch her, to wipe her tears, to push the hair away from her face, but he didn't. "Not everyone, Olivia."

She turned around, bending over to wipe her nose on the edge of her T-shirt. "Even Ben thinks I'm totally hopeless. He's pretty much given up on me."

"Then Ben is stupid."

She stared at Armando for a moment, and then to his surprise she actually laughed. "Yeah, maybe you're right. Ben *is* stupid!"

"So, what are you going to do then?"

She looked down at the ground. "I don't know for sure. I thought I knew this morning, but now I feel kinda confused all over again."

"Do you really want to keep taking that crud, Olivia?"

She didn't answer.

"Honestly, do you really think it's the best thing for you? Does it make your life any better? Are you happy with how things are going right now?"

She slowly shook her head. "No, of course not. I'm not a total idiot, Armando."

"Do you want to go to that rehab place the doctor told you about? I could drive you over there—tonight if you like."

She shook her head again. "I don't think that would work for me."

"Well, what then? You have to do something to make this change. I've seen it happen over and over again. Someone wants to quit and they say they're through with it, but before you know it they're back at it again, usually worse than before."

"I know." She looked up at him now. "But I haven't taken anything since Saturday night. That's two days."

He smiled. "That's great. But what about tomorrow?"

She sighed. "I don't know."

"You've got to make some changes, Olivia. Big ones."

"I went to NA last night."

"Narcotics Anonymous? Really?"

She nodded. "I felt like a fool at first. But then I listened and the people seemed fairly normal and actually pretty nice after a while."

"But is that enough? Just going to NA?"

"I also asked Grandma if I could live out here for a while."

"Really? You'd leave your apartment?"

"I think it might help, at least for the time being. There are people, you know, who live at the apartments . . . you know what I mean. I'm sure you met some of them at the party that night. . . . "

"Yeah. But would it be enough for you to stay out here?" He studied her closely. "What if you got tempted to go into town and, well, you know, make a score?"

"You could keep my car keys for me."

"You want me to be your jailor?"

She almost smiled. "Sort of. I mean it might help."

"Does Dora know about any of this?"

She firmly shook her head. "No, and I don't want her to know.

Grandma is the only one who believes in me. I think I'd die if she knew."

"Okay." He thought for a moment. "I guess it might work, if you're really willing that is." He peered into her eyes. "Are you?"

"I think I am."

He glanced into the backseat of her car. It was heaped with clothes and boxes and bags and stuff. "Are you moving in tonight?"

She smiled. "That was my plan."

He held out his hand.

"What?"

"Your keys."

She handed him the keys and he pocketed them. "Want some help?"

"Sure. Grandma told me I could have the upstairs, but she said I'll have to share the bathroom with you." She looked at him. "Is that okay?"

"Sure, it's okay. But just be warned, if I see any . . . uh . . . you know, controlled substances, they'll be going straight down the toilet."

She shook her head. "Honestly, Armando, I don't have anything on me."

He shrugged. "Well, I know enough about addiction to know you might be lying right now."

She nodded. "Yeah, I might be. But really I'm not. I don't have a thing, well, besides cigarettes that is. And you can't expect me to give up everything all at once."

"No, not everything."

"Even at NA they said to take this thing one day at a time."

"Yeah, that sounds wise." He opened the back door to her car. "How about if I help you take this stuff upstairs now."

She looked into his eyes. "Thanks, Armando."

After they unloaded the car, he parked it on the other side of the barn, where it would be out of sight and hopefully out of mind. Then he locked it and hid the keys in an old tin pail that he slipped beneath a loose floorboard in the barn. Just in case she went looking in his room while he was out in the fields.

Later that evening the three of them sat out on the front porch, sipping decaf coffee that Olivia had made and listening to Dora reminisce about life on the farm.

"That was one of the happiest times of my life," she continued, "back when your daddy was a little tyke and the three of us would meet down at the creek for lunch." She laughed. "I'd pack up a picnic basket and take Henry's fishing pole along with me—the big heavy one that his father used to use for deep-sea fishing. Then, after lunch, I'd tie one end of the line around little Charlie's waist and let him go wading up and down the creek, and I'd just reel him in whenever he got too far off. 'Course, the water was only a few inches deep that time of year, so I really didn't have anything to be too worried about, but after losing little Susan, well, you never knew."

Olivia took in a deep breath and slowly exhaled. "I just can't understand why Dad ever quit liking it out here."

Dora shook her head. "I don't know for sure, honey. But I think it started out when he was going to school and trying so hard to fit in with the town boys. They liked making fun of country folk."

"You mean they picked on Charlie because he lived on a farm?" asked Armando.

"Yep. They called him names and made jokes. They did it to all the country kids. Henry said it had always been like that, even back when we were kids. Guess I just never noticed."

"Maybe nobody ever picked on you," suggested Armando.

"Maybe not."

"Yeah, but lots of people get picked on," argued Olivia. "It doesn't have to turn a person against everything, especially his own parents." She turned to Armando. "I'll bet you've been picked on before."

He laughed. "Oh, yeah. I've heard my share of wetback jokes."

"But you don't seem angry and bitter."

He shrugged. "What good would that do?"

"None, I guess. But it proves my point. You don't have to change who you are or how you think just because you get picked on."

"Maybe people can't always see it," he countered her, "but I think you *do* change—on the inside anyway."

"What do you mean?"

"Well, you know that old saying about sticks and stones?"

"You mean they'll break your bones, but words will never hurt you."

"But the thing is, words *do* hurt," Armando continued. "They always take their toll. But I guess some of us simply choose not to show it."

Olivia nodded. "Yeah, I suppose you're right."

Armando knew he was right. And as they watched the rose-colored sky fade into deep shades of purple, he realized that words had probably hurt Olivia too. Her father's words, telling her she was useless and a failure and a grasshopper, and maybe even Ben's sharp words of criticism. And perhaps her escape, her way of fending off the harsh criticisms, had been to turn to drugs. Who knew? Or maybe he was feeling sorry for her tonight and making up excuses. But just the same, he wished there was a way to protect her from Charlie's unfeeling words, although he knew that was next to impossible. After all, Charlie was her father. And Armando was little more than a farmhand, not to mention a "dirty Mexican" in Charlie's opinion—or at least that's how those icy looks and barbed words made him feel.

But what would old Charlie think if he knew how Armando really felt about his only daughter? What kind of words would be flung around then? Of course, such feelings would remain Armando's secret. He had no reason to reveal anything to anyone. Olivia had simply come to him for help—that was all. And it would be wrong for him to think it was anything more than that. It was quite likely that when she got better—clean and free from her addictions— that perhaps Ben would come back for her. And maybe they would both be happy then.

Chapter Twenty-Seven

*A*rmando no longer relied on the little alarm clock to rouse him each morning. He automatically rose with the sun now. This eagerness to get outside and start the new day felt foreign to him, yet exhilarating. It reminded him of the carefree summer days of boyhood, back before his grandmother had died. Except that now he looked forward to work not play. Before going to bed last night, he'd jotted down even more ideas, like Dora had suggested. And after reading more in Henry's book and some careful thinking, he felt he knew the perfect spot to build a greenhouse. Today he would pace it out and see if it really worked.

Just as he pounded in the last wooden stake, roughly outlining his proposed site, he heard the sound of vehicles turning off the road and onto the gravel driveway. He glanced up to see a familiar-looking SUV and Charlie's white Buick parking near the barn. Two men climbed out of the SUV, and Charlie emerged from his car and peered at the house. All three men had on suits and one from the SUV carried a large roll of paper. Armando dusted the dirt off his hands, picked up the sledgehammer he'd used to pound the stakes, then slowly walked toward the men.

"Hey, Charlie," he called out in a neutral voice.

Charlie jerked his head in his direction with a slightly surprised expression then frowned. No response. He quickly turned to the other two men, speaking to them in hushed and confidential tones.

"What's up?" asked Armando as he continued to approach them.

"We have some important business to attend to," said Charlie in a dismissive voice, as if he were speaking to a young and bothersome child.

"And that would be?"

"None of *your* business!" snapped Charlie. One of the other men snickered.

Armando held up his chin as if preparing himself for another blow, verbal perhaps but fairly potent just the same. He cleared his throat. "Is your mother expecting you today, Charlie?"

"This *isn't* any of my mother's business either."

Armando firmly shook his head. "That's where you're wrong, Charlie. As long as this is your mother's property, I'd say it's her business."

"The court will decide exactly *whose* property this is." Charlie fished in his pocket for sunglasses.

"What do you mean?"

"Not that it's any of your business—" Charlie slipped on his sunglasses—"but since you seem determined to stick your nose into where it obviously doesn't belong, I have filed for my mother's guardianship and it's only a matter of time before I'll be handling all of her affairs—including this property."

Armando thought for a moment before he spoke. "Well, if that's true, Charlie, if it's *only a matter of time*, then maybe you'd better cool your jets and wait it out until the court actually decides."

Charlie's expression tightened. "Like I said before, this is none of your business."

"That's not how I see it. I work for Dora, managing this farm. And as long as this is her land, I'd say it *is* my business." He forced a stiff smile to his lips and absently swung the hammer back and forth along his side.

Charlie glanced quickly to the sledgehammer then back to Armando. "Are you threatening me, boy?"

Armando blinked then looked uncomfortably down at the hammer hanging loosely in his hand. "Of course, not, Charlie. I was just pounding in some stakes."

Charlie pointed toward the freshly planted field. "And what exactly do you think you're doing over there?"

"Farming."

"Well, you can stop wasting your time, not to mention my mother's money. This place is going to be developed for an industrial site and the sooner you get that through your thick skull the better." Armando knew that Charlie was glaring at him from behind the protective dark glasses.

"Well, until you have an official document stating—"

"Don't you have someplace you need to be, *boy?*"

Armando didn't budge but continued to look straight at Charlie. "Just right here."

"Well, then stay out of our way." Charlie glanced toward the other men, who seemed slightly less amused now and perhaps even a little concerned. "Sorry about this, guys. Time's wasting. Let's get to work now."

Armando stepped out of their way. "If you'll excuse me for a moment, I'll go inside and let your mother know you're here, Charlie." He paused and studied Dora's son. "Say, do you want to stop by the house and pay your respects—"

"No I do not!" He pointed to the field in front of them. "Come on; we have business to take care of."

Armando nodded. "Well, watch where you step, guys. We've got things growing out there that we don't want disturbed."

Charlie swore. Armando turned around and headed quickly for the house. His heart pounded and once again he fought back the urge to retaliate against Charlie with anger or even violence. He knew it was only the foolish way out, and probably the way Charlie would like him to react. It would help Charlie's case against his mother if he had witnesses who could testify to an attempted assault from the wild Mexican man. As he bounded up the porch steps, he wondered how to tell Dora. Should he protect her feelings? or simply report the truth? As he stepped through the door, he knew he could only do the latter. Dora was always straightforward and no-nonsense with him. Why should he play games with her now?

"Charlie's here," he announced when he found both Dora and Olivia in the bedroom. Olivia was pinning up Dora's hair.

Olivia groaned. "Oh, what does he want now?"

"He's got his developmental buddies with him and they're—"

Dora started to stand, making the loose hair slip from Olivia's hand. "For land sakes, Howie and I already told him to stay outta here!"

"I tried to tell him as much," said Armando. "But he wouldn't listen."

"Dad *never* listens—to anyone." Olivia placed her hand on her grandmother's shoulder. "Just sit still a minute and let me finish here."

Dora pressed her lips together, closing her eyes as Olivia put in the last few pins.

"There's something else," began Armando. "Something you should know, Dora." He leaned against the dresser so that she could see him, waiting until he knew he had her full attention. "Charlie says he's filed for legal guardianship of you."

Olivia slammed her fist into the dresser top then swore loudly. "Oh, I'm sorry, Grandma. But that man makes me so mad!"

Armando sadly shook his head. "Now I don't know exactly what that means, Dora, but Charlie claims he'll be managing your affairs as well as your property before long. At least, I think that's pretty close to the words he used."

Dora sat quietly, staring at her cast as it rested in her lap. Finally, she spoke. "Well, I figured it would come down to this sooner or later. I guess Charlie won't be happy until he's got everything—his way."

"But surely you can fight him?" Olivia set the box of hairpins down. "Doesn't Daddy have to prove you're incompetent or nutty or something to get guardianship?"

Dora nodded. "Yes, and I 'spect he's been building his case for some time now. Howie told me to prepare myself for this possibility—he thought it might come to this. And he warned me to be ready. He also said it can get pretty ugly if it really goes to court."

Olivia bent down and wrapped her arms around Dora. "I'm so sorry, Grandma. But, don't worry; we'll stick with you through the whole thing. She glanced up. "Won't we, Armando?"

"That's right, Dora. And I think old Charlie's going to be hard-pressed to prove you're incompetent."

She sadly shook her head. "Oh, don't be too sure about that. Sometimes folks think you're getting senile just because you're getting old—or because you forgot where you put your house key or left the water running or walked outside with no shoes on—"

"I think Dad's the one who's crazy!" Olivia headed for the door. "And I'm going to go out there to tell him so!"

Armando shook his head. "I don't think that's such a good idea—"

"He's *my* father, Armando! I can tell him off if I want to!"

"But it'll only make things worse."

She turned to Dora. "What do you think, Grandma?"

Dora grew thoughtful. "I think I want him and his men off of my property right now."

"You and me both, Grandma."

Dora stood. "And I don't care who tells him so."

Armando watched as the two women headed to the front door. He knew there was probably no stopping them now, but he also knew their outrage would most likely backfire on them. "Hey, you want me to call Howie, Dora?" he asked before they were completely out the door.

"Good thinking, Armando. The number's right there by the phone."

He found the number and dialed, waiting impatiently for the old man to answer. "Howie?" he said quickly. "Charlie's out here with some development guys, and Dora and Olivia are going outside to give 'em what for."

"I'll be there as soon as I can," said Howie. "You just try to keep things calm until I arrive, Armando. It sure won't help matters to set off the fireworks."

Armando hung up the phone and raced outside to catch up with the women. Fortunately they hadn't even reached the barn yet, and Charlie and his men weren't anywhere in sight.

"Hey," he called out as he jogged to catch them. "I just talked to Howie."

Dora paused to listen. "What'd he say?"

"He said he was coming over right now and he wants you guys to cool it until he gets here."

"*Cool it?*" Dora frowned. "Did Howie actually say that?"

Armando smiled. "Not exactly. But he wants everyone to stay calm. He said it won't help anything to get all excited."

"But I want them *off* my property!" exclaimed Dora.

"Yeah, they have no right to be here!" agreed Olivia, shaking her bandaged fist in the air.

Armando looked at the pair of them and suddenly, despite himself, he started to chuckle.

"What in heaven's name is so funny, Armando?" demanded Dora.

"Just you two." He pointed to Dora's cast and then to Olivia's bandage. "You look like the walking wounded about to go into battle against the big guns."

"Well, somebody's got to stand up for Grandma!"

"Yeah. But maybe you should wait—" Just then he spotted all three men coming their way. They were still a ways off, but it looked like they were coming from the direction of his garden project over by the creek. And this made Armando angry.

"What's wrong, Armando?" asked Olivia.

"Oh, nothing." He attempted to divert his eyes, but not fast enough.

Olivia turned to see. "There they are, Grandma!" She took a step toward them. "Here come those dirty stinkin' rats!"

"Looks like they've been over by the creek too," said Dora, squinting in the sun toward them. "Hope they didn't tromp all over your flowers again, Armando."

He felt his fists clinch, but remembering Howie's warning, Armando forced himself to take in a slow deep breath. "We need to remain calm," he said quietly, mostly to himself.

So Armando and the two slightly disabled women stood their ground, waiting by the barn for the interlopers.

"What's going on here, Mom?" asked Charlie in a voice that seemed to suggest that absolutely nothing was out of the ordinary.

"That's just what I was about to ask you, Charlie." Armando thought he saw a steely glint in the old woman's eyes.

Charlie smiled as if nothing was wrong. "I'm showing the guys the lay of the land again. Like I told you a couple weeks ago."

"You did nothing of the sort—"

"Aw, Mom, there you go forgetting things again." He turned to the other two men, holding up his hands apologetically. "She's getting on in years, you know; she has a hard time remembering—"

"I remember this is *my* property!" Dora spat out the words. "And if I have to I'll defend it with everything I've got against the likes of you, Charles Lawrence!"

"Now, don't you go flying off the handle, Mom. You don't plan on getting out your old shotgun again, do you?" He chuckled for their benefit. "She even tried to shoot Armando here once, didn't she, boy?"

Armando didn't answer. Instead he met Charlie's gaze evenly, his face like a stone.

"You've gone too far this time, Dad!" Olivia stepped up to him now, putting her face less than a foot from her father's. "You leave Grandma alone or you're going to be sorry."

"This is none of your business, Olivia." Charlie took on a bored tone now, as if he'd rehearsed this all beforehand. "But if you must know, I'm only trying to help your grandmother. We all know she's too old to keep this place up, and besides, I'm worried about her safety."

"You're a big fat liar, Dad!"

"Olivia!" He shook his head sharply, appearing to be shocked. "How dare you speak to me like that."

"Why's that, Daddy? Am I embarrassing you in front of your new buddies?" She turned and looked at the men now, and it was plain to see they were growing increasingly uncomfortable. "Don't you guys realize you're wasting your time here? This land is not for sale! Not today, not tomorrow, not ever! The sooner you figure that out the better off we'll all be."

Dora took a step forward and nodded firmly. "That's right, fellas. This land belonged to my husband, Mr. Henry Herman Chase. He built it from nothing into a farm—"

"A *farm?*" Charles let out a cynical laugh. "You call *this* a farm? Oh, sure, you pull a few weeds and plant a few seeds and—" Suddenly he turned and looked at Armando as if this unhappy confrontation was all his fault. "And what on earth do you think you're doing digging that great big hole over there by the creek? You trying to flood the place?" He turned to his mother now. "Do you know what this kid is up to over there?"

She glanced uneasily at Armando but didn't answer.

"I asked you a question, Mom. Did you have any idea that he's digging the whole place up and—"

"Maybe he's hunting for the treasure," she said quickly.

"The *treasure?*" Charlie made a mocking sigh now. "Good night, I think all three of you have gone completely mad!" He turned to the men, who appeared fairly uneasy with this little family dispute. "Hey, don't worry, guys. According to my attorney, this land is as good as mine. Let's go back to my office now and work out the details on paper." And with that, the three men climbed back into their vehicles and drove off, leaving nothing but a cloud of dust behind them.

Armando looked at Dora. She was shaking. "Are you okay?"

"I'm so angry I could spit!" Her wrinkled face was pinched into a tight little knot. "How can it be possible that that horrible man is my very own son?"

Olivia took her by the arm and slowly led her back toward the house. "Calm down, Grandma." She spoke soothingly. "Maybe Armando was right. Maybe it doesn't do any good to get all worked up like this. I think we need to get some breakfast into you. And pretty soon Howie will get here and we can discuss this whole thing calmly."

Armando followed behind them, relieved to see Olivia finally showing some good sense. Because right now, he wasn't so sure he could continue to remain calm. He felt enraged by Charlie's arrogance and disrespect of Dora, and despite himself Armando almost wished he'd allowed his temper to flare too. The things he'd like to say to that ignorant selfish man! But what good would come of it? Come to think of it, what good had any of their words done today? If anything, it seemed likely that they'd only tossed Charlie more ammo to shoot back at them with. But even so, Armando wished he'd given old Charlie boy a great big piece of his mind— along with a piece of something else!

They'd sat down to a little breakfast when Howie showed up.

Armando went to get the door, giving him a quick report before he invited him to join them for breakfast. "It's only oatmeal, but we made a big pot."

"Oatmeal sounds real good to me," said Howie, hanging his hat on the hook by the door. "Sorry it took me a while to get here, but I stopped by the hardware store to pick these up." He opened up a brown paper bag and removed several No Trespassing signs and laid them on the kitchen table. "Hello, ladies." He smiled at Dora and Olivia.

"What are those for?" grumbled Dora.

"I want Armando to post them by the entrance from the road as well as on the fence that borders the highway," said Howie. "Posting these signs makes it illegal for Charlie or any of his boys to come in here without permission. They'll be trespassing and we can press charges."

Dora smiled. "Good."

"And we can take it a step further if you like, Dora." Howie paused as Olivia set a bowl of oatmeal before him; then he bowed his head and said a quiet prayer.

"A step further?" repeated Dora in an impatient tone. "What do you mean?"

"We could get a restraining order against your son." Howie picked up his spoon. "But that might be overkill."

"A restraining order?" Dora set down her coffee cup. "What exactly does that mean?"

"It means that Charlie would be breaking the law if he came round here uninvited or otherwise, and he could be fined or even put in jail for harassing you."

She frowned. "I don't really like the sound of that, Howie. I know he's a bad egg and all, but it just goes against the grain making it illegal for your own flesh and blood to come calling. Somehow I don't think my Henry would like it."

Howie smiled. "I don't think he would, either."

"*I'd* like it," said Olivia.

"Those No Trespassing signs ought to do the trick," said Howie. "Now as far as Charlie's petition for guardianship, I'll draw up our response to him this afternoon. And when I convince him that he's going to have a long, drawn-out, and expensive court battle on his hands, he might think twice about this whole thing. 'Course, I'm sure he's hoping to wear you down, Dora, to coax you into just giving in."

"He'd have better luck charming the stripe off of a skunk."

Olivia laughed. "He's already done that, Grandma. You didn't see any stripe on his back, did you?"

They discussed their strategy further and Howie assured them that everything would be completely under control by the end of the day. "That computer company isn't going to want anything to do with Charlie once they realize that there's a court dispute tied to the deal. Mark my word, they'll be looking elsewhere before lunchtime."

"Good." Dora held her cast up in the air. "And we can all celebrate because I'll have my cast off by then too." She glanced at Olivia. "Speaking of that, why don't you help me finish cleaning up so I'll look respectable for my doctor's appointment?"

Howie stayed for another cup of coffee while Armando cleared the table. "I'm sure glad you're staying out here with Dora," he said.

"Yeah, I'm glad too."

"Is Olivia staying out here too?"

"Just for a while." Armando wiped off the table.

Howie nodded. "I know Olivia's had some problems." He cleared his throat. "But all in all I think she's really a good kid— just a little mixed-up."

Armando didn't know what to say, and he wondered exactly how much Howie actually knew about her situation.

"You haven't met her brother yet, have you?"

"You mean Charlie's son? Dora told me a little about him, but I haven't met him. Doesn't he live in Seattle?"

"Yeah. He's barely thirty but already big in the banking business. Takes after his great-grandpa, I suppose."

"And his dad?"

"I guess so."

"It's funny how they're so different," said Armando as he rinsed a juice glass.

"You mean Dora and Charlie?"

"Yeah. And Olivia too. It's hard to believe they're all related sometimes."

"Maybe. But in some ways Charlie and Dora are a lot alike too. They're both pretty stubborn and set in their ways," Howie observed.

"I suppose. But at least Dora's not trying to take something away from someone else."

Howie stood and carried his empty coffee cup over to the sink. "Not everything can be seen with your eyes, Armando."

"Huh?"

"You know, sometimes things aren't exactly what they appear to be." He patted him on the back. "You're a good kid, Armando. Now don't forget to post those signs where I told you."

"Sure, I'll get right to it."

"You take care now, and call me if anything new comes up."

"Thanks, Howie."

Armando quickly finished the dishes and hurried outside to post the signs along the fence. As he pounded a nail into the fence, he considered Howie's words about not seeing everything with your eyes. Although he sort of understood what the old man was insinuating—because there were things in life that you can sense or feel without actually seeing—he still wasn't completely sure how that all applied to Dora and Charlie. Was Howie suggesting that Dora had taken something away from Charlie too?

And yet it seemed that the only thing she had that Charlie wanted was her property, and if he'd be patient and play his cards right, he'd probably get all that someday anyway. Armando just hoped that day was a long way off.

Chapter Twenty-Eight

Armando felt bad to hear Olivia snapping at her grandmother, but he also knew she was fighting her own demons right now. Still, how could poor Dora understand why her granddaughter didn't want to drive her into town for her doctor's appointment? In exasperation, Olivia made some lame excuse that finally satisfied her grandmother and Armando went outside to start the pickup.

"Don't know what's wrong with my girl," said Dora after he'd helped her into the cab. "Guess she's just moping over her goofy Ben fellow." Dora puckered her lips into a frown. "Don't know why that should trouble her so. I felt it was a poor match right from the start."

Armando shrugged and put the truck into gear.

Dora pointed to the No Trespassing sign at the entrance of the driveway. "You really think that's going to stop Charlie?"

"Howie seems to think so." He turned onto the highway.

Her chin jutted out in determination. "Well, Howie knows about these things. I 'spect he's right."

"I hope so. But, Dora, I don't understand why Charlie's so determined to turn your farm into a stupid industrial site." He shook his head sadly. "It doesn't make a bit of sense."

"It makes sense to him," said Dora sharply. "*Dollars* and cents!"

"But it seems so disrespectful—to you and his father. It even makes Olivia angry. Doesn't Charlie care about family at all?"

"Charlie left his family far behind a long time ago. He cut his ties to us when he took off to college and never looked back. Why, other than a wedding announcement and a couple of birth announcements, we hardly heard a word from him for years. Sometimes I think that's what killed my Henry—the poor man died of a broken heart. Oh, he wouldn't have admitted it, no matter how bad he felt. He always made excuses for his boy, saying how Charlie was only chasing after a dream just the way Henry had chased after his own dreams. But it hurt him deeply. I know it did."

"Did it hurt you too?"

She was silent for a while, just staring out at the highway in front of them. But then she spoke in a voice so quiet he could barely hear her words. "I 'spect it did some."

He glanced over at her and suddenly felt guilty for making her sad—especially after she'd already suffered through a pretty hard morning. "Lots of good people get hurt when families break apart. I know it hurt my grandmother when her daughter left and never looked back."

"You mean your mother?"

He nodded. "Yeah. My aunt managed to locate her when my grandmother was dying. And we all hoped she'd come pay her final respects. But she never did."

Dora made a *tsk-tsk* sound with her tongue. "That's too bad."

"But my grandmother never held it against her—even as she was dying. In fact, that's when she made me promise that I'd forgive my mother."

"And you really believe you did?"

"Like I said before, it's something I'm still working on. Sometimes I think I forgave her, and sometimes, like if things are tough and I'm feeling down, I have to forgive her all over again."

"Well, I think it's easier said than done."

"Maybe Howie was right about that too."

"About what?"

"Maybe it does take God's help to *really* forgive someone."

"Humph." She turned and looked out the side window. "Don't know about that."

They were coming into town now and she focused her attention on directing him toward her doctor's office. "You see that big stone church over there?" She pointed to an impressive tall building across from the medical complex.

He nodded. "Nice."

"That was my dad's church."

"It looks old."

"It is. The windows are real pretty when the sun comes shining through. We used to go every Sunday when I was growing up. But after I got married, well, things changed."

"Did you get married in that church?"

"Land sakes, no!"

"Why did you stop going?"

"It was easier not to go. Besides, that's where my dad attended."

"Oh."

"And that's where Charlie and Audrey go now."

Armando parked in front of the medical complex and helped Dora from the truck then walked her into the reception area. "I'll just wait outside," he told her once she was seated with a recent issue of *Ladies' Home Journal.* "Maybe I'll check out that old church."

She nodded. "You do that."

The sun shone brightly outside, and Armando wished he'd thought to put on a ball cap as he crossed the street to get a closer look at the big stone church. He walked up the wide front steps, also made of stone, and examined the enormous double doors, intricately carved with images of trees and leaves and flowers. He ran his hand over the surface of the wood and wondered how long it took to carve such a piece.

"Armando!" called a woman's voice. "Is that really you?"

He turned to see Olivia's mother coming up from behind him. She had on a white pantsuit and carried a large flat box in both hands. "Do you need help?" he asked.

She smiled. "Yes. Could you get the door for me?"

He pushed open the heavy door and held it open as she walked in. "Do you want me to carry that for you?"

"No. I'm fine now. Do you want to come inside and see the place?"

"Sure." He smiled. "Dora said the windows are pretty."

She nodded. "Oh, they are. I need to take this cake down to the basement. We're having a women's tea this afternoon and I have to get things set up. But you go ahead and look around all you like."

"No one will mind?"

"Of course not. This is a church. Everyone's welcome here."

Armando wondered if her husband would be in agreement with that, especially after this morning's confrontation. But since old Charlie wasn't anywhere around to make a fuss, he decided to take her up on the offer. He listened as her footsteps echoed down the stairwell then turned toward what he assumed was the direction of the kitchen. He paused before he went in, taking time to read the shiny brass plaque displayed prominently on the wall. The name "Lawrence" caught his eye. It was a memorial to the pioneer family who had helped found the church more than a hundred years ago—Dora's ancestors. Armando wondered what it would feel like to have such an important family in the community. Then he shook his head. It sure didn't seem to make much difference to Dora. Her family obviously had as many troubles as any other family, if not more.

He pushed open another carved wooden door, not as large as the exterior ones but just as beautifully carved, and entered the sanctuary. Of course, he knew this wasn't a Catholic church, and according to some people he probably shouldn't even go in here, but to his surprise there was something familiar and slightly comforting about the space. Maybe it was the high ceilings or the rows of polished wooden pews or pieces of religious art, but something about the hushed stillness and holy quiet brought an unexpected sense of reverence to him. And before he even realized what had happened, he found himself in a back pew, kneeling. He wasn't actually praying—not with real words anyway. But something in his heart felt like it was opening up, or maybe it had already been open, but for the first time in a long time, maybe even since he'd been a boy, he felt like he was actually in God's presence.

He looked up at the stained-glass image of Jesus, portrayed as a shepherd, and considered once again what Howie had said about believing in Jesus and having a personal relationship with Him. It seemed unlikely that Jesus, the Son of Almighty God, really wanted a personal relationship with a nobody like Armando Garcia. Was it even possible? He looked down at his hands lying limply in his lap, stained from work, and perhaps the dirtiness of life in general. *Is it even possible?* And yet he knew he needed *something* in his life. Something beyond the haunting taunts of Tio Pedro. Something beyond the encouraging yet fading memories of Abuela Maria. And something beyond his current precarious relationship with Dora. He knew that his longing for family, longing to belong to something bigger than himself, was probably unrealistic. And yet it never left him. He wondered if what he really longed for was that relationship that Howie had described. A faith that was bigger than Catholicism, deeper than religion, something he could hold on to with both hands. Something that could hold on to him. But was it even possible?

He wasn't sure how long he stayed there like that, with his head bowed down as he silently pondered these things. But finally he looked up. And when he saw the stained-glass shepherd—all lit by the sun, like Dora had described, and pouring out an image of light—it was as if Jesus Himself were smiling down on him. It felt like something in him was both being broken and clicking right into place—in the same moment. Just like that. And in that moment, he prayed—he felt sure it was a prayer—and he asked Jesus to come into his heart. And then he said, "Thank You." As simple as that.

Armando felt certain he would never be able to explain this phenomenon to anyone. And yet he believed it was for real and not just a figment of his imagination. He had no idea what the next step would be, but as he quietly slipped out of the church, it felt as if some weight had been lifted. He felt hopeful. His steps lightened as he headed back toward the medical complex and he smiled to himself as he waited out in the parking lot until Dora emerged with her arm finally free of the old cumbersome white cast. Her arm looked thin and pale and slightly shriveled, the way his finger might look after leaving a Band-Aid on too long.

"How's it feel?" he asked as he gently helped her into the pickup.

"Just fine."

"So you're all healed up okay?"

"The doctor gave me some silly exercises to do and a little red ball to squeeze and play with." She laughed. "I guess he thinks I'm a little child."

"You need anything in town?"

"No. I just want to go home."

They rode home quietly. Armando appreciated the silence. He didn't want to tell Dora about visiting her childhood church. Not yet anyway. He didn't think she'd quite understand. In fact, he doubted that anyone would fully get it. He knew he didn't. It just felt like he was returning to what he'd been taught from his earliest days of boyhood, lessons he'd learned at his grandmother's knee. Lessons that had been meaningful, yet never completely absorbed. And somehow he felt that Abuela Maria was smiling down on him right now. And that in itself was reassuring. It'd been a long time since he'd really felt like his life would please her.

Olivia was out on the porch pacing nervously when they got back. Her expression was clearly troubled.

"Something wrong?" asked Dora as she climbed up the steps.

Olivia frowned. "I guess I shouldn't be surprised."

"About what?"

"Dad just called to inform me that he gave notice on my apartment today. I have to be out by tomorrow."

Dora shrugged. "Oh, is that all? Well, don't worry; you can stay out here with me for as long as you like."

"I know, Grandma. But it really irks me that he'd do that."

"Well, you said yourself you're not taking classes this summer. And your folks got you that place while you were going to school—"

"I know. But can't you see that he's only doing this to be vengeful?"

"Maybe it's for the best," suggested Armando.

Olivia scowled as she nervously chewed on the side of a cuticle.

"You want me to help you move your stuff?" he offered.

"I don't know!" she snapped. Then she went into the house and slammed the door behind her.

"Goodness," said Dora. "She's sure in a snit."

Armando shrugged. "Well, I'm going to work now."

"Wait a minute." She held up a finger. "You and I have some unfinished business to attend to first." She sat down in the rocker and put her oversized purse in her lap. "I'd meant to do this in town, but it doesn't matter." She pulled out a slip of official-looking paper. "This is the deed for the pickup. I've already signed on this line." She pointed to her shaky-looking signature. "And Howie said you're supposed to sign right there." She dug in her purse until she found a ballpoint pen.

He sat down and signed his name then smiled. "Thank you, Dora. I promise to take really good care of it."

She nodded. "I know you will."

He started to stand.

"Now, hold on there a minute. I have something else too." She fumbled around in her purse until she finally pulled out a dog-eared white envelope. "Here. I know that old pickup isn't worth much. And if you hadn't rescued it, well, it'd just be going to rack and ruin anyway." She handed him the envelope. "This is your real wages."

"But—"

"No *buts*. I told you we had an agreement. And I mean to treat you fairly." She waved her hand. "Now, go on, off with you. I know you have work to do."

"Thank you—"

"Don't thank me." She stood now. "But I do have a question for you."

"What's that?"

"Well, you heard as well as I did what Charlie said this morning. He was complaining about how you were digging something up down by the creek." She frowned. "What exactly are you doing down there anyway?"

He grinned. "You mean like am I looking for the hidden treasure?"

"Oh, you know good and well I just said that."

He tried to appear surprised. "But what about the old gold miner and his buried treasure you told me about?"

"Oh, I knew you wouldn't fall for such nonsense." She paused for a moment with a worried expression. "You didn't, did you?"

"I don't know . . . " He played her along. "Finding a lost treasure could be pretty exciting."

"I know you're just fooling with me now."

He smiled. "Well, you already know how I'm working on a little garden area over there, but it's meant to be a surprise. Anyway, it's almost ready now and I wanted to invite you back there to see it, maybe later on this week. I thought maybe we could invite Howie too. And Olivia, of course. Would that be okay?"

"It's okay by me."

He didn't count the money until he got back to his room. By his calculation it was a generous wage, enough to cover the entire time he'd been working here—and far more than he'd expected. In light of this, it seemed the pickup was actually more like a gift. And for some reason that had nothing to do with money that made him very happy. It was as if she had wanted him to have the truck all along.

He noticed the small stack of letters left behind by Manuel, the farmhand, still sitting on the chair by his bed. Just last night he'd been translating another one of the old letters, and in it, Manuel's wife had said how much she needed extra money for the children. Of course that had been more than thirty years ago, but the urgency of her plea reminded him of his own aunt and her three little girls. And for the first time since leaving L.A., he felt seriously concerned for their welfare. With Tio Pedro in jail, maybe even sentenced by now if he'd been convicted, along with the absence of Armando's monthly financial contributions, they might really be hurting. And despite Tia Marta's faults—mostly loving a good-for-nothing man— she had opened her home to Armando at a time when he needed family. And he had been fond of his little cousins. Last night he had longed for something he could do to help them and now he set aside a portion of the money, determined to somehow get it to them, hopefully without revealing his whereabouts. Maybe he could send a money order through Mickey. He felt pretty sure he could trust his old friend.

Armando worked harder than ever for the rest of the day. Barely stopping for lunch, he worked to clear out overgrown brambles and weeds from another section of field and prepared it to be plowed under. His plan was to dig up various seedling trees that had sprung up here and there along the creek and to bundle their root wads into burlap bags like he'd seen in the book, and then move them to the cleared section where they could grow straight and tall and perhaps one day be sold individually to landscapers. Suddenly the possibilities on this small farm felt endless to him—only as limited as his imagination, which seemed to expand daily.

That evening after supper, he sat at the kitchen table with Dora and went over his lists and plans with a fervor and excitement that he hadn't felt since he'd been a boy anticipating his tenth birthday and the brand-new dirt bike he knew his grandmother had hidden in the neighbor's garage. "I know it's a lot to do all at once," he finally said to Dora after they'd gone over the whole thing. "So I've tried to break it up into stages—stage one, two, and three. I figure each one could take up to a year, maybe longer."

Dora studied the last page of his plan and nodded. "Looks sensible to me."

"I thought I could talk to George at the Feed & Seed some too. He seems to know a lot about growing, and he could probably give me a pretty good idea about how much this would cost to get going."

She nodded. "You might even ask him to come out here and look around. Henry used to do that with George's father. I think Bill Foster used to call it a 'field consultation' or something official sounding like that." She laughed. "But I used to say that it was just an excuse for him to get his hands on my hot cinnamon rolls. Henry used to always have me make a big batch before Bill came out here."

Armando smacked his lips. "Sounds good to me. I wonder if George has the same sweet tooth as his father."

"I'm sure I could dig up that old recipe." She glanced toward the stairway. "And maybe if Olivia can get out of her foul mood, she'd give me a hand too." She lowered her voice. "She really seems upset over Ben. I didn't realize they were so serious."

"Did she say anything more about what she wants to do about her apartment?"

"I can hear you two down there talking about me," Olivia called from the top of the stairs. "It's not like I'm some crazy person, you know."

Armando glanced up to see her emerge from the shadows. She had on cutoffs and a paint-splotched T-shirt. Her face looked taunt and especially pale in the dim light of the stairway.

"Hey, how's it going?" he asked in what he hoped was a friendly tone. "We missed you at supper."

"I set you a plate in the fridge," said Dora. "You feeling any better now?"

Olivia made a smirky face. "I'm fine, Grandma. And contrary to what you think, I'm *not* pining away over Ben. I haven't felt like myself, is all." She sat on the bottom step, pulling her knees to her chin and reminding Armando of a little girl—a lost little girl.

"Did you want me to help you get your things from the apartment?" he asked. "I bet we could do it with a couple pickup loads."

She nodded. "Yeah, I was thinking it might be good to do that." She looked at her watch. "You want to do it tonight?"

"Sure, if you feel like it."

"Yeah. I guess I better. Otherwise Daddy dearest might send someone in there and have it all carted off to Goodwill or who knows where."

"Well, don't wear yourselves out," warned Dora. "And you make sure you get something to eat first, Olivia."

"Yeah, yeah." Olivia nodded.

And so they spent the rest of the evening going through Olivia's apartment, packing up the items she wanted and loading them into the back of the pickup. To Armando's relief, she decided to leave most of the large furniture behind.

"These pieces really belong to my parents anyway," she

explained. "I don't want my dad coming over to Grandma's and accusing me of stealing any of his precious belongings." She kicked the sofa with her tennis shoe then cussed as she rubbed her injured toe.

"I think we can do this in one trip," said Armando as they loaded a couple more boxes into the nearly full pickup bed.

Olivia sighed and leaned her head back, gazing at the star-filled night. "Seems a waste of a beautiful spring night to be stuck moving all this crud."

He looked at her and hoped that some of the old Olivia would be returning soon. "I don't mind," he said quietly.

She turned and looked at him, then suddenly laughed. "Armando, sometimes you just seem too good to be real."

He laughed. "Guess you should get to know me better then."

"Guess so."

They finished loading the truck then drove back to the farm. The cab was so silent that Armando thought maybe Olivia had fallen asleep, but when he sneaked a glimpse he saw her sitting there with her eyes wide open, staring through the windshield, up at the sky.

"Maybe we should wait until morning to unload it," he suggested as he parked in the driveway and turned off the engine.

"Yeah. It looks like Grandma's gone to bed. No sense in disturbing her."

They stood outside the pickup for a moment, just listening to the night—to the rhythmic sounds of frogs and crickets, before Armando finally spoke. "I know your apartment was real nice and everything, Olivia . . . but it sure wasn't as peaceful as it is out here."

She nodded. "Yeah. I won't miss all that traffic noise and the neighbors."

"Sometimes I feel so at home here that I can hardly believe I spent my whole life living down in L.A. It's weird."

"You don't miss it ever?"

"Not yet."

"That's good." She sighed. "Thanks for your help tonight, Armando."

"No problem." He looked down to her still-bandaged hand. "Was all that lifting and carrying hard on your stitches?"

"Nah. I think it's about time for them to come out." She laughed. "Doesn't that whole thing at the hospital seem like a long time ago now?"

"Sort of."

She reached over and put her hand on his arm. "And I really do appreciate your help with *that* too."

"Are you feeling okay?"

"Getting better. I know I was kinda witchy today. And I can't guarantee that tomorrow will improve. Honestly, there were times today when I felt like I could've torn somebody's head off or chewed on nails. That's why I didn't come down for dinner—I knew I'd do something unforgivable. And I feel really bad for Grandma. I'm sure she thinks I'm a total mess."

"She just thinks you're sad about Ben."

Olivia didn't say anything.

"So do you think you guys will get back together in time?"

"I don't know."

"Well, I'm sure it's getting pretty late." Armando stretched his arms to get the crick out of his shoulder. "I guess we should be hitting the hay."

"Yeah. But thanks again. And if I'm a grump tomorrow, I'll tell you that I'm sorry in advance, okay?"

"Hey, don't worry about it. I'm sure you'll be back to your old sweet self before long."

She laughed but there was a cynical edge to it. "Now, we're not really sure what that might be, are we? I mean I could be an absolute monster without my little happy pills and go-to-sleep pills and all those feel-good-in-between pills."

"Somehow I don't think so."

"You're such an optimist, Armando."

He thought about that as he walked to his room. Maybe she was right. Maybe he was something of an optimist. Abuela Maria had always told him to look for the bright side of things. And he usually tried to find the good in people. But he also knew that his optimism had gotten him in trouble a few times too. Sometimes he'd believed in the wrong people—trying to see the best in them—and then been let down. And sometimes even worse than that. He wondered if that's not how he was seeing Olivia now. Hoping the best for her, and, well, who knew what else? But perhaps he was only setting himself up for another great big letdown. And somehow he suspected it would be a hard one. But then that would be his own fault.

He sat down on his bed and picked up the old Bible again, opening it up to where he'd last read—in Ephesians. He continued reading there, stopping at the part where it spoke of being dead in sin but alive in Christ. And for some reason that actually made sense to him tonight. He wasn't sure why, since a lot of what he'd been reading felt rather cryptic and murky. Maybe it was the experience at the old church today, or maybe it was something that had been happening for a while and he hadn't even noticed. But when he came to the part that said "by grace you have been saved through faith; and this is not your own doing, it is the gift of God—not because of works, lest any man should boast," he had to stop and read those lines again and again and again. And somehow it finally sank in and actually made sense.

So for the second time that day, Armando prayed. Only this time he got down on his knees and prayed in real audible words. He asked God to help him understand these things as well as what had transpired in the church, and to make these things real in his life. And he asked God to help him return to the faith of his childhood.

And when he said, "amen" he realized that perhaps he'd never really left that faith in the first place, but had only suppressed it and ignored it. Perhaps his faith had been like a dormant seed, planted deep within his heart and quietly waiting—not unlike the sunflower seeds he had so recently sowed—to sprout forth when the time was right. He went to bed that night with a strong sense of hope and peace—and an indescribable assurance that all would be well.

Chapter Twenty-Nine

By Thursday morning, Armando was ready to go to town and talk to George about what was needed at the farm. But first he went to the automotive store and picked up a few parts for his pickup. He didn't buy the things he'd originally planned to get, back when he'd imagined getting the truck into perfect shape. Now he'd simply settle for having it running well. The paint and extras would have to come later.

After that he went to Foster's Feed & Seed and talked to George about some of his ideas, including the greenhouse and several other things.

"And Dora really wants to do all this?" George looked curiously at him.

Armando nodded. "She thought you might even be willing to come out for a consultation and she offered to make cinnamon rolls."

George laughed. "Well, if that don't beat all. How old is old Dora now anyway?"

"She's eighty-one but pretty spry, especially now that her broken arm is better. This morning she was outside working in her flower beds, up to her elbows in dirt and happier than ever."

"I can just see her." George handed him some plant catalogs. "Well, take a look in these and see if that doesn't help you some." He looked in a little notebook. "And I could come out for a field consultation the middle of next week. I'll give a call first."

"Sounds good." Armando glanced around the barnlike store. "I'm wondering, do you have anything for a pond?"

"A pond? You mean an irrigation pond?"

"Not exactly. It's more of a decorative pond in an area that I've been working into a garden."

George nodded. "Hey, that's a great idea, Armando. Lots of nurseries have ponds these days. They use them to grow pond plants and stock them with fish—it's a good business. I have a few things over here, some pumps and liners and whatnot. I heard you can get goldfish to stock your pond with over at the pet store on Main Street. They're nice and cheap, but they can grow pretty big if you feed them regularly. And, if you want, I'll give you the name of a lady I recently met who sells pond plants like lily pads and what have you. She was in here last week telling me all about it."

"Sounds great."

"I'd like to see that pond myself when you're all done. I've been thinking about putting in something like that in my own yard. Maybe with a fountain too; I like the sound of water."

"Well, I'm having sort of a grand-opening party tomorrow evening at seven," said Armando. Suddenly he felt a little self-conscious. Why would an important businessman like George Foster want to come see Armando's little garden?

"Hey, that sounds interesting. I don't have any plans tomorrow. I might drop by."

"Great. I'm sure Dora would love to see you." Then Armando poked around in the pond supplies a bit until he found a few things he was looking for, then took them up to the counter.

"These go on Dora's account too?" asked George.

He shook his head. "No. Keep this separate from the fertilizer and other stuff. I'm paying for this myself. Cash."

Armando loaded up his supplies into the truck then went down the street to the pet store where he bought a couple dozen goldfish.

But as he came out the door he was practically run down by Ben Sheraton, causing him to nearly drop one of the plastic bags containing fish.

"Sorry, man," said Ben, helping him to hold on to the slippery bag before it fell to the ground. Then Ben looked up at his face and recognized him. "Hey, Armando, I didn't realize it was you. How's it going?"

"Okay." He held up his bags of fish and smiled. "I just got these little guys to put into my pond."

"You have a pond?" Ben looked surprisingly interested.

"Yeah. I'm filling it up today, well, hopefully anyway."

"Cool. I'd love to see it sometime."

"Come on over, if you want. In fact, I'm having a little get-together tomorrow evening at seven. It's no big deal really, just a few friends." Yet even as he said it, he wondered why in the world he'd invited Ben of all people—and what would Olivia think? But he felt pretty sure Ben would decline anyway. It seemed beneath him somehow. "Of course, I'm sure you're probably busy with your art show and—"

"Actually, it's been cancelled." Ben scowled. "Due to lack of interest or so they say. Now they've got this lame collection of collectible dolls in there—I mean ones like Barbie and Chatty Cathy. Like anyone's interested in that." But then he brightened. "So, sure, maybe I'd like to come check out your pond. Did you say seven?"

"That's right." Armando forced a smile.

"By the way, have you seen Olivia around? I hear she moved out of her apartment."

"Yeah, she's living with her grandma for a while."

"So she'll be at your party too?"

"Yeah. And Dora too, as well as some other older folks." For some reason Armando wanted to clearly convey that this was *not* going to be anything like the party Olivia had hosted last week. Maybe he hoped that in itself would make Ben lose interest.

"Sounds nice." Ben nodded. "Maybe I'll see you around then."

Armando was still chastising himself for inviting Ben as he followed the directions that George had given him to the pond lady's house. What was Olivia going to say? But perhaps Ben wouldn't even come at all. Surely he'd get a better offer for a Friday night than going to a garden party with a bunch of old people.

The address took him to the outskirts of town, but it wasn't exactly a farm like he'd expected, although it did appear to have a couple of acres. And even though the sign in front said Plants for Sale, Armando still felt uncomfortable and conspicuous as he rang the front doorbell.

"Yes?" A middle-aged woman stuck her head out the door and looked at him suspiciously.

"Uh . . . George Foster from the Feed & Seed gave me your address," he said quickly. "He said you sell pond plants and I'm making a pond and I need—"

"Yes, yes." She nodded impatiently to a gate off to the side of the house. "Go around there and I'll meet you in back. And be careful not to let my dog out."

Armando went over to the gate, and checking for the dog, let himself in. He stared at her backyard in wonder. Everywhere he looked there seemed to be something amazing growing. This woman clearly had a green thumb!

"Come on over here," she called to him.

He looked past a blooming rose arbor to see her sitting on a bench beside a large pond. She was tugging on a pair of tall rubber boots as a small brown dog looked on with interest. As Armando came closer, the dog ran from her and started to bark at him.

"He's harmless," she called. "Come here, Harry. Stop your yipping."

Armando bent down to let the dog sniff his hand. "This garden is amazing," he said. "Did you plant all this yourself?"

She nodded. "Yep. I've been working at it for about fifteen years now—about the time my husband took off and left me with three teenage boys to raise. It's been my therapy, cheaper than seeing a shrink."

"And a lot better payoff too. It's really incredible. And your pond—" he stared in wonder at the reflective water spotted by blooming lily pads and irises and all sorts of other growing things— "it's beautiful."

Now the woman actually smiled. "Do you have a pond?"

"I'm building one. I got a liner and some fish to put in it today. It's right next to this creek, and I dug two canals that I can open and close, to adjust the water level, you know, and I'm hoping I can work it out to be sort of a fountain, but I'm not too sure about that yet."

"That sounds clever. But if you want to keep your fish, you'll have to make sure to keep a piece of wire mesh in the canals or they'll swim away."

He nodded. "I hadn't even thought of that."

She told him a few more things about ponds, then stepped into her pond and helped him to select a nice variety of pond plants, even explaining how to put them into his pond. He asked lots of questions then finally realized he'd taken up a lot of her time. "Thanks so much. This is going to be great."

"Keeping a pond is really pretty simple," she said as she pulled off her boots. "And keeping fish and plants together creates a perfect ecological balance. It's all about balance, you know. Sunshine and shade. Fresh water and old water. A real ecosystem."

"Thanks again. You've been really helpful."

"Well, it's nice seeing a young person interested in these things."

"I never introduced myself," he said, wishing that he could

befriend this interesting woman, especially since she seemed
to know so much about plants and ponds and the things that he
wanted to learn more about. "My name is Armando Garcia. I work
for Dora Chase—she has a farm. Do you know her?"

"I think I've heard of Chases' farm, back when I was a girl.
Didn't they used to grow a lot of produce?"

"Yes. But now we're trying to turn it into a nursery—or a nursery
supplier. We're still not completely sure which. But we want to grow
plants and shrubs and flowers, you know."

"Sounds exciting." She smiled again and held out her hand, still
damp from pulling out the pond plants. "And I'm Frances Bodine.
Sorry to be so rude earlier, but you never know who might come
knocking at your door these days."

"It's okay. And if you ever have the time, I wish you'd come out
and see what I'm working on." He glanced around her yard in admiration. "It's not nearly as nice as what you've done, but I'm trying."

"That's all you can do." She pushed a short strand of dark gray
hair from her eyes. "I'd like to come see your place."

"Really? I'm having a sort of grand-opening party tomorrow
evening at seven. Mostly older folks, like George Foster; I think you
know him. I know it's short notice and it won't be much, but—"

"I'd *love* to come."

"Great." He gave her directions, but even as he spoke he wondered if he wasn't biting off more than he could chew. Having Dora
and Olivia was one thing, but the party seemed to be growing by the
hour. Still, if all went well, it could be fun. It might be. He paused
to point at what looked like little buckets on top of bamboo poles.
"What are those for?" he asked.

She laughed. "Those are tiki torches. They were popular during
the sixties. But I still happen to like them. You put oil in them and
then burn them for light in the evening—or to keep the mosquitoes
away."

"Oh, yeah." He nodded. "I guess I've seen them before."

"You can get them real cheap at ShopMart right now. They're on sale this week."

So he thanked her and paid her, then loaded up the pond plants and headed on over to ShopMart, where he found tiki torches, lawn chairs, and a few other things to complete his special garden. Finally, he stopped at the grocery store and got a few items to use as refreshments for his little gathering. After he paid the cashier he looked down at his nearly empty billfold and sighed. Oh, well, it would be worth it. And even though he was almost broke, he was still glad he'd already sent the money order to his aunt, care of Mickey, because now it might've been tempting to hold on to it. And he suspected they needed it more than he did right now.

Then he went right back to the farm and returned to the field that he'd been preparing to transplant trees into and began applying the fertilizer that George had recommended. He worked until supper time, and then stopped only briefly to eat before he excused himself to go back outside again.

"You're sure working hard," said Dora. "I hope you're not over-doing it."

He smiled. "Actually, this evening I plan to work on my garden project until it gets too dark to see. I just hope I can get everything done."

"You still planning on having your big grand opening tomorrow evening?" she asked with a raised brow.

"Grand opening?" echoed Olivia. "What's up with that?"

"Remember," said Armando. "I told you how I'd invited you and Dora and Howie, and, as it turns out, a few other people too."

"A party?" said Olivia. "You're throwing a party?"

He laughed. "Sort of. I'm not really sure what it is. But hopefully it won't be a total disaster."

"Can I help with anything?" she asked.

"Sure, if you want to. I got some things to fix for refreshments. They're in the fridge. Do you want to help with that?"

"Yeah. I can handle that."

"I can help too," said Dora, holding up her hands. "I got two good hands now."

Armando laughed. "This party can be a celebration of two things—the garden and Dora's recovery."

So feeling like maybe this thing was under control, Armando loaded up the wheelbarrow and headed over to his garden area. He'd already put the fish into a five-gallon bucket of water and so far none of them had perished. And after several trips he was ready to start laying out the pond liner. He anchored the liner along the edges with the large smooth stones that he'd already collected from the creek, placing them evenly around to hold it securely in place. And then, practically holding his breath, he went over and opened the shunt on the upper canal and waited as the creek water flowed slowly at first, then more quickly, to gradually flood the pond cavity. He watched with wonder as the waterline steadily rose. He even took off his shoes and rolled up his pant legs and got into the pond in order to smooth out the wrinkles in the liner and reposition the rocks. And finally, when the water level was high enough, clear to the rocks, he went over and replaced the wooden shunt to so that the water continued its normal flow on down the creek.

He'd expected the pond water to be brown and muddy at first, from the dirt in the canal, but he hoped the sediments would eventually settle to the bottom. Hopefully by tomorrow and in time for his little gathering. In the meantime, he situated the pond plants in the way Frances had suggested and after a while he released the fish. Then he set up the tiki torches along with the lawn chairs and a few other things he'd managed to scrounge around the farm to make the place more comfortable and interesting. He'd even brought matches to try out the torches, and as it was getting dusky, he took a moment to light them.

To Armando, this quiet little out-of-the-way place was without a doubt the most beautiful garden on all the earth. And in his heart, he thanked God, for he knew that this was a true gift—a treasure that could have only come from heaven. Even when he looked over to his sculpture—a rustic angel forged out of an odd variety of recycled items—it too seemed somewhat magical, or perhaps it was spiritual, as its metal finish glowed warmly in the flickering torch-light that burned at the edge of the pond.

And that's when he decided the garden must have a name. And since it was Henry's idea from the beginning, and it was Henry's beautiful flowers that adorned it now, it seemed only fitting that Henry's name should be involved. So, after sitting on a log bench for a good while and enjoying the garden in the dusky twilight, he finally blew out the torches and went back to the barn to prepare a special sign to grace the entrance—a sign that would announce to everyone who entered in that this was indeed "Henry's Garden."

Chapter Thirty

$\mathcal{A}$rmando could hardly focus on his farmwork the following day. Not that he didn't enjoy it, because he did. It took all of his self-control not to sneak over to the garden and see how his pond was doing, but he had promised himself he would stay away until all his work for the day was complete.

"Do you want me to go over and help you set up the food?" asked Olivia at lunchtime.

He shook his head. "No. I want to set it up myself. I want it to be a surprise."

"You're being so mysterious," said Dora. "Almost makes me start believing that you really did dig up a hidden treasure over there."

"Maybe I did." He winked.

Olivia laughed. "No way. If you'd dug up a treasure you'd be long gone by now. *Adios, amigos!*"

He frowned. "Why's that?"

"Duh! If you had a bunch of money like that, why would you want to hang around here anymore?"

He felt slightly defensive. "Maybe I *like* it here."

Dora's face grew stern. "Olivia, you surprise me. Are you starting to think like your father now?"

Olivia made a face. "Not hardly! I was just jerking Armando's chain, Grandma. I remember one time when he told me that his goal in life was to get rich."

"Maybe I'm starting to find out there are some things in life that are worth more than money," he said.

Dora nodded. "That's what Henry used to say. And he was right too."

Armando smiled to himself. He wondered what Henry would say about the garden. Somehow he thought that he would be pleased.

Armando turned off the tractor at five o'clock then went to the barn to retrieve the sign he'd created last night. It was rustic looking, but it seemed to fit with the garden. He'd scrounged an old piece of wood from the shed then nailed small sticks to it to form the letters to write "Henry's Garden." He planned to nail this to one of the tall aspen trees that stood like sentries, marking the entrance to the garden. He followed the trail to the garden. He'd taken time to mow it a few days ago, but now he stopped here and there to pick up a rock or a stick—anything that might cause someone, particularly one of the older folks, to stumble. He didn't want anything to spoil this evening.

Before he nailed up the sign he went straight to the pond, worried that it might have leaked during the night or that the fish would all be dead. But not only had the pond remained full, the water had completely cleared and he could easily see the fish swimming around now. With the pond plants, as well as the blooming flowers all around, it was really quite beautiful. At least he thought so. He wasn't sure what anyone else would think. He quickly put up the sign then hurried back to the house to shower and gather up the refreshments for the party.

"Aren't you even going to eat supper?" Dora asked as Armando carried another tray of food out to his wheelbarrow, now draped in an old tablecloth that Olivia had provided.

"I'm not that hungry," he called. "And besides there'll be food at the party."

"And I stuck a ham sandwich in there for him," said Olivia as she carried out a jug of lemonade. "You got everything now?" She peered with interest at his wheelbarrow, now transformed into a heavily laden food cart.

He grinned. "I think so. Hopefully I won't dump it all out before I get there."

"Okay then, I'm going to go clean up and change. I want to look nice for your big wingding."

Armando considered telling her that Ben might come. But he wasn't quite sure how she'd take it. She could be either elated or infuriated by the news. And, anyway, he didn't even know if Ben would actually show. No use getting her excited over nothing. "All right. I'll come back over here just before seven and we'll wait for everyone to get here and then all go out there together." He frowned. "Do you think that's okay? I mean will people get impatient or want to—"

"Don't worry so much, Armando; it'll be just fine."

He spent the next hour setting up the food and drinks on his makeshift table of a board stretched between two sawhorses. Then he arranged and rearranged the chairs and the small stumps that were meant to be used as coffee tables until he was finally satisfied. He even took time to pick a few of the abundant blooms to make small bouquets that he placed in paper cups filled with pond water. He set these on the various tables then stepped back to take in the scene. A little rustic perhaps, but pretty. He hoped the others would like it too. Mostly he hoped Dora would like it. For some reason that was really important to him. He knew this had been Henry's special place and he didn't want anything he'd done to dishonor him.

Finally it was almost seven, and he knew it was time to go back. Feeling like a nervous bridegroom, he walked slowly toward the house. Maybe no one would show up except for Dora and Olivia. And, really, that would be perfectly fine with him. Maybe even for the best. But as he came out into the open, he saw a couple of cars parked out in front. He recognized Howie's Cadillac and suspected the green pickup belonged to George Foster, and as he neared the house an unfamiliar car was pulling into the driveway.

"Hey, Armando," called Olivia. "We were just starting to wonder about you."

"Sorry. I got busy—"

"Who's that?" asked Dora, pointing at the older Mercedes that was pulling in.

"That's the woman with the amazing garden," he quickly explained. "Remember, I told you about her. Her name's Frances Bodine."

As introductions were being made, Armando noticed a bicycle turning from the road and remembered that Ben didn't drive a car. Fortunately Olivia hadn't seen him yet, so Armando got her attention and whispered in her ear, "I hope you don't mind that Ben's coming—"

"Ben?" Her eyes grew wide. "But why?"

Armando shrugged uneasily. "I'm sorry. I should've told you. I ran into him in town yesterday and mentioned—"

"Oh, don't worry, Armando." She smiled, but he detected a stiffness in it. "It's perfectly fine. I'm sure Ben will be very interested in your little garden project."

Soon everyone that Armando had invited was milling around on the porch and he felt it was up to him to make some sort of announcement, something to get them on their way.

"Well, thank you all for coming," he said. "I'm a little embarrassed now because . . . well, it's only a small garden . . . but I hope you'll all enjoy it." He held up his hands self-consciously. "And without further ado, come right this way." He took Dora by the arm, and together they slowly led their small entourage toward the garden.

"Oh my," said Dora when she saw the sign nailed to the aspen. "Henry's Garden. Now, wouldn't he be pleased?"

And suddenly they were in the garden and Armando looked around, watching everyone, studying their expressions to see what they thought.

"Oh, this is beautiful," said Dora with a happy smile. "Oh my, look at those calla lilies up against the valerian and the hibiscus out in front—oh my, the flowers look absolutely gorgeous. Henry would be so proud."

"And will you look at that pond!" exclaimed Howie. "It's even got real fish in it. I didn't even bring my pole."

"Nice work, son," said George with a pat on Armando's back. "It looks like you're headed down the right road going into the land-scaping business."

"Your pond looks lovely," said Frances. "And already the plants look like they're doing quite well. Look, that lily pad even has an open bloom on it."

Armando smiled in happy relief. "Thanks."

Then he glanced back to see Olivia and Ben still standing on the trail. They appeared to be deep in conversation and he wondered if they might be making up after their last big blowout. And although he knew it was selfish and wrong, he hoped not.

"There's food and drink over here," he said, indicating the table. "Just help yourselves and feel free to look around or sit or whatever."

"I think I'll just rest here a bit," said Dora as she settled herself onto the lawn chair directly across from the pond.

"Can I get you some lemonade or something?" offered Armando.

"That'd be nice."

He went and filled a cup and even put some cheese and crack-ers on a paper plate then carried them back to her, setting them on the stump to her side. "Do you really like it, Dora?" he asked, kneel-ing next to her.

"I love it, Armando. It's like paradise." She sighed. "And that funny angel by the pond—where did that come from? Did Ben make it?"

Armando laughed. "I'm glad Ben didn't hear you say that. I put it together myself with some things I found lying around the farm. I call it the Garden Angel."

She patted his arm. "You're a real clever boy, Armando. You remind me so much of my Henry."

Before long, Howie came over and sat in the lawn chair next to Dora. They began chatting of old times and how they thought Henry would appreciate what Armando had done. And on the other side of the pond, it seemed that Frances and George were enjoying each other's company too. She seemed to be explaining the workings of a pond to him and he seemed very interested. But it bothered Armando that Ben and Olivia hadn't joined them yet. And suddenly he grew worried. What if they'd made up and left? Olivia hadn't been off the farm in days. Would she be tempted to go back to her old drug-dependent ways again? While he didn't really think so, and it's not as if Ben had been a bad influence exactly—at least Armando didn't think so—still it concerned him. And besides, he wanted Olivia to see the garden.

"I can feel Henry here," said Dora suddenly, reaching over to grasp Howie's hand. "Do you feel it too?"

Only a few feet away, Armando couldn't help but listen.

Howie nodded. "Yes, I believe I do. Perhaps God's allowing him to enjoy this moment with us."

"Do you really think so?"

"I think that God is trying to tell you something, Dora."

She reached for a handkerchief and dabbed her eyes.

In that same moment, Armando began to pray for Dora. It felt as if something inside him, maybe even the Lord Jesus, was urging him in this way. He prayed that Dora would experience God in the same way that he'd been doing these past few days. He prayed that somehow God would use this garden to open her heart.

"What is it, Howie?" she asked in a trembling voice.

"It's the same old thing, Dora. I think you know by now." Howie smiled. "God wants you to let go of those old things, to forgive others in the same way that He's forgiven you—completely."

"But how does a person do that? It sounds impossible!"

"Like I've said before, Dora, you ask God to help you."

"Just like that?" She shook her head. "There must be more. It sounds too simple."

"Simple maybe, but not easy." He patted her hand. "I know it's hard letting go of old hurts and wounds, Dora. And no one would deny you've had more than your fair share of loss and disappointment. But God *will* help you, if you'll only ask Him."

She nodded, ever so slightly. "Well, Howie, I know you wouldn't lie to me. And I've been thinking a lot about these things of late. I promise you, I will continue to give it my full consideration."

He chuckled. "Well, now, that's all I can hope for, Dora."

She sighed and looked toward the pond. "I sure hope Henry is watching."

Armando smiled to himself as he went over to the clearing to watch for Ben and Olivia. He hoped they hadn't left already. But as he stepped out he noticed that they were now coming his way. "Hey, I thought maybe you two had taken off," he said in what he hoped sounded like a casual voice. He didn't want them to know that he'd been concerned.

"No way," said Olivia as she entered the garden. "I'm not going anywhere without first seeing the mystery gard—" she stopped and looked around. "Armando," she said in a quiet voice. "This is incredible. Did you really do this yourself?"

He nodded.

"This is totally amazing." She walked over to the pond and looked around. "Wow. I mean it; this is really fantastic."

"Thanks." He knew he was probably beaming now, but what else could he do?

"Isn't it wonderful?" called Dora. "Did you notice the Garden Angel?" She pointed toward the pond.

Olivia stared at the sculpture. "Where did you get that?" She turned and looked at Ben as if he had something to do with it. But he just shrugged. "Armando?" She turned to Armando now. "Really, where did you get that?"

Armando felt his cheeks growing warm and he knew the others were looking at him. "I . . . uh . . ."

"He made it!" said Dora triumphantly. "He found a bunch of old things just lying around the farm and just stuck them all together. Isn't he smart?"

Olivia laughed, then reached over and pinched Armando's cheek like he was five years old. "Yes, Grandma, he's very smart."

He grinned. "There's food over here, if you guys want something."

"This is nice, Armando." Ben spoke in a quiet voice.

"Thanks. It's a good place to come and be quiet, you know." Armando filled a cup and held it out to him. "I think the lemonade is all natural," he said with a grin.

"Good."

Olivia came over and joined them. "Isn't this incredible, Ben?"

He nodded. "It's nice."

"Nice? Is that the best you can do? This place is like a fairyland, an oasis, a real work of art—honestly, don't you think so too?"

Ben shrugged. "It's just a garden."

Armando saw Olivia's eyes flash and decided to jump in before she said anything regrettable. "Yeah, and it'll get better with time. I plan to put some paths around over there and—"

"Ben!" Olivia's voice sounded shrill. "Can't you even give an honest compliment? Why can't you just admit it; this is a beautiful place. Armando worked this ground with his own two hands and he made something—"

"Hey, it's okay," said Armando lightly. "This is only the beginning, you know. Someday we'll have greenhouses and all sorts—"

"It's *not* okay," she continued. "I want Ben to give you an honest-to-goodness compliment. Everyone can see that this place is fantastic—"

"Olivia." Ben glanced around as if to clue her in that others might be listening.

"I don't care who hears me." She folded her arms across her front. "Besides, everyone here can see you're acting like a total jerk."

Armando put his hand on her arm. "Olivia, really, it's okay. Ben has a right to his own opinion—"

She shook her head. "No, it's not a matter of opinion, Armando." She lowered her voice now. "Ben just can't stand to admit that someone else might have succeeded at something." She turned and glared at Ben. "Can you?"

"Oh, Olivia," he rolled his eyes. "Here you go again."

"No, it's true, Ben." She pointed to the angel by the pond. "Take Armando's sculpture there. It's really good, isn't it? And he doesn't even claim to be an artist."

Armando forced a laugh, for Ben's sake. "Hey, compared to Ben I'm like a preschooler. It's okay though. I only did it for the fun of it. Come on, lighten up, Olivia. He's right; it's only a garden."

Now she turned to Armando. "It is *not* only a garden. It's something my grandfather started long ago and now it's something even more—it's almost spiritual. I just want Ben to respect that."

Armando didn't know what more to say. He felt bad for Ben, but his interference didn't seem to be helping anything. "I'm glad you like it, Olivia. Really. Now, I think I'll go talk to George and Frances." Then he turned and walked away.

Armando enjoyed playing host. He refilled drinks and passed around platters of appetizers, chatting with everyone as he went.

But he tried to avoid Ben and Olivia, and he felt relieved when they finally began visiting with others and hopefully leaving their petty differences behind. Then as the sun began going down, he remembered the tiki torches and went around lighting them, delighting in the pleased *oohs* and *ahs* from his guests.

"This is so beautiful," said Dora again. She turned to Howie. "Now, we used to have some pretty good picnics down here with Daisy and Henry, but we never thought to come in the evening."

He shook his head. "A shame, isn't it? Imagine how they would've loved it."

"Well, I hope they can both see this right now." Dora spoke in a hopeful voice. "I believe they'd enjoy it.

He nodded. "Yes, I believe they would."

Armando noticed Ben standing alone by the Garden Angel and decided to join him. "Hey, I hope you didn't take what Olivia said—"

"I'm used to her, man." Ben crunched his empty cup into a tight wad. "It's just how she is. She's got to have it her way or no way."

Armando frowned. "Well, she's been having a tough time of it lately."

"Hey, you don't have to defend her to me. I know how she is."

Armando looked at his angel sculpture and wondered if Ben really did know. He wondered if he even knew himself. "She's been pretty down lately and I don't think—"

"Look, I know you're trying to help, but we can work this thing out perfectly fine without you."

Armando held up his hands. "Hey, I'm not trying to get in the middle of this. I thought you should know she's had a pretty tough week."

"*She's* had a tough week?" Ben laughed cynically. "I just got my art show shut down without selling a single piece, and I'm not even sure how I'll pay next month's rent on my studio, and if things keep going like this I'll probably be back teaching art at Treasure High by fall."

"You teach high school?"

Ben groaned. "Please, don't remind me. I took a couple years' sabbatical to try and make it, and now I'm ready to throw in the towel."

"You're going to give up?"

Ben laughed now, but it was a bitter laugh, harsh with a sharp edge to it. "And what do you think I should do?"

Armando shrugged. "I don't know. But it seems kind of strange to give up in a small town like Treasure. I mean it's not like they're the art mecca of the West Coast. Have you ever thought about taking your exhibit to a big city like Seattle or L.A.?"

"It's not that simple."

"Yeah, I'm sure it's not. I really don't know anything about it. But I'm thinking if I had a dream—like, say, making it in the land-scaping business—I wouldn't give it up just because it didn't work out in one place." Armando looked around. "Like as much as I love it here, it still might not work out for me to stay on indefi-nitely. I mean Dora's pretty old and Charlie's breathing down her neck like a hungry wolf. Who knows what's around the next corner?"

"So you're thinking you can take your dreams wherever then?"

"I don't really know much about it, but I don't see why not." Armando pointed to his chest. "Seems to me they're all inside here anyway."

Ben patted him on the shoulder. "You're a good kid, Armando. A little wet behind the ears perhaps, but a good kid." Then he turned and walked over to Olivia.

Armando didn't hear their conversation, but he noticed the expression on Ben's face and it wasn't happy. Then Ben left—with-out even saying good-bye to the others. Olivia went around picking

up cups and things and chatting with people in a much more pleasant manner than she'd done before.

As it began getting dusky, Dora stood up. "I hate to break up this
lovely party, but I think I better trek back to the house while there's
still enough light to find my way."

"Don't worry, Dora," said Armando. "I'll make sure you don't get
lost." He went over and took her by the arm.

"I better be going too," said Howie, slowly standing. "I don't see
that well in the dark myself."

Olivia stepped over and took his arm. "Why don't we walk back
together?"

Then George and Frances paired off and followed behind them
and the little entourage made their way back to the house where
good-byes and thank-yous were said, and the visitors climbed into
their cars and drove off one by one into the summer's night.

"That was the nicest evening," said Dora, still standing by the
front door. "I thank you, Armando. It was truly a delight. I'm sure
I'll sleep well tonight."

"Good night, Grandma." Olivia kissed her on the cheek.

"Sweet dreams, Dora," called Armando.

Armando and Olivia stood on the porch for a few minutes
before Armando spoke. "I guess I better go back and clean
things up."

"You need any help?"

"Nah, it's okay. You've already helped enough."

"I'm sorry I acted up at your party," she said in a quiet voice.
"I didn't mean to spoil things for you."

"You mean the thing between you and Ben." He shrugged. "Hey,
that's no big deal. Looked like you guys worked it out anyway."

Olivia frowned. "Yeah, maybe."

"Other than that, don't you think it went okay tonight?"

She smiled now. "Of course, it was absolutely wonderful. Really,

Armando, what you've done out there—well, it's nothing short of amazing."

"Thanks." He sighed. "Guess I better go blow out those tiki torches. Wouldn't want to see the place burned down by morning."

She laughed. "It's a little early for fire season around here."

He knew she was right about that, since everything on the farm was still fresh and green and moist. But he thought to himself that there was more than *one* kind of fire. And it disturbed him more and more to consider the kind of white-hot heat that seemed to smolder inside of him every time he was around her. What a tiny breath of air it would take to burst that spark into flames.

Chapter Thirty-One

They'd just sat down to lunch when they heard a car pull up in front of the house. "Wonder who that is?" asked Dora.

"I'll check." Olivia hopped out of her chair and went to the open kitchen window to peer out. *"Oh no!"*

"What is it?" asked Armando.

"Daddy dearest." She turned and frowned. "Grandma, I thought those No Trespassing signs were supposed to keep him out."

"Is anyone with him?" asked Dora.

Olivia looked again. "No, looks like he's alone."

"Maybe he's come to make a truce," suggested Armando.

Olivia laughed. "That'd be the day."

"Go see what he wants, Olivia," commanded Dora.

Armando stayed at the table with Dora, and they both listened as Olivia talked with her father at the front door. "What do you want?" Olivia asked him for the second time, her voice even more aggravated than before.

"Let me in. I need to speak to your grandmother."

"Didn't you see the signs on the fence?"

"It's a little late to keep out trespassers," he said gruffly. "Kind of like closing the barn door after the horse has escaped." And suddenly he was in the kitchen, planted at the end of the table and staring at them.

"What are you doing here, Charlie?" Dora's voice sounded fairly even, but Armando thought he detected a note of weariness in it and he wondered how much of this bullying she could take.

"I've got news for you, Mom." Charlie pulled out a chair and sat down as if he'd been invited. And in all fairness, Armando had to admit that the man looked slightly less imposing in his yellow polo shirt and khaki pants. But the expression on his face was grimmer than usual.

"What is it?" she asked with an air of disinterest.

"It concerns your migrant worker here."

"Armando is *not* a migrant worker," snapped Olivia. "And don't you—"

"Call him what you like," said Charlie. "But let me speak."

Dora glared at her son. "If you've come out here to make more trouble for me, you can leave right now."

"I think you've already got plenty of trouble, Mom." He laughed in a cynical way. "And I think it's about to get a whole lot worse."

"What on earth are you talking about?" demanded Dora. "You know I don't like playing silly games with you, Charlie. If you have something to say, then just get it out into the open—otherwise you can beat it."

"Fine." He looked at Armando with a dark scowl. "Seems your little friend here has a history. Do you want to tell them or should I?"

Armando studied Charlie. "I don't know what you're talking—"

"No, I figured you wouldn't." He turned to Dora. "I've just learned that your boy here has a warrant for his arrest down in California."

Armando stood up and stared at Charlie. "*What?*"

"Oh, nice touch, boy. Try to act like you're surprised; maybe they'll fall for it."

"Charlie, you've gone too far this time." Dora pushed herself up from the chair and shook a small wrinkled fist at her son. "You need to leave right now—"

"Not so fast, Mom." He turned back to Armando. "Why don't you tell them what your warrant is for?"

Armando shook his head. "I don't know what—"

"Fine!" Charlie narrowed his eyes. "I'll tell them myself. Your good little Mexican boy here is involved in drug trafficking. He's wanted in Los Angeles right now. Seems he was in possession of about eighty kilos of cocaine when the cops unexpectedly dropped in to break up the party, but he hightailed it out of there and left his buddy holding the bag."

"That is *not* true!" shouted Armando. "That's *not* what happened at all."

Charlie laughed. "Right. Isn't that what all felons claim?" Then he turned to his mother. "So, I guess this proves my point. Can't you see you're not thinking straight when you go and hire a dangerous criminal to come out here and live with you, Mom? Honestly, do you realize you're harboring a wanted felon right under your own roof?" He shook his head. "Let's set breaking the law aside for a moment, but do you know what kind of danger you could be in? This is exactly the kind of unpleasantries you read about on the front pages of small-town papers like ours: 'Elderly woman slain by—' "

"I don't believe you." Dora's voice trembled. "You're—you're making this up to upset me."

For Dora's sake, Armando felt desperate to say something—anything! He wanted to explain this or defend himself, but no sensible words would come to him. In fact, the only words spinning through his jumbled mind right now were in Spanish—a language he rarely spoke and would be of little use to him in this situation.

"I was afraid you'd say that." Charlie looked down at the table as if her words had wounded him. "It figures you'd believe a lying criminal over your own flesh and blood." He slammed his open palm on the table, making them all jump. "But that's why I've got the sheriff coming out here. He's on his way and he'll explain the warrant as well as all the legal details."

Dora appeared stunned now as she looked silently at Charlie and then to Armando. Her lips were pressed together in a tight pale line and her eyes were bright with anger, or perhaps it was disappointment or even fear. No matter. Armando knew he couldn't bear to watch it for another minute. He couldn't stand to hurt her like this.

"Excuse me!" he said abruptly. The small kitchen chair fell backward as he rose from the table. Then he pushed past Olivia, still standing in the doorway, and hurried through the living room, but as his hand reached the front doorknob, he looked back, and the look in Olivia's eyes felt like it was being burned into his memory like a red-hot brand. The hurt and confusion, perhaps even accusation, he saw there cut him as deeply, maybe more so, than what he'd just witnessed in Dora's eyes. His chest felt so tight that it seemed he couldn't breathe as he ran down the porch steps and across the yard, through the barn and into his room. Without even thinking, he crammed his few belongings into his backpack. And other than the old worn Bible, he left behind everything else that Dora had given him—somehow he knew he didn't deserve any of those things.

Then running full speed, he cut diagonally across Dora's property until he came out on the highway that led west toward the interstate. Not wanting to draw attention to himself, he stopped running and walked fast, his left thumb sticking up in the air each time a car passed, and he never paused once to look back.

Chapter Thirty-Two

*I*t took about thirty minutes before Armando finally got a ride. And by then he was steadily glancing over his shoulder, certain that the first car to pick him up would have the markings of the law on it—the sheriff that Charlie had mentioned. Not that he was surprised that so many vehicles passed without stopping, since many people in these parts, as well as lots of other places, seemed to have strong biases against Latinos—especially young men. But fortunately an old Ford van filled with what looked like about a dozen migrant workers took pity on him.

"You heading for Arcadia Farms?" asked the man at the wheel.

"Nah." Armando threw his backpack on the floor and climbed in. "Just going south."

"Well, we can take you as far as Arcadia, that's near I-5. You might be able to get another ride from there."

"*Gracias.*" Armando sat forward on the edge of the middle seat, trying not to take up too much space in the already crowded van. Even with the windows open the smell in there was a mixture of sweat and tobacco and unwashed clothing, and there was an empty tequila bottle sliding across the floor at every curve. Armando looked around to see mostly middle-aged and younger men, except for in the back where an older woman and two younger ones sat quietly, their heads back and eyes closed as if they were sleeping.

"They need strawberry pickers right now." The older man next to him spoke in Spanish. "Good crop of berries and they need to get them in—pronto."

"*Gracias,* no," said Armando, forcing a smile to his lips. He politely explained how he needed to get down south right now. Then, leaning forward and planting his elbows on his knees with his chin cupped in his hands, he wondered how on earth he would ever begin to untangle this crazy mess. But somehow he knew he must try. And maybe God would help him. And there, in the midst of companionable strangers, bumping along the highway together in an overloaded old van, he closed his eyes and prayed. He wasn't even sure how to pray exactly, but mostly he asked God to help him through this thing. And he didn't stop praying until the van quit moving.

"Everybody out," called the driver. "And get what you need now 'cause I'm locking this up."

Armando grabbed his backpack and thanked the driver, slipping a couple of bucks into his hand. "*Gracias, amigo.*"

"No problem, man." The man smiled to reveal a missing front tooth. "We got to stick together."

Armando nodded, then turned toward the traffic noise of the nearby interstate. He noticed an on-ramp and headed in that direction. He knew that hitching on the freeway was illegal in this state, but hopefully he could catch a ride near the exits—maybe with a trucker on a long trip in need of company to keep him awake.

But after waiting near the on-ramp for more than twenty minutes, he became nervous and impatient, and decided to take his chances walking. He wouldn't stick out his thumb now, just in case a cop was passing by, but maybe he'd get lucky and be picked up anyway. Otherwise, he'd have to hoof it clear to the next set of exits to look for a ride.

He walked for two hours in the hot afternoon sun without a single offer of a ride. The blaring noise of big diesel engines and the sound of spinning tires speeding past him only a few feet away made his head throb and his ears ring. And his throat felt like sand as he longed for a sip of water. He'd worked on the tractor all morning without pausing once for a drink and then he'd barely touched his iced tea before Charlie's unexpected visit had interrupted their lunch.

Even so, he tried not to be too angry with Charlie. For one thing he didn't want to waste his precious energy on that selfish little man. Besides, he told himself, it might be that Charlie was only looking out for the welfare of his mother. Yet somehow Armando didn't really believe this. He wondered where old Charlie had gotten his information. And he wondered if it was really true that there was a warrant for his arrest. And if there was a warrant, how could Armando possibly fight it? How would he even begin to prove his innocence? These questions seemed to pound themselves into his brain with each step he took on the sunbaked asphalt. After a while, he wondered if perhaps he was crazy for doing this. What chance did he have against the L.A. legal system anyway? Maybe he shouldn't even try to clear his name. Maybe he should turn around and head north. Try Lucky this time—although his luck seemed to be running out fast right now.

But he didn't turn around. Instead he kept putting one foot in front of the other and walking steadily south. Somehow he knew he wouldn't turn back. For whatever reason, and despite the odds, he knew that he must do the right thing this time. Even if it killed him trying, he was determined to continue.

It was close to four when he heard a car pull off the freeway and slow to a stop behind him. He could tell by the sound of the engine and the wheels that it was a car. Not a truck or the wished-for semi. His heart began to pound as he imagined a black-and-white patrol car and a uniformed officer standing outside the door with his hand hovering over his loaded revolver before he gave out the warning call.

"*Armando!*"

But it was a woman's voice calling out to him. And when he turned around he saw Howie's light blue Cadillac parked on the shoulder of the freeway and Olivia hurrying toward him. He thought he must be seeing another mirage—like the puddles of water that he'd felt certain he'd seen along the edges of the freeway but every time he got there they were gone. Well, perhaps this was it. Maybe he'd come to the end of himself already. He looked at the mirage but continued to walk backward.

"Wait!" she called.

He stopped and squinted now, peering hard to see if he could make the mirage disappear.

"*Armando!*" she screamed. "*Stop!*"

Suddenly he knew this was no mirage and he started to walk toward her. "What . . . what are you doing—"

"Don't ask questions now. Just get in the car."

Feeling as if in a dream, he followed Olivia back to the car. He saw Howie sitting in the passenger seat, a satisfied smile on his face as he nodded a greeting. Armando got into the backseat and waited silently as Olivia got into the driver's seat, checked her rearview mirror, turned on her signal, and reentered the freeway, her foot pressing hard on the ignition to make that powerful engine roar as she quickly got the car up to seventy-five.

"Like I said, Olivia—" Howie spoke in a matter-of-fact voice— "you'll pay for your own speeding tickets."

"I'm barely over seventy."

Howie chuckled. "Wish I could say the same."

Armando sat there, still feeling as if this wasn't real and wondering if he hadn't actually passed out alongside the freeway and was now hallucinating from heat exhaustion and dehydration.

"You hungry, Armando?" asked Howie.

Armando wasn't sure how to answer. He still felt confused and wondered why they'd tracked him down and picked him up like this. What if they were working with the police to bring him in?

"Of course, he's hungry," said Olivia. "He never got to eat lunch."

"Let's stop at the truck stop ahead. As I recall they used to have a pretty good diner there."

Suddenly, Armando no longer cared about anything. He simply leaned back into the cushy seat and sighed. Let them turn him in if they wanted. What difference did it really make whether he was caught up here or down there. Maybe being picked up now would save him a long miserable trip of hitching rides down the interstate.

Olivia parked the car and started to hand the keys to Howie.

"Why don't you hold on to them, dear." He picked up his straw hat and slowly climbed from the car then headed for the entrance of the diner.

"Are you coming?" she asked from outside, staring at Armando still sitting in the backseat and feeling like he didn't have good sense.

"Yeah." He climbed from the car and looked around, trying to appear casual, as if he were only stretching his stiff neck. Still, he didn't see any patrol cars.

"If you're looking for the cops—" she took him by the arm and led him toward the entrance—"we didn't invite them along."

Howie was already being seated at a table by the window. The two of them joined him as the waitress set the menus and water on the table. Armando downed his water in one long swig, hoping she'd get the hint and refill it. But before she did, Olivia slid her glass over to him and nodded. He downed that one too.

"I'd like coffee and pie," said Howie, smiling at the young wait-ress. "You got any blueberry pie this time of year?"

"You bet. Not fresh blueberries, of course, but it looks pretty good just the same. A la mode?"

He nodded. "That'd be perfect." He turned to Armando. "You

know what you want, son, or do you need a minute?" Without looking at the menu Armando ordered a cheeseburger and a chocolate shake. Then Olivia ordered a chicken-salad sandwich and iced tea and the waitress left.

Howie looked across the table to Armando. "Sounds like you're having a pretty hard day, son."

"Yeah, I guess you could say that."

"You want to tell us what's going on?"

Armando sighed. "Where do you want me to begin?"

"How 'bout the beginning?"

He nodded. He felt ready to confess—everything and anything. And if they wanted to lock him up, well, then fine. "Okay, let's see. Well, I used to live with my aunt and uncle. And my uncle, Tio Pedro, wasn't exactly what you'd call a law-abiding citizen, if you know what I mean. Like he didn't really want to work regular jobs, you know? And it's not like I didn't know about some of the stuff he was into, but I mostly just tried to steer clear and live my own life. My aunt, Tia Marta, sort of pretended like she didn't know what was going on. But I think she did. Still, Tio Pedro brought home money from time to time and she needed it to survive—it bought food and paid the rent for herself and their three little girls."

The waitress refilled his water and Armando paused to drink it down. "Anyway, my uncle would sometimes be gone for a long time—like doing a short jail sentence or whatever—and I would try to help out a little more financially. I always paid my share of the rent and I bought groceries a lot of the time, but I was thinking more and more about leaving and getting on my own. Except it's hard to leave, you know, when they're the only family you have."

The waitress brought their drinks now and Armando took a long sip of the shake before he continued. "So, anyway, Tio Pedro wrenched his knee—I'm not sure how exactly, but it was all swollen up and he could barely walk. He asked me to drive him to a friend's house where he was going to borrow a set of crutches, or so he said. And I guess I felt sort of sorry for him, so I agreed. But once we got going I got suspicious. I think it was something in his eyes or the way he kept turning up the stereo real loud and changing the stations—like he was all hyped about something.

"We went into what I knew was a pretty bad neighborhood, but that didn't surprise me so much because Tio Pedro's friends come from all walks of life. And he had me pull into a driveway of a real dump and then he just sat there. I asked him if he wanted me to go get the crutches for him, but he said the guy would bring them out, to pop open the trunk and wait. Well, in a minute a guy came out carrying two big duffel bags—*no crutches*—and he dumped the bags into the trunk then slammed it shut and sort of nodded at my uncle. I knew right then that it was a drug deal, and my uncle was probably acting as the middleman. But I was so angry I couldn't even think straight. I started to get out of the car right there in the driveway, but my uncle yelled and cussed at me, telling me I couldn't just leave him there in a bad neighborhood with his hurt knee and all. So I started driving. I knew it was wrong. I should've bailed while I had the chance, but like an idiot, I wimped out. I gave in to Tio Pedro's bullying." He shook his head.

"That's understandable," said Olivia.

Armando sighed. "Yeah, but you know what the real honest-to-God truth is?"

"What?" asked Howie.

"The truth is: part of me was thinking, *Hey, if I help Tio Pedro with this, he will have to pay me off.* I was thinking I could profit from this deal, you know? Get rich."

"That seems fair," said Olivia; then she frowned. "I guess."

"How did that make you feel?" asked Howie.

Armando wadded the paper napkin into a tight little ball. "Like I was just like him."

"So what did you do?" demanded Olivia.

"I kept driving and I felt partly furious and partly excited by the prospects. But I was also pretty scared."

He stopped talking as the waitress set down their orders. Then even before she left, Howie bowed his head and prayed. "Lord, bless this food, and help us to help our friend Armando here. Show us what's best to do and then help us to do it. Amen."

"Man, I'm dying to know what happened next," said Olivia with wide eyes, "but you better eat something first."

Armando willingly obliged her, taking several big bites before he set down his burger and continued. "You can probably guess the rest of the story. I drove for about a mile, but by then I felt almost certain we were being followed. It wasn't a marked car or anything, but something about it felt like it was the police, and I started to freak. I told Tio Pedro, but he said I was just being a big chicken. Suddenly the idea of his dirty drug money didn't matter to me. And I didn't even care what he thought of me anymore. I pulled diagonally into an alleyway, using the car to block it off so I couldn't be followed; then I jumped out and just ran for it. Maybe it was stupid; maybe it was disloyal to my uncle. I didn't really know at the time. All I knew was that I couldn't explain how it was that I was driving a car with all that dope in the back. And, believe me, it doesn't help anything being Latino down there, especially when it comes to drug trafficking. Anyway, I just wanted to get far, far away—from that place and my uncle and even L.A.—at that moment I'd totally had it with the whole scene."

Olivia picked up the second half of her sandwich. "Where did you go from there?"

"First I went to my friend Mickey's and just laid low for a couple hours. Then he called my aunt and found out that my uncle had been arrested and she was on her way out to see if she could find somebody to help her post bail. I was able to sneak back home while she was gone and grab a few things, and then Mickey drove me out of town a ways and waited with me until I caught a ride with a trucker heading to San Jose. After a couple days of hitching I finally made it up here."

Olivia turned to Howie. "See, I told you he was innocent."

Armando poured some ketchup on his fries. "Innocent?"

"You weren't intentionally involved."

"Maybe not at first." He shook his head. "But what really bugs me is that if those cops hadn't been on us . . . what would I have done? Would I have gone along with the whole thing—for the money? It's an easy way to make a bunch of money—quickly."

"There are never any real answers to those 'what if' questions," said Howie. "Sometimes we need to remember that God can intervene—He can change the course of our lives in an instant."

Armando nodded. "Yeah, I believe that."

"But why did you feel like you had to run?" asked Olivia.

"I knew I couldn't trust my uncle."

"What do you mean?" Howie set down his coffee cup.

"I knew he'd be really furious at me for ditching him like that, and I knew I couldn't trust him not to try and pin the whole thing on me—if nothing else but for plain revenge."

"Your own uncle would do that to you?" said Olivia.

"Remember, he's only my uncle by marriage." Armando picked up his hamburger again. "And he doesn't treat his own blood relatives any better."

"Do you have any other criminal records?" Howie laid his fork on his nearly empty plate and stared intently at Armando.

He shook his head. "Just a speeding ticket from when I was a kid trying out my aunt's new Camaro. Man, I had that thing going one-twenty!"

Olivia chuckled. "Guess we won't be letting you drive the Caddie."

"Hey, I don't drive like that anymore."

"Well, then," said Howie, patting his mouth with his napkin. "What are your plans now, son?"

"I was heading down to L.A." He picked up a fry. "Not sure what good it'll do, but I thought maybe I could at least try and clear my name."

Howie smiled. "A good name's worth more than riches."

Armando shrugged. "Don't know about that. But I don't like the idea of being locked up in prison much either."

"You got any legal representation?"

"What do you think?"

"Well, how about if we three make this little trip together?" Howie waved to the waitress to bring him the check.

"You're kidding?" Armando stared at the old man in amazement. "You'd be willing to go all the way down to L.A. just to help me out of this crazy jam? Do you know how long that drive is?"

"I've been hankering after a good road trip." Howie pulled out his billfold and laid some money on top of the check.

"Better finish your food, Armando," said Olivia. "I'm going to go call Grandma and let her know the good news."

"It was Dora's suggestion that we come look for you," said Howie as Olivia left. "Of course, Olivia was eager to come. That girl thinks a lot of you, son."

So Armando, still feeling slightly dazed, finished his food, down to the last drip of ketchup, and then the three of them piled back into the old Cadillac and headed on down the freeway.

"I figure you two can take turns driving," said Howie as he unfolded a road map. "We'll make better time that way. We'll stop for food and gas and a chance to stretch our legs from time to time. But if my calculations are correct—and if you kids drive the way I'm guessing you will—we should be there by tomorrow afternoon. That'll give us plenty of time to get a motel and have a good night's rest and then clean up before we go in and talk to the DA about dismissing this whole thing."

For the next few hours, Olivia drove while Howie asked Armando specific questions about possible witnesses, past employers, or trustworthy friends who could testify in his behalf. Howie made lots of notes on a yellow legal pad, and for the first time that day, Armando actually began to feel hopeful. Oh, he knew it was still a long shot for an eighty-three-year-old attorney from the sticks of Oregon to finagle a Latino boy facing serious drug charges through the Los Angeles legal system. But maybe— like Howie kept assuring him—maybe God was at work here. Maybe there was a miracle in sight. And finally Armando decided it was time to tell someone about that day in the church. He told it fairly quickly and in a rather matter-of-fact way, and yet Howie's reaction was anything but.

"Well, hallelujah!" he exploded from the backseat. "Nothing you could say would make me any happier. Welcome to God's family, son. I figured it was only a matter of time."

Olivia said nothing, but kept driving, her face expressionless, her eyes fixed on the freeway before her.

They finally stopped for gas and food as the sun was going down, and Armando offered to take the next driving shift. Then as they were preparing to leave, Olivia dashed into a twenty-four-hour drugstore and emerged with several pillows and a pale blue blanket. "To make you more comfortable in the backseat," she told Howie. "We need to take good care of you so you can do your best job helping Armando."

Armando was careful not to speed as he drove south on the interstate. Traffic began steadily thinning as the hour grew later, and he had no intention of drawing any undue attention to the easy-to-spot Cadillac. Both Howie and Olivia appeared to be sleeping comfortably and he kept the radio playing softly, carefully scanning for a new-jazz or a soft-rock station as the other station faded out. It still amazed him that these two people were willing to help him like this. What had he ever done to deserve such good friends? In a way they seemed closer than family. He sighed. More than ever he hoped this thing would work itself out just like Howie was saying, not only for his sake but for theirs as well. And for Dora's.

Suddenly he felt a stab of concern. If the three of them were here, who was left to help Dora? Oh, he knew she was pretty capable of caring for herself, especially now that her arm was better. But who would help fend off the assaults of her son? Who would come to her defense if he got on her case again or accused her of being senile? Armando swallowed hard, then prayed for God to watch over his dear friend and protect her and keep her. And at the moment, he didn't know what more he could do.

Chapter Thirty-Three

$\mathscr{D}$ora sat on the sofa and stared blankly at the TV as her favorite game-show host droned on about tonight's winner. She stroked Homer's coat. "It's just you and me, old cat." She glanced out the window and sighed. "But I suppose we could go out and breathe some of that fresh evening air before we call it a night." She gently shoved the cat from her lap and went out on the porch and looked across the field to her right. Armando had made good progress with it and it looked nearly ready to plant now.

She thought about Armando and sighed sadly. Hopefully he wouldn't be gone for good. Surely Howie, of all people, ought to be able to help the poor boy. Somehow she believed, despite what her son had said, that Armando must be innocent. He seemed such a good boy. Oh, she knew he wasn't perfect, but then who was? Except for maybe her Henry. And, to be honest, she had to admit that even dear Henry had a flaw or two. She looked off to the aspen grove and suddenly longed to see Henry's Garden once more. It was as if her beloved were beckoning—come meet him there.

"I'm taking a little walk," she told Homer, carefully making her way down the steps so as not to be tripped up by the feline again. She'd learned that lesson. Slowly she walked through the plowed field and then followed the mowed-down trail that Armando had so thoughtfully created.

She smiled when she saw the crude sign—Henry's Garden— then touching her hand to her lips, suppressed a girlish giggle as she entered the garden. Everything looked much the same as the previous evening when she'd seen it for the first time, only all was quiet and still now, except for the gurgling sound of the nearby creek and an occasional bird twitter or cricket chirrup. She paused to watch the fish swimming, happily it seemed, in one flashing swirl of fluid orange, as if they too were afraid to be left alone—isolated from their companions in some dark corner of the pond.

"No one likes to be alone, Homer," she said as the cat rubbed against her legs. She strolled around and admired the flowers and plants, pausing to pick several sweet violets that were still faithfully blooming. Violets had always been one of her favorite flowers. She'd always looked forward to their early appearance after the long winter, so bravely poking their heads out and turning their sweet purple faces toward the sun. They wouldn't be around much longer with summer's heat starting to bear down upon them.

Finally, tired from her walk, she sat down on the lawn chair directly across from the pond and looked over at the funny angel sculpture. Hadn't Armando called it the Garden Angel? Or was it the *Guardian* Angel? She couldn't remember for sure. Perhaps it was meant to be both. She wondered if there really were guardian angels that actually watched out for people, or was that just some old wives' tale? And then she wondered if there were real angels in heaven, and even more than that, she wondered if there really was a heaven. Or did people simply go into some deep sleep when they died?

"Are you sleeping, Henry?" she asked in a weary voice. "Or is it like Howie says? Are you up there having a good old time and looking down on me and wishing I'd hurry up and figure things out so I could come and join you?" She looked at the sky and sighed. "Oh, Henry, can't you send down an angel to show me the truth? Or better yet, why don't you come on down here yourself? I fear I'm getting closer and closer to the end of my life, and sometimes it seems like I don't know a single thing anymore."

She leaned her head back and closed her eyes. Tired. She was bone tired. Sometimes it seemed like she was too old and weary to even go on for another day. And yet how could she stop when she felt so unsure as to what lay ahead for her? Of course she'd listened to Howie explaining all this to her, and some of what he said made sense—especially lately. But some of it was confusing too. Oh, if only her Henry could send her some sort of sign. Some kind of assurance that would convince her that there truly was a heaven— and that, somehow, she might be welcome there too. Perhaps then she could finally rest.

Just then a soft summer breeze stirred, and the aromatic smell of the violets in her hand wafted up to her nose. She opened her eyes and looked at them. Something about that smell suddenly reminded her of a day during that last spring. Henry had picked her a little bouquet of violets very much like this one, perhaps even from this same place, and then he'd whispered in her ear: "Forgiveness is like the violet that puts forth a sweet fragrance on the heel of the one who crushed it."

"Forgiveness." She said the word slowly, letting it roll off her tongue as if it were completely new and foreign to her. *"Forgiveness."*

She lifted her tiny bouquet to her nose and breathed in its sweetness. She had plucked these pretty flowers, torn them from their comfortable bed, and consequently ended their little lives in this happy garden. And yet they thanked her—thanked her with this delightful fragrance! The fragrance of forgiveness was completely undeserved by the one who received it, but given freely just the same. And suddenly, right there in Henry's Garden, she knew that Henry had sent her the answer—*forgiveness.*

Oh, Howie had tried to tell her, but she'd been too stubborn and dense to really see it. Now she knew—somehow she knew—that she was meant to forgive those who had crushed her . . . whether or not they deserved it. Just as the little violet gave up its fragrance to its abuser—or the way the Lord Jesus had died on the cross.

Suddenly it all made sense. Oh, not to her head perhaps, but to her heart. Her heart understood perfectly.

She bowed her head. "Dear Lord . . ." She sighed deeply. "I know I haven't spoken to You for a long, long spell. Not really anyway. And I 'spect I've been mad at You over the years. But somehow I'm not mad anymore. I'm just old and tired and sad in my heart. I 'spect You know how I've tried to live a good life and do what's right, but I'm afraid I haven't done too well. I can see that plain as day now."

Tears streamed down her face as she considered all the memories that had come her way recently, reminders of how things had really been. "There's so much that I did all wrong." She dug in her pocket for her handkerchief and wiped the tears from her wet cheeks, once again smelling the violets still clutched in her hand. "I know You're a forgiving God. Howie's told me so dozens of times. And I know that's why You let Your own Son die on the cross. Well, the fact is, I need a whole lot of that forgiveness right now and I'm asking You—" she let out a small sob—"I'm begging You. Please forgive me."

She took in a deep jagged breath and then she sat there for a long moment. And suddenly she felt a cool breeze waft over her— clean and fresh—like forgiveness. "Thank You," she whispered. And then she sat there in a deeply contented silence, just drinking it in. It felt even better to her than her long-awaited bath back when her arm was in the cast.

"Oh, thank You, Lord," she said with her eyes turned to the sky. And then she bowed her head again and asked for His help so that she might somehow forgive others in the same way that He had forgiven her. "I 'spect it'll take some time, Lord," she said in a matter-of-fact voice. "But I also 'spect, like Howie says, You'll help me to work this thing out."

She sighed as she opened her eyes once again and felt surprised to see that it was growing dark already. She must have been out here much longer than she realized. She stiffly pushed herself up from the lawn chair and began to walk through the shadows toward the entrance of the garden. But after only a few steps, her foot stumbled on something and she crumbled to the ground in a heap. As she lay there, she felt a sharp pain shooting through her leg like a bullet. It tore through her right hip clear down to her ankle and then it burned like fire.

She tried to get up, but instantly knew it was impossible. And so she lay there, the violets still clutched in her hand, and prayed that God's will be done. If it was her time to go, perhaps she was ready. She felt fairly sure that she was ready. Before long Homer came over and curled up against the warmth of her midsection, and even the pain seemed to subside after a bit or perhaps she was simply growing numb. And Dora, for the first time in her life, felt herself totally letting go of everything and completely trusting God. She felt completely at peace and ready for whatever lay ahead.

Chapter Thirty-Four

Olivia awoke around three in the morning and sleepily offered to relieve Armando and drive for a while.

"That's okay. I'm all right," he quietly reassured her. "You keep resting."

"Are you sure?"

"Yeah, really, I'm wide-awake right now. You sleep until the sun comes up, and then we can switch."

"Okay." She rearranged her pillow and leaned back.

"Olivia?" he asked.

"Yeah?"

"Do you think your grandmother is okay?"

"Oh, sure. She's fine. She sounded really glad that we'd found you and that we are going to help you."

He nodded. "Okay then. I'll try not to worry about her."

"We can call her when we stop for breakfast if you want."

"Yeah. That'd be good."

They were a couple hours north of L.A. when Armando stopped for gas and breakfast. Howie, although a little stiff, seemed to be faring the best of the three of them. "I was always good at sleeping in cars," he told them over hotcakes. "Something about the noise of the road and the purring of the engine puts me right to sleep."

"I tried to call Grandma," Olivia told them as they finished their breakfast. "But no one answered. She might've been outside though. I'll try again before we leave."

But Olivia's second attempt to reach Dora was unsuccessful too, and Armando felt a gnawing concern growing within him. "Is there someone else you could call?" he asked. "Someone who could check in on her and make sure she's okay?"

Olivia glanced at her watch. "Well, my parents wouldn't have gone to church yet. But I hate getting my dad involved."

"How about your mom?" Armando suggested. "She and Dora seem to get along all right."

"Yeah. As different as they are, Mom actually likes Grandma. Maybe I could get her to go over there without letting my dad know what's up."

So Olivia tried her parents and somehow managed to convince her mom to go check on Dora without disclosing their whereabouts or informing Charlie of her phone call.

"Good girl," said Howie when she told them the news. "Now, if we hit the road, we ought to make Los Angeles before noon."

Armando took his turn to sleep while Olivia drove, not even stirring until she stopped at a rest area right before the Grapevine. She tried once again to reach her grandmother, but still no answer. Then Armando, being familiar with L.A. freeways and traffic, offered to drive the last leg of their journey. It was almost noon by the time they checked into a Best Western motel.

"Everybody should take a little nap," suggested Howie. "Then we'll start working on our plan."

But Armando had trouble going to sleep. He glanced over at Howie, peacefully resting on the bed across from his, already snoring lightly. So Armando decided to pray. And after an hour or so, Howie woke up, and they got Olivia and all three went down to the hotel restaurant to get something to eat.

"I phoned Grandma again," said Olivia with a worried brow. "But she still isn't there. And I left a message at my parents', but

I was worried about revealing exactly what we were up to. I mean you never know what Dad might do."

"I hope Dora's okay." Armando pushed his plate away from him.

"Well, hopefully we can wrap this up quickly," said Howie. "I'll make some phone calls and leave some messages, but it's hard to accomplish much of anything on a Sunday. Tomorrow we'll start early and see how far we can get." He glanced out at the bright blue swimming pool, clearly visible from the restaurant. "And if I were you kids, I'd want to try out that pool."

Olivia frowned. "I didn't bring a suit."

"I'll bet they have some in that gift shop," said Howie. "It looks like they have almost everything you could imagine in there."

Armando felt concerned. "I know this trip is costing a bundle, Howie, and as soon as I can, I want to pay you—"

"No need for concern, Armando. Fact is, Dora's the one funding our little expedition." He smiled. "Not that we want to be extravagant with her money. But, trust me, you don't need to worry about the cost right now."

Olivia laughed. "Yeah, and knowing Grandma, she'll get the work out of you when we get back anyway."

Armando smiled. "I hope so."

Before he met Olivia at the pool, he decided to call Mickey and see if he could learn anything about his uncle.

"Hey, man," said Mickey. "What's up?"

"I'm in town," he explained. "I heard there's a warrant for me and I wanted to—"

"Yeah, that uncle of yours is a total jerk." Mickey swore. "I heard he's trying to make it seem like you were behind the whole thing. Your aunt is furious at him."

"Tia Marta?"

"Yeah, she knows it was Pedro's own stupid mess, not yours."

"Did you get the money order I sent for her?"

"Yeah, I gave it to her last week. That's when she told me about all this crazy mess. But, hey, she really appreciated the help, man."

"I wanted to go see her, but my . . . uh . . . my attorney says to wait."

"You got your own attorney?"

"Well, he's more like a friend."

"You hanging with lawyers now? Whoa, man, you've really come up in the world."

Armando laughed. "It's not really like that. The guy is retired and he's a friend of this lady I've been working for."

They talked a while longer. Then Armando made sure they could reach Mickey the following day in case they needed him to make a statement in his behalf.

"Good luck, man," said Mickey. "If anyone deserves a break, it's you."

"Thanks. Same to you."

Then for several blissful hours, Olivia and Armando forgot about their troubles as they acted like children, swimming and playing in the pool. They took naps in the shade and even ordered dinner to be served poolside. Howie sat on the deck, far enough away so as not to get splashed, as he read a paperback mystery, sipped on iced tea, and caught several well-deserved catnaps.

"Is the sky always that color?" asked Olivia as the two were toweling themselves after their final swim.

Armando looked at the dusty yellow sky, now growing orange along the edges as the sun dipped into the horizon. "Yeah, pretty much so."

She shook her head. "Kinda weird, huh?"

"Yeah. Does it make you appreciate your blue sky back in Oregon?"

"Oh, our sky can look like this too, but not usually in June. It doesn't usually get like this until late summer when farmers start burning grass fields or there's a forest fire or something, but even then it doesn't usually last for long."

"Well, it can look like this any time of the year down here. Once in a while we'll get a nice breeze off the ocean and it'll actually clear up for a day or two. But mostly it's like this if not worse."

"Don't know about you kids, but I'm ready to call it a night." Howie closed his book and slowly got up. "It's almost nine, and we've got a busy day ahead of us tomorrow."

"Shoot," said Olivia. "I forgot to try Grandma again. And by now she'd already be in bed."

"Don't worry, Olivia, she's probably fine," Howie assured her. "Besides you can check on her first thing in the morning."

Then the three of them headed for the elevator, and Armando and Howie told Olivia good night in front of her door.

"I'm worried about Dora," confessed Armando as soon as he and Howie were in their room.

Howie nodded. "To be honest, I am too. I've been keeping a stiff upper lip so as not to upset Olivia. But it's not like Dora to be out all day like that. I've been praying for her, and I know the good Lord is watching out for her, but I'd sure like to hear that everything's okay."

"Do you think you should call Charlie and see if he knows what's up?"

Just then the phone rang and Armando picked it up to hear Olivia on the other end. "It's Grandma!" she cried. "She fell down and broke her hip! Mom found her outside this morning and called an ambulance."

"Is she okay?"

"I guess she's as okay as possible—*after spending the night outside!*"

"She was outside all night?"

Howie's eyes grew wide with concern as he listened.

"It's Dora," Armando explained quickly. "She fell and broke her hip."

"Poor Grandma," said Olivia with a sob. "She's barely over breaking her arm and then this happens."

"Where is she now?"

"She's in the hospital, but Mom says they'll move her to Shady Acres in a day or two."

"*No way!*" Armando shook his head as he fought back a landslide of guilt. "That's the place where Dora says old people go to die."

"Mom told me that Grandma was okay with this."

"That doesn't sound like Dora to me." Armando motioned to Howie. "I think you need to tell Howie exactly what's going on, Olivia."

"Yeah, put him on."

Armando paced back and forth as he listened to Howie trying to soothe Olivia. Finally it sounded as if they'd decided that she should fly home and be with her grandmother as soon as possible.

"And instead of worrying," said Howie in a calm voice, "why don't you try praying, Olivia?" He paused as if listening for her response then said, "Oh, God doesn't care about all that stuff, honey. He loves you and will listen to you no matter who you are or what you've done. Just give Him a try and see." Then he hung up.

"So is Olivia going home?" asked Armando.

"Yeah, we think it's for the best."

Armando shook his head. "I feel like this is all my fault—like if I hadn't made such a mess of everything—"

"Son, there's a verse in the Bible that says that 'God causes everything'— even bad things—'to work together for the good of those who love God and are called according to His purpose for them.' And that's what I'm going to believe in this case. I would suggest you try to do the same. In the meantime, like I told Olivia, you could be praying for Dora."

"I have been."

Howie smiled. "I figured as much."

The next morning, Howie had Armando drop him off at the DA's office as soon as the doors were open. "And while I start untangling this mess, you can take Olivia to the airport and get her on the next flight home."

"But shouldn't I stay here with—"

"No. I'll explain that I'm taking full responsibility for you and that you'll be back shortly to turn yourself in."

Armando nodded. He didn't really like the idea of turning himself in, but he knew it had to be done. Hopefully, they wouldn't lock him up and throw away the key forever.

Howie handed Olivia his Visa card. "Now, don't go hog-wild with this."

She laughed. "Yeah, like maybe I'll run down to Rio and have myself a good ol' time."

"Call and let us know how she's doing." Howie tipped his hat as he turned toward the large foreboding building.

"Are you scared?" asked Olivia after they got onto the freeway.

"Huh?"

"You're being so quiet. I just wondered if you're worried about getting put in jail."

"Yeah, I guess I am. But the truth is I'm even more worried about Dora. I'm glad you're going back to help her."

"Me too. I don't want her going to Shady Acres. I know that would kill her for sure."

Armando bit his lip. Once again, he tried to tell himself this wasn't his fault, but he still felt guilty.

It took longer than he'd expected to park and get Olivia's airline ticket. But finally she had the ticket in hand and they were standing at the final security check before the gates.

"Only passengers can go through here," she told him.

"Yeah. Well, have a good flight then." He felt a lump growing in his throat but wasn't sure why. Yet for some unexplainable reason he felt as if this could be the final good-bye for them.

"Don't worry, Armando." She smiled. "Everything's going to turn out okay."

He nodded. "Yeah, but if I don't . . . well, you know . . . if things don't work out and I have to stay down here—"

"No, Armando!" she grabbed him firmly by the arm. "Don't even think that!"

"Hey, it's possible." He shrugged, trying to act tough or nonchalant or maybe even macho. But he really felt like crying. "This is L.A., you know. And you can never tell what might happen—"

"Don't say that!" She clung tightly to his arm now and suddenly she was the one who was crying. "I can't do this thing without you, Armando. You—you've been the only one keeping me going. I know I can't do this without you. I'm afraid I'll go back to my old ways—my old stuff—"

He wrapped his arms around her and pulled her close to him. "You *can* do this, Olivia. You've been very strong. Believe me, you can do this without me."

"I'm afraid." She looked up with watery eyes. "I'm scared to death that I'm going to fail—that I'll fall right back into my old messed-up life."

"It's like Howie said: you need to ask God to help you." He spoke in an even voice now. "I know this might sound strange. But I mean it, Olivia. Honestly, God is the only thing that's keeping me going right now. I've been praying more than ever and I'm really trying to trust Him—for everything. And it's honestly making a difference."

"Really?" She peered at him with what seemed a faint trace of hope. "Do you *really* believe that?"

"I do."

"That's interesting because I tried praying last night, after I talked with Howie. And I have to admit that it felt really weird and sort of phony at first. But I kept going and suddenly it seemed really real— I mean like God was really listening. I even got goose bumps. But then I wondered if I was imagining it." She stepped back now and let go of his arm, wiping her wet cheeks with her hand.

He firmly shook his head. "I know what you mean. I felt like that at first too. But more and more I believe it is real. I believe God is listening and that He's going to help us through this. I really believe it, Olivia."

"But what if, like you said, you have to stay down here. What if Howie can't clear you?"

"Then I'll have to trust God for that too." But even as he said the words, he wondered if they were true. Could he really trust God while serving an unfair jail sentence? Maybe only time would tell.

"But what about us, Armando?"

He felt his brows rise. *"Us?"*

She looked down now, fidgeting with her bag as if she were embarrassed.

He reached over and touched her shoulder. "Olivia?" he asked. "Do you really mean there's an *us?*"

She looked back up at him and nodded. "I want there to be an us." Then she frowned. "You honestly didn't know that?"

"Well, there was Ben—I didn't want to—"

"But what about *you*, Armando?" She set her bag down at her feet and folded her arms across her chest. "What about what *you* want?"

He looked down at her and grinned. "Hey, I wanted you even before I'd ever met you. I was hooked on you from the time I first saw your picture on Dora's mantel on the same day I'd actually considered stealing her truck."

"You were going to steal her truck?"

He laughed. "I tried to make myself think I was."

She shook her head. "You couldn't do it though."

"I guess not. But somehow that old pickup stopped me, and then I saw that picture of you and was blown away."

She tossed him a coy look. "Oh, go on."

He pushed back a stray strand of hair from her eyes. "Of course, back then I thought you must've been a perfect angel."

"And now?"

He smiled. "I know you're human and make mistakes—just like me."

She shook her head again. "No, I think I've done a much better job of making mistakes than you have."

"I don't know. My mistake might land me in prison."

She threw her arms around him. "No way! That cannot happen." Then she held out Howie's Visa card, still in her hand. "Hey, we could go get tickets, Armando, to anywhere on the earth. We could run away to some deserted beach in Mexico and never come back. Of course, we'd pay Howie back in time and—"

He laughed at her. "I know you don't mean that, Olivia. You couldn't run out on Dora and Howie like that."

She slowly shook her head and handed him the card. "No, you're right. Please, don't tell Howie that I—"

"Don't worry." He reached up and touched her cheek then studied her face for a long moment. "I need to remember how you look, just in case—"

"Don't say it, Armando." She put her hands on either side of his face, and pulling him toward her, she kissed his mouth, warmly and tenderly. "But you better remember this." Then she stepped back. "And so you know, I'm taking this God thing seriously, I'm going to be praying real hard that God brings you back—and soon!"

He nodded, unable to even speak.

"Good-bye, Armando!" She picked up her bag and walked through the suddenly vacant security line.

He stayed and waited until she was on the other side of the gate. He wanted to yell out, "I love you, Olivia!" but somehow he couldn't get the words to form themselves in his mouth. Instead he just waved and wondered if he would ever see her again.

Chapter Thirty-Five

Armando, as he'd promised, returned to the DA's office. He felt his chest tighten as he walked through the heavy glass doors and began explaining his situation to the receptionist. She got on the phone, keeping a wary eye on Armando as she spoke, almost as if she expected him to bolt. He waited, wondering if an armed guard would soon be escorting him to a police car, where he would be quickly transported to jail—perhaps in a cell with Tio Pedro, although that seemed unlikely.

Then the receptionist gave him directions to an office on the third floor. Thankfully when he arrived, Howie was already there, sitting comfortably in a chair with a small stack of papers in front of him. And seated at the desk across from him was a middle-aged African-American woman.

"This is Marsha Adams," said Howie. "And this, Armando Garcia."

Armando shook hands with the woman. "Nice to meet you, ma'am."

"You have a good lawyer here, son." She peered at Howie from above her narrow glasses as she shuffled through some papers. "And very persuasive too."

Howie chuckled. "Marsha has been very kind to take the time to see us today, Armando. She's an important woman with a very busy schedule, you know."

"I really appreciate it, ma'am."

"Well, your story intrigued me." She studied Armando closely now. "Your aunt stopped by to see me last week."

"Tia Marta?"

With no show of emotion, she nodded. "She has given me her statement."

"Statement?" Now Armando wasn't sure if this was good or bad. It seemed impossible that Marta would stand up against her husband.

"Yes. She is willing to swear under oath that Pedro lied about your involvement in the cocaine bust."

"Cocaine?" His eyes widened.

"Yes. Quite a lot of cocaine. Street value of about five hundred thousand."

"Half a million?"

"You didn't know?"

"I knew the instant I saw those bags that they didn't contain crutches. And I knew it couldn't be good. That's why I wanted to get out of there." He slowly shook his head. "But half a million dollars' worth of cocaine . . ."

"We've already begun to prepare your statement," explained Howie. "But we need some more information from you."

So Armando and Howie spent the next couple hours with Marsha's assistant, Betty, answering questions and filling out paper-work. Finally, in the middle of the afternoon, Marsha stuck her head in the little cubicle. "You guys about done in there?"

"I think I've got what I need," said Betty.

"I'd like to see the guys in my office then."

Armando followed Howie back into Marsha's office, his heart pounding with apprehension. Was this going to be it? Was he going to be carted off to jail now to await sentencing?

"Have a seat," she said as she sank down into her chair with a sigh. "Let me cut to the chase, okay?"

"Sure." Armando swallowed hard.

"All charges will be dropped in exchange for your statement and testimony."

"Praise the Lord!" shouted Howie.

Armando blinked. "Just like that?"

She leaned forward. "You are willing to testify against your uncle, right?"

He considered this for a moment, imagining himself in the witness stand, Tio Pedro sitting and glaring at him from across the room. "Yes. I am willing to tell the truth."

"That's all we ask."

And so it was settled. A few more papers were signed, and then Marsha bid Howie and Armando, *"Adios."* She winked at Armando. "That means 'go with God,' you know."

He nodded. "Yeah, I know. *Adios* to you too."

* * * * * * * * * * * * *

Howie decided it was too late in the day to begin their trek back to Oregon. But just the same, it seemed nothing short of a miracle that the two of them were heading north on I-5 first thing the following morning. There seemed no doubt that God had helped them out on this. They started their trip before sunrise in order to beat the morning commuter traffic and were safely out of town by dawn.

"I'm perfectly willing to spell you on the driving," offered Howie. "I'll admit I'm not the fastest thing on the road, but I do know how to keep it between the lines."

Armando chuckled. "Don't worry, Howie. I feel like I could drive from here to New York if I had to today. I'm so thankful not to be locked up or caught in the L.A. judicial system right now."

Howie nodded. "All I can say is that I think God was on your side, son. Things happened at the courthouse yesterday that you don't expect to see. It was quite heartening to an old coot like me. Almost makes me want to take up my practice again."

"Why don't you?"

Howie laughed. "Well, other than Dora and a couple other old cronies, I might be a little-hard pressed for clients."

"I'd hire you in a heartbeat." Armando smiled. "If I needed a lawyer, that is, and if I could afford it."

"Hopefully you won't be needing a lawyer again anytime soon."

"But what about Dora? Last night, Olivia said that she seemed completely resigned to the idea of going into Shady Acres, and Olivia's actually having to talk her into going back home again."

"I don't fully understand it myself. Unless she's been so worn down by Charlie that she simply doesn't care anymore. Did Olivia say whether she seemed depressed or despondent at all?"

"No, but she said that Dora seemed different. And, naturally, it sounded like she was still pretty worn-out by her ordeal of spending a night outside with a broken hip."

"A broken hip can be bad news for old-timers like us."

"Why would it be any worse than a broken arm? I mean I realize it's a bigger bone, but wouldn't it heal in time?"

"I can't even begin to recall how many times I've seen an elderly person go steadily downhill after a broken hip. It starts out with a broken hip and then one thing leads to another, but it's usually pneumonia that gets them in the end."

"Well, we'll have to help her fight it." Armando nodded firmly. "Dora needs to know that we're all here for her, that we'll take care of her and keep things running until she's better."

"That might be just the ticket, son." Howie leaned his head back and closed his eyes. "Might be just what the doctor ordered."

Armando drove the fastest he dared to without risking a speeding ticket. He felt he'd already narrowly escaped the law once and wasn't about to take any more chances, no matter how small. As he drove, he thought back to the previous evening when Howie had let him borrow the Caddie to pick up his things as well as visit with Tia Marta and the girls. They'd all been so happy to see him. With screams of delight his little cousins had thrown themselves at him, wrapping their arms around his waist and legs as they told him that they'd never let him go again.

"You girls go outside and play," scolded Tia Marta. "Let us have some peace."

"Sorry, I won't be able to stay longer," he told the girls as they scurried out the door. "But I'll stay in touch."

"Will you?" Tia Marta's dark eyes were somber.

"I'll write," he promised. "And I'll send you money when I can."

She shook her head. "No, you don't need to worry about us, Armando. I have a job now and I should get a raise at the end of the month."

"But I'll help if I can. You guys are my only family."

She glanced at her daughters, now happily playing outside in the wading pool. "I've heard from Rita, Armando."

He tried not to register too much interest in the woman—his own mother—who'd sold him to his grandmother more than two decades ago. "How is she?"

"She's okay, I guess. She has a good job, and she even offered to help me out a little when I told her about Pedro's latest fiasco."

"That's nice."

"She asked about you."

"Did she?"

"Yes. And when I told her that you'd left, she sounded a little concerned."

"I wonder why that should concern her."

"I don't know. But something about the way she spoke sounded like maybe she had some regrets or something. I don't quite know how to describe it. Anyway, I told her if I heard from you I'd let her know. But is that okay with you? I mean I would totally understand if you don't want anything to do with her, Armando. Sometimes I don't want anything to do with her myself. Except she is my only sister, and well, like you said, we're family."

He nodded. "Yes, I can understand that. And I don't mind if you tell her what I'm doing. It's nothing to be ashamed of."

"No, no. Of course not. Farmwork is good honest work."

He thought about trying to explain to her that it was more than that—that he and Dora had dreams of making it into something far bigger. But the truth was he wasn't sure what he was going back to, only that he was going back.

"What if your mother wants to write to you or be in contact?"

He shrugged. "I doubt that she will, but if she does, it's okay. You know that I don't hate her, Tia Marta. Abuela Maria made me promise to forgive her, you know. And I have done that—am doing it."

"Do you know what her name means? Rita?"

He shook his head.

"Saint Rita is the patron saint of lost dreams."

"Lost dreams?" He laughed. "Well, that sounds about right."

His aunt smiled then hugged him with fresh tears filling her eyes. "I would be proud to call you my son, Armando."

"Thanks."

"And—" she stepped back and wiped her eyes—"I am so sorry for what Pedro did to you. When I think that you could be locked up right now—" She swore quietly in Spanish. "Oh, it makes me so furious!"

"Yeah, I know what you mean, but we've both got to forgive him."

"Forgive him?" She scowled. "I'd rather spit on him—or worse."

He smiled. "Well, that's understandable. But try to remember what Abuela used to say about forgiving others—and what the Bible says."

Tia Marta narrowed her eyes. "When did you become so reli-gious, Armando Enrico Garcia? I don't ever remember you going to church when you lived in *my* house."

"It's not so much about being religious, I think, as it is about living your life for God. That's what I'm trying to do now."

"So are you going to become a priest?" Her eyes grew hopeful. "Mama always thought you'd make a good priest."

He thought of Olivia then laughed. "No, not if I can help it."

Once again, he thanked her for her statement and promised to stay in touch. Then he took a few minutes to stop by Mickey's place before he headed back to the hotel for the evening. Mickey's life appeared to be going along exactly the same route as before, but at least Mickey seemed happy with it. And he had a new girlfriend who seemed pretty nice. But when he left, Armando couldn't help but feel a strong sense of relief that he wasn't still stuck there with him. It suddenly seemed strangely ironic that something as wrong and senseless as Tio Pedro's spoiled drug deal could change Armando's life in such a positive way. But perhaps it was like Howie had said. God can use all things to bring good if you trust Him.

And now, as he sped down the highway, he felt even more relieved to know that they would be *home* before midnight. Yet even as that word flashed through his mind, he wondered. Was his destination really *home?* Or was he just like his mother, or was it her patron saint, chasing after lost dreams?

* * * * * * * * * * * * *

The last couple hours of driving became a blur in Armando's mind, but somehow they made it safely back to Treasure, and he accepted Howie's generous offer of a bed and probably fell asleep before his head ever touched the pillow. But he was up with the sun the next day, ready to seek out Dora and Olivia as soon as possible.

"You been up long, son?" asked Howie when he finally ambled

out of his room, still wearing a worn plaid bathrobe and a sleepy expression.

"An hour or so." Armando held out a half-full pot of coffee. "I took the liberty of making myself at home. Want some?"

Howie grinned. "Sounds good."

Armando handed him a cup of coffee then sat down. "I wonder if Olivia was able to convince Dora to go home or not."

"One way to find out."

"Think it's too early to call?"

"Nah. You know Dora; she's a farm gal through and through—gets up and goes to bed with the chickens."

Armando dialed the number and waited for several rings. Then just as he was about to give up, Olivia answered.

"You're there?" he exclaimed. "So did you get Dora to come home too?"

"Yeah. I was just helping her out of bed. Man, we could really use your muscles right now."

"I'm at Howie's."

"You're kidding?" Her voice grew loud with excitement. "You guys are back? You want me to come pick you up? I mean after I get Grandma settled and everything."

"Sure, that'd be great."

To show his appreciation to Howie, he insisted on fixing breakfast and then cleaning up. He was finishing when Olivia knocked on the back door.

"I can't believe that Howie already has you on KP!" she exclaimed as she let herself in.

"Hey, I insisted," said Armando as he hugged her. "I owe this man everything."

Howie laughed. "Better watch yourself, son. That was a delicious omelet you made me. I might not want to let you go back to Dora."

"Hey, anytime you want a home-cooked meal, you just give me

a holler." Armando smiled as he hung up the dish towel. "Or better yet, stop on by the farm."

Olivia grabbed his arm. "But for now I'm taking him with me."

"You tell Dora that I'll drop by this afternoon to check on her as well as to talk business," called Howie. "And the key to my car is on that hook by the back door, in case you want to unload your stuff now."

"Thanks," called Armando.

They were barely out the door when Olivia threw her arms around him and kissed him on the cheek. "I missed you *so* much!"

He looked down at her as if he were drinking in her face. "I was worried that I wouldn't get to see you again, Olivia. I mean everything between you and me seemed too good to be true—and you know what they say about that."

She laughed. "But we don't have to listen to them now, do we? And besides, I was really praying that you'd get off."

"Really?" He blinked. "You actually prayed?"

"Yeah." She nodded as she took his backpack from him. "You surprised?"

He shook his head in amazement. Then opening the trunk of Howie's Caddie, he grabbed an armload of his stuff and headed toward the street. "Hey," he called when he saw the pickup. "You're driving my truck."

She dropped her own load into the back of the pickup. "Yeah. I couldn't find *my* keys anywhere and yours were sitting right there on your dresser."

He smiled sheepishly. "Oh, yeah, I forgot about your keys."

"That's okay. You can hang on to them for a while. There's no place I want to go anyway." She handed him his keys. "But you can drive—unless you're worn-out from your trip—"

"No way." He held firm to the keys. "I can't wait to drive my own pickup again." Together they quickly loaded all his stuff and were soon on their way home.

* * * * * * * * * * * * *

Dora was sitting in a wheelchair at the kitchen table when they got home. Armando went straight to her and gingerly gave her a hug. "I don't want to hurt you," he said apologetically. "But it's so good to see you again."

She smiled. "It's good to see you too, son."

He knelt down in front her. "And are you feeling okay? I mean besides your hip; I know that must hurt."

"I guess I should've been taking those calcium pills like the doctor told me before."

"Are you taking them now?"

She glanced at Olivia. "Yes, Nurse Olivia is seeing to that."

He pulled a chair over and sat down beside her. "Are you happy to be home, Dora?"

She nodded. "Oh, yes. I love my little farm."

He sighed in relief. "Oh, good. I was worried when Olivia said you were ready to go to the nursing home."

"Well, I guess I was trying to be cooperative—not so stubborn, you know. I didn't want to make it difficult for everyone."

"Oh, Grandma." Olivia took her hand. "You know you're no trouble. I love being out here with you. And so does Armando."

"That's right, Dora. And we're going to take such good care of you that you'll be outside dancing a jig in the rain in no time."

She smiled then shook her head. "Oh, I doubt there'll be much dancing for me. Not on earth anyway."

"Oh, Grandma."

Dora held up her hand. "No, I want to have my say. You two are young and strong and I remember how that felt back when—why, you think that you'll live forever. But the truth is you won't. We all have to die sometime. And the good news is that I finally think I'm ready. That's why I decided it didn't matter so much if they took me to Shady Acres after all."

"But you don't *want* to go there, do you?" Armando studied her face. "I mean, I know we're not professional nurses or anything, but I think we can take pretty good care of you—if you'll let us."

Dora laughed. "Of course I'll let you. And of course I want to be in my own home on my own farm. There's no better place on earth. I just can't figure out why two young, healthy things like you would want to be tied down with an old, good-for-nothing piece of baggage like—"

"Grandma!" Olivia wagged her finger under Dora's nose. "I don't want to hear that kind of talk."

Dora smiled. "Yes, yes. You've already told me that. Now why don't you run off and do something useful like the laundry. I want to have a private word with Armando here."

Olivia stood. "Okay, then, I guess I can take a hint."

Armando laughed. "That wasn't exactly a hint."

Dora reached for his hand. "I was doing some thinking while you were gone, Armando. Like I said, it's occurred to me that I'm not going to last forever. The truth is, I thought I was a goner that night in the garden." She sighed. "But I felt ready to go. And what a beautiful place to breathe your last breath—Henry's Garden."

"Well, I'm going to go over that path, really carefully this time, and I'll make sure there's nothing to trip you up, ever again."

She held up her hand. "Don't you worry about that. It was pure clumsiness on my part. But while I was out there preparing myself to meet my Maker, it occurred to me that I was leaving you high and dry. And I got to thinking: what would my Henry do under these same circumstances? I remembered what high stock Henry put in having a good education. He never got to go on to college himself, but he was well read and what you might call a self-taught man.

And I never thought less of him for a single minute. Still, I thought to myself that Henry would say you should go to school, Armando. And I got to thinking we've got that nice college nearby—where Olivia goes sometimes, when she's a mind to—and I remembered hearing they have some sort of agricultural program and I got to thinking that's just what you need. So I'm setting aside enough tuition money for you to attend college. I realize that you might want to work on the farm too, so I 'spect you can take it at your own pace if you like."

"Dora . . . " Armando shook his head. "That is so generous of you. I don't even know how to thank you—"

"Well, then, don't." She pressed her lips together. "In fact, it would make me happy not to hear another word of it, other than your promise that you'll do it—go to college I mean. You seem like a smart young man to me. And it's something I want to do."

"Yes, of course, I promise I'll go. It would be an honor. It's something I only dreamed of."

She smiled. "Good. No reason you can't start in September. Talk to Olivia about the details of getting signed up and all. I'll arrange the finances with Howie the next time I see him."

"Oh, that's right. He said he'd be coming over this afternoon."

She clapped her hands together. "Perfect."

"And unless I'm needed in here, I think there's work to be done outside."

"Yes, I figured you'd be anxious to get back out to the soil." She smiled.

Armando thought about his childhood dream as he walked across the yard to the barn. He'd dreamed of going to college, encouraged by his grandmother and the nuns at school, who always told him he was brighter than average. He'd even thought that his dream might've been possible. But it seemed that dream had become lost after Abuela Maria died and his life had become hard. He thought about his mother's patron saint again—Rita, the finder of lost dreams. Maybe there was still a chance for him. And, who knew, maybe there was still a chance for his mother, and she too would find her lost dreams. Miracles happened.

Chapter Thirty-Six

$\mathcal{A}$t dinner that evening, Dora was quieter than usual, and Armando noticed that she only ate a few bites of food before she said she was full.

"You feeling okay, Dora?" he asked as he and Olivia started clearing the table.

"I guess I'm just thinking." She folded her hands in her lap.

"About what?" he asked.

"About having another garden party."

"Really?" He studied her. "Are you sure you're up for it?"

"Why not? All I need is someone to wheel me out there."

"I think a garden party would be fun," said Olivia. "Who shall we invite?"

"Charlie and Audrey."

"Mom and Dad?" Olivia's voice sounded horrified. "Why on earth would you want to invite *them?*"

"They're family."

"I know, but—"

"And we need to talk."

"I think it's a good idea," said Armando as he wiped down the table.

Olivia frowned at him. "Well, I think you're both getting a little loopy."

"Let's plan it for Saturday evening," said Dora in a firm voice. "You can call them for me, Olivia."

"Yeah, sure." Olivia scraped the leftover food off of a plate.

Armando slipped behind Olivia and gave her a gentle squeeze. "Come on; give it a try."

She smiled. "Okay. But don't blame me if we have a fireworks show and it's only June."

"And we can invite Howie too," said Dora. "He's like family."

Armando felt relieved at this, since he knew he wasn't exactly family himself. "You want me to give him a call?"

"Yes, thank you. Let's plan it for seven, just like last time."

"But what if Dad refuses to come?" asked Olivia.

"I think he'll want to be here." Dora nodded then wheeled herself into the living room and turned on the TV.

As it turned out, no one declined their invitation. And so a small party for six was planned for Saturday evening. Olivia and Armando took charge of the refreshments and even spent a couple hours sprucing up the garden that morning. And although they weren't sure why, they both knew this evening was very important to Dora.

"I want you to use my best dishes and silver," Dora informed them that afternoon as they were putting together the food and drinks.

"Out in the garden?" Olivia shook her head. "Don't you think that's a little over the top?"

"And there's a linen tablecloth in the bottom drawer there." Dora pointed to the china hutch. "And maybe some candles would be nice too."

Olivia tossed a questioning look at Armando, but he just smiled. "That sounds like a good idea, Dora."

After an early dinner, Armando and Olivia made several trips before they had everything they wanted in the garden and began to set things up. They had made Dora promise to have a little rest before the evening's activities began.

"I really don't see why Grandma wants to invite more conflict with my dad," said Olivia as she spread the white tablecloth over Armando's makeshift table. "She seems so much happier lately. Why spoil it? And then we go to all this trouble—for what?" She turned and looked at Armando.

He shrugged. "I'm not sure, but something about Dora is different. I think she wants a chance to make her peace with Charlie."

"But does that mean she's caving?" Olivia's eyes grew wide. "Do you think she's going to give up her fight and just let him sell her place after all?"

"I don't know. But it's her place. If she wants him to sell it, I guess it's up to her."

Olivia firmly shook her head. "No way! I know she wouldn't do that. This farm was Grandpa's dream. She wouldn't do that to him."

A little before seven they returned to the house, and Olivia helped Dora get ready for the party while Armando waited on the porch for the guests to arrive. He was thankful to see the low blue Caddie pulling into the driveway first. Howie's presence would be valuable tonight. Armando waved and walked over to the car to greet him.

"So this is the big showdown?" said Howie as he climbed from the car.

"Showdown?"

Howie chuckled. "Well, that's probably not the right word. But I get the feeling there will be some word slinging here tonight."

Armando frowned. "I hope it doesn't get too heavy. Dora seems a little frail lately."

"That's too bad. She seemed pretty perky a couple of days ago— she was so happy to have you two kids back with her again."

Armando nodded. "Maybe it's just her hip. I know that it hurts a lot and she's so stubborn about taking those pain pills, but we made her promise to take one tonight."

"We might all wish we'd taken a pain pill before this evening is over."

That's when Armando noticed Charlie's car turning from the highway. "Here comes the rest of the party."

"Is it party time yet?" asked Dora as Olivia wheeled her onto the porch.

"My, don't you look lovely, Dora," said Howie, removing his hat and bowing like a true gentleman.

She waved her hand then grinned. "It's Olivia's doings. She thought I should get prettied up for the big evening."

"Couldn't hurt." Olivia winked at Armando. "Sometimes you feel better when you look better."

"You look pretty good yourself," whispered Armando as he stepped onto the porch next to her, giving a slow nod of admiration for her flowery sundress.

"Here come the parents," said Olivia in a flat voice. "Oh, the fun's about to begin."

"Olivia." Dora shook her finger at her granddaughter then smiled. "This might go better than you expect."

Olivia leaned against the porch railing and sighed. "Miracles can happen."

Charlie got out of the car then went to the other side to open the door for Audrey. "Hey, everyone," called Audrey in a happy voice. "Sorry we're a little late, but Charlie had to listen to the end of the *Wall Street Report.*" She went up on the porch and grasped Dora's hands. "My, but you look pretty tonight. That hat is lovely on you."

Dora smiled. "Olivia dug it out of the closet. I'm sure I haven't worn it in fifty years—don't know how we missed it for the rummage-sale things. How did that go, by the way?"

"Oh, it was a real success. I can't remember the exact numbers, but I know it was enough to build a new children's wing at the mission we support down in Bolivia."

Dora turned her attention to Charlie now. "I'm so glad you could make it, Charlie." She smiled up at him.

"How are you feeling, Mom?"

"I've been better. But all in all, not too bad." She looked around the group. "And it's so good to have my family all gathered around me. I just wish that young Charlie could be here too."

"I'm sure he would've liked to come, but he and Tiffany are taking a cruise right now," said Audrey. "To celebrate their fifth anniversary. Imagine my little boy has already been married five years. Seems like yesterday."

"Better watch out, Audrey," warned Howie. "He could make a grandma out of you in no time."

She frowned. "Oh, now I don't know about that."

"Well, are we ready?" asked Dora. She pointed toward the garden. "The party is that way."

* * * * * * * * * * * * *

Dora braced herself as Armando and Olivia each grasped a side of her wheelchair and lifted her down the stairs. "Armando already started making Grandma a ramp," said Olivia to no one in particu-lar. "It's out in the barn."

"That's nice," said Audrey as they started walking along the path.

As planned, Armando led the way, pushing Dora in her wheel-chair. "Watch your step," he warned the others. "I've tried to make the path as smooth as possible, but—"

"If you're as clumsy as me," finished Dora, "you better watch out." She laughed. "Of course, I don't have to worry about that now. This riding around in a chair is starting to grow on me." Still, she held on to the wheelchair's arms as she rumbled along.

"Hopefully you won't have to be in that thing for too long," said

Audrey from behind. "Has your physical therapist been out here to visit this week?"

"Yes. He'll come on Tuesdays and Thursdays and the nurse will come on the other days. Olivia has it all written down for me, nice and neat. But Olivia's my best little nurse and she'll even put me through my exercises on the days when the therapist doesn't come."

Charlie cleared his throat as if he was going to say something, but instead he kept walking. Finally they reached the entrance to the garden and Dora pointed up to the sign. "See that," she said with more enthusiasm than she'd felt in years. "Armando made that to remember Henry by."

"How sweet," said Audrey. "I never knew Henry, but I'm sure he'd be happy with this."

"Oh, yes," agreed Howie. "He would've loved what Armando's done with the place."

Charlie cleared his throat again, but this time he spoke. "So, did you ever find the hidden treasure, Armando?"

Dora sensed derision in her son's tone, but Armando seemed to ignore it. "I guess there's more than one kind of treasure, sir."

"Okay," said Dora. "Come into the garden."

One by one they entered the garden, and Audrey, the most congenial guest by far, immediately began to gush over the beauty. "Why, it's marvelous, Armando. Did you really do all this yourself?"

"Well, the flowers were still here from when Henry planted them. But I moved them around a little."

"And he built that pond," said Olivia with pride. "See—it even has fish in it. And he made that sculpture—isn't it great?"

"It's very good." Audrey chuckled. "I hope Ben didn't see it. I'm sure it would make him jealous."

"Speaking of Ben." Charlie entered the conversation again. "What's become of the young man anyway?"

Olivia shrugged. "I don't really know, Dad. Haven't you heard that Ben and I are history now?" Then she reached for Armando's hand and slipped hers inside it and smiled.

Dora thought she saw Charlie's nostrils flare slightly, but then he pressed his lips together and simply stared at the couple.

"We have refreshments over here," called Dora, hoping to distract her son.

"That looks lovely," said Audrey as she picked up a fragile china plate and began filling it. "Oh, this is so fun, Dora. I haven't been to a good garden party in ages."

"Dora is going to become legendary for her garden parties," joked Howie. "This is her second one of the season."

"Really?" Charlie's voice sounded skeptical, and he looked at his mother as if seeing a stranger.

"Oh, yes," said Dora. "Although to be fair, the first party was hosted by Armando. It was his grand opening of Henry's Garden."

"And it was very nice," added Olivia as she filled glasses with strawberry lemonade. "Everyone said so."

"But the garden is good for more than parties," said Dora, as Howie sat down in the lawn chair next to her. "I like to come here in the mornings to just think and pray and be quiet. Olivia brings me out here and I sit and enjoy it." She sighed. "Everyone should have a garden like this."

"Armando and I have been talking about making a small pond in my backyard," said Howie. "He said he could make it with a fountain and fish and everything."

"Ooh," said Audrey. "I'd love to have something like that in our yard too. Can you put me on your list, Armando?"

By now everyone was comfortably seated in the casual circle of chairs next to the pond. Everyone except Charlie, who stood off to the side with his arms folded across his chest and a scowl carved into his brow. "Well, you'd better check with me first, Audrey. I'm not ready to have someone digging holes in my backyard anytime soon."

Dora laughed. "Well, Charlie, sometimes you've got to do a little digging before you find the treasure."

"Come on over here and sit down and join the party," urged Audrey, patting the empty chair beside her. "You look like an old ogre over there."

"I'm not sure I want to join this party."

"Oh, Charlie," said Dora. "I know we've had our differences. But tonight is about forgetting those things."

He shook his head. "There are some things I can't forget, Mom."

"Oh, I know." She nodded. "I've felt like that myself. But lately I've learned a few things. And if an old woman like me can change, surely you can too, Charlie."

"Maybe I'm not the one who needs to change."

"Dad!" snapped Olivia. "Can you even hear yourself? After all you've done, Grandma is trying to reach out to you and you're—"

"That's okay, Olivia," said Dora in a quiet voice. "Let your father and me sort this out for ourselves."

Charlie came over now and pulled the empty chair out of the circle, and setting it just on the outside, sat down, still scowling. "Look, Mom. I've tried and tried to reason with you. And you *never* listen to a word—"

"I'm listening now, Charlie." She leaned forward in her chair. "What do you want to say?"

He ran his hand over his balding head. "What *can* I say? That you're too old to be running a farm like this? That you need to be someplace where people can take better care of you?"

"I resent that, Dad!" Olivia stood now. "Armando and I are taking really good care of—"

"Olivia." Howie reached over and touched her arm. "We all know that. I think Charlie is talking about something else. What do you really mean, Charlie?"

Charlie shook his head. "I mean my mother isn't thinking straight. She's getting senile and—"

"Tell us specifically how you think she's getting senile, Charlie," said Howie.

Dora looked evenly at her son, waiting for him to go on.

"She's forgetful. She goes outside barefoot. She falls down and hurts herself."

"But *everyone* does those things," said Armando suddenly.

"And *you!*" Charlie pointed at him. "*You* can stay out of this. I don't even know why you're here. You're part of the problem—"

"Charlie!" Dora took in a deep breath. "Don't speak to Armando like that. He's like one of the family now." She smiled at her young friend. "As welcome as the rain on a hot parched day."

Charlie's face only grew darker.

"Yeah, and Armando's absolutely right, Dad. If he and I did any of the things you're accusing Grandma of, no one would even look twice. I mean, sure, if you're twenty you can go around acting crazy and or even messing up your life and it's just okeydokey. But if you're eighty, well, then you better watch your step or someone will stick you in the funny farm for sure."

"She makes a good point," said Audrey.

"So that's it then?" Charlie stood now. "You're *all* against me. Was this some sort of setup? Get everyone out here and jump all over Charlie? Maybe I should've brought along *my* lawyer."

Dora shook her head. "That's not it, Charlie. I just hoped we'd talk honestly and enjoy a pretty summer's night together."

"Talk *honestly?*" His voice sounded tight, like he was squeezing the words through his vocal cords. "You want me to talk *honestly*, Mom? Right here in front of your . . . your *family?* Well, if I were to talk honestly, I'm sure you wouldn't be able to take it."

"Try me." She looked at him and waited.

"Fine!" He sat back down in the chair, his fists clenched tightly on his knees. "Okay, you want honesty, Mom; well, how about the honest fact that Dad *never* loved me. Or that he always put the farm and the farmwork ahead of me. You wonder why I hate this farm so much? Well, it's because it was always more important than me. And, it's true—I couldn't wait to get away from here. And here's some more honesty. How about *you?*" He pointed at Dora. "You never loved me either. Oh, sure you might've said that you did and, yes, you took care of me, but it *never* felt like real love to me. Don't kid yourself, Mom. I saw how much you loved my father, but I never ever got love like that from you. You guys had each other and this stupid farm—you didn't need me!"

Dora sat a bit straighter, eyes unblinking, and studied her son. All she felt was compassion and pity. But even so she didn't speak. Finally, after what seemed a long time, Charlie started to stand.

"Wait a minute, Charlie." She held up her hand to stop him. "You spoke your truth, and now I will speak mine. Sit down, Son."

To her pleased surprise, Charlie sank back down into his chair and just stared at her.

"I'm sure you are right about some things, Charlie." She nodded slowly, giving him plenty of time to take this in. He looked somewhat surprised, but then she continued. "It may have seemed that your father didn't love you at times. But he did. *I know he did.* You see, Henry was raised in a family that worked hard just to scrape by, and his father never had time to be much of a father or to show what you call love. And so this was all new to Henry. But, mark my word, he loved you. And I know it frustrated your father that you showed so little interest in farming—the thing he loved so dearly. But even so, he loved you, Charlie. You'll have to trust me on that. When you went away and stayed away, it broke your father's heart. Oh, he tried to hide it, but I saw him sometimes, just staring at your graduation picture with silent tears coming down his face. Don't kid yourself, Charlie; your father loved you."

Charlie shook his head. "Fine. Maybe he did. But it didn't seem like it to me, back when I was growing up."

Dora nodded. "I'm sure we've all felt that way. I know I rarely felt that my father loved me."

"And I still don't feel like my father loves me," added Olivia in a quiet voice.

Charlie turned and stared at her. "That's *not* true."

She shook her head. "It's true to me, Dad."

"So you see, Charlie," said Dora. "I'm learning there is more than one side to every story. And each side seems true until you've seen the other side. Now, as far as what you said about me, I will be completely honest; you are partially right. But you don't know the whole story. You see, before you came along, I had lost two other babies. One before it was born, and your sister, Susan, just after she'd turned one. And it broke my heart—just shattered me—to lose those children. When I became pregnant the third time, well, I thought I didn't have it in me to love another child—a child that I felt certain I would lose—again."

She pressed her hand to her lips for a moment then continued. "It shames me to admit this, Charlie. But I was young then. I'd lost my mother as a girl and Henry was busy with the farm, and I didn't have anyone to talk to about these things. So, you're right, Charlie; it took me a while before I allowed myself to *really* love you. And I'm sure you must've sensed this, even as a little baby. Then when I got over it some and I allowed myself to love you, well, I'm sure even then that it was a frightened and overprotective sort of love. But I didn't know how else to do it. And for that I'm sorry. But I did love you, Charlie. I can remember when you were a little boy and we'd play hide-and-go-seek in the cornfield, and you would just giggle and laugh and you loved it. But the older you got the more you became like my father—and he and I already had our problems. And it felt so complicated to me sometimes that I didn't even know what to do. So, yes, you are right, Charlie. I had difficulty showing my love to you. But I *did* love you. And I still do." And now Dora couldn't help herself. She began to cry. Covering her face with her hands, she sobbed quietly.

Olivia stepped up from behind her and set her hands on Dora's shoulders, squeezing gently. Everyone else remained silent. Only the sound of water and crickets broke the stillness.

"Isn't this what family is supposed to be?" Armando spoke suddenly, surprising Dora. "You love each other and you hurt each other and then you forgive each other?"

"That's true." Olivia nodded. "And then you do it all over again."

Dora looked up now. "They're right. But it took me a long time to get to the forgiving part. It wasn't until recently, the same night that I fell down and broke my hip, that it started becoming clear to me. Oh, people like Howie and Armando have tried to tell me before, but I guess I wasn't ready to hear the truth. I couldn't let go of the hurts that I'd borne for all these years—old things I'd been carrying far too long—but that night I just let them go." She held up her empty hands as she looked around at the group. "And when I forgave others and asked God to forgive me, it was like a ton of boulders had been lifted off of me. And even when I fell down and busted up my hip, I felt all right somehow. Like I had finished something—some last bit of earthly business—and I was ready to go."

Now she looked directly at Charlie. "But, let me tell you something else, Son. I wish I'd figured this out a whole lot sooner. It wearies me to think of all the years I wasted being weighed down by all that nonsense. And because I love you, Charlie, I don't want you to go through the same thing that I did. You say you're a Christian, and I know you go to church real regular, but you need to remember what that Cross was all about, Son. You need to remember what the Bible says about forgiving others as God has forgiven you. I know it seems a little late for me to be preaching forgiveness to others. But I 'spect what I'm saying is don't make the same mistake I did." She reached up for Olivia's hand, still resting on her shoulder, and gave it a squeeze. "Don't any of you fall into that nasty ol' trap."

Epilogue

The summer days had grown steadily shorter and cooler, and the sunflowers were in full bloom now, a glorious array of color—orange, yellow, russet, and gold. Armando had gotten up early this morning, eager to cut more flowers for the florists who were paying top dollar for the pretty blooms.

After cutting several bucketfuls, he slipped into the house, in search of a cup of coffee. But Olivia wasn't up yet. Not so unusual since she was by nature a late sleeper, but he'd expected to see Dora puttering about, pushing her walker and maneuvering around. It wouldn't be long now, the doctor had said last week, until she could get along without it. He went into the kitchen and started the coffee. Waiting for it to perk, he decided to check on Dora, to see if she could use a hand. Although her progress improved daily, she still had difficulty getting out of bed on her own.

But she was sound asleep—or so it seemed—and Armando turned to leave. No harm in sleeping in. But he stopped by the door. Something about the room seemed very quiet to him. Too quiet. He went back over to the bed and bent down to look. A sweet smile was on her lips, but when he reached to touch her cheek with his fingertips, it was cold. And he knew she was gone, had probably died peacefully during the night. But just the same, he crumpled to the floor and sobbed the same way he'd done when he'd lost Abuela Maria. And that's exactly where Olivia found him.

Together the two of them sat on Dora's bedroom floor and held each other and cried until there were no more tears left. Of course, they knew she was old and frail and ready to go. They just hadn't been ready to let her. Then Armando got up and called Howie to see what should be done.

* * * * * * * * * * * * *

The funeral had been well attended by family and friends. Olivia and Armando had created a large bouquet of flowers from Henry's Garden to place on her grave that day. And the following morning, Armando had slipped up to the cemetery again. This time he brought a large bouquet of sunflowers. He sat on the bench and told her how much he loved her and how much he missed her, and then he thanked her for believing in him and left.

But now, only three days later, he felt completely lost—not much different than when his own grandmother had passed away ten years earlier. Of course, he had Olivia, but even so, he felt somewhat deflated and slightly confused as he wondered what he should do next. He prayed that God would lead him, and yet he still wasn't sure which way to go. He'd already preregistered at the local college, back when Dora was still alive and when he still had hopes of working on the farm and developing a nursery. But now he wasn't even sure if going to college was really the right thing to do. And to study agriculture? What would be the point of that?

"Of course, it's right to go to school," Olivia urged him earlier that morning. "It's what Grandma wanted. I thought it's what you wanted too."

"It was. But now I feel like everything is changed. Agriculture seems a little far-fetched. And I should probably get a real job and become more, you know, responsible."

She laughed. "Oh, puh-lease. You're sounding like my father now." She pointed to the transplanted trees, the newly begun green-house. "Are you saying that this is not a *real* job—not *real* work?"

"That's not what I mean, Olivia. It's just that I figure your dad will be in charge of things now. And who knows what he might do with the place now that Dora's not here."

Olivia frowned. "Yeah, it's hard to say."

"I guess I should've known this was a possibility. But I had hoped—"

"Yeah, me too." She wrapped her arms around him. "Well, before you go packing your bags, let's find out what Howie's got to say about everything."

"When's he coming?"

"He said tonight. He said that we're supposed to meet in the garden. Grandma wanted it to be sort of a memorial—her final garden party."

Armando smiled sadly. "I wish she could be here too."

"Maybe she will."

And so they all gathered in the garden, much like they'd done in June, only this time with one noticeable absence. Armando leaned back in the lawn chair and waited for Howie to begin. He'd overheard bits and pieces of conversation between Dora and Howie during the past couple of months, and he knew how she was patiently trying to patch things up with her demanding son. As a result Armando expected that she'd left the farm in its entirety to Charlie. And it seemed only right to do so. In Armando's culture, the eldest son was always the one to inherit the estate. But there was no way that Armando could see himself working for someone like Charlie, that was assuming that Charlie would even want to keep the farm. Armando sighed as he watched Howie open his briefcase and shuffle through some papers.

Of course, Armando already knew there was a provision in the will for him. A straightforward woman, Dora had plainly told him that she'd had Howie write up a promissory note for Armando's college education so there would be no disputing this decision later. But she'd also said there was to be no time limitation on it. That way Armando could schedule schooling around his seasonal work. Armando felt fairly certain he'd have to do that now, although he'd have to look into another line of work. Maybe he could get a job as a mechanic.

Without much ado, Howie adjusted his glasses and began to read a letter, handwritten, he assured them, by Dora's own hand.

Dear Loved Ones:

If this is being read, it's because I am gone. Although I'm sorry to leave my loved ones behind, I am finally ready to go. I am ready to meet my dear Lord Jesus and to thank Him for His great mercies upon me. And I am ready to see my sweet Henry and all those who have gone on before me. And I'll be waiting up there for the rest of you to join me someday. I imagine you now, sitting in the lovely garden (hopefully it's not pouring down rain in December, but maybe Howie can make some provision for that if it is). But I want you to know that I love each and every one of you. And I have carefully considered what should become of my property. I have prayed to God, and discussed this situation with Howie, until I finally feel I know what I want to do. Don't worry, this is all written up nice and legal like, by Howie, but I wanted to leave a personal letter of explanation in my own simple words.

First of all, I leave the farm, all the land, house, and outbuildings to my granddaughter, Theodora Olivia Chase, because I know she loves it as dearly as her grandpa and I did and because I think that would make my Henry happy. Next I leave all my monetary resources, previously stored in my mother's pink hatbox, in a trust fund to be managed by Howie (or his preappointed replacement should he succumb to his age and join me). Now this trust fund will be for the sole purpose of supporting and developing the farm into a thriving nursery business managed by Armando Enrico

Garcia (bet you thought I'd forget your full name). And in the event (which I am predicting) that Armando and Olivia wed, the farm will become jointly owned between the two of them. No sense in letting Olivia run the whole agricultural show when we all know she'd really make a better artist, which is what I'm hoping she'll do. Paint those sunflowers, Livvie!

Now, the reason I didn't leave any of this to my son, Charlie, or his son, Charlie, is because both my Charlies have already benefited from the fairly large inheritance left to them by my father, as well as the fact that neither of them ever cared a lick about farming. Now I don't mean this to sound disrespectful or unloving, but we all know it's just the way things are. And, don't worry, I understand. I am proud of both of the Charlies and all their fine accomplishments in the financial world, as I'm sure my father, Charles Lawrence, must also be.

The other smaller details of my will can be read in the official and somewhat overwhelming (and boring) legal document that my dear friend Howie has so professionally drafted. But finally I must say this: I love you all very much and pray that you will live your lives to the fullest, that you'll love each other wholeheartedly, like Henry and I always tried to do, and that when you make mistakes and hurt each other (like I know you will) that you'll be quick to forgive and forget. For that is the secret treasure that my dear Henry buried on this property so long ago. I discovered it only recently when I picked the sweet violets transplanted by Armando's shovel. It's the treasure we've all been looking for and it is found only when we love and forgive—again and again just like the seasons—until the good Lord calls us home to His treasures above!

Lovingly,
Theodora Olivia Lawrence Chase

About the Author

$\mathcal{M}$elody Carlson is the award-winning author of more than seventy books for adults, teens, and children. In other words, she loves to write! But more than an author, she considers herself to be a story-teller and feels the power of fiction can be as life-changing as anything. After all, Jesus Himself utilized stories to make some of His most valuable and memorable points.

Melody's most recent novels include *Looking for Cassandra Jane; Blood Sisters; Finding Alice;* and for teens, the Diary of a Teenage Girl series.

When not writing, Melody likes to spend time with her husband and Labrador retriever, enjoying the natural beauty and outdoor activities so readily available in central Oregon.

TURN THE PAGE

for an exciting preview from

looking for cassandra jane

by
MELODY CARLSON

Available now at a bookstore near you.

ISBN 0-8423-4098-X

chapter one

MY DADDY USED TO SAY I had the devil in me. My grandma said it was only because I was a highly spirited child, yet as time went on I figured my daddy might've been right after all—especially seeing as how he and the devil were already on a first-name basis anyway. I was fifteen years old before anyone told me that Jesus loved me— and even then I didn't believe it.

I can still recollect my daddy's face reddened by whiskey and rage. "I'm go'n' to beat the devil outta you, Cassandra Jane Maxwell!" he'd bellow in a slushy voice. Then with his usual drunken awkwardness he'd yank off his leather belt and come after me.

Of course he only did this after the empty Jack Daniel's bottle went spinning across our cracked linoleum floor, and that bottle gave me the advantage because it's not that tricky to elude a drunk—especially if you're fast. And I was fast. But even to this day I still sometimes see my daddy's face when I hear a TV evangelist going on and on about the devil and evil and all.

This is not to make it seem that my daddy was a truly wicked man. The fact is I mostly loved my daddy. And when he was sober he was a fine-looking and well-mannered gentleman. He liked wearing a freshly pressed shirt with a neatly knotted bolo tie and he believed in polishing his shoes. And his dark hair, like his shoes, would gleam in the sunlight, combed through with Brylcreem ("just a little dab'll do ya"). And when my daddy walked through town he'd hold his shiny head up high, almost like a cocky rooster strutting through the chicken yard, and seemingly oblivious to all those quick side-glances or knowing nods coming from our fellow townsfolk.

Maybe this was his way of making up for all that was wrong in his life, or more likely he was telling himself that he would do better that day, that he wouldn't give in to his weakness again. And like his hair and his shoes, my daddy talked real smooth and slick too, when he wasn't under the influence. He sold top-quality used cars at Masterson Motors on Main Street, and on a good day he could easily best any other salesman on the lot. My grandma said Clarence Maxwell could charm the stripes right off of a snake—and she meant it as a compliment. But his life was full of sorrows. And his escape in those days was always the bottle.

My daddy used to say that I killed my mama. Of course he only said this when he was under the influence, but my best friend, Joey Divers, told me that whiskey never lies. And I suppose in some ways it was true, because if I hadn't been born my mama wouldn't have died. But then I never asked to be born and there were plenty of times when I surely wished that I hadn't been. (My grandma said that's like wishing you were dead and it's an insult to your Maker.)

My mama died when I was only three days old, and years later I overheard my grandma saying that if my daddy hadn't been out drinking he might've taken my poor mama to the hospital before she bled herself to death. But I would've never dreamed of saying that my daddy killed my mama. Truth is, I know firsthand how bad it feels to lug *that* kind of guilt around with you. I would never wish *that* upon anyone, no matter how pitifully wicked they were.

Since my daddy was pretty much useless after my mama died, my Aunt Myrtle looked after me some. I guess I was a real fussy baby and I suspect I was fairly trying for poor Aunt Myrtle, but I reckon the reason I was so cantankerous was because my mama was dead. To be honest I don't remember that far back, although I've heard said that hidden somewhere deep in our subconscious we do remember such things. I do, however, remember my Aunt Myrtle looking at me with those pale blue eyes. The corners of her lips might turn up into something of a smile, but her eyes were cold and hard like the surface of the park pond those few times it froze over. And her smile, like that brittle veneer on the icy pond, was deceiving. As kids we always knew that even though the pond looked like it might support your weight, you never could count on it and only a plumb fool would go out beyond the edge. One year an unsuspecting deer wandered out and the ice gave way and the poor, confused animal went right down into the freezing dark depths below. And that's about how I felt around my aunt.

Aunt Myrtle usually came over to our house to take care of me. She always had her hair fixed up and lacquered with Aqua Net hair spray you could smell before she even walked in the door. I think she fancied herself to be a Donna Reed look-alike wearing all those shirtwaist dresses and high-heeled shoes, but now that I think about it those outfits don't seem like the best kind of housekeeping clothes. She'd tie one of my dead mama's aprons around her thick middle and do a little cleaning and cooking if it suited her. But mostly she just watched the television (shows like *As the World Turns* and *Search for Tomorrow*) or else she just walked around the house like she had a corncob stuck somewhere inside her anatomy. And I knew to stay out of her way.

My earliest memory of Aunt Myrtle was being scolded and pushed away from her long full skirt. My hands were probably sticky or dirty and she was afraid I'd muss her all up, but even when I was squeaky clean she always kept me a good arm's length away. I don't think she was ever real comfortable around kids, and although she did eventually marry, she never bore children of her own. Back when I was little I thought maybe she hated me because I had killed her only sister by being born. But I later on I learned that my mama was only her stepsister and no blood relation at all. And as it turned out, my Aunt Myrtle never really liked her much anyway, and I figured that was why she didn't like me either.

Joey Divers told me that his mama told him that my Aunt Myrtle had been in love with my daddy at one time. I couldn't understand this because my Aunt Myrtle seemed like an old woman to me, almost as old as my grandma, I thought when I was little. But one day I asked Aunt Myrtle how old she was, and she told me she was almost exactly the same age as my daddy and that they had even gone to school together as kids! The way she said this to me was strange, with those pale blue eyes of hers looking almost dreamlike. It made my skin feel creepy and I wondered if Joey hadn't been right all along.

About that time I became fearful that she might actually be in love with my daddy still, and even though she'd been my mama's step*sister*, I didn't for the life of me want Aunt Myrtle to become my step*mother*. But perhaps her infatuation for my daddy might explain why she put up with me all that time, since I knew she could hardly stand me. And I remember how she'd go on and on, talking like she had my best interests at heart, but in the next breath she'd be telling me how I was a *bad little girl* and how I'd never amount to anything. I know she'd heard my daddy say I had the devil in me and naturally she believed him. But for all her hard work and self-sacrifice it never got her anywhere with my daddy. And I must credit him with that. In fact, although I know he was "involved" with a few women here and there, he never actually fell in love or remarried. In his own way I believe he remained true to my mama's memory. And perhaps that was the main part of the reason for his sorrows.

My grandma would've taken care of me more of the time if she could've, but she had her little grocery store to tend to. Her first husband, my mama's daddy, had built that store from scratch with his bare hands just before the Great Depression. It was an old, boxy wooden building not much bigger than a small house, but with a little apartment above. Situated on a corner downtown, its only windows faced the street, reaching from the ceiling clear down to the floor, and it was all shadowy and dark toward the rear. The store had the smell of oldness to it, as if the bygone years of apples and pickles and sliced bologna had somehow soaked right into its wood plank floors. But it wasn't an unpleasant odor, and it always made me feel comfortable and right at home, like it was a part of me and my history. It was usually nice and cool inside, even on a hot summer day.

Grandma said they used to rent out the apartment before my grandpa died, but it was a real blessing for her to have it when she and my mama were left alone and the Depression set down upon them like a hungry, old bear. She said that little one-bedroom apartment gave her and my mama a safe haven and a roof over their heads, and I think those were happy times with just the two of them. I never quite understood why she upped and married Myrtle's daddy just shortly after the Depression ended—just when things were finally looking up for her. And the saddest part about that "blessed union" was the way her second husband just emptied her cash-register till, as well as her two bank accounts, and then ran off and left old Myrtle behind. But my grandma was a good woman and believed that the good Lord would see her through those fiery trials, and I never once heard her complain about getting stuck having to raise her stepdaughter.

My grandma's luck improved slightly after that, and her store held its own and even prospered during and following the war. But shortly after I was born (back during that big baby boom in the fifties) a chain-owned supermarket moved into town, and as a result, competition got something fierce. Brookdale wasn't the kind of town that could support a big supermarket as well as the several little "mom and pops" that had been around for decades. Most of the smaller markets surrendered, but my grandma hung in there, working long and hard just to make ends meet. Sometimes my Aunt Myrtle worked at the store too, and then my grandma would stay home and take care of me. Those were the good days with hugs and cookies and walks to the park. Unfortunately there just weren't enough of them to go around.

Sometimes my grandma would tell me stories about my mama, and when I was five years old she gave me a framed photograph to keep as my very own. And I would look into those dark soulful eyes in the black-and-white photograph and think she must've been the most wonderful woman in the whole wide world. Her skin looked as smooth as my grandma's favorite cream pitcher, and her hair was thick and dark and curly. And even though her dress was all out of style with those big, puffy shoulders and no one ever wears their hair like that anymore, I know with a certainty in my soul that my mama would still be a knockout if she suddenly appeared on the street today. I used to think I'd grow up to look just like her. But like so many other dreams, it hasn't really come true.

My grandma said that my mama's daddy died when she was just a little girl, and that Mama never really got over losing him. It seemed to comfort Grandma that at least the two of them were up there in heaven together now.

However, I found no consolation in this. I'd have much pre-ferred to have her down here on earth with me, because I'm pretty sure my mama and I would have gotten along real well. Naturally I came to this conclusion from looking at her photograph. I'd pre-tend to have these long, wonderful conversations with her, and she always said really intelligent things (like she'd been around some to know instead of just growing up in Brookdale where everyone is pretty average and normal).

And since she was sort of exotic looking, I liked to imagine she'd been a princess from the Far East, kidnapped at birth and sold to my grandparents because she was so beautiful. She was sure lots prettier than old Aunt Myrtle. I suppose that's why my daddy liked my mama better. My grandma told me I resembled her, but I still can't see it. When I was little I'd climb up onto the bathroom sink and look into the murky mirror in front of our medi-cine cabinet, but all I saw was a pale, pinched face with two dark holes for eyes and a mop of black hair sticking out all over. My grandma said the black hair and dark eyes came from my mama's daddy. He was full-blooded Cherokee, which makes me one-quar-ter. The first time I saw an old photo of my mama's daddy, I was sadly disheartened. He didn't have long braids or beads or feathers or anything that looked the least bit like a real, true Indian. Instead he had on an old-fashioned soldier's uniform. My grandma said that was because he'd been in the army and fought in World War I a long, long time ago. I thought it would've been much more exciting if he had fought against Colonel Custer at the Little Bighorn, and I even told Joey Divers that he had. And Joey actually believed me—until he told his mama, that is, and of course she set him straight.

Joey then pointed out that I was a liar, and I didn't argue with him on that account, but in my defense I did tell him that I had what my grandma called a very fertile imagination. Now I wasn't exactly sure what *that* meant just then, and neither was Joey (although he did look it up later) but it seemed to smooth things over just fine. And Joey forgave me, which wasn't surprising, because I was, in fact, the only friend he had.

Joey Divers was what my grandma called "a poor lame duck." He had suffered from polio when he was just a baby and consequently had a useless left leg and was forced to wear a stainless-steel brace connected to an ugly black shoe. And therefore he couldn't run and play with the other boys, and sometimes they even teased him about it. But not when I was around. That's because I was never afraid of them. In fact, I don't think I was afraid of hardly anything—except for my daddy, that is, but only when he was drunk. Anyway I would stand right up to those stupid boys, fists doubled, eyes squinted up real mean, and I would tell them that I was one-quarter Cherokee Indian and that my grandpa had whupped Colonel Custer at Little Bighorn, and that I could beat up every single one of them!—one at a time, of course. Fortunately they never took me on. I suspect they thought they might get in trouble for fighting with a girl, especially when the fight was due to the fact that they'd been picking on a little lame boy. I guess I was mostly relieved that they didn't want to fight with me. Although I did get a reputation for being pretty tough and, I suppose, pretty weird as well.

That reputation helped me to get through a lot of hard times. After all, it wasn't easy having a drunk for a father in a small town like Brookdale, where everyone knows everything about everybody. And besides that, sometimes being tough is all a girl's got anyway.

degrees OF guilt

Sammy's dead ... they each played a part.
Kyra, his twin sister. Miranda, the girl he
loved. And Tyrone, a friend from school.

WHAT'S THE REAL STORY?

There's always more than
one point of view—read all three.

kyra's story
{DANDI DALEY MACKALL}

miranda's story
{MELODY CARLSON}

tyrone's story
{SIGMUND BROUWER}

For a sneak peek into Miranda's life,
turn the page . . .
www.degreesofguilt.com

A Sneak Peek at Miranda's Story...

It's 10 minutes before fifth period when I get to school, and the halls are fairly vacant because kids are still at lunch. As I walk to my AP history class, it occurs to me that I could drop this class and still graduate. In fact, I could easily drop three classes and graduate. I only took these AP classes because Ms. Whitman said it would increase my chances of getting into a good college, possibly even on a scholarship. Funny how that used to be terribly important.

No one is in the classroom yet, and instead of finding a front seat, I go for the back row, far corner, next to the window. I open my history book and pretend to be reading, but my eyes don't focus on the page. I remember how I used to do this on a regular basis back in middle school—pretend to be invisible—and it usually worked. No one ever wanted to sit next to me, or converse, or even look at me back when I was a nobody. I want to be a nobody again. It shouldn't be that hard.

TYNDALE
FICTION

Other Great Tyndale House Fiction

- *Safely Home*, Randy Alcorn
- *The Sister Circle*, Vonette Bright and Nancy Moser
- *'Round the Corner*, Vonette Bright and Nancy Moser
- *Out of the Shadows*, Sigmund Brouwer
- *The Leper*, Sigmund Brouwer
- *Crown of Thorns*, Sigmund Brouwer
- *The Lies of Saints*, Sigmund Brouwer
- *Looking for Cassandra Jane*, Melody Carlson
- *Armando's Treasure*, Melody Carlson
- *A Case of Bad Taste*, Lori Copeland
- *Child of Grace*, Lori Copeland
- *Into the Nevernight*, Anne de Graaf
- *They Shall See God*, Athol Dickson
- *Ribbon of Years*, Robin Lee Hatcher
- *Firstborn*, Robin Lee Hatcher
- *The Touch*, Patricia Hickman
- *Redemption*, Karen Kingsbury with Gary Smalley
- *Remember*, Karen Kingsbury with Gary Smalley
- *Return*, Karen Kingsbury with Gary Smalley
- *Winter Passing*, Cindy McCormick Martinusen
- *Blue Night*, Cindy McCormick Martinusen
- *North of Tomorrow*, Cindy McCormick Martinusen
- *Embrace the Dawn*, Kathleen Morgan
- *Consuming Fire*, Kathleen Morgan
- *Lullaby*, Jane Orcutt
- *The Happy Room*, Catherine Palmer
- *A Dangerous Silence*, Catherine Palmer
- *Fatal Harvest*, Catherine Palmer
- *Blind Sight*, James H. Pence
- *And the Shofar Blew*, Francine Rivers
- *Unveiled*, Francine Rivers
- *Unashamed*, Francine Rivers
- *Unshaken*, Francine Rivers
- *Unspoken*, Francine Rivers
- *Unafraid*, Francine Rivers
- *A Voice in the Wind*, Francine Rivers
- *An Echo in the Darkness*, Francine Rivers
- *As Sure As the Dawn*, Francine Rivers
- *Leota's Garden*, Francine Rivers
- *First Light*, Bodie and Brock Thoene
- *Shaiton's Fire*, Jake Thoene
- *Firefly Blue*, Jake Thoene
- *The Promise Remains*, Travis Thrasher
- *The Watermark*, Travis Thrasher